GEIGER

GEIGER

GUSTAF SKÖRDEMAN

Translated by Ian Giles

GRAND CENTRAL
PUBLISHING

New York   Boston

Grand Central Publishing
Hachette Book Group
1290 Avenue of the Americas, New York, NY 10104
grandcentralpublishing.com
twitter.com/grandcentralpub

Originally published in Sweden by Bokförlaget Polaris in 2020
First North American edition: May 2022

Grand Central Publishing is a division of Hachette Book Group, Inc. The Grand Central Publishing name and logo is a trademark of Hachette Book Group, Inc.

The publisher is not responsible for websites (or their content) that are not owned by the publisher.

The Hachette Speakers Bureau provides a wide range of authors for speaking events. To find out more, go to www.hachettespeakersbureau.com or call (866) 376-6591.

Library of Congress Control Number: 2021948567

ISBNs: 9781538754375 (hardcover), 9781538754368 (ebook)

Printed in the United States of America

LSC-C

Printing 1, 2022

For Cecilia, with love

1

The Royal Copenhagen coffee cups were still on the table, with just the dregs in the bottom; the cake dishes were cleaned out and the glasses of juice empty. Blue polka-dot napkins—both fresh and soiled—were lying all over the place. The tablecloth was covered in coffee stains and crumbs, and here and there were red rings left by the glassware. The youngest children had rushed off, leaving the chairs pulled out from the table.

Half of the children were now on the Josef Frank sofa. The other half were running around shrieking, caught up in a heated sugar rush. A tennis ball came out of nowhere, fortunately hitting a gap between the souvenir plates hanging on the wall depicting different cities in Europe: Berlin, Prague, Budapest, Paris, Rostock, Leipzig, Bonn.

During the last week of school, the grandchildren had stayed with their grandparents so that their parents could take a holiday to Brittany. Sisters Malin and Lotta wanted to do it before the summer holidays began, and half of Sweden went down to France.

During the past week, Grandpa Stellan had taken refuge in the study while Grandma Agneta had made breakfast and dinner and driven the kids to and from school and their leisure activities. Not to mention keeping an eye on them as they bathed off the jetty in the unusually warm early summer evenings. It was also Grandma who'd gathered up and packed away the snorkels, flippers, swimwear, goggles, toys and what was left of the sun cream. As well as all the clothes, tablets, chargers and schoolbooks.

And now both of the sisters were there with their husbands, to take their children home again. It was almost as if the house was breathing a sigh of relief at the fact that peace would soon reign supreme and everything would return to normal.

The garden door was open and Lotta was outside, walking by her aging father's side while he pointed out the latest additions to the flower beds and planters. She knew most of the flowers, but some had been added. Her dad liked to have a few ever-present favorites while varying the rest.

He thought the flowers were at their most beautiful just before they came into bloom. When the buds were beginning to burst open. On this, father and daughter differed.

Lotta listened attentively to her father as he enthusiastically exhibited his floral splendor: coneflowers, hollyhocks, blue delphiniums, bittersweets that had germinated by themselves, oregano, mint, yarrow and lady's slipper. He loved his flowers, and Lotta thought about how much time he'd spent in the garden during her childhood. Dad was not to be disturbed out here—but you always knew where he was.

While Dad stopped to catch his breath, Lotta turned around discreetly and pretended to size up the house—the stylish, functionalist home that she knew inside out and really had no good reason to stand looking at. The large windows and the two terraces with the amazing views over Lake Mälaren and Kärsön Island.

Then her gaze settled on the garden path, the twelve heavyset stone slabs that she and her sister had run along so many times. Their dad jokingly called them the twelve-step model to a better life, because they led to the garden shed. Inside it, he could dedicate himself to what he loved most, undisturbed.

The stone slabs had been so awkward to lay that Stellan had decreed that they would remain there forever. And they already had forty years on the clock, so her father's prophecy was probably going to be borne out.

She looked at her father. He was eighty-five years old, and just as lucid as ever, but his body was tired, and advanced in years, so much so that he missed parts of his throat while shaving. He had always been tall, but now he was stooping. The big pair of spectacles that had been his distinctive attribute for as long as she could remember often ended up crooked, and the eyes behind the frames were cloudy.

Lotta was almost as tall as Stellan, but they were otherwise not particularly alike in appearance. Her father's hair had been ash-blond, while his daughter's was black—a legacy from her strong-willed grandmother, according to Stellan. And if his gaze was friendly and warm, then Lotta's was scrutinizing and skeptical.

"Can't we sit down for a bit?" said Lotta, because she noticed that her dad was tired and knew he would never acknowledge it.

They sat down on the flaking green bench outside the garden shed. Stellan fanned himself with a paper plate that had been heaped with bulbs, and Lotta wiped the sweat from her brow. The heat felt almost unnatural. It had had the whole country in its grip throughout May, and showed no signs of dissipating now it was June.

How many times had they sat here together? A bench for rest, but with all the tools within reach—a place where one recovered while also being ready to get working.

That was the theory, at any rate.

Inside the shed were stacks of garden furniture and tools that hadn't been used in decades: weed hoes, sprinklers, a copper watering can, a now-moldy striped hammock and the creak-ingly old sunbeds that the sisters had loved playing with when they were little. They had sunbathed between the snowdrifts on the very first days of spring, "cloudbathed" on cloudy summer days, and spent entire summers pretending the sunbeds were boats, cars, planes, space rockets or jetties from which they could jump into imaginary water.

When the sisters had got too big to play, the sunbeds had gone into the garden shed, and there they had remained ever since. Instead, Dad had secretly used them for resting during his gardening, but had been given away by the light squeaking audible through the walls.

Now the shed was more of a monument to a bygone era. Only the garden table was brought out each year by the gardener, Jocke, who continued to put in appearances as regularly as clockwork, despite having retired many years ago. He wouldn't accept any payment, either. He'd been coming weekly ever since Stellan and Agneta had moved into the house as newlyweds in the early seventies, and he'd carried on after retirement without either asking or being asked to. Perhaps he needed the steady routine to maintain his sanity.

Lotta nudged the door to the shed ajar and the heat struck her. The warm summer meant it was like an oven inside.

"Aren't you going to open up that window again?" she said, pointing at the plywood board nailed to the back wall. "We're not little anymore—there's no risk of us spying."

"No, but now there are new small spies," Stellan said with a smile.

"They only care about their screens."

"I'll ask Jocke to take it down. The window looks on to a lovely beauty bush, but I don't come in here as much as I used to."

"Not at all, I'd say," said Lotta, her gaze lingering on the rusty sunbeds.

"This is for you," said Stellan Broman to his daughter, holding out a flower.

Every time she visited, he gave her a plant or a bulb from his garden for her small kitchen garden, and she was grateful to receive them.

"What is it?" she asked.

"I don't know. Clarkia, I think. Jocke planted it."

"You always blame him."

Lotta smiled at her father.

Joachim—"Jocke"—had always been a natural part of her life, and he and Dad had always bickered gently over who knew the most about flowers. If she were honest, she'd probably learned more about plants and flowers from Jocke than she had from Dad.

But she still had very affectionate memories of her father's passion for gardening during her childhood, since it had meant he had been at home. Not at work, not in the house surrounded by friends and colleagues. No grandiose partying, no job, just quietly pottering about in the flower beds.

His life must have been much calmer over the last thirty years. Did he miss the old days? Being at the center of attention?

If nothing else, it had provided her and Malin with a different childhood—an existence that all their friends had envied. And what difference would it have made if Dad had been at home more— if he hadn't shut himself away in the recreation room or fled into the garden as soon as he came through the door? They'd always had Mum.

And it had all been very exciting without a doubt: all the well-known faces that had turned up at the house, all the parties and frolics, and all the grown-ups doing strange things.

Perhaps it was their parents' intense social life that had made her into such a recluse? The workaholic within her was definitely thanks to Dad, but even when she wasn't working she preferred not to see people. She just wanted to settle down with a book. Or perhaps meet a friend to talk. *One* friend.

The shrill cry of a child signaled that it was time to go back inside to the others.

As usual, Malin had stayed inside with their mum. She had never liked the garden. "Urgh, worms and woodlice," had been her judgment as a six-year-old—and she'd stuck to it.

Dark-haired Lotta and blonde Malin. The responsible big sister and the spoiled little princess.

Like a parody of a typical little sister, Malin hadn't helped her mother with the cleaning, packing or dishes, Lotta noticed. Instead, she'd fetched a box of old clothes from the attic and was hunting for vintage treasures for her children.

"Do they really want old clothes?" Agneta asked.

"They're lovely," said Malin, holding up a pale blue plush playsuit from her own childhood.

With her blonde hair and dark eyebrows, Malin was a copy of her mother. It was obvious that Agneta had been a stunning beauty, and despite being almost seventy she still attracted glances when out and about. Even if she didn't notice them herself. Both mother and daughter were beautiful in a way that made the people they met instinctively wish them well. It was as if their beauty radiated from within, and people therefore didn't begrudge them anything.

While Malin and Lotta had spent time with their parents and the kids had run around, the sisters' respective other halves had—as usual—withdrawn. There was always something about work or the car or a bathroom renovation that they could discuss to one side: Christian, in his neatly pressed shirt and patent leather shoes, Petter in shorts and sandals. They weren't altogether comfortable with each other—a financier and a cultural bureaucrat—but neither of them was at all comfortable with their great father-in-law, the legendary TV presenter, so they sought each other out. Neither of them was especially invested in the issues that interested Stellan: TV in the 1970s and 1980s, European travel or how classical culture, entertainment and public education were connected. Neither of them could quote Schiller.

After noting that the brothers-in-law had followed their usual pattern, Lotta noted that the kids were following theirs. Her own sons were sitting staring at their mobiles, and Malin's two kids were fighting. Molly was screeching because Hugo had thrown a tennis ball at her forehead and told her to head it. The ball had bounced against the wall and then on the table between two coffee cups.

It was high time to drive the boys to training and get away from Malin's badly brought-up brats. She had masses of meetings—being away for a whole week was a long time in her job. It was lucky that Petter could manage his own hours, and that the kids had activities all summer.

"Time to go. Say thank you to Grandma and get dressed."

Leo shook back his fringe. He went to his grandmother, took her hand and thanked her. Sixten needed telling again, but then he went and thanked her too.

Malin rifled through the remainder of the clothes, threw a few garments into a bag and put the box to one side. She didn't take it back up to the attic again, Lotta noted. And she was convinced that the bag of old clothes from their childhood that her sister had taken would remain untouched for years to come.

Lotta opened the front door and let her sons out. Petter took the hint immediately, came inside and thanked his parents-in-law and then went out to sit in the car. In the meantime, Lotta helped Malin's children to get dressed. Her sister had to find Christian and tell him to come inside and offer his thanks, then Lotta herded them all out to the two cars on the driveway, while Malin hugged her mother.

Stellan returned to the armchair in the living room, a well-used Pernilla from Dux, with a protective auditory accompaniment in the form of the *St. Matthew Passion*: John Eliot Gardiner's classic recording from 1988 with Barbara Bonney.

Agneta came out onto the front step to wave off the retreating hordes. Then the sound of the telephone ringing inside the house cut through the air, and she told her daughters she had to take it. Malin couldn't help but comment with a smile that her mother and father were the only people she knew who still had a landline at home. She said she would never be able to explain to her children what a landline was.

"It's your father," Agneta said apologetically. "He absolutely wants to keep it."

Then she went back inside the house, while her younger daughter joined her waiting family.

Agneta went into the study and picked up the big receiver attached to a spiral cable that led to an old Ericsson Dialog phone with a dial. She answered with her surname, just as she always had done.

"Broman."

On the other end of the line, a man's voice spoke in heavily accented German.

"Geiger?"

It was as she'd feared.

Good God.

The grandchildren.

But she heard the cars start outside, and realized she didn't have much choice.

She quickly calculated, then she answered curtly "Yes" and hung up.

Then she went upstairs and into the bedroom, opened the drawer in her bedside table, pulled out the instructions for the clock radio and the bathroom scales, and then got out a big, black Makarov pistol and a silencer that she screwed onto it.

On the way back to the living room, she cocked the weapon and noted that it seemed to be functional, despite having lain unused for so long. At least it had been cleaned and oiled.

She approached her husband diagonally from behind, pressing the muzzle against the side of his head.

And then she squeezed the trigger.

Blood spattered onto the book, which fell out of Stellan's hands: Goethe's *Faust* in the original German.

It hadn't been a loud bang, but louder than she remembered—so for safety's sake she lowered her weapon and went to the living-room window.

Outside, the sisters seemed to have been conferring on something, because they still hadn't left. But now Lotta walked away from Malin's car to her own and got in.

Lotta looked back toward the house again from the driver's seat, caught sight of her mother peering out and waved cheerfully. Malin followed Lotta's gaze and did the same.

The weapon concealed behind her back, Agneta waved back with her empty hand. Her daughters let down the rear passenger windows so that the kids could also wave to Grandma one last time. They did, and their grandmother smiled and reflected that with such wonderful grandchildren, she must have done something right.

2

"They've called."

Karla Breuer looked up from her book and fixed her gaze on Strauss, who was standing in the doorway to her office. The Cannonball, as she called him. Short, rotund and deadly efficient.

She knew that he called her the White Ghost because of her long white hair, ice-blue eyes and white clothes. And because he considered her to be a remnant of the past, a specter from a forgotten time.

"Who?" said Breuer. "And where?"

"Beirut. To Stockholm," said Strauss, who saw that the White Ghost hadn't been expecting that.

It was one of many numbers they were monitoring, and one that no one had thought would be used again. That was probably why Strauss and Breuer's department was going to be one of the last to be transferred: no one thought their targets were current. It felt as if when the BND had deserted Pullach for Berlin they had wanted to leave the old world behind them. But Breuer stubbornly maintained that the past never disappeared.

Breuer was the only person in the department who'd been working in intelligence when the number in Stockholm had been classified as active. And that had been many years ago. But now it was apparently active again, against all the odds.

"Then we have to go."

Breuer got up and walked straight past Strauss without looking at him. They had never become friends during the four years they'd worked together, but now they were jointly responsible.

Although the final decision was up to Schönberg.

Strauss glanced into Breuer's office as she swept past him. Not a single one of the monitors was illuminated; none of the computers were on. On the other hand, there were heaps of books and reports.

He couldn't grasp how a completely analogue operative was allowed to remain. Whom did she have a hold over? During her four decades in the intelligence service, she'd probably gathered all sorts. Then he turned on his heel and hurried after her.

There weren't many people left in these buildings now, he thought to himself as he looked around the corridor. Most people had already moved to the new complex in Berlin, the country's biggest administrative building, with a price tag of half a billion euros.

Its size and location in central Berlin should really have reminded the architects and drivers of the project of the East German Stasi's old headquarters, but apparently that issue had had no impact—or they simply hadn't cared.

In an open society, there was no longer such dread of activities behind closed doors.

Six doors down the corridor, Breuer knocked on Schönberg's door and went in before Strauss could catch up.

Schönberg had a stack of files in front of him, three of them laid out side by side but with the covers closed. He must have shut them when he heard the knock. Even here on the inside, people kept secrets from each other.

"Geiger is activated," said Breuer.

Schönberg didn't reply, but simply gave her a look that said, *So what?*

"That means that Abu Rasil will be activated," said Breuer. "We can take him now."

"You think he's still alive?" said Schönberg. "After more than thirty years of silence?"

"He's alive. He withdrew, but now he's been activated again. They wouldn't have called Stockholm if Rasil wasn't alive."

"And what can he do nowadays?"

"If he's been activated after three decades, it's likely to be something spectacular. We need to go."

Schönberg sat in silence.

"What's the point of our department if we don't take our warning systems seriously?"

Schönberg merely stared at her.

"This is exactly what they're counting on," Breuer continued. "That no one thinks Rasil is alive. That no one will do anything."

"How certain are you about the indication?" Schönberg said finally.

Breuer looked at Strauss.

"Completely certain," said Strauss, because he understood that was what Breuer wanted him to say. It was standard practice for the outgoing head of unit to recommend their successor, and Strauss was keen to take over from her. And it wouldn't be many years until Schönberg's post as head of department would be vacant. Strauss could see his career trajectory clearly before him.

"You've got four months to retirement, Breuer. Send Strauss."

Breuer didn't dignify that remark with a reply.

Schönberg sighed.

"How long have you been after Abu Rasil? Forty years?"

"I was after him for ten years, then he disappeared. And I was close to catching him several times."

"That's what you think, anyway."

"Are we going to let the biggest terrorist we've ever tracked get away?"

Schönberg took off his reading glasses and rubbed the bridge of his nose. Then he looked at his subordinates.

"Abu Rasil is a myth," he said. "A legend that the Palestinians launched in the seventies to scare the West."

"And that's exactly what Abu Rasil wants you to think."

"The superhuman terrorist. That one single brain was behind practically every terrorist attack in Europe at the time—the story's just too good to be true."

"As a parting gift, then?" said Breuer, locking her eyes on her boss. Both Schönberg and Strauss realized she wasn't going to give up.

"Go," said Schönberg. "Take Strauss and Windmüller. But you've only got a week."

"We'll leave straightaway."

"Straightaway?" said Strauss.

"Straightaway. Rasil is naturally already en route."

Breuer turned around and left, and Strauss ran into his own office to grab his jacket and service weapon. He could buy everything he needed on the road—except a Glock 17 and a customized Zegna in size 60.

There were no stacks of books in Strauss's office. Instead, there were the same number of computer monitors as in all the other offices, but unlike Breuer's, they were switched on. Plus the Nick Cave posters and Strauss's beloved Devialet Phantom Gold—the world's best wireless system for playing music. As his colleagues had moved across Berlin, Strauss had been able to turn up the volume more and more.

He hesitated for a second in the doorway, but then he couldn't help himself. He turned on his Phantom with the remote control and started playing "The Good Son" from his mobile.

Heavenly.

Then he quickly left and hurried down the corridor to inform their colleague that he was coming with them to Sweden. Windmüller was one of the many well-trained operatives whose task was to guarantee security and protect their lives.

Breuer's fixation on Abu Rasil was well known, and questioned by all at the BND. This would be her final chance to prove the legend was true and that she'd been right all along.

Strauss didn't know what to think, but he would never dare question the White Ghost. Not openly at any rate, and certainly not while she was still on active service. Breuer knew a lot of bigwigs.

None of the three had any family to notify, so all they had to do was get moving. Windmüller got into the mobile operations van, while Strauss opened the door of the BMW for Breuer. He couldn't judge how serious the assignment was. But *if* Abu Rasil existed and *if* he had been activated, then something big was happening right now.

Something really big.

3

As soon as Agneta's daughters had left, everything became urgent.

She grabbed a rucksack from the hall and hurried upstairs. Way back when, the bathroom had felt like the safest place—for three reasons. You could lock yourself in, there was no way to see in, and no one would ask what you were up to inside. And the many visitors to the house always used the toilets downstairs.

Burying things in the garden or heading off into the woods might seem smart in the heat of the moment, but when the equipment came to be needed, it might not be possible to retrieve it at once. She'd got that far in her thoughts, even back then.

Now she didn't have much time. Naturally, there would already be people on the way.

The only question was: how far away were they?

And who was coming?

The toilet roll holder wasn't up to the job no matter how hard she wielded it, so she had to run down to the basement to fetch a hammer. She hadn't given any thought to how she was going to break up the tiling—nor how noisy it would be—so long ago, when she'd deposited the package in the bathroom wall and tiled over it.

But there was no one to hear her now.

She swung the hammer as fast and hard as she could and cracked the tiling on the first attempt. She continued striking it to remove all the rest of the tile, worked at the seam of the carefully fitted damp-proof membrane underneath and then shoved in two fingers to pry out the emergency package, wrapped up in waxcloth.

A fat bundle of thousand-krona notes—but they were no longer valid, she realized. She would have to make do with the cash she had in the house. Fortunately, they'd always kept some in the metal tin in the kitchen.

Three passports in different names, but all with expiry dates long since passed.

The codeword for the radio transmitter.

Car keys—was the car still there? When had she last checked?

An instruction booklet on how to survive the collapse of civilization, which she reluctantly took.

Cyanide capsules.

Good God.

The pistol had never been hidden here—she had wanted that close to hand, and had settled on the bedside table. She'd come up with a labored story about it being passed down from her father, in case anyone found it. But no one ever had.

She stopped. Was that a car?

She quickly ran to the window on the upstairs landing, carefully lifted the edge of the curtain and glanced down to the street.

Nothing there.

But would they really park outside the house? Wouldn't they park nearby and then sneak up? Although what would people think if they saw mysterious men creeping through their gardens in this well-heeled neighborhood?

No, it would clearly be easiest to drive up to the house and park on the street, looking as though one had legitimate cause to be there. Perhaps they would even use a courier's van or a pickup truck with the word "plumber" painted on the side. Something no one would remember.

But they weren't here yet. She had no idea whether she had hours, minutes or seconds.

She needed to get back to work.

"My banana doll!" Molly called out.

"We'll have to get it next time we see Grandma," said Malin.

"*No!*" Molly screamed.

Malin sighed.

"I think we need to go back," she said to Christian.

She knew how fixated Molly was on her oblong, yellow plush character with its wide smile. The banana doll served as both playmate and cuddly toy, and if they didn't fetch it at once their daughter would never stop screaming.

Christian glanced hastily at his Rolex GMT-Master II. It was the Pepsi edition, and he was more than a little proud of it.

Jesus.

This was going to take all day.

But there wasn't much they could do about that.

They'd just gone past Brommaplan, where he could have turned around, but he'd realized too late. He had to carry on to the round-about and do a full lap of it instead—then they were on the way back.

Bloody doll.

The clock was ticking, so Agneta went back into the bathroom, took the packet of quick-drying cement and mixed it with some water using the toothbrush mug. She spread the mixture onto the back of the spare tile that had been at the bottom of her drawer in the bathroom cabinet all these years along with the cement, and then she put the tile over the hole and pulled the basket of towels in front of it. It wouldn't fool anyone if subjected to thorough examination, but she might win a few days and that could be enough. It was all about buying time.

She put the toothbrush mug and tile pieces in her rucksack, along with the money and the passports. Then she went down to the kitchen and made up a bag of food. A sudden impulse made her run to the garage to add the battery charger to her bag.

Good. And now what?

Confuse matters a bit.

How?

The jewelry box. Stellan's wallet. Something else.

The little Munch painting hanging in the guest toilet.

All of it went into her rucksack.

And now to pull out some drawers and mess things up a bit.

What else?

Of course. The reason for all of it. It took her a minute to fetch it.

She checked the time.

Too much time had already passed.

She needed to go.

She couldn't take her and Stellan's car—she knew that much. So she went into the garden shed and tugged out the old bicycle that had been there for decades. Pink with white handlebars. It must have belonged to one of the girls, even if she couldn't remember ever seeing either of them riding a bike.

Over the years, the bicycle had slowly disappeared behind rakes, shovels, trimmers, a wheelbarrow and various planks of wood that might come in useful one day. A broken garden hose was tangled around the frame, handlebars and front wheel. The chain wasn't oiled and the tires were almost flat, but it could be ridden.

Were any of the neighbors watching? They would be questioned, and she didn't want any of the operatives currently being set in motion finding out about her two-wheeled escape vehicle. Given how rarely her daughters usually got in touch, she ought to have upward of a week before one of them got worried. For that long, at least, the police would leave her in peace.

The others were more of a problem.

The ones who had called.

And the ones who might have been listening.

She had no idea how much time she had.

Hours or days?

Or perhaps they would be content with the conversation and simply await the result?

She went back inside for one final check. Then she glanced through the pane of glass in the front door. There was nothing out of the ordinary outside. She buttoned up her parka and put the hood over her head. She would be hot, but she had to disguise herself somehow.

Finally, she went over to her dead husband and kissed him on the top of his head.

"Thanks for all the years. Cross your fingers for me."

She patted him on the cheek and then vanished outside to the bicycle, before pedaling away.

At the very moment Agneta Broman disappeared round the bend of Grönviksvägen on her old bicycle, Malin Broman-Dahl's black BMW M550d xDrive Touring came rolling along Nockebyvägen before turning on to Grönviksvägen, with just a few hundred meters to go until it reached the parental home at number 63.

4

The sound was deafening. Cars honking, trucks with students on the back and sound systems worthy of a festival. Old classics and pumping house. Each vehicle was playing music so loudly that the windows of the magnificent stone buildings rattled.

Balloons, champagne bottles, blue and yellow flags. A crowd.

Young people filled with hopes and expectations.

Parents and grandparents and wealthy old aunts were arriving at the school that was always the first to let its graduating students out. There were placards with first names and baby photos and class affiliations. School class, that was. Other class affiliations were marked using watches, clothes and bags—and the makes of the cars that were misparked with malicious disrespect on all the streets around Östra Real upper secondary school. Parking wardens circled until the mandated five minutes had elapsed and they could start ticketing, like hyenas waiting for a lion to have satisfied its appetite on the dead zebras so they could have their turn.

Even the usually deserted upper section of Artillerigatan was crammed with people on the way toward the playground of the exclusive school. Here were aging directors in yellowing peaked graduation caps, over-made-up trophy wives unhappy that they couldn't wear their fur coats in the heat and young men with slicked-back hair who in their first years after graduating from high school had already had time to found two or three of their own companies. Green and red trousers were still popular among the men here, Sara noted.

All this circus because a bunch of teenagers were finishing school. Heading nowhere.

Enjoy this day, she thought to herself from her position in the sauna-hot car. Because tomorrow you'll be a statistic. Unemployed, without a place of your own. A problem for society. Enjoy it while you can.

When a three-year-old "Ebba" floated past on a student placard in the hands of a proud father, Sara realized she hadn't ordered one like it for her own Ebba.

She noted it in her mobile calendar. As soon as her shift was over: get a placard for her daughter.

Sweat ran from her brow, sliding down her cheeks. The small of her back was completely soaked.

Sara and David had made an early start, so they'd secured a legal parking spot opposite the door they were now watching at Artillerigatan 65, just by the long wall running toward Östra Real. Now they were surrounded by empty plastic drink bottles and greasy fast food packaging, and feeling an increasing need for a wee.

David Karlsson. And Sara Nowak.

Sara had put her hair up in a bun and put on a Ralph Lauren baseball cap in order to blend into the neighborhood. When she lifted the cap to wipe the sweat from her brow, she saw in the rearview mirror that it was time to dye her hair again. Her hair was brown, but the roots were fiery red. It looked as if her scalp was on fire.

As a child, Sara had been called "the Indian" because of her red hair. Not particularly logical, and very tedious in the long run. She'd also been called "the giraffe" since she was taller than most of the boys in the class—177 centimeters, just like Naomi Campbell and Linda Evangelista. Her height and distinctive cheekbones meant she'd spent her teens on the receiving end of hundreds of clumsy chat-up attempts, telling her that she looked like a model. So many that Sara had eventually tried out precisely that career, despite mostly thinking that she looked odd.

Modeling had gone fairly well, but she remembered what it had been like sitting around waiting for assignments, feeling uncomfortable. Offered up like a product in a catalog, while customers sat there, picking and choosing uncertain girls. A clothes horse with the right length legs.

Being dependent on others' appreciation and opinions about her outer appearance hadn't suited her at all. So she'd terminated the contract with the agency and started training in the martial arts instead, in order to find an outlet for all the rage that the selection processes and touchy-feely photographers had built up in her.

Now she was proud of her height and her hair color, but she still dyed her hair brown to avoid being easily recognizable during reconnaissance work. She really didn't like having people's gazes on her. Particularly men's, since her job in the prostitution unit meant she'd come to associate covetous glances with very unpleasant people.

"Jesus Christ, it's hot," said Sara, closing her eyes as she held the small handheld fan they'd bought in Clas Ohlson to avoid draining the car battery by using the air conditioning.

"It'll be fun to see how long it takes for people to start complaining about the heat," said David. "The first hot summer in decades."

He looked from the door to his watch and back again.

"How long has he been in there now?"

"Don't know. Too long. He's probably done. We'll go in on the next one instead."

"OK."

"But maybe we could scare this one a bit when he comes out? Try and put him off, even if we can't get him done."

David gave Sara a look.

"Harassment?"

"No, just show him that we have an eye on him. Check his ID, hint that his wife might find out. They think they can carry on without any consequences."

"Either we catch them red-handed or we leave them alone."

"Look at us now," Sara said. "We can take down a bloke, but this girl has ten other clients today. And around the rest of town, hundreds of other girls have thousands of clients. Just today. And we're taking down a handful. Who get fined. And then carry on as before. It's just crazy."

"That's how it is."

"And it's shit!"

"What's up with you?" David asked. "Why are you so angry?"

"Is it so strange? Isn't it stranger that you're not angry?"

"I don't think you can do a good job if you're angry."

"It's bloody brilliant being angry," she said. "Gives you energy to carry on. What am I supposed to be otherwise? Happy? 'Hurrah! What awful people there are in this world!'"

"I think it's stupid. You work less efficiently and you burn out. You can't deal with this job if you get angry at everything you see."

"It's about bloody time someone got angry at this shit. Instead of just trying to understand and reason, they should get totally raging. Fucking furious."

"We need to work with a long-term view."

"I don't want to work for the long term, I want to work for the short term. Like this—'Stop it! Now!'"

David shook his head.

"We need to get them to understand what they're doing is wrong. Anger isn't a good way to communicate. It creates distance, conflict. They won't listen if you shout at them—they'll just become defensive."

"But do you think what we do actually matters? Everything just keeps going on anyway."

"What is it you want most?" said David. "To rescue the girls or take down the punters?"

"Both."

"But which is most important?"

Sara shrugged.

"If you had to pick one."

She thought about it. But she already knew the answer.

"Take down the punters," she said. "Without villains there are no victims."

"I want to rescue the girls."

"But they don't want help. They refuse to testify. Refuse to move to safe houses. Refuse to bloody speak to us."

"We need to gain their trust," David objected. "It takes time."

"'Trust'? Shouldn't it be pretty bloody easy to choose between us and a bunch of violent pimps? Between us and being raped ten times a day by disgusting johns? With the possibility of being killed at any moment?"

"This doesn't sound like you, Sara. Has something happened?"

"No, not a fucking thing. That's the problem. No matter how many buyers of sex we arrest, there are thousands more standing in line with their dicks in their hands. All ages, all sorts, all of them. Nothing helps. What's the point? And the girls don't even want to testify—not against the pimps or the punters."

"They're scared of what happens next," David said, "once the perpetrators are in jail and we're otherwise occupied. Scared of revenge—that something might happen to their families."

"I know that. And that's why we can't help them. Can't put away the guilty. Why not jack it all in, if we don't stand a chance? Maybe we just shouldn't bother anymore?"

"If we don't, who will?"

"Why doesn't God do something?"

David sighed.

"Not again—"

"Yes, again. I get really worked up when you talk about God the same day as you take care of some teenage girl who's been gang-banged to pieces. How the hell do you do it?"

David didn't reply. This wasn't the first time Sara had challenged his faith. More like the seventieth time. By a factor of seven. She didn't even seem to want to understand what his faith was about. He understood it wasn't part of their line of work, but without his faith he wouldn't have been able to cope.

"Faith in a God that means you don't even dare come out to your family!" said Sara. "What kind of God is that, really?"

"It's not about my family. I've told you that! I can tell them anything. It's everyone else."

"That's what I mean. Free Church congregations in some backward hole that force families out if they have a homosexual son. In Sweden, today! Not to mention other countries. The American Deep South, Saudi Arabia, Poland, Russia. It's not about religion, it's about legitimizing hate, controlling fellow human beings. Freely attacking gays and women and…"

Sara fell silent. David looked up and saw her staring at the door.

"Check on the girl!" she shouted, leaping out of the car.

David saw Sara run down Artillerigatan toward Karlavägen. Then he hurried in through the door they'd been watching. He knew the flat was up one story, facing the inner courtyard. It wasn't their first visit.

He tried the door. Locked.

"Open up! Police!"

He could only hope there was someone inside who was capable of opening the door. He thumped hard on the door and called out again, and after a minute or so he heard steps on the other side and a click from the lock.

The door slowly swung open.

David knew that the girl who lived and worked here called herself Becky, so he assumed that it was her opening the door. But it wasn't all that easy to tell, because she was holding her hand in front of her face. And what little of Becky's face he could see was completely bloodied.

"Are you injured?" said David. "Seriously, I mean," he added, as he saw the woman's eyes flash. It was pretty obvious she was injured. "Are you OK? Can I look?"

David carefully took Becky's hand and she let him move it aside. Her nose appeared to be broken. One eyebrow was split. And two teeth had been knocked out. Others might be loose.

"I'll call an ambulance."

But Becky waved her hand dismissively.

"Haxi," she mumbled as she took her handbag from the coat rack. She pulled out her mobile, entered the PIN and handed it to David.

"What? Oh, right—you want me to call?"

"Mmm."

"Taxi to pick up from Artillerigatan 65. Becky. Going to Danderyd Hospital." David looked at Becky quizzically to check whether the choice of hospital suited her. The woman nodded in response. "The emergency room."

Then he ran back down to the street.

How had Sara known?

The punter had already realized at Tyskbagargatan that he was being chased by Sara, so he dashed toward Karlavägen. Pushing aside all the families carrying their graduation placards. Stopping cars, which couldn't actually do more than a couple of kilometers an hour in the throng.

Sara ran after him along the footpath running up the center of the lush avenue on Karlavägen. Several student trucks were heading for Östra Real: families and friends en masse.

The man zigzagged between the revelers, shoving them aside so he was practically pulling himself through the crowd.

Sara ran, jumping and dodging.

"Move! Idiots!"

Some protested loudly, others pulled unhappy faces. People weren't accustomed to being run into in these parts.

On Sibyllegatan in front of the kiosk there was a Chevrolet Bel Air '56 decked out for graduation, its driver impatiently waiting to turn on to Karlavägen. He took his chances when a gap that was barely big enough appeared. The young man floored it, but was stopped by Sara landing on the bonnet.

"Idiot!" Sara cried out, but carried on without stopping.

She registered pain in her ankle and shoulder as she ran on past the ICA Esplanad.

The punter was pulling away.

Jesus—she wasn't going to make it.

Sara plucked a champagne bottle out of the hands of a dumpy middle-aged gentleman with a pointed beard, and threw it with all her might at the fugitive.

And she hit her target.

A bullseye on his back.

Sufficiently hard to make him stumble, which resulted in him running into a gaggle of young lads and tripping over.

As he struggled to get up, Sara caught up with him.

She threw herself down, wrapping her legs around his stomach and squeezing—a scissors move she'd used a lot when training in the Russian martial art of Sambo. She'd learned that her strong legs were particularly useful in that position. Numerous burly blokes had been forced to tap out when they'd been caught in her iron grip during training.

"I surrender!" the punter cried out, and Sara loosened her grip slightly. There was a stinging feeling in her leg, and she saw that the punter had something shiny in his hand. A flick knife. He'd stabbed her with it. Fortunately not deeply, just a scratch. But still...

Sara bent forward, grabbed the little finger on his empty hand and bent it backward. He screamed with pain, and then she struck his knife hand from behind, making the weapon fly out of it.

Then she squeezed even harder with her legs.

"Let go!" the punter shouted. "Let go! You're suffocating me!"

"And you stabbed me with a knife," said Sara, pulling out her handcuffs. "Give me your hands!"

"Fucking whore!"

Sara squeezed even tighter.

"Let go!" the idiot cried out. "Police brutality!"

Then he turned to the people standing nearby and exhorted them:

"Video this! Video this!"

At the same time, he carefully concealed his own face.

"Give me your hand," said Sara.

Finally he obeyed.

"And the other."

When Sara had locked the handcuffs, she released him from her scissor hold and the punter gasped for air, as if he'd been underwater and needed to catch his breath.

"Did you think you could run away from me? Huh?"

But he was too exhausted to answer, and she leaned forward and bellowed into his ear.

"Idiot!"

Then she found his wallet, pulled out the driving license and took a photo of it.

Pål Vestlund.

The name of a bloody john. Ring on his finger and everything.

"You never give up."

The words came from David, who'd come running through the sea of student graduation revelers.

And it was true, Sara thought to herself. She never gave up.

"How is she?" she asked, her eyes on the captive punter.

"Two teeth, nose, eyebrow."

"Bloody swine," said Sara, grabbing Vestlund by the hair and pulling his head back.

"I'll report you," he managed to say.

"For what?" said Sara. "For this?"

And then she kicked him in the ribs.

"Or this?"

Then she kicked him right in the crotch. Vestlund screamed and curled up into the fetal position.

"Sara!" said David, stepping between them.

He looked around to check whether anyone was filming. But everyone seemed to have their sights set on the front doors of Carl Bildt's old school, which were about to open.

"I slipped," said Sara. And then she added: "Why should he get off more lightly than Becky?"

"Stop it."

"He stabbed me," said Sara, showing the bloody wound on her thigh.

"OK, but we shouldn't be like them," said David. "How did you know he'd hit her?"

"Blood on his knuckles."

"Just that?"

"'Just that?'"

"No, I mean that was enough, was it? For you to realize. And you saw it from that distance."

"See for yourself."

"Yes, I can see it now. But I wouldn't have seen it from across the street."

"OK, let's get this swine on his feet and bring him in. Buying sex, grievous bodily harm, violently resisting arrest. I struck the knife out of his hand—it should be over there somewhere."

David found it and then they pulled Pål Vestlund to his feet.

Sara could still feel the adrenaline pumping through her body. She didn't have a lot of time for the theory of catharsis—the idea that implementing violence was an outlet that made one calmer, used by many martial arts trainers as an argument in favor of letting young criminals train at their clubs. Instead, Sara was convinced that it just built it up. The more she trained, the more she let the anger emerge, the more aggressive she became. Even Martin and the kids had begun to notice her increasingly short fuse. And you only had to look at football hooligans—no bloody way did they become less violent by fighting each other. No, sometimes she regretted accepting violence into her life—but on the other hand, it was good to be able to channel it at times like this. There were two sides to it.

They headed back toward the car, with Vestlund ducking his head in order to hide his face from any passing acquaintance.

As they walked past Café Foam, Sara's mobile rang. The ringtone told her it was Anna, her old study buddy at the police academy, who now worked in homicide in Västerort to the west of the city. Anna had been assigned "Somebody That I Used to Know" by Gotye as her personal ringtone—although it was mostly a joke. Truth be told, Sara knew her pretty well. Anna wasn't her only friend, but she was one of just a few.

"Nothing bad," said Sara into her mobile.

"Yes, I'm afraid it is," said Anna.

"I wanted a proposal that we grab a beer or something."

"And you're getting a murder in Bromma."

"OK. Of a prostitute?"

"Only for very kinky customers in that case," said Anna. "An eighty-five-year-old man with a bullet in his skull."

"OK...A john?"

"It actually has nothing to do with your job—this is purely private. I think you know the old man. Or knew him."

Family, neighbors, friends, old colleagues—names and faces rushed through her head. An old man murdered. Someone she knew.

"Who...?" was all she managed.

"Uncle Stellan."

"Uncle Stellan?" said Sara, trying to take it in. Struggling to fit it into the right place in her brain. But Uncle Stellan didn't seem to sit right. There wasn't a spot for him anywhere, actually.

"The old television presenter," said Anna. "You knew him, right?"

"Yes. Well, his daughters. Yes—him, too. I was there constantly when I was a kid."

"Well, then. Perhaps you can help."

"But hang on—has Uncle Stellan been murdered?"

"Shot in the head."

"You're kidding."

"No."

"By who?"

"No idea. Some dissatisfied ex-viewer? I thought you might know something. An old threat. Row in the family. Crazy neighbor. Bonkers admirer. I don't know."

"I'm on my way."

By the time Anna said "No," Sara had already hung up.

5

The driveway to the grand white villa was besieged by police cars, the street was cordoned off with blue and white tape, and police officers were coming and going. Neighbors and curious onlookers were standing at their garden fences and on the pavement, staring. They were trying to pump passing officers for information without seeming nosy. There weren't any journalists yet, but it was only a matter of time.

Sara parked a short distance away and walked up to the house. Even from a distance, she could feel herself being transported back in time and she had to stifle the impulse to check she hadn't turned back into her childhood self.

She flashed her police ID and stepped over the cordon.

"Sara!" someone called out behind her and she turned around. A white-haired man in dungarees and gardening gloves was looking at her.

"It's me. Jocke."

Jesus Christ. Jocke. The gardener.

"What's happened?" he said, the worry audible in his voice.

Sara could see how those around him pricked up their ears with curiosity. All in vain.

"I can't say anything," she said.

"But I'm part of the family."

"I know. But still. I'm sorry."

Sara continued toward the house. Jocke had seemed like a ghost from the past. So much older, but still the same as ever. It was remarkable that he still worked for the Bromans.

On the way to the front door, she glanced toward the garden and directed her steps that way instead. Perhaps it was the close encounter with the past that influenced her.

She could also feel how she was still buzzing with adrenaline following the arrest. She thought she probably needed to calm down before speaking to her childhood friends Malin and Lotta about their father's death. But it was mostly a pretext.

The Bromans' garden would always live on in her memory as the emblem of a paradise lost, a symbol of the innocent games of childhood. Perhaps she should take a look at it first, try and find a little respite from the crap she had to put up with in her job. Perhaps this was exactly what she needed just now. Well, if she ignored the awful reason for her visit, anyway.

The waterside garden was just as wonderful as she remembered. She walked past the small cabin for guests and onto the jetty. She hadn't stood here since she was a child. In her mind's eye she saw three little girls sitting and laughing and chucking cheese sandwiches into the water. Happy and carefree. Dark-haired Lotta, blonde Malin and red-haired Sara.

They had complemented each other. Formed a team.

She supposed it was here that they'd first heard the Swedish expression for skimming stones: "sandwich throwing." And they'd thought it sounded fun—especially if you used real sandwiches instead of stones. It had been a sunny day, just like this one. But it was an eternity ago. In another world.

What happened to all that? Sara thought to herself. *Why couldn't it carry on?*

They'd spent their days hanging out here, on this jetty, all through the warm summer months.

Had they ever actually swum?

Sara couldn't remember for sure, but they must have done. Yes, she could definitely remember swimming costumes and the smell of sun cream. She'd never been able to stand the scent. Why? Was it perhaps because they'd spent their days sitting here covered in sun cream, but never swimming?

Suddenly, she was uncertain—probably because she had remembered the reason for her visit. She turned around and headed toward the house.

Big, white and stylish. Expensive even back when the Bromans had bought it, and probably worth a fortune today.

It felt wrong not to ring the doorbell and wait for Aunt Agneta to open the door, or for the sisters to tumble out and hang on to the door handle, scrutinizing their summoned playmate. Those moments on the porch steps had always seemed like an entrance exam. After that, everything was normal.

But Sara didn't ring the bell. She opened the door and stepped inside. She looked around.

Nothing had changed.

It was almost literally like stepping into the past.

The hall was exactly as before, with the same coat rack, the same stool and the same telephone table. The same photos of Stellan with celebrities and politicians lined the walls. Everything she could see of the house's interior from here was the same as it had been thirty years ago. Everything was in the same place—even the smell was the same.

Was it possible for time to stand still?

Sara remembered exactly what it had been like to cross the threshold into the house, how Agneta had always come to meet her, even if one of her daughters had opened the door. She was substantially more inclined to be welcoming to guests than the rest of the family were.

In the living room, Forensics were working on the victim. The armchair was turned the other way, but Sara noticed an arm hanging lifeless on one side. She didn't want to see any more. Not now. Instead, she asked one of the forensics team where Anna was and received a gesture toward the kitchen in return.

As Sara approached the kitchen, she heard Malin's piercing voice.

"You have to find her!"

"We're working on it," Anna replied, in a slightly resigned tone.

Malin was shaken and disoriented when Sara came into the kitchen. As soon as she caught sight of her childhood friend, she got up and hurried toward her, with her hands extended in a gesture to ward her off.

"Sara, you can't be here," she said, shaking her head. "Something terrible has happened."

"It's OK. I'm a police officer," said Sara, showing her ID.

Malin stopped herself.

"Yes, of course—that's right, so you are. Sorry, it's so...Are you here on official business?"

She looked afraid, as if the fact that Sara was there in her capacity as a police officer, and not as a childhood friend, made the nightmare situation even worse.

"You didn't have to come here," said Anna.

Sara looked at Anna: short, fit and rapid in her movements. She inspired respect despite her diminutive stature. She had thick, black hair, brown eyes and dark skin, and she radiated decisiveness. They had often been at odds, but neither of them had previously got involved in the other's job.

"Yes," said Sara. "I did. It's Stellan."

Malin emitted a sob when she heard her father's name and Sara turned to her. Who had her childhood friend become?

To begin with, she saw that Malin was no longer a natural blonde. Her roots were mousy-colored, while the rest of her hair was platinum blonde. As expected, she was wearing expensive clothes. Sara guessed that Malin spent a lot of time shopping on Birger Jarlsgatan. Schuterman, Gucci, Prada—maybe even Chanel. Her handbag was Louis Vuitton. A little dull for Sara's tastes. She remembered the sisters as big brand snobs and harsh judges of taste—remembered how happy she'd been on the few occasions she had won their approval.

"Sara, they have to find Mum," said Malin in a small voice.

"Is Agneta missing?"

"Yes. And Dad is—"

"I know. It's completely insane. Stellan—shot."

"Where can Mum be?" said Malin, looking at Sara.

"Don't know. But they'll find her."

"How?" Malin's fear was turning into agitation. "She might have been shot, too. Or kidnapped. Or maybe she's lying injured somewhere, and she'll bleed to death if no one finds her."

Anna interrupted—perhaps more for Sara's sake than Malin's.

"As I've said, we've got uniformed officers out searching the area," she said. "Questioning people and looking for clues. We've got a boat out on the lake. We're trying to secure a helicopter. And if we don't find her, we'll bring in dogs."

"It's my mum!" said Malin.

"I know. But we can deal with this. Trust us."

Malin looked at Sara, who nodded reassuringly. When they were little, it had been the sisters who had been in charge, but now Malin had to be gracious and trust that she and her colleagues knew best.

"Is she dead?" said Malin, looking Sara in the eye.

"Don't you think she might have hidden somewhere? Given what happened to your dad."

"Yes. But then surely she could come out now?"

"Perhaps she doesn't know we're here. Where do you think she might go if she wanted to reach safety?"

"No idea. My house?"

"Might she be there?"

"No. Or... Well, we're here. She might be there waiting for us." Malin's eyes widened. "Is she there, Sara? Wondering where we are?"

"Do you think she has a phone with her?"

"No, it's lying in the kitchen. We called it."

"Is Christian here?"

"He was the one who called the police. I was... I just couldn't."

"Can I ask him to go back to yours and check whether Agneta's there?"

Malin had no objection, and Sara turned to Anna.

"What do you think?"

"Absolutely. I'll ask them to pick him up."

"He's with the kids at C.M.'s," said Malin. "The neighbor."

Anna nodded curtly and left.

Sara remembered C.M.: Carl Magnus something or other, an old friend of the family. He had lived in the house next door throughout her entire childhood and was apparently still there—a retired CEO who even during his working life had spent a lot of time playing tennis, golfing, and hunting with the king. He was renowned for having the most expensive rifle in the hunting club—more expensive than the king's, which according to Stellan was something of a violation of etiquette. Fabbri—Sara remembered that the gun had been called that. As a child she'd thought it sounded like *fabrik*, the Swedish word for "factory."

She also remembered that C.M. had been fairly clueless on those occasions when Stellan and Agneta had asked him to check on the girls when they were away. But Christian was there, too, and the grandchildren doubtless sensed the gravity of the situation. If kids were good at one thing, it was reading adults' state of mind. C.M. wasn't needed as a babysitter—the important thing was that he offered the family a little calm in the midst of everything else.

Sara examined Malin as she sat on a chair, staring vacantly into space. Underneath the makeup, her face was completely pale. What did it do to someone to find their father murdered? In their childhood home, too. Sara thought it would be better if Malin got professional help dealing with the trauma, but for the time being she, Sara, would try to calm her down by focusing on specific things.

"Why did you come here?" said Sara. "Were you visiting?"

"We'd already been here. Us and Lotta and her family. Mum and Dad looked after the kids while we were in France, and we came back today to pick them up. We waved goodbye and left, but Molly had forgotten her banana doll, so we came back."

"Where did you turn back?"

"Brommaplan."

"And when you came back, Stellan was already...?"

"Yes."

"That's only ten minutes—maybe fifteen—for everything to have happened."

"Yes. It doesn't make sense. It doesn't make sense..."

"What does Lotta say?"

Malin was silent as the words sank in.

"Don't know. She...I don't know if Christian's called her."

"He's on the way—I'll check with him...Malin?"

"Yes?"

"I have to go and...look at him. Will you be all right?"

"Absolutely."

Malin sounded absent, as if the answer was nothing but a reflex.

Sara went into the hall and then into the living room.

And there he was, sitting in the old Bruno Mathsson armchair. Uncle Stellan.

Lying on the floor beside him was a blood-spattered book. Goethe.

And next to the stereo there was a CD case—the *St. Matthew Passion*.

He had died surrounded by beauty.

Stellan Broman had been shot diagonally from behind, one of the forensics team advised, sweat running down her brow in the heat. The bullet had gone into the left-hand side of the back of his head, not far from his ear, and out of the side of his forehead, just above the end of the right eyebrow. Straight through the brain. Blood and brain matter had splattered onto his shirt, his cardigan, the armrest, the book and the floor.

Shot while he was sitting reading. Hadn't he heard the murderer?

Surely Stellan hadn't gone deaf? No, she couldn't see a hearing aid.

And what about Aunt Agneta? Where was she?

If she had hidden, surely she ought to have ventured out by now. It must have been a couple of hours since Stellan had been shot, and the police had searched the house several times, according to Anna.

So where was she?

One option was that the murderer had taken her with them—an unpleasant thought, to say the least.

A hostage drama with her friends' aged mother. But why? Kidnapping was one of the toughest crimes to pull off successfully—Sara knew that much. It almost always went wrong.

She looked around the room. It seemed so much smaller now than when they had been little. People had been born, grown up and had their own kids since she'd last been here.

The Mathsson armchairs, well-filled bookcases, the sofa and coffee table from Svenskt Tenn covered in Josef Frank fabric—had they been reupholstered, or just carefully used?

Everything in perfect order.

She recollected that you didn't play just anywhere at the Bromans'—it wasn't like at Sara's, where there weren't really any boundaries between Sara's world and her mother's. Perhaps because it was such a squeeze with toys and adult possessions on top of each other, despite the fact that Sara spent most of her waking hours at the Bromans'. Now she couldn't understand how her mother had put up with it, but she was grateful that she had done, and that she had shown Sara a freer world—a home in which Sara was allowed to be present and to help set the rules.

But at the Bromans', you played outside or in the girls' room. And if the weather or space requirements ever meant you needed to use the living room, you tidied up carefully afterward.

She remembered that it was never as much fun to play in the rest of the house as it was in the girls' room or in the garden. But the sisters demanded that they did sometimes, in some sort of protest against the established order. They were always uninspired games whose rules were invented after the fact. Games that were never played twice.

How could she have foreseen that she would be standing here today, with Stellan murdered in his armchair? Same house, same people, but nothing else the same…

She had run into Aunt Agneta and Uncle Stellan a couple of times at the NK department store and at the market stalls at Brommaplan, and in those instances Agneta had seemed happier than Sara remembered her being during her childhood. When the girls were little, Agneta had seemed resolute, almost strict, with her big seventies-style glasses, carefully styled hair and elegant dresses from Paris. In the company of adults, she took a step up and became the perfect hostess. Stellan had been playful and inventive in an educational way—but only for brief periods. Then he had preferred to read or talk to a grown-up. He'd probably carried on being like that, Sara thought to herself. A man who only really cared about his job and his books. Unless the subject at hand was him, of course. Then he could talk forever.

Uncle Stellan. When the girls were little, he had been the most famous person in the country, alongside Palme and the king. Everyone had watched Stellan's shows, everyone had talked about them the next day, everyone had quoted them and been amused by them. *The Happy Country, Good Neighbours, Sheer Madness.* Televised entertainment with loads of practical jokes like "woolen cap day"—when everyone had to wear a woolen cap on a set day. Or "let's all be kind"—greeting strangers and asking whether you could help them with anything. And who could forget "electrical fault," when all the viewers had been encouraged to flash their lights at home simultaneously?

All of Sweden had taken part.

And loved it.

Sara had always been jealous of her friends for having Stellan as their father, while she only had her mother. At the same time, she'd been grateful that *she* got to play in the home of the great man. He had become at least a partial replacement for the father she never had.

Uncle Stellan. Cheerful Stellan, Playful Stellan, Sweden's Stellan.

Why would someone want to shoot him dead?

When Anna came into the living room, Sara couldn't stop herself digging a little, despite it not being her case. She reasoned that it was—on a personal level.

"So what do you think?" she said.

"Break-in gone wrong."

"Stellan caught a burglar? But he was shot from behind, sitting down."

"Maybe he didn't notice the burglar, but the burglar saw him and panicked. We're in Bromma—there are burglaries all the time. There are often two or three different gangs working simultaneously."

"But they must have come in just as the families left," Sara objected.

"They might even have seen the cars leaving and thought they had a green light. It might be some real brutal bastards—maybe one of the gangs from the east. They might have come into the house, despite knowing someone was at home, because the alarm wasn't on. And then the first thing they did was get rid of a potential witness."

"And Agneta saw that and fled?"

"Or they took her with them. Did they have a safe deposit box?"

"Don't know," Sara said. "Do you think they went there with her to empty it?"

"They might even have known that he kept something specific in it. Have any of the papers written about something expensive he owns?"

"Not a clue. But is there anything to suggest it was a break-in?"

"His wallet is missing. Maybe a few valuables. We've not yet had the daughter check."

"What an unnecessary way to die," said Sara.

"What were they like?"

"As people? Stellan was friendly, but completely focused on his job and career. He loved being famous. Agneta was a bit reserved when we were little, but she was always nice to Stellan's guests. And a dutiful mother. I think she turned into a bit of a doting granny when the grandkids came along. I suppose she was busy supporting Stellan's career when we were little."

"Managing the home?"

"And hosting parties and being a hostess. Wandering around with a long, brown More cigarette and a drink and talking to everyone, introducing them to each other. She was the one who came up with all the themes and rounded up whatever was needed—catering staff, musicians, entertainment, props."

"Props?" Anna asked.

"They always had themes for their parties. The Roman Empire, the Twenties, Dracula. Full costumes and matching music. And the whole house was done up. It was a massive job—they might have hundreds of guests. Artists, politicians, businessmen, authors, celebrities, researchers, foreign diplomats. Like Bindefeld's bashes, but more fun. Something always happened. Naval battles in the lake, snowball fights in the middle of summer, wine fountains. Everyone loved the parties. Once, they built a water slide from the roof of the house into the lake. Another time, they filled the house with balloons—every single room—from floor to ceiling, and the guests had to fumble their way around. And things could get pretty wild. It's said that Rita Berg once went waterskiing naked right in front of all the guests."

"And you were right there, in a corner?"

Sara laughed. She'd never really grasped how unusual her childhood had been.

"As kids, we mostly just watched. Until bedtime. And as I got older, I lost touch with Malin and Lotta."

"So you didn't go to any celebrity parties?"

"My husband's are quite enough."

"That's right—you really do move among the upper echelons."

"Well, higher up than at work—but not that high."

Anna grinned.

"He's in the kitchen."

A female uniformed officer with a black ponytail and hawkish nose stuck her head into the room, addressing Anna. Sara realized she meant Christian.

"And some journalists have turned up," said hawk-nose as the three headed for the kitchen. "They want to know if something's happened to 'Uncle Stellan.'"

Did "Uncle Stellan" still sell papers?

"Yes, of course they do," said Anna. "Just say that something's happened, that we have no comment to make and that we'll make a statement soon."

When they reached the kitchen door, the policewoman peeled away from them like a fighter jet breaking out of formation to pursue its own assignment.

Before entering the kitchen, Anna stopped and grabbed Sara's arm.

"Don't you feel something?"

"What?"

"A presence. I feel a presence."

Anna's hocus-pocus. Sara had forgotten that side of her friend. She wasn't just an effective and analytical police officer—she had a fuzzy, witchy side too.

"He hasn't passed over," said Anna. "You touched him—you ought to be able to feel that."

"Sorry," said Sara. "I can't feel a thing."

"I'm getting a lot. This house is full of memories—energies."

"Not surprising, given all their parties," said Sara.

Anna looked deep into her eyes.

"Nothing?"

"No."

"There's someone here who doesn't want to talk to me. I think they want to speak to you."

"Give him my mobile number," Sara said with a smirk.

"Maybe it's best if you stay a little while," said Anna, ignoring Sara's grin. "Is that all right?"

"Of course."

Ghost or not, Sara thought she could be of some assistance.

In the kitchen, Christian was holding his wife's hand. Sara had only met him a few times: once at the shopping mall in Sickla when she'd run into them by chance, and then of course at their wedding, which had been an odd experience. A clear reminder of a part of Sara's past that was gone—beyond reach.

She had never felt so dictated to, so unwelcome, while it was also demanded that she be there. The perfect wedding required that all periods of the bride's life be represented, but it felt as if it bothered Malin that Sara was one of those parts. The childhood friend. The friend who had fallen—degraded from the idyllic Bromma to the miserable Vällingby, according to Malin. So Sara thought.

Christian extended a hand, and Sara got the impression that the serious expression was a pose he'd chosen to adopt. The same could probably be said of the rest of his exterior: well-ironed shirt, dress trousers with Hermès belt and an expensive watch. There were thousands of financiers just like him. Drove a BMW or Audi, worked out twice a week, used as many skin products as their wives. But he doubtless earned loads of money, and that was probably important to Malin. It could hardly be his personality she'd fallen for. Sara doubted whether she would be able to pick Christian out of a line-up a minute after meeting him.

"Hi. Have you called Lotta?" she asked.

Christian looked from Sara to his wife and then back to Sara.

"No. Sorry. I didn't think of that. I—"

"It doesn't matter. I was going to ask you something else—could you go back to yours and check whether Agneta has gone there?"

"Absolutely...Can I take the kids with me?"

Sara looked at Anna.

"Of course," she said.

"You don't need to ask them anything? It's OK for them to leave?"

"You're free to take them with you. Where is it you live, by the way?"

"Lidingö."

Of course.

"Will *you* be all right, darling?" Christian said to Malin.

"Yes. Sara's here."

Sara couldn't help being surprised by the sudden confidence in her—almost a little moved. But then it struck her that Christian might now play the same role in Malin's life that Sara had done in childhood: someone who did as she told them to, someone who could admire her and fetch her things. Provided that there was someone like that nearby, Malin was probably OK—perhaps it was that simple. That thought wasn't as touching.

"I'll call later," said Christian to Sara, before looking at his wife again to show that the words also applied to her. Annoyingly, he made the gesture with his thumb and little finger held out.

"Shall I call Lotta?" said Sara once he'd left.

"I'll do it. I just don't know what to say."

Sara pulled out her mobile and got Lotta's personal number from Malin. Lotta answered after two rings.

"Hello, this is Sara Nowak."

"Hello."

She paused briefly to give Lotta the chance to say something, but she didn't so Sara carried on.

"Have you heard from your mother recently?"

44

"Yes, we were there today."

"But not since you left here?"

"No. What do you mean 'here'? Are you there?"

"I'm a police officer nowadays, as you might know. I'm here with Malin at Stellan and Agneta's. I'm afraid I've got bad news. Your father is dead. And your mother is missing." A new pause to give Lotta the opportunity to take in what she'd just heard. After a period of silence on the line, Sara spoke again. "We're assuming your mother is unharmed. That she's just hiding somewhere. When people are scared and upset, it's easy for them to make slightly irrational decisions."

"'Hiding'? Why?"

"Because Stellan's been murdered. And we think Agneta may have fled from the murderer."

There was a long silence before a sound was heard on the other end.

"Are you joking?"

"Absolutely not."

"Murdered?"

"Yes. It doesn't make sense. Maybe a burglar. We don't know. We're making inquiries and trying to find out if anyone saw anything."

"I'm on my way."

Sara ended the call, which gave a male uniformed officer the opportunity to report to Anna.

"We've now dealt with all the nearest houses—no one heard or saw anything. We'll continue working outwards over a wider radius. Unfortunately there's no public CCTV here. The boating club has a system, but only overlooking the jetties, and we don't think the murderer arrived by boat, or that the missing person left by that route. We'll still request the tapes, just to be sure. There are a lot of homes with CCTV, but they're directed at doors and gardens. And no one reported their alarms going off, so our hypothesis right now is that Agneta Broman went along Grönviksvägen—presumably in the opposite direction her daughter came from when she returned. Either alone, or together with the perpetrator. If she was taken hostage, that is."

Anna looked at Malin, as if she thought that the final remark had been rather a harsh thing to say in front of the daughter of the missing person. Sara also looked at Malin to see whether anything the policeman had said had caused a reaction. But she seemed to be absent.

"Do we want to put out an appeal in the press to find her?" the uniformed officer asked.

"Not yet," said Anna.

Then there was silence until Malin startled everyone by crying out: "But where *is* she?"

6

All the air had escaped en route.

The back tire was empty by the time Agneta reached Drottningholm, and the front tire by Nyckelby—so she cycled the final kilometers on the rims alone. She hoped that no one would notice her because of it. But then again, a pink bicycle with no air in the tires didn't exactly scream "murderer on the loose," so she crossed her fingers.

With the collar of her coat turned up and her hat pulled down as far as it would go, Agneta had at least made it hard for passersby to get a good look at her. There was more of a risk that someone would think she was a mad old bat who'd escaped from her old people's home as she pedaled on, panting and her face bright red. Wrapped up in furs in this heat! If they thought that, they might try to return her against her will.

It was at least twenty years since she'd last been on a bicycle, if not longer. The sweat was running down her brow and soaking her back, and she had been obliged to stop and rest several times. Her heart was pounding so hard that it felt like being punched by a fist.

All the other cyclists on Ekerö had racing bikes and shiny, skin-tight lycra clothing. Agneta was wearing ECCO shoes and riding an old bike with a puncture.

Hopefully, they would all just take her for an old dear who had never got her license and cycled everywhere instead. A local born and bred—there were still plenty of them on the islands in Mälaren. In just a decade or so, they would all be gone—house prices had tripled, and many homes were now occupied by displaced city dwellers who drove much too fast on the winding country roads, careless of local wildlife.

Only when she turned down the narrow gravel track toward the barn in the woods did she ask herself whether everything would still be there.

When had she actually last checked?

Ten years ago? Twelve? It hadn't been as long as fifteen, in any case. Was it as recently as five? The years all merged into one, flashing by like the landscape outside the window on a train journey— hard to take in, impossible to stop, and you soon forgot the details. All the houses, trees and vehicles turned into one single blur, leaving your thoughts to wander. You were everywhere except the here and now. You forgot that you were on your way somewhere. That was how her life had passed by.

Until now. The train had stopped and she had got off in a place she hadn't seen for a long time.

Agneta's legs were trembling with overexertion when she finally propped the bicycle against the wall of the barn. Her throat was on fire and her lungs felt as if they were going to explode. Her level of fitness was dismal, but was that any surprise at this age?

In the life she had chosen long ago, there was no retirement age— and now she realized all too clearly the downside of that.

There was a small padlock key attached to her car keys. She had no idea what the farmer who rented out the spot in the empty barn made of it all, but she hoped he'd bought her story about a nostalgic car owner in long-term care who refused to die—which was why his car remained here, year after year. As long as the money kept arriving in his account, he probably didn't care, she thought to herself.

The padlock was a little stiff, but eventually it opened. She unhooked it and swung open the doors. An old, pale blue Volvo 245 estate model. KOA 879. Chosen because it was easy to drive, reliable and simple to repair. Good as new, albeit covered in a thick layer of dust.

It struck her how old-fashioned this entire safety net was. But no one had counted on time galloping away like this, or thought that it would be relevant after so many years. But now things were how they were. And she needed to check the crumbling remains of the once well-oiled machine to see whether there was anything that might be of use to her.

Of course, the car wouldn't start—so she opened the bonnet, attached the battery charger and plugged it into the wall socket.

The fact that she had picked a barn with an electricity supply all those years ago had been an inspired decision. Secluded location, uninterested owner and an electricity supply. Just as she had so often done before, she wondered exactly how good she was compared with others in her world. She knew that she was skilled, but perhaps all her old colleagues had been even better?

Perhaps she had merely been a cheerful amateur? A useful idiot. The fact that so many people had seen her had been entirely deliberate and necessary, but what was the truth of the situation?

If nothing else, Agneta would need to deliver a top-level performance to pull off what was expected of her.

In all likelihood, she was under time pressure too. But you couldn't rush everything. Eight hours was how long it would take to charge the battery, according to the manual, and her arthritis meant she wouldn't be able to move for several hours after the bicycle ride.

Sometimes it helped to apply liniment before the aches set in, so Agneta got out her Siduro and a tin of the old classic, Sloan's— the one that Stellan had always borrowed to avoid buying his own, thus acknowledging that he, too, had grown old.

Then she got out her blood sugar monitor—a Mendor Discreet— pricked her finger and checked the sensor. Good results. Perhaps she should have waited a little longer before testing. The exertion might not have taken its toll yet.

She got out the food bag she had put in her rucksack. Apples, biscuits and some tinned sausages—but no can opener. It would have to be apples and biscuits. And hopefully some sleep.

Eight hours alone in a barn with the back seat of a car as the only place to rest. A serious delay, but there was nothing to be done about that.

She was tired, so she welcomed the chance to sleep. And hopefully no one had found Stellan. They weren't expecting visitors. No one had any reason to come to the house.

That gave her the days she needed, and she didn't need to worry about her other targets being tipped off.

The only question was how quickly Suleiman could get here.

Suleiman, or Abu Omar, or Abu Rasil—whichever name he was using this time.

The legend that she'd never met, although he'd supposedly been watching at a couple of training camps that Agneta had attended during the 1970s. Even back then, he'd been an icon about whom significantly more stories were told than could possibly be true. The myth who was always one step ahead of the Israeli Mossad and the Western intelligence agencies. The one who avoided hundreds of attempts to arrest or kill him. Was he still alive? Was he going to turn up?

Agneta knew the phone call meant he was on his way.

Was he already in the country? If so, things were bad. But she was counting on him having been somewhere far away—probably living under a false name in the Middle East. But perhaps he'd been living his new life in Europe, which would mean he could get here much more quickly.

People like Abu Rasil weren't normally able to travel all that fast. It wasn't just a case of hopping on the next flight to Sweden. Naturally, everyone had their eyes on one another.

So perhaps she had a few days after all.

She needed all the time she could get, especially at this age. She needed to rest in advance of what was coming.

What she had just begun.

Her own mission.

It was still hard to take it in after all these years.

Now it was actually happening.

Until now it had merely been a distant threat, a catastrophic scenario, an unpleasant fantasy.

After thirty years of a completely different life—a normal life—she was suddenly back to being the person she had been in her youth. The person she had been drilled from childhood to become.

Would she pull it off?

7

"This is crazy!"

Less than half an hour after their call, Lotta stormed into the kitchen.

"Police everywhere. At Mum and Dad's."

Trailing in her wake was a skinny young woman with a huge underbite and a careworn air about her. She was weighed down with double shoulder bags plus a separate laptop bag, and was presumably an ambitious assistant whom Lotta was leaning on rather too heavily.

"Sara," said Lotta, giving her a quick hug before embracing Malin. Then she shook hands with Anna.

"Lotta Broman."

"Detective Inspector Anna Torhall."

Sara examined her friend from childhood and saw that she'd gained a few gray hairs since they'd last met. Lotta would never dream of dyeing her hair. And the few wrinkles she had were probably a source of pride. They showed that she was serious. A professional woman. Director General of the Swedish International Development Cooperation Agency, with many years ahead in her career.

"What's happened?" said Lotta, turning to Sara. "How is this possible? Is it really true? Where is he?"

She looked around, as if her father might appear in the kitchen— perhaps looking a little embarrassed that they'd been brought here for his sake.

"Sit down," said Sara, while Anna loitered in the background. She was leaning against the kitchen counter, listening. Agneta had never liked her doing that, Sara thought to herself.

"Coffee?" said the downtrodden assistant.

"Yes, put some on for everyone," said Lotta. "The coffee is in that cupboard over there."

"I don't think we should touch anything," said Malin.

Lotta looked at Sara.

"A pot of coffee should be all right," she said, after checking with Anna, and the assistant turned away.

"OK," said Lotta. "Talk."

"Your father was shot," said Anna, stepping into the center of the room. She waited a second before continuing. "In the living room. We don't know by whom or why. And Agneta is missing. We're searching for her, and we're assuming she fled when she heard the shot, and that she's hiding somewhere."

"But where?"

"We don't know."

"You have to find her!" Malin leaped up, looking as though she wanted to run away, but didn't know where to. "It's been several hours!"

"There are police patrols out there searching the area," said Sara, updating Lotta. "Making inquiries and looking for evidence."

"Sara," said Lotta. "It's our mum."

"I understand that it's a lot to take in. But they know what works best. Trust them."

"'Them'? Aren't you working on this?"

"No. I'm just here as a friend of the family."

There was silence for a moment, as if everyone needed to digest what had just been said.

"Shot?" said Lotta.

"Yes, I'm afraid so. It's hard to get your head around."

"Is he still in there?" Lotta added, pointing toward the living room.

"No. They've just driven him to the forensic medicine center."

"Are they going to cut him up?"

"You mean an autopsy? Yes."

Naturally, it was impossible to contemplate one's father not only being dead, but shot, Sara thought to herself. And then cut open on a stainless steel bench, with strangers turning the body inside out and examining, weighing and measuring. One's father taken apart. And just a couple of hours after seeing him and everything being normal.

"I need to ask, even if it might sound strange," said Anna. "But have there been any threats against Stellan?"

"Threats? No. Of course not." Lotta couldn't help laughing incredulously.

"Did he get into any disputes with anyone? A quarrel? Maybe he received some angry emails? Had anyone made threats?" The sisters shook their heads time after time. "Was he honked at while out driving? Might he have driven in a way that upset someone?"

"Would someone have shot him for driving badly?"

"You've no idea what kind of disturbed people there are out there. High as a kite, pumped up on adrenaline, stuffed with anabolic steroids. Honking at them or overtaking them might be all it takes. Road rage is much more common than you'd think."

"We can't possibly know," said Lotta. "But he didn't drive aggressively, or slowly like an old man. Anyway, he barely drove at all. He can't have upset someone."

"Did he receive any strange letters? 'Presents' on the doorstep or in the garden? These days, practically all celebrities have a stalker or two. It's nothing new, really. Just remember Evert Taube."

"But it's been thirty years since Dad was last on television. Why would a crazy stalker wait until now?"

"Maybe they've been inside. Or in a mental hospital."

"He's always had nothing but love from people. I've never heard an ill word against him."

"What about the person who tried to burn down the shed?" said Malin. "Might that have been a stalker?"

"Odd way of showing adulation," said Sara.

"Did someone try to burn down the garden shed?" said Anna.

"In the eighties," said Lotta. "It'll hardly have been the same person after thirty-five years."

"He used to get letters and flowers and stuff like that," said Malin. "On the *Allsång* show, we receive loads of emails and presents for both the guests and Sanna, who presents it. Some of them are sick, although there are some sweet ones too."

"Perhaps it was a case of mistaken identity," said Anna. "It's happened quite a few times in Sweden—if someone with the same name owes money to some dangerous people."

"But in that case, they surely ought to have realized they had the wrong person when they saw Dad?"

"He was shot from behind," said Sara, immediately regretting that she'd so clumsily mentioned the details of their father's murder.

"A mistake?" said Malin, shaking her head. "How awful."

"What a horrible thought," said Lotta.

"We're knocking on every door in the neighborhood—both to find Agneta and to get information about the murder. Violent crimes are often solved because someone happened to see something. A car parked somewhere odd. Someone throwing away their coat. Or dropping their mobile."

"But that doesn't change the fact that our dad's dead."

"No."

The three childhood friends sat silently in the Broman family kitchen, just as they'd done so many times before, but now with an entirely different reason for the shared silence.

"I went down to the jetty earlier," said Sara, smiling slightly. "I haven't been there since middle school. Do you remember when we wanted to skim stones, but instead we threw sandwiches in the lake?"

"Yes, it was really nice," said Malin.

"No," said Lotta. "I don't remember that."

Without saying a word, Lotta's grim-faced assistant put coffee and a carton of milk on the table, and without asking she poured milk into Lotta's cup while the others were left to help themselves. Sara sipped the hot, black coffee—a sign that they were all adults. No hot chocolate now.

"Did you look in the guest cabin, too?" Lotta asked Sara.

"No. Didn't have time."

Lotta's gaze lingered on Sara before she turned to Anna.

"You don't have any trace of Mum?" she asked.

"Not yet. But we will," said Anna.

"We'll find her," said Sara.

"I'm sorry, but I need to ask some more questions." Anna turned to Lotta. "The more we have to work with, the better."

"Go ahead."

"Did you notice anything at all strange or different when you were here? The atmosphere, something that was said, some new object or one that had moved from its usual spot? Anything?"

"No."

"It was just as usual."

"No other visitors or calls?"

"Well, the phone rang," said Malin. "Just as we were leaving."

"Did it?" said Lotta. "I didn't hear that."

"No, you'd got into the car. It was when I was saying bye to Mum."

"And the phone rang?" said Anna.

"Yes, so Mum went inside to answer as we left."

"It was Agneta who answered? Not Stellan?"

"She said she was going to answer it." Malin couldn't help smiling. "They still have a landline."

"But you don't know anything about who it was or what was said?"

"No, we left."

"It *may* have been a burglar calling to see if anyone was at home," said Anna.

"But in that case they wouldn't have broken in, would they?" Malin said. "If Mum picked up?"

"Or the person calling wanted to be certain that they were at home," said Sara.

The implication hung over them for a while before anyone said anything. Lotta looked thoughtful.

"We'll check the phone records," said Anna, in an attempt to placate the sisters.

"Do many people call here?" Sara asked.

"No, almost never. They mostly see C.M. these days, and he lives next door. And Mum has her mobile. I don't know why they still have the landline."

"And we know she's not at C.M.'s?" said Sara.

"We've already checked with all the neighbors," said Anna.

"Order to the slave—find Mum," said Lotta, smiling forcedly at Sara.

"Order to the slave."

She'd completely forgotten about that game, and she realized that it made her feel ill at ease.

Why?

Because of an old game?

Lotta had probably intended it as a friendly allusion to their childhood, but the reminder had made Sara uncomfortable. Now that she thought back, she realized that the games had been solely based on her obeying the sisters and being forced to do lots of humiliating things. That innocent childhood had encompassed more than sunshine and swimming. Some of her memories were darker than others.

Anna received a call and when she ended it, she turned to Sara.

"We're going to focus on a gang responsible for a wave of break-ins in this neighborhood. They stabbed a man in his own home when they happened upon him."

"Stabbed?" said Sara. "They didn't shoot him?"

"Burglars who resort to violence when they're interrupted, in this neighborhood. I think we can consider your father's murder solved." Anna turned to the sisters.

"And Mum?" said Malin.

"We'll find her soon."

"Then they can..." said Sara to Anna, who nodded.

She turned to her childhood friends.

"Listen—go home to your families. Take care of each other. They'll call if they need to ask you anything else."

"And when we find your mother," said Anna.

Sara hugged the sisters, and then Anna escorted them out.

Sara looked around the kitchen. Every single detail—every tile, every spice jar—served as reminders of her childhood. Sara couldn't help looking in the cupboards. Nothing had changed.

It felt as if she'd traveled back in time and soon she would meet all of the house's occupants, looking just as they'd looked when she'd said farewell to them more than thirty years ago. Would she warn them, or just take the chance to be a child and avoid thinking about all the things that filled her brain these days?

Sara shook off these thoughts. A longing for the past meant that she was wishing away her own children and family—her entire adult life and the experiences she'd gathered over the course of it. And she didn't want to be without them.

It was high time she returned to her own life. To her own family, and the present.

But she would do that with a new perspective on existence—the insight that anything could happen at any time.

Sara looked around one last time and shivered slightly.

Anna would have said that Sara could feel Stellan's presence, but she knew better.

If there was one thing she could feel, it was Stellan's absence.

8

Forest.

Forest, forest, forest.

How on earth could her fellow countrymen love this godforsaken backwater so much?

Why would anyone buy a summer cabin in the middle of an ancient forest stretching for kilometers in every direction? No views, no space, no air. Trees, forest, darkness.

And apparently Sweden was only properly hot for a week or so every year. It sounded very much like her own private vision of hell.

You were supposed to go south on your holidays—not north. To light and warmth, not cold and darkness. The Swedes were slow, antisocial and bad at languages. They only spoke English. Not a word of German. There was no reason whatsoever to come here.

The dark landscape flew past the car window. Tens of kilometers without buildings or people.

"Jönköping." How the hell did they name their towns in this place? It was unpronounceable. "*Jöön-kööpink*."

Karla Breuer didn't like traveling for work, she didn't like traveling by car, and she didn't like her fat colleague Jakob Strauss. Naturally, he'd questioned the entire mission, wondering what harm a gang of senile old spies could do.

She didn't dignify that with a response.

Almost 200 kilometers an hour. It was time he contained himself. Their job was *not* to draw attention to themselves. They'd left the operations van a long, long way in their wake. What would they do in Stockholm without it? Sit there twiddling their thumbs, waiting?

And he couldn't shut up either. He rambled on about everything from the medieval crusades to the dip in form experienced by Borussia Mönchengladbach. Things she either knew more about than he did or was completely uninterested in.

And there was the bloody music he felt obliged to play at top volume. "Papa Won't Leave You, Henry." You don't say.

Finally, a view.

A big lake with a big island, and the ruins of an old castle.

And then more forest.

If she had been able to, she would have banned Germans from buying cabins in Sweden. She would have banned Sweden in its entirety.

And she would have banned men from driving cars, apart perhaps from small electric cars that couldn't do more than 50 kilometers an hour.

That damn need to stimulate a rush of blood to the head by doing everything in excess! Sex, alcohol, sport, work, speed. All in doses that were too high. Too much, too fast, without interruption.

Never stopping.

Never thinking.

Never accepting the meaninglessness of life.

Just working. Competing, maximizing and, deep down, screaming in panic.

She had never understood the point of reunification. It was responsible for this type of person. A childhood characterized by discipline and gloominess, jealousy of the West, and the desire for capitalism. And now that all of this was available to the "German Russians," as the former East Germans were referred to, they couldn't handle the freedom—everything had to be as expensive as possible, as ostentatious as possible, as eye-catching as possible. Branded fashion with bold logos, expensive cars with huge engines, big brash wristwatches, exclusive restaurants. All to show the world that they were definitely not some pipsqueak from the East with a bowl haircut and fake jeans. At least, not any longer.

It takes time to merge two countries—to unify two cultures that are so different. If it is even possible.

Ten years ago, when she'd found out that even in her department they would have to accept a number of employees with East German backgrounds, she'd expected a small flock of gray-haired, bureaucratic office rats. Deep-sea fish, barely capable of surviving without external pressure.

Instead, they'd been given delayed teenage rebellion. A bunch of adrenaline-filled Dobermans hungry for revenge, who put all their energy into being more stereotypically Western than Westerners could ever be. Now that they'd finally been let into the real security service, they wanted to be tougher and more efficient than all their new colleagues. They turned into stereotypes, and in her eyes they brought nothing of value.

She hoped that Strauss wouldn't ruin this for her. This was her final chance to prove that the legend of Abu Rasil was true, while also burying him. To show everyone that her theories were correct—that one single man, with just one aim, had been responsible for most of the terrorist attacks in the 1970s and 1980s. She wanted to show the world that she wasn't mad, and she wanted to rescue her legacy. It was all connected.

Her entire career had been characterized by the mysterious terrorist. There had been many witness accounts of his existence, yet her colleagues refused to believe them.

Breuer did, though.

She'd written report after report, tied witness statements to technical evidence and grainy photos to signatures on hotel bills and car rental agreements. In vain.

Someone had pointed out that Breuer herself was helping to build up the myth surrounding the terrorist, but the more frightening

Abu Rasil appeared, the better, in her view. If the threat became big enough, her colleagues' eyes might be opened.

Despite the lack of interest from those higher up, she had chased elusive shadows across continents, following in his footsteps, trying to think his thoughts. But Karla Breuer had always arrived too late. Had always missed him. Now she knew that she would be in the same place as Abu Rasil for the last time. Soon, her career would be over. Before that, the world needed to believe in the ruthless terrorist called Abu Rasil, and Breuer needed to deliver if she was to stand a chance of getting out with her honor intact.

She'd been looking forward to growing old on a beach somewhere hot, but that dream had faded when she'd heard about the call to Stockholm. Now Breuer understood that the instinctive reluctance she'd felt about retiring was connected to her colleagues' view of her as being fixated on a figment of her imagination. They believed her opponent had died long ago, if he'd ever existed in the first place. But Breuer was trying to warn them that he was waiting in the shadows, planning one last act—worse than anything they'd seen before.

Just like her, Abu Rasil was considering his legacy. Naturally, he didn't want his work to be forgotten. The world would remember him. As the greatest terrorist ever.

9

Sara couldn't stay at a crime scene if she wasn't part of the investigation, but neither could she let go of this incomprehensible murder.

Who had shot Stellan?

And why?

Outside the house, the curious onlookers had been joined by reporters. A couple of them recognized Sara, and called out her name as if they were old friends.

"Is it Stellan?" one shouted.

"Is it to do with prostitution?" said another.

Sara didn't reply, but they wouldn't give up. The moment she got into the car, Tillberg tapped on the window.

"You don't have to tell me," she said. "Just say no if I'm wrong. Is it Uncle Stellan? Is he hurt? Is he dead?"

Sara started the engine, put the car into drive and put her foot down.

This wasn't just about the murder; an important part of her childhood had been erased. Instead of going home, she drove along Grönviksvägen to Rättviksvägen, then past the square at Nockeby and on to Drottningholmsvägen. There she took a left when the lights turned green, and went across the bridge.

In the middle of Kärsön, she indicated left, crossed the opposite carriageway and drove down to Brostugan—the cafe beneath the bridge. She could sit here and think in peace and quiet while still being close to Stellan's house—it was almost visible across the water. It felt good not to leave the Broman family quite yet.

Sara stepped out of the car's air-conditioned coolness into the sauna of summer. The only thing disturbing her peace was the traffic up on the bridge.

She walked toward the main entrance, stopped outside and checked the menu. Alongside her were people in shorts and vest tops doing the same—hungry despite the heat.

A group of middle-aged bikers meekly carried their trays inside. Then they put on their helmets, making themselves look dangerous again, before rumbling away. The other patrons didn't seem able to make up their minds, so Sara decided to go ahead of them.

Inside, the cafe felt like the quarters of a well-to-do farmer from another era. The fact that all the customers were sitting outside in the sunshine reinforced the slightly unreal feeling of the inside. In the queue at the till was an older man, joking with the woman in front of him that he got a discount because he was a regular, before quickly adding that he lived alone beside Mälaren because his wife had dementia and had moved to a home. Perhaps it was a clumsy chat-up line, Sara thought to herself. But on the other hand, why not try your luck?

Sara took a large glass of water and a coffee with too much milk and headed outside to sit in the sunshine—as far from the other patrons as possible. She ended up next to a dull gravel car park in which Pontiacs and modern Mustangs were overrepresented. Together with the gray-haired bikers, the cars gave the impression that Brostugan was a gathering place for men in late middle age who were still keeping their boyhood dreams alive.

Sara wondered fleetingly what her own girlhood dreams had been, but she couldn't think of any. Did that mean she would avoid a midlife crisis? Or did she simply have a lot of repressed dreams?

The sun was practically burning her skin and a couple of wasps were circling her coffee cup, followed by the classic solitary fly that buzzed right in front of her eyes. She wafted it away, but knew it would return. Sara had never been here before, so she carried on looking around. A deserted mini-golf course. Canoes on the shore. A flag advertising an ice cream brand, fluttering down by the water. Maybe it was to tempt boaters, otherwise its position was odd.

A single bead of sweat trickled down her brow. The sun was shining properly—maybe she would end up sunburned. Like most people nowadays, she was mostly worried about the climate, rather than pleased about the heat now that they were finally getting a proper summer.

She sat quite still for several minutes, just breathing. Then thoughts about Stellan's death began to creep up on her. A break-in gone wrong didn't seem to fit with the way the murder had been committed. Sara was convinced that someone had shot Stellan deliberately and willfully. That he'd been the target.

But why?

Were there any scandals in his past? Could it have been someone seeking revenge?

She couldn't think of anything, so she got her mobile out to search for "Stellan Broman" and "crime." Then "Stellan Broman" and "scandals," as well as "reports" and "police." Most of the articles she pulled up mentioned Stellan's old television pursuits, which had annoyed some viewers and led to reports and complaints. But there was nothing serious enough to merit murder thirty or forty years later.

One of the complainers was upset that Stellan's "greet a stranger" initiative had led to strangers greeting her constantly; she wanted to be left alone when she was out and about.

When Sara searched for "Stellan Broman" and "accusations," she got an unexpected hit. A link to an article about a book by a Swedish researcher. The subject was the Cold War.

"Former TV presenter Stellan Broman denies that he was identified in scandalous book."

Sara scrolled on and searched for the researcher's name. Eva Hedin was a retired professor of history who'd written two books about Swedes who worked for the Stasi—the East German security service. According to the article, which had run in one of the nationals, Stellan Broman had been identified as one of them—something he denied.

There was just one article in which Stellan was named specifically, but another half a dozen or so about the books, and the fact that Swedes had been identified as Stasi accomplices.

No matter how far-fetched it seemed, the Stasi connection was the only thing Sara had found that could in any way be tied to the murder. She called Anna.

"Yes?"

"Stellan seems to have been identified as a Stasi spy."

"Stasi? But that was—"

"In the eighties."

"If there's anything in it, surely he would have been murdered back then."

"Just thought it might be worth checking out."

"I'll add it to the list."

Sara knew what "adding something to the list" meant. They'd both used the expression when tips came in that they didn't believe, and which they put to one side until they had nothing else to go on. It was effectively saying "I don't believe this."

After she'd put away her phone, Sara couldn't quite drop the Cold War connection—mostly because she'd felt a bit silly when Anna had so quickly dismissed the suggestion. She was used to her ideas being taken seriously.

The fly was still buzzing around Sara's face; sweat was running down her spine and her blouse was sticking to the small of her back. She glanced down to check whether the sweat had soaked through to form dark patches.

She had nothing urgent to do at work since David had volunteered to write the report, so Sara decided to try and find out whether there might be anything behind the East German connection. If nothing else, she could use it to argue against Anna if she continued to ignore the tip and they didn't get anywhere.

Sara used Wikipedia and the phone book to find an Eva Hedin with the right year of birth living at Åsögatan 189 on Söder. She called the number listed, but got no answer.

Sara got into the car and drove along Drottningholmsvägen toward the city center. It didn't cost anything to check.

After passing Lindhagensplan, she drove through Marieberg and across the Västerbron bridge to Hornstull. Then via Ringvägen and Bondegatan to Åsögatan.

Once she'd arrived in the neighborhood often called SoFo by pretentious Stockholmers with a New York complex, Sara did a U-turn and double-parked outside Hedin's street door, before getting out of the car. She wondered what she was doing.

Åsögatan 189. All of the city center was like a photo album in which every block was associated with memories. Right across the street was number 192; she remembered from her single days that two lads had lived there, with four bathtubs in their flat—one that actually worked in the bathroom and three in the living room that weren't plumbed in. And they'd had three restaurant-style espresso machines in the kitchen, in an era when home espresso makers hadn't yet become a thing. They needed a lot of space for their gadget hoarding—or was it a disorder that had been given a name by now?

They'd either changed the police entry codes that day, or the code lock was broken. She could not get in.

Sara glanced through the pane of glass in the door and caught sight of the name board in the hallway. "Hedin" was clearly listed on the lower ground floor. She took a few steps back on the pavement and saw that there were windows on both sides—she picked the left-hand side first.

It was clearly a studio flat, because the room facing the street contained a bed, desk and television. At the table, there was a woman in large spectacles sitting and typing on an old laptop.

Sara tapped gently on the glass so as not to scare her, but the woman turned quite calmly toward the window to see what the noise was. Sara waved her hands and hoped she would understand.

She clearly did, given that she got up and went into the hall. A few seconds later, the street door was opened by a short woman with a determined gaze. Her hair was slightly wavy, as if it had been set in a perm a long time ago.

"Hello—sorry if I alarmed you," said Sara, even though the woman didn't look in the slightest scared. "Are you Eva Hedin?"

"Yes."

"I called but you didn't pick up."

"I have my phone on silent when I'm working."

"My name's Sara Nowak and I'm a police officer," Sara said, showing her police ID. "Can I come in?"

"Not when I'm working."

Based on what she was saying, it was clear that Hedin didn't want to be disturbed, but otherwise she gave no impression of this. She simply stood there in silence, looking at Sara.

"I have a few questions about Stellan Broman."

She noticed that she'd caught the woman's attention.

"What sort of questions?"

"Can you keep a secret?"

"Ask the Security Service," said Hedin. "Yes, I can."

"Stellan Broman is dead. Murdered."

"And what does this have to do with me?"

"I saw you identified him in your books."

"Not by name."

"Can you tell me more about it? I've not read the books."

"They're available in libraries and used bookshops."

"Don't have time."

Hedin remained silent for a moment while looking at Sara.

"Come in," she said at last.

Sara followed her into the small flat. The square hallway was painted blue and lined with overfilled bookcases that ran along all of the walls. Hedin turned to Sara.

"You said murdered?"

"Yes, but as I said, it's not official yet. The investigators think it's a break-in gone wrong, but I—"

"Don't think that."

"No. It's too weird. Shot in his home without any trace of a struggle, decades after he was in vogue."

"What do you know about the Cold War?" said Hedin.

"Well, a bit…"

"There are things in Stellan Broman's past that would give a motive for murder."

Sara looked at her.

"May I sit down?"

Hedin gestured at the one armchair in the room. She sat down on the edge of the bed.

"Stellan Broman was a so-called informal collaborator—or an IM as they called it—for the East German Stasi," said Hedin. "You can read about it in my books. I couldn't include his name, but I reproduced his details as they appear in the Stasi archives—the ones I could find. There's no doubt about it. I don't know why the media haven't picked up on it more. One single article in which he got to deny everything."

"But the Cold War was a long time ago—in the seventies."

"It lasted until 1991, when the Soviet Union collapsed. Long after Stellan Broman retired. And many believe it's still going on today. Cold War 2.0. There's a good book with that title."

"But why do you think that Stellan was a spy?"

"I don't think. I know. Read my book."

She went over to the bookcase and took down a large hardback that she passed to Sara. *The Swedes Who Worked for the Stasi*.

"But '91 is thirty years ago. Why would someone murder him today for something that happened then?"

"Geiger ruined the lives of many of the people he reported on," said Hedin. "Just like all other Stasi agents. Someone may have decided to seek revenge. They may have read my book and only then realized who Geiger was."

Hedin looked almost exhilarated at the thought.

"Geiger?" said Sara.

"That was his code name."

Geiger.

It sounded like an old black-and-white movie from the 1940s.

"Stellan Broman was one of Sweden's best-known television presenters," said Sara. "The only mega-celebrity there was back then. Like a combination of Ernst Kirchsteiger and Zlatan. Why would he be a spy?"

"Ideology. He believed in the East German project. A lot of people did. Sweden had a tremendous amount of cultural exchange with the DDR, and the Swedish education system was developed using the East German one as a model. There are many teachers, politicians and cultural workers who were given prizes and distinctions in East Germany, who visited the country, who were working to get the DDR recognized as an independent state. Stellan was one of them."

"Would Stellan have been murdered because he wanted to recognize East Germany as an independent state?"

"His mission as an informant would have included identifying East Germans who'd managed to escape, and those who were still in the country but had plans to leave. Those who were given away had their lives ruined."

"But why now?"

"Because it's only lately that many of them have been identified. I've had to go head to head with the Security Service and right to the Supreme Court just to get a look at the documents, but I'm still prohibited from copying them or even taking notes."

"And you're absolutely certain that Stellan Broman was an East German agent?"

"Informal collaborator. IM. Committed friend of East Germany. There's lots of evidence for the latter in freely available sources."

Hedin went over to the bookcase again and took out a folder that contained copies of old newspaper articles about cultural exchanges with East Germany and political delegations. In the pictures, Sara saw the Stellan of her childhood—Sweden's "Uncle Stellan"—shaking hands with East German politicians and diplomats and poets, receiving prizes and opening festivals. Agent or not, he certainly appeared to have been a very good friend of East Germany, and Sara began to wonder whether this strange woman might not have a point.

"IM," she said.

"Yes," Hedin confirmed. "But in several respects, he functioned as a spy. He gathered information and facilitated contact between East Germany and key Swedes."

"What kind of information?"

"Almost everything was of interest. Sweden's views on the DDR, Sweden's views on NATO and the EC, as it was known then. Research and business. Cultural policy. A major issue was the acknowledgment of the DDR as an independent state, and Sweden was at the vanguard of that, thanks to all of East Germany's good friends here. We were the first to legitimize oppression."

"But what did he know about all of this? Research and business? And politics?"

"He knew everyone. As the biggest celebrity in the country, he was friends with everyone in the elite. Other celebrities, financiers, cultural types—and politicians. He's supposed to have had big parties at his house where he invited all the important people."

Sara remembered once again how she and the sisters had lain watching, spying down the stairs or from the garden on all the grown-ups who'd been so happy and noisy. They'd witnessed all sorts of peculiarities during those parties, even though they'd only been there at the beginning.

"What did he do then?" said Sara. "Capture secret documents on microfilm?"

"Perhaps. At any rate, he passed on information verbally and in writing to his handler. And reported on how he'd tried to promote a positive image of the DDR. That much is in the archives."

"Handler?" said Sara, almost certain what that meant although she saw no reason to divulge her familiarity with the term.

"The Stasi officer who recruited him, and then served as his point of contact."

"I still don't understand what *Stellan* could have done."

Hedin heaved out a plastic folder stuffed with copies of old reports in German, leafed through them and read aloud.

"Source Erik, CEO in the maritime industry, reluctant, material secured," she said. "Source the Cat, air force colonel, receptive, material secured. Source Hans, ambassador, accommodating, material secured. A total of fifty-six code names for different sources with different degrees of willingness to cooperate."

"'Material secured'? What material?"

"I don't know. Something that influenced their willingness to cooperate, maybe. Sensitive information about them."

"Extortion?"

"Yes."

"Was that how they recruited spies?"

"Normally, they used a combination of flattery and questioning. And threats, if necessary. Bribes, obviously. Geiger was part of a group all recruited by the same handler—a spy ring, if you want to make it sound dramatic."

"Do you know who else was in it?"

"I've got the names of a couple of them, but as I said, I'm not allowed to give them to anyone."

"Didn't they open up all the records when the Wall came down?"

"Yes, but when the DDR was collapsing, Stasi officers initiated operation Archiv Berlin in order to destroy all sensitive documents. They managed to burn a lot of it before their headquarters were stormed by crowds wanting to open up the archives. The CIA may have more on the spy ring in the Rosenholz files, but for some reason they seem to prefer to suppress that information."

"So Stellan Broman wasn't just an agent for East Germany, he was also in a spy ring controlled by a Stasi officer?"

It was hard to take it all in, but Sara thought that Hedin's books looked solid and serious.

"Just a second," she said, getting her phone out and going to Wikipedia. She couldn't help doing a little research right in front of Hedin. Hopefully, Hedin wouldn't see what Sara was looking up.

Eva Maria Hedin, born 24 July 1945, is a researcher currently active at the Centre for Research on Eastern Europe at Mälardalen University, and a retired Professor of History.

Then an article about her career, and a list of published works. And finally, the most important passage as far as Sara was concerned.

Hedin has researched the Stasi archives and is the only outsider to have been granted access to the Swedish Security Service's records taken from the Rosenholz files concerning people in Sweden who were named in connection with collaboration with the Stasi, following a Supreme Court judgment in 2015.

This wasn't just any old conspiracy theorist—this was someone who clearly knew what she was talking about. The only question was whether the information was relevant.

"You've seen the Rosenholz files," said Sara.

"You've been googling, eh?" said Hedin, grinning.

Sara waited for an answer.

"I've been allowed to see small excerpts. About other Stasi collaborators. And detailed information about Geiger. There are some clues about the other people in his spy ring. But nothing about Ober, who was the leader of the spy ring."

"Do you think one of their members might have murdered Stellan?"

"No, but if Geiger's death is linked to East Germany, there's a chance they know why he was killed. And by whom. In any case, the ringleader would know. And if it is part of a bigger plan, he or she would know that too."

"A bigger plan?"

"If an old IM is suddenly brutally murdered after thirty years, it may be the beginning of a much bigger chain of events. Don't forget that Russia still has sleeper agents all over the world—ones planted by the KGB and simply transferred to the FSB, the current Russian intelligence service. They may also have taken over the East German agents, too."

"And what chain of events might that be?" said Sara.

"No idea."

"Then we need to find out who this Ober is."

"Can't. The CIA refuses. Won't even confirm that they know."

"I'm sure they'll help us."

Hedin shook her head.

"A murder investigation," said Sara, her eyebrows raised.

The retired professor merely looked at her, and Sara thought for a moment.

Could Uncle Stellan's murderer really be some kind of spy from the eighties?

How old would he be in that case? If the person in question was thirty or thirty-five when the Wall fell, he would only be sixty-five today. Maybe seventy.

It was quite possible.

"And what if it isn't 'a bigger chain of events'?"

"Revenge."

"Someone whose life he ruined?"

"As I said, things often went very badly for those he reported on. During the visits to the DDR, he and his family got to know a lot of people—ordinary East Germans. Some of them were young East Germans who wanted to go west. Geiger's files contain a lot of names of those accused of saying they wanted to leave the DDR. And things did not go well for them. Some went to prison, many were bumped off. Their families were punished, too. Lost their jobs and privileges and had to move to worse housing. In one case, the man managed to get to Sweden and the woman was to follow, but Geiger reported them and the woman was arrested and took her own life. You could imagine that the man in question may always have wanted to avenge the death of his loved one."

"And who was that man?"

The same silence. The same fixed gaze.

"I can't give you any names," Hedin said eventually. "But I've got them in my papers."

"This is a murder investigation."

"A Supreme Court ruling takes priority. Much higher priority."

"So you're on their side?"

"They'll have to stay here in my papers," said Hedin, patting a blue file tied with string she'd just placed on the bed. "Excuse me, I need to use the bathroom."

Sara waited until Hedin had locked the door to give her deniability, and then she opened the file.

Excerpts from records in German.

On the page titled "IM Geiger" there was an annotation in pencil: "Broman." Against "IM Kellner" it said "Schulze"; against "IM Koch" it said "Stiller." Against "IM Ober" it said "Ringleader" and "Name" with a big question mark after it. Sara took out her mobile and photographed the pages.

She leafed onwards. Thanks to her schoolgirl German, she was able to find a couple of files about young East Germans who'd ended up in prison after Geiger had reported their plans to leave the country, although the punishment was doled out for some made-up crime. Next to one name there were details of a male "friend" in Sweden—one Günther Fricke. Sara also photographed those pages, as well as some she didn't have time to interpret, and then she quickly put the folder back when she heard water rushing through the pipes.

While Hedin washed her hands, a memory cropped up in Sara's head of how she and the Broman sisters had played capitalists and workers when they were little. She hadn't thought about it for years. And previously she'd interpreted it as a tragicomic reflection of the fact that they'd grown up in a thoroughly politicized society, where children's television could be about capitalism's hunger for profits or the Vietnam War. Now, however, it felt as if there might be another explanation for why they'd played that particular game in well-heeled Bromma.

Sara always got to be the evil capitalist who was lectured by the sisters, who were on the side of the workers. She remembered that Stellan had got very angry when he'd found them playing that game. Sara had thought it was because they were in Bromma, where all forms of Red influence were to be prevented—but perhaps Stellan had been worried about being uncovered as an East German agent?

"Was there anything else you wanted to ask me about?" said Hedin once she was back. "I need to get back to work."

"How sure are you that Stellan was Geiger?"

"I can actually show you that," said Hedin, taking out a red file tied with string. She leafed through the papers and pulled out a dozen sheets of A4 attached in the corner—copies of files from a German archive. The Stasi archive, judging by the heading.

Sara glanced through the text and tried to understand as much as possible. German was tricky enough anyway, but bureaucratic German—communist bureaucratic German to boot—was even worse.

But she understood some of the information. The house in Bromma, contacts with the Swedish elite, intense socializing. There was no doubt that Uncle Stellan had been Geiger—however that was possible. But the name wasn't written down, so she had to assume that none of the newspapers had dared to run with the story.

Sara held up the bundle of papers.

"I need to take copies of this," she said.

"Take them. I've got others."

Sara got up.

"There's just one more thing," she said. "If Stellan Broman's death had anything to do with the Cold War, with this spy ring, or with someone he hurt—what might have happened to Agneta?"

"Which Agneta?"

"His wife."

"Don't know. Is she dead? Or missing?"

"Missing. And this is top secret. It can't get out to anyone."

"Who would I tell? When did she disappear?"

"In connection with the murder. Could someone taking revenge have kidnapped her? Might it be connected to the spy ring? Why would someone attack his wife?"

"Sometimes spouses knew what the spies were doing, sometimes not. But I've not seen anything about his wife in the archives."

Agneta's disappearance was still a mystery.

10

The Kalashnikov was still there in its waterproof bag under a heap of old rag rugs. She took it apart, oiled all the components and then put it back together again. She could have done it blindfolded. She had actually done it blindfolded—but that had been forty years ago.

She needed to test fire it, and she wondered how far away the nearest house was. At a guess, it was a couple of kilometers, and even if someone happened to be passing right now, there was no one who would investigate the sound of shots this far out on Ekerö, given how much game was shot unlawfully with the silent blessing of the residents.

She made the weapon ready and fired three shots in rapid succession, although without the automatic element since she didn't want to attract any curious witnesses.

The old Kalashnikov worked just as it should. There was a reason this was the world's most widespread automatic weapon.

The barn was now fragrant with gunpowder, and the smell took her back in time. Once again she felt the heat, the sand in her eyes and the strong winds—at once warming and frightening. She heard the commands being shouted in foreign languages—languages of which she remembered only fragments today.

As a matter of reflex, she secured the weapon again, put it down on the floor butt-first and stood to attention—in three rapid steps.

It had stuck.

The question was whether everything had stuck, or only enough to encourage her to set off on her mission in the belief that she was equipped for it—only to discover en route that she was nowhere near good enough. That she had forgotten. That she couldn't do it.

That she was too old.

Doubtful of her own abilities, but at least satisfied with the test firing, she put the rifle back in the bag and stashed it in the boot of the car along with the box of ammunition. She got out the mobile phone she'd bought ten years ago—an insurance policy that had made her feel faintly ridiculous—even then the old world had seemed increasingly distant, almost unreal. Today, she was glad she'd made the purchase. Her own mobile was out of the question, and now she didn't have to cycle to some nearby farm to make a call. An old woman knocking on the door in the middle of nowhere would have drawn attention, even if she could have come up with some story about being out in the woods and losing her mobile. But she would probably have struggled to talk uninterrupted, and she definitely didn't want anyone listening in on her next call.

A ten-year-old Ericsson without any smart features was exactly what she needed. Long battery life, plenty of calling time. Charging it a couple of times a month had become a ritual, an invocation of times gone by—although it was unclear which ones. But in any case, it was a brief opportunity to look back at her life and her mission. To remember who she'd been.

Now that her mission had suddenly become reality, all the years of waiting were suddenly over and the other life had been forgotten. It was like returning through Professor Kirke's wardrobe, or waking up from a dream in which you'd lived a whole life and realizing that just a few minutes had elapsed.

Apart from her body.

Her damn body. Deserter. Traitor.

As a young woman, it had been impossible to imagine how decrepitude would feel. As an old woman, it was almost impossible to think about anything else. The muffin top tummy, the flaws and droopy breasts. Her body, which had been her most effective weapon, was now a burden. Like going to a ball in knight's armor.

In terms of her mission, she had always found the objectification of women useful—and had been able to use her attractiveness to get men where she wanted them. It was a sort of sexual aikido—using the attacker's force against himself. She'd seen her body as a tool—at the cost of always maintaining a distance from it, not experiencing it as her own. But she couldn't help but miss that desirable body a little now—when she could have used it the way she wanted to.

Four rings, then he answered.

"Yes?"

"Geiger is dead."

A brief pause, too brief for most people to notice it, but it told her everything she needed to know. Just half a second before the other speaker replied had given away their hand. Not one second or two seconds—just half of one.

"Never heard of him. You must have the wrong number."

And with that answer, he sealed his own fate. He was still ready, true to his old loyalties. The ring was still very much active, just as Agneta had feared. Now she had no choice.

"Listen up," she hastened to say before he had time to hang up. "You need to cooperate if you want to live. We're in the same situation. Geiger is dead. I know who did it and they'll carry on. Stay inside, don't open the door, don't answer the phone. I'll be with you in eight hours. I'll text from this number when I'm outside the door."

Then she hung up.

She was certain it would work. You couldn't give them the feeling that they had any other options—she'd learned that much. And since she'd practiced the tactic so many times, she knew that it almost always worked. The few times it didn't, you had to improvise on the spot. Now she knew that he, at least, was still loyal, which meant she had to act.

She had eight hours, then she absolutely had to be at his door. She ate the last of the biscuits, urinated in a corner of the barn and covered it in old straw. Fortunately, she always had tissues in her pocket. Given she was stuck here until the car was charged, she preferred not to show herself outside the barn unnecessarily.

The test firing of the gun had been a risk of its own. There were more people out and about in the woods around here than you would think, and she knew how often it was passing members of the public who, by chance, put police on the trail. But she'd chosen to take that risk.

There were around seven hours until the battery would be charged, if the instruction manual was right. She might as well gather strength. She contemplated the straw and the car, and eventually opted for the car. She folded down the back seat and lay down in the boot with her coat blanketed across her and the AK-47 her bedfellow. Her legs still hurt. She would need to take painkillers before she left, otherwise she wouldn't be able to walk.

But that was then. This was now.

Fatigue washed over her, soft and comforting, like waves on a white beach in the West Indies. If she'd been born a few decades later, she might have found it highly stressful, being pulled back into a life she'd finished with—a life suited to a forty-years-younger version of herself. In addition, she'd shot dead her husband of almost half a century, undeniably an act of some importance. But that wasn't how she thought.

She had a mission. Her whole life had been one long preparation for this day.

And now the day had come.

Two minutes later, she was sound asleep, snoring.

11

Sara sat in her car for a long time, thinking about what Hedin had told her. It was a lot to take in—not just what had happened to Stellan and Agneta, but also the fact that Stellan had supposedly been a spy for the DDR.

After so many years together, Martin was still the one Sara called when she needed perspective and some contact with reality. Her husband was in a meeting about an impending concert tour, but he left the room to answer his phone, as if he'd sensed something unusual had happened.

Martin came from the same neighborhood as Sara and the Bromans, and like every other Swede of the same age, he'd grown up watching Stellan's shows. He tried to grasp what Sara told him.

"How are you?" was his well-meaning question, but Sara struggled to answer. "Where are you? Do you want me to come to you?"

"No, it's fine. But I might react when it all hits me properly."

"Are you sure? I'll come to you now if you like."

"No, you look after your artists. I just wanted to talk a little. Process it."

"But it's not your case, is it? You're not a police officer now—just a friend. Well, just and just... You know what I mean."

"That's exactly why I might know something that could help them. Anna and I have always helped each other out."

And they had. Ever since the police academy, they'd been in a pact to help each other. And Anna probably knew exactly how important this was to Sara—that was why she'd been so open toward her.

"See you later, at home. Love you."

"Love you."

Sara realized that she really wanted to end the call so that she could think more about Uncle Stellan's death. She didn't want to admit to Martin how obsessed she could get with a case, even when—as now—it wasn't her own. Sometimes it just felt like things depended on her if they were going to get solved. She found it hard to relax and trust others. And she didn't think Anna had any objection to a little extra help.

Anna was done at the Bromans' house and was heading back to the station in Solna, so when Sara called her they agreed to meet at Brommaplan.

Once there, they couldn't decide between McDonald's and a coffee from Pressbyrån. They opted for the latter. Then they settled down on a park bench in the sunshine and watched the stream of passengers heading in and out of the underground station.

"We found something in the upstairs bathroom," said Anna. "Some kind of hidden compartment, which had recently been covered up. The adhesive was still wet."

"What was in it?"

"Nothing. But it could have been where they kept their valuables. That would suggest a break-in. A home robbery."

"Why would the burglar cover the hole back up again?" said Sara.

"Maybe as a diversion—to create confusion. Perhaps it was something very particular, like jewelry or watches that could be traced, and they wanted to buy some time before we put an alert out."

Her mobile beeped four times almost simultaneously, and then twice more. Newsflashes from *Aftonbladet*, *Dagens Nyheter*, *Svenska Dagbladet*, *Expressen*, *Omni* and *Dagens Eko*.

"Uncle Stellan dead. Thought to have been murdered."

"Unclear if Stellan murdered."

"Uncle Stellan found murdered in his home."

"Uncle Stellan dead. Found by daughter."

Well, it was only ever going to be a matter of time.

Anna's mobile rang. The ringtone was a song by some stupid talent show winner that her friend apologized for every time it rang, but never changed.

"*Expressen*," she said, hanging up. "And I *am* going to change it."

"And there was nothing in the hidey-hole to suggest what had been in there?" said Sara.

"Something wrapped in a waxcloth, according to Forensics."

A secret hiding place correlated well with Hedin's theories about espionage, Sara thought to herself. The question was simply what had been kept in there. Microfilm? Weapons? Radio equipment?

And why had the murderer taken it? And then covered the hole back up?

To buy time, obviously. So far she agreed with Anna. The murderer had perhaps not expected the espionage trail to become known quite so soon.

Was that why Stellan had died? Because the murderer needed to get at what was in the secret compartment?

What could be that valuable?

Money?

"Instead of putting cash under the mattress, perhaps he'd hidden it behind a bathroom tile," said Anna, as if she'd been reading Sara's thoughts. "He must have made a fair whack in his time. He might have gone a bit gaga in his old age and stopped trusting banks. We're checking similar cases now. Armed robberies in domestic homes, with or without deadly violence. And we've raised a search party. Missing Persons have rounded up almost a hundred people."

"It's easier when a celebrity is involved."

"Definitely. Although it might be tricky to persuade everyone to keep their mouths shut about the wife being missing."

"It'll get out sooner or later," said Sara. "How's it going with the gang of burglars?"

"We're checking up on where they all are. Then we'll bring them all in at the same time. That was the plan."

"OK. But look, I had another possibility I wanted to put to you."

"Shoot."

"I met a researcher. A professor of history. She's written books about Swedes who were spies for the Stasi—and according to her, Stellan was one. An informal collaborator, they called it."

"Uncle Stellan? A spy?"

"Informant slash collaborator."

"You think that might be why he was murdered?"

"Seems more likely than a break-in that Stellan didn't notice. Don't you think?"

"But the Stasi...East Germany hasn't existed for fifty years."

"Thirty."

Anna was silent for a moment.

"I don't know...I think we've got a better theory. And it's not actually up to me what we focus on."

"But you can have a word with Bielke? I assume his lordship is running the show?"

Sara liked Bielke as a preliminary lead investigator, but couldn't help making fun of his noble ancestry.

"Absolutely. I'll pass it on."

It didn't sound as though Anna would. Even if the information was a little unexpected, it bothered Sara that it wasn't being taken seriously.

If she wanted the spy theory to be followed up on, it seemed she would have to do it herself. And that wasn't her job.

At the same time, Sara realized that the murder of Stellan Broman wasn't work, as far as she was concerned. Not in the slightest. It was extremely personal.

12

Lotta seemed to be the more lucid of the sisters, and Sara didn't want to have to go all the way out to Lidingö where Malin lived, so she called Lotta and agreed to meet her in Vasaparken outside her home, next to the renowned Sven-Harry Art Museum.

Sara understood that Lotta wanted to be with her family, given that her father had just died, but she also needed to find out more about the spy theory—if nothing else, because it upended her own perception of the family with whom she had spent so much time as a child.

"Did you know there was a hidden compartment in the upstairs bathroom?" said Sara. "Behind a tile?"

Lotta looked at her. Scrutinizing her, almost slightly annoyed, as if Sara was bothering her with stupid jokes when the family was grieving.

"What hidden compartment?" she said. "What was in it?"

"Nothing," said Sara. "It was empty. So you've no idea what might have been hidden in there?"

"No."

"The theory is that the murderer took the contents with them. Might your parents have put money in there?"

"No, Mum usually kept her money in a metal tin," said Lotta.

Sara remembered the metal tin in question—black, red and gold with some kind of Chinese motif on it. Almost certainly the kind of stereotypical design that would have drawn negative attention nowadays.

"But I don't actually know if she still does that," Lotta continued.

"The compartment had been covered back up," said Sara. "The murderer had replaced a tile and used adhesive around it." She was unsure what you called the stuff you used to stick bathroom tiles to the wall.

"Where did he get it from?"

Sara didn't have an answer to that. Lotta undeniably had a point.

"And why cover the hole?"

"To conceal that the theft was the real reason for the murder? Do you know whether Stellan and Agneta hired any contractors recently?"

Lotta shook her head. It was unclear whether she didn't know or whether they hadn't, but Sara didn't ask her to specify. She seemed impatient to wrap up and return to her family, which was understandable. For Sara, the problem was that Lotta's expression made her feel as if she was twelve years old and being difficult again. Her childhood friend had always been good at that.

"OK," said Sara. "It's a new lead to follow, at least."

"Was that all?" said Lotta, looking at her with a frown. "You could have asked me that on the phone."

Just as in childhood, Sara felt a knot in her stomach because Lotta was annoyed with her. But she did actually have something else she wanted to bring up.

"One more thing. East Germany."

"OK—what about East Germany?"

"Does it bring anything particular to mind when I mention it?"

"We went there a few times. And Dad was awarded prizes and so on. But what does that have to do with this?"

"There's a researcher who believes that your father worked for the Stasi, and that he reported people who wanted to leave."

"Never."

"Are you sure?"

"It sounds mad. Why would he do that?"

Sara didn't have a good answer to that. She couldn't remember a single thing that indicated anything like that, and now she was simply presenting facts about Stellan from what was essentially a complete stranger to one of the people she'd known the longest in her whole life. Sara stayed silent while she thought about what to say. Perhaps she should just apologize, forget all about it and be on her way? Or would that be giving in just because she'd always given in to Lotta in the past?

"Because he believed in the East German project," Sara said at last. "But I'm going to look into this in further detail before we assume that it's true. It's a fairly well-known researcher who's identified him as an informant, so regardless of whether it's true, it's possible that revenge could be a motive. I just wanted to ask whether you had any recollection of any threats toward Stellan? In more recent years, or back in your childhood? Letters, phone calls, someone who bumped into him out and about?"

"No, nothing like that. People always approached him and wanted to say hello—but it was always friendly. These days, he would have been constantly stopping for selfies."

"Didn't they show East German kids' films on his show?" said Sara.

"Yes. *The Little Sandman*. But that was how it was back in those days—lots of stuff came from there. *Bolek and Lolek. Drutten and Jena.* And we traveled to lots of countries—not just East Germany."

Sara remembered very clearly how often the sisters were away traveling with their parents. Other children never got time off during term time, but presumably the school didn't dare turn Uncle Stellan down. Malin's and Lotta's rooms were filled with toys and souvenirs from different countries and other parts of the world, in an era when charters to Majorca and weekends in London were the standard fare for Swedes. Sara felt ashamed when she remembered how many tiny souvenir trolls and foreign princess dolls she'd stolen from the sisters. Often, she hadn't even played with them—she'd just thrown them away, frequently off the Nockebybron bridge. But they'd never noticed that anything was missing, so no harm was done.

"He took part in a lot of demonstrations," said Lotta, after a period of silence. "And he was very engaged in the peace movement. Anti–nuclear weapons and all that. But then, so was everyone back then."

"Things were more political then," said Sara.

"What else has he said?" said Lotta. "This researcher."

"She."

"OK, she. Why does she think Dad was a spy? Are you sure she's not just some tinfoil hat conspiracy theorist? There were people who thought they were Dad's kids or his secret wives. Celebrities have always attracted a lot of crazies."

"I've got copies of the papers from the Stasi records for Stellan."

"Show me," said Lotta, and Sara got them out in response to a childhood reflex that made her obey. As she handed them over, she wondered what it might feel like, first to have one's father murdered, and then to have him knocked off the pedestal he'd spent his whole life on. Would Lotta refuse to change her worldview, or would she accept the truth? Did she realize that she was fortunate to have had a father at all? What he had been like to his daughters couldn't be changed by any spy revelations.

Her childhood friend examined the papers closely, as if reading the judgment after an unexpected verdict against her in the hope of finding some formal errors that invalidated it. Her gaze seemed to linger on every single word. Perhaps she had a better grasp of her school German than Sara did. Her job at the Swedish International Development Cooperation Agency probably demanded more of her English and French, given all the former colonies that now received aid.

"There seems to be no doubt about it," she said at last, putting down the papers.

"No," said Sara.

Then they sat in silence for a long time. Mothers pushed their buggies through Vasaparken, people sunbathed on blankets on the grass, a young girl from a nearby kennels passed by with half a dozen dogs. Everyone was sweating in the heat but wanted to take the opportunity to be outside, Sara thought to herself.

"Does this need to come out?" Lotta said at last, which was when Sara realized what had been occupying her thoughts.

Her own position.

Being the child of Uncle Stellan was a plus, even when you had a career in the public sector. Being the child of a national traitor was very much a minus. It was rumored that Lotta was a candidate for a significant ministerial post in the coming government reshuffle. If that was true, then this had come at an inopportune moment, to say the least.

"It's already out—there's an article with his name in it. Although in that, he obviously denies it."

"It's completely unknown," said Lotta. "But now he's been murdered, this is front page stuff. I'm thinking about the kids. They shouldn't have to see their grandfather hung out to dry in the media after his death."

"I'm not going to spread it around. I'm just curious whether this might be linked to the murder."

"It's such a long time ago. And I doubt it was all that serious."

"OK, but let me know if you do think of anything."

"Dad was naive," said Lotta. "Saw the best in everyone. He was probably tricked into this. I don't think he saw himself as a spy or informant. He probably just thought he was being nice to people and answering questions and facilitating contact. Like his work with the peace movement, for instance."

Sara nodded, and a memory of Stellan with a big anti-nuclear weapons symbol around his neck appeared before her.

"They were busy with marches and demonstrations and lists of names. For peace and disarmament and against nuclear weapons," Lotta continued. "I think he started some game on television too. 'It's bombed with bombs' or something like that."

Typical Uncle Stellan. Everything he did, he did with an amusing and educational slant.

"But he got all sorts of people involved in that. Ministers and celebrities. Even Palme."

"You never noticed any hatred toward him because he took such a clear position? I mean, Palme was very much hated for his part in the commitment to peace."

"No, no one hated Dad. Uncle Stellan was the only thing that was any fun in Sweden in the sixties and seventies. The only thing that wasn't gray and depressing or hyperpolitical. Being against nuclear weapons back then was basically like being in favor of democracy today."

"Who did he mix with? Apart from celebrities at his parties?"

"Colleagues. People he worked with."

"And a lot of politicians, right?" said Sara. "People in power."

"Yes, absolutely. Celebrity Sweden was so small back then—everyone knew everyone. And given that he was popular across the board, I think our home became something of a haven. Reds and blues could mix and forget about politics. Relax and let their hair down a bit—without being watched. Well, 'a bit'... Sometimes things went spectacularly wrong."

"Any scandals?"

"No," said Lotta. "I'm sure there could have been lots, if people had seen how things ended up going sometimes—but it never left the house. I remember Dad saying, 'Now we're going to turn off the camera'—that meant that everything that happened from then on was top secret."

"That's right—he filmed a lot."

Sara remembered Stellan with the Super 8 camera glued to his face at every family gathering. The same old camera throughout all those years, and endless film showings every time the Broman family had been away on their travels. Indescribably dull depictions of the banks of the Dalälven river combined with exciting films from exotic locations like London, Rome, Berlin, Paris, New York or Beijing. The former made one burst with ennui, while the latter made one cry tears of jealousy.

The first time Sara went abroad, she and her mother had taken the ferry to Åland, and she still hadn't been to more than half a dozen countries in her life. The Broman sisters had probably reached that figure before they had even started school. Worst of all, friends of Malin and Lotta sometimes got to go with the family on these wonderful trips, but only girls who were popular at school. Never Sara. The trips with the famous father were a way to score points in the social game being played in class, and taking Sara the slave along didn't have any upsides.

But she was good to have around when playing at home, because she did as she was told and was close at hand. All they had to do was summon her. "Order to the slave."

And there and then, Sara realized that there was a small part of her that actually *liked* the thought that Stellan Broman had been an East German spy.

That there was something to crack the facade.

The perfect, enviable, loathsome facade.

And in a way, Stellan's being drawn to East Germany didn't seem that illogical. Maybe he'd been tempted by the image of the dictator as the great Father—the one who took care of his people, and demanded absolute obedience and devotion in return.

He had probably been able to relate to that.

Spending time on television could twist the mind of the most sensible person, and Stellan Broman had been synonymous with Swedish television for decades. He had adorned magazine covers, been on the radio, been talked about in workplaces and every single school. He had been worshipped as a demigod in twenty-six-inch format. No matter where he went, he was stopped, thanked, feted. He signed autographs and shook hands, and every time he left the capital city to make a visit somewhere else around the country, the local papers would plaster the visit all over their front pages.

It wasn't Uncle Stellan who invented color television, but in Sweden it had been he who received the praise for this new form of technology. In the eyes of the people, he'd brought both color and life to the whole country.

His phenomenal memory had its own role to play. He seemed to remember every face, every name, every anecdote he'd ever encountered. People he'd only met in passing would be remembered years later—even details like where they lived. He could reel off telephone numbers and door numbers that people had once chosen on his shows. All of Sweden watched Uncle Stellan, and all of Sweden felt seen by him. Whether Stellan had actually cared about all the people he met, Sara had no idea. But he had benefitted enormously from it seeming as if he did.

In her mind's eye, an old black-and-white television clip played. She hadn't even been born when it was broadcast for the first time, but she'd seen it repeated dozens of times, if not hundreds. Seen it reproduced in the weeklies, television supplements, morning papers, business magazines, specialist texts—she'd even heard that it had been analyzed in a couple of academic dissertations. The clip was from back in the era when there was only one television channel and everyone watched the same program.

A grainy black-and-white picture, a sprightly tone, wide smiles and gentlemen in jackets and ties—despite the light-hearted atmosphere. Uncle Stellan was in the studio with the young singer Barbro "Lill-Babs" Svensson, the quizmaster Nils Erik Bæhrendtz and the minister of finance, Gunnar Sträng. As part of a good-natured parody of his own show, Double or Quits, Bæhrendtz had been quizzing Sträng about the new tax laws and had found a gap in his knowledge. Sträng had been given a dunce's cap as punishment, and had not only laughed at the silliness, but, to the boundless joy of the audience, he'd even put the cap on. The peals of laughter would never stop. There were sensational front pages across all the country's newspapers the next day with the finance minister in his dunce's cap. A historic moment.

After *Tivoli* in the 1960s, it became *Stellan's Place* in the 1970s, and the morning show *Up with the Cockerel* in the 1980s and right up until the 1990s. Then commercial television arrived on the scene, and the newspapers began to write about viewer figures; when each small decrease led to malicious speculation that Uncle Stellan was losing his grip, that he might be "finished" and that he was past his sell-by date, he eventually gave up. Stellan Broman wanted to be loved and admired—not scrutinized and compared.

The reason he gave was that he wanted to spend more time with his family after all his years of hard work. But Sara knew it was too late for that. His daughters were almost grown up. They were more than used to their father's physical absence, even if he had always been a presence psychologically. They'd been able to see their father on television more or less every night as they grew up. and everyone knew they were his daughters. Friends, colleagues, employers.

So things had worked out for them.

Lotta was an A-grade child from the start. Top marks, scholarships, chair of the student council, solo performances at every end-of-year assembly. She played basketball in the national league, studied in America for a year, graduated in political science in record time despite being involved in Amnesty at the same time. Then she got involved in the sporting movement, and applied to the Ministry of Foreign Affairs, but was headhunted as an expert for the Ministry of Communications; there, she soon became an undersecretary of state before becoming the Director General of the Swedish International Development Cooperation Agency just a couple of years ago. A DG who was tough as nails, but respected by her subordinates. A presence in debates. A name increasingly mentioned in connection with the government.

Malin followed in her father's footsteps. Script supervisor for SVT in her early days, then producer of an entertainment show under the legendary entertainment boss Linde Berg. An embarrassing stint as presenter on *Sommarbubbel*, a hasty return to behind the camera, a brief marriage to a male presenter, a romance with another. Now married to her rich financier, and for many years in charge of producing the old classic *Allsång på Skansen*. Sara assumed that Malin was surrounded by many competent colleagues.

What secrets—if any—were hiding in this envied and feted family?

She wanted to find out the truth—if only for her own sake.

Had she effectively grown up in the home of an East German spy?

13

Just as Sara got into the car in the car park at Sabbatsberg, Anna called and told her that her colleagues had brought in the gang they'd been monitoring—one of the ones running riot in Nockeby and Höglandet. They were known for their violence, which made them very interesting suspects in relation to Stellan's murder.

Unlike many of the foreign gangs active in the area, these burglars were a group of eighteen- to twenty-year-olds from Hässelby-Vällingby who'd been under surveillance for a long time. It appeared that they were involved in everything from drugs to carjacking and burglary. They had threatened witnesses and harassed the police, and the fact that the police hadn't acted against them sooner had caused muttering among the force. But now the decision had been made to arrest them immediately. A murder took priority over gathering evidence before an almost-guaranteed drugs raid.

The apprehended were four lads—two "ethnic Swedes" and two "of foreign heritage." They all denied everything, even those break-ins where their DNA had been found at the scene or they'd been captured on CCTV. Two of them had alibis for the time of Stellan Broman's murder, but Bielke—head of the preliminary investigation—took the view that this simply meant that other members of the gang had carried out the break-in. That was probably why it had gone off the rails—the leaders of the gang hadn't been there to keep their underlings in check.

The atmosphere at the station in Solna had been one of high spirits. The general feeling was that they'd solved the murder of Stellan Broman, and in just a few hours. Someone probably ought to let the papers know so that they could write something positive about the police for once...

The key thing now was to find Agneta Broman. The search party still hadn't found anything, and Anna was forced to admit to Sara that they had no clues. But they'd begun checking CCTV across a much wider area.

Sara asked Anna whether she'd brought up the spy theory with Bielke, but since they'd arrested a group of suspects, Anna hadn't thought there was any point. Personally, Sara found it hard to accept that they weren't pursuing all avenues of inquiry simultaneously—if only to avoid ending up with a new Palme investigation and some new cock-and-bull theory about Kurdish rebels.

Anna agreed with Sara, but it sounded as though it was only to bring the conversation to an end. Her friendly openness about the investigation had apparently drawn to a close—presumably because Anna was convinced that they'd found the guilty parties. Sara thanked her and ended the call.

Nevertheless, it was time for her to go back to work. David had said he would cover for her, since it was personal, but Sara realized there were limits to collegial helpfulness, just as had been the case with Anna. She drove across the Barnhusbron bridge, along Scheelegatan and Hantverkargatan as far as Fridhemsplan, and then turned into the police car park, where she parked up and headed straight for her office.

She read through David's report, changed a couple of sentences relating to the arrest of Vestlund and then tried to focus on work—future plans and the impending review of the prostitution unit's structure. She called Becky, the woman at Artillerigatan who'd been assaulted, to check if she was OK. All important parts of an important job, Sara thought.

But eventually she couldn't contain herself any longer. She pushed her own work to one side and returned to the Cold War. Using the photos she'd taken at Hedin's flat, she went online to merinfo.se and began to search for the names from the files. Some had too many hits, while others were less common, and in several cases the combination of name and age were enough to find the right person.

Then she set about searching using different directory inquiry services and social media. Eventually, she had a list of five names and numbers.

Gerhard Ackerman, Günther Dorch, Fred Dörner, Angela Sundberg and Hanne Dlugosch. All she had to do was call.

Ackerman hung up before Sara had finished introducing herself, and didn't pick up when she tried calling again.

Dorch was silent while she told him she'd received information that he'd once run into trouble after an East German informant disclosed information about him. Then he explained very calmly that he had nothing to say on the matter and wanted to be left alone.

Dörner was full of bile that he wanted to spew up: hatred for East Germany and for Sweden's compliant attitude, and fury that the guilty had never been held accountable.

Sundberg didn't answer the phone and didn't have voicemail.

Dlugosch was more than happy to talk. She'd fled East Germany, and when she tried to get her mother out of the country by inviting her to a wedding in Sweden, someone had given them away. Not only had her mother been prevented from traveling, but she'd been given a six-month prison sentence for some made-up offense, and had been so broken by being incarcerated that she'd fallen ill and passed away half a year later.

"Was it him?" said Dlugosch.

"Who?"

"Uncle Stellan? Was it him who reported us? I've always wondered."

"Why do you say that?" Sara asked.

"Because I met him on the street outside the SVT studios, and I said I thought he should stop praising East Germany because it was a dictatorship. And I said I wanted to get my mother out. He said he would try and help me, and asked for my mother's name. He said he had contacts there. Knew important people." Dlugosch paused. "He must have known a lot of important people there—they arrested her right away."

So there was something in what Hedin had said, Sara thought to herself. There were people who had cause to harm Stellan.

It was odd to picture a snitch and spy behind the television personality's laughing, father-of-the-nation face. She realized that the truth about Uncle Stellan was probably going to ruin the cherished childhood memories of many Swedes.

But surely that was how it was with everything when you were growing up? Adults' secret lives. Sex, alcohol and sweets whenever you wanted. Imagine if children knew what adults got up to when they were out of sight...

What did Sara do when her children weren't watching?

After the call to Dlugosch, she dialed the number for the Security Service, stated her inquiry—the Cold War—and requested that she be connected to someone who could help.

"Brundin."

Sara had always thought it was strange to hear women answer the phone using only their surname.

"My name's Sara Nowak and I'm calling about the murder of Stellan Broman."

Sara took care to avoid saying she was working on the investigation—better safe than sorry, she thought.

"OK."

"We've received information indicating he was an informant for the DDR back in the day, and we're looking into whether that may be related to his murder."

"OK."

"What do you have on Broman? If this was in fact the case, do you know who he harmed with his activities? Have you identified any threats?"

"No comment."

"What?"

"No comment."

"To what? That he was a spy, or whether there was a threat?"

Silence was the only response.

"Come on—a murder! Of one of Sweden's most famous people ever."

"I'm with you so far."

"Help me out, then! Do you have evidence that he worked for East Germany—yes or no?"

"Listen to me. You're asking about old Stasi collaborators who've remained undiscovered and unpunished. Anything relating to such issues is top secret. That means I can't even confirm whether any such investigations exist, and in the event that they do exist, I can neither confirm nor deny whether certain named Swedish citizens appear in these investigations, quite simply because if we said who wasn't in them you would soon be able to work out who was. Ergo, all those people we haven't cleared. And as I said, I can't even confirm that any such files exist, let alone what it might say in them. This is about Sweden's relationship with another sovereign state, which means there is absolute secrecy."

"A state that no longer exists."

"Germany exists."

Sara sighed as exaggeratedly as she could and hung up. She'd never encountered anything like this before.

Why were they refusing?

What did they want to hide?

Had they missed Hedin's research?

No, she'd been forced to take legal action against the Security Service—so they must be aware of it.

Did they have something bigger in play with relation to Stellan Broman?

Or was it simply that they knew Hedin's conclusions were wrong?

Did they know that Uncle Stellan's death couldn't be connected to the Cold War?

"Got a minute?"

The text message from Lindblad was friendly, as ever, but Sara knew a question from her was never a question.

She walked down the depressing gray-brown corridor with its fabric wallpaper and plastic flooring toward her boss's office, while thinking about what to look at next. She wasn't going to waste time just sitting around and waiting for the leader of the preliminary investigation to realize that the burglary line of inquiry was wrong. And she couldn't really see how she could help in the search for Agneta.

What was it David had said?

You don't give up.

"Do you mind?" said Lindblad as she stepped in. As if Sara could genuinely have said "yes" to her without any consequences. "I just need to get this sent."

Sara sat down while her boss typed away for another thirty seconds. Then the swoosh of an email departing was audible, and Lindblad leaned back and looked at Sara.

Åsa-Maria Lindblad was a woman of about fifty with fine, brown hair cut short, cold hands and a sharp gaze. Her constant smile never reached her eyes.

She was someone who'd made a career by pushing diagonally upward, over and over again, until she'd become a chief inspector and head of the prostitution unit—mostly because her superiors thought that was where she would do the least harm. The officers in the unit were sufficiently experienced that they could get by on their own.

Lindblad believed she was a committed and inspiring boss. Her approach to leadership was primarily about writing jaunty posts on Facebook:

"So proud of my colleagues out on the streets making a difference."

"ProstU—you're the best!"

"My heroes!"

She was always first to congratulate her colleagues on social media when it was their birthday, but she never understood what they were talking about when they had problems.

She'd never accompanied any of them in the field. In fact, she hadn't done any real police work for twenty years.

And she spent most of her working hours checking her subordinates' schedules and attendance, so that she could make deductions from their salaries if they were late or absent.

"Good work," said Lindblad.

"With what?" said Sara, thinking about the call to the Security Service.

"That you spotted the blood on his knuckles. Not many people would have done."

Lindblad always copied what other people said and then repeated it as if she knew what she was talking about. But Sara knew what the situation was.

"David told you?"

"Yes. He was impressed. Me too."

Bollocks.

Lindblad had no clue what was impressive. She was equally lyrical whether you'd made coffee or saved a life. Always hysterically encouraging—she seemed to think that drove the people around her. She probably believed that everyone around her thought she was a great boss, when in practice everyone knew that nothing came out of her mouth but empty words. It was chaos in there, and she was fighting desperately not to go under.

She clasped her hands and leaned forward.

"But he's also somewhat worried about you."

Sara didn't reply. She looked expectantly at Lindblad.

"You were reportedly rather heavy-handed with the man you apprehended."

"He ran, I chased—when I caught up, he fell over and hit himself pretty hard."

"Not according to the report," said Lindblad, pushing a file across the desk.

"Report?"

"The man has reported you for excessive violence. Grievous bodily harm. He says you didn't identify yourself as a police officer before knocking him down. And then you kicked him repeatedly when he was in handcuffs."

"Absolutely not. He just wants payback because we arrested him."

"David is partially able to confirm the complainant's statement."

Sara didn't know what to say.

"David?"

"He's worried about you, like I said. He says he hasn't seen this side of you before. And before you get angry at him, remember that he was the one who praised you for the thing with the blood on the knuckles."

Sara stayed quiet. If you had views on your colleagues' conduct, then you took it up with them, not with the evil boss. Lindblad must have pried it out of him. Or he was genuinely worried.

"If no witnesses come forward, he'll struggle to get much of a hearing with his report," she said. "But that doesn't make much difference to me. For me, the worst thing is that the report exists at all."

"What do you mean?"

For a brief moment, Sara thought Lindblad was going to ask her to put pressure on Vestlund to withdraw the complaint.

"I don't want to hear about any excessive violence," the chief inspector said instead. "It makes me look like a bad boss. It's like this—if I get praise for our work, then you get praise from me. If I get shit, you get shit."

"OK."

Lindblad was mad—everyone knew that—but no one dared raise it with management. People were afraid of what she'd do if they did.

"And that brings us to the question of what we can do to help you," Lindblad continued.

"With what?"

"To get a handle on this behavior. As I said, David's worried about you. And I am, too. But I don't want to point fingers and make people out to be villains. I want colleagues who are happy, and who are able to perform at work."

"I can perform," said Sara.

"But at what cost? This job wears you down. It eats into you."

Sara shrugged her shoulders. Lindblad had no idea what Sara's job did to her.

"I've personally heard you talk about how the perpetrators should be punished," said her boss.

"And about how the victims should get help."

"Mostly about the perpetrators, if I'm honest."

"I'm just so sick of seeing so many of the johns coming back time and again. They get their letters at work so that their families don't know, they pay their fines and then they start buying sex again. And degrading the girls. Assaulting them, beating them, pissing on them. And there's a constant stream of girls forced to come here from Bulgaria and Romania whose lives get ruined, just because Swedish men can't be satisfied with wanking off."

"You'll have to talk to Udenius. That's an order. Every week until she says you're better."

Sara had no intention of talking to Udenius, but she didn't tell Lindblad that. Why blab to a psychologist who reported right back to the boss?

"Can't you put me on secondment? I could help with the Stellan Broman murder inquiry."

"We need you here."

"They're stuck on the wrong line of inquiry. They think it's some teenage boys. And now they're wasting time."

"But you know what they should be looking at?"

"Yes. Well, at least what they should check out."

"Pass your information on to them and they'll get to it as soon as they can."

"But I know the family. I know things."

"Tell them to the leader of the preliminary investigation. And if he doesn't want to listen, then I promise to have a word."

"Don't you want to know what they are?" said Sara.

Lindblad raised her eyebrows.

"Stellan Broman was an informant for the DDR and the Stasi," Sara continued. "He ruined lots of lives."

"A spy?" said Lindblad, looking skeptically at Sara.

"Eva Hedin is a highly regarded researcher who—"

"One," her boss interrupted her. "You work here, not in the Western division. Two—you're overworked and need to talk to a therapist. Three—you need to control yourself. There will be zero tolerance of violence. Four—forget this spy theory."

"Can't you listen?"

"Listen? I'm listening! Are you saying I don't listen? Are you dissatisfied with the way I lead the prostitution unit? Are you sitting there saying I don't give a damn about my colleagues? You have no idea how much I suffer when you're out working on the streets! I cry through sleepless nights—that's how worried I am about you. That's why I'm here with you right now. Because I'm worried about how you feel. And all I get in return is a spit in the face—stuff about how I'm a bad boss who never listens to my subordinates. It really upsets me when you say that."

Lindblad had now worked herself up to the point where tears had formed in her eyes. Uncomfortable... But the worst thing was that Sara knew that she would get payback somehow. Some really awful way.

"No, you listen," Sara said, getting up and leaving.

Once back in her office, she searched online for information about the Cold War, the Stasi, informal collaborators and Uncle Stellan.

His entire television presenting career, the dominance of Swedish television entertainment that was incomprehensible by today's measures, and his political engagement on behalf of East Germany and peace.

His career had even run in parallel with the Berlin Wall. His first presenting slot had been in 1961, the year the Wall went up. And his final television program was broadcast in 1990, just a few months after the fall of the Wall and two years after the commercial channel TV3 launched. His era was that of the Berlin Wall and television monopolies.

But what was this country that Stellan Broman had been so passionate about?

Sara wasn't all that clued up on the DDR, and essentially only knew that it had been communist and a Soviet vassal. But now she was going to do some research.

Following the Second World War, defeated Germany had been divided into four zones overseen by each of the four conquering powers: Britain, the USA, France and the Soviet Union. In recognition of their help in defeating Hitler, the Soviets were allowed to establish their own country in their zone. And it was the Soviets who were then in charge, via their puppets in the government. The Russians chose who led the country and which decisions were made. It was a controlled economy and a constant fight on behalf of socialism.

The result was that millions of East Germans fled west. The mass flight came to pose a threat to the very existence of the country. So the Communist Party in East Germany were obliged to build a wall to prevent people from escaping—a wall straight through the divided capital city. Berlin, where it had previously been possible to move freely between the countries.

But how could anyone defend a dictatorship? It took Sara a while to get to the bottom of this.

The dominance of the USA following the Second World War made some people dream of something else—a counterweight. And thanks to its propaganda and its false statistics relating to economic success, the Soviet Union became just such an alternative for many people. It showed there were other paths that could be followed.

And since Sweden had been just as influenced by Germany before the outbreak of war as it came to be by America following the war, there were many who felt sympathy for both halves of the country and its highly developed culture—music, literature, philosophy, design, theater. What was more, East Germany had distanced itself significantly more from the Third Reich than West Germany had. Officially, at least.

Sweden's declared neutrality meant, among other things, that they wanted to keep an open mind when it came to the construction of socialism in the East—perhaps in order to counterbalance the powerful American influence. Whatever the reason was, there was excessive lenience in relation to shortcomings in freedom of expression and movement in the Eastern Bloc. They were regarded as childhood illnesses that would be grown out of.

Another important explanation was that many people quite simply believed in socialism. They looked to the utopian theory, and overlooked the violations of freedom and oppression that were the practical outcome.

At the same time, the Cold War was the age of secrecy and double-dealing. Sweden's official neutrality concealed an expansive, secret partnership with NATO. And this was in parallel with the export of arms to a string of dictators and warmongering countries, in contravention of what was prescribed by law and formal declarations. Another example was IB—the spy organization that not even everyone in government knew about, and whose primary purpose was to aid the Social Democratic Workers' Party to identify and work against political opponents.

Sara couldn't help being fascinated by all the mysterious deaths in the 1980s that could be connected in one way or another, and via different forums, to the export of arms and other secret dealings with East Germany, even if it had nothing to do with the murder of Stellan. The prime minister shot in the open street; the reporter dropped into the Hammarby harbor in her car; the arms inspector pushed in front of an underground train; the UN assistant secretary-general whose plane was blown up: they all had connections to arms exports, as inspectors or witnesses, and a large proportion of those exports went via East Germany. And in none of these cases had those responsible been found.

But if it was Stellan's past that had caught up with him... was it a former East German he'd harmed who had killed him? Or a family member, like Dlugosch? Someone who'd lost someone?

Or was there something else in his background? Could old agents still be active? If so, why would they want to kill him?

And what had they done with Agneta?

14

Sara emerged from the Gamla Stan underground station by Mälartorget, walked along Munkbroleden and past Tyska Brinken as far as Kornhamnstorg. She avoided the narrow alleyways. She'd never liked them, which was strange for someone who'd opted to live in the old town. As usual, she'd left the car in the police car park.

She passed the Chinese restaurant and the corner shop where newspaper placards were already proclaiming the passing of the people's favorite.

STELLAN BROMAN DEAD—MURDERED AT HOME.

UNCLE STELLAN MURDERED—FOUND BY DAUGHTER.

In the latter, the word "found" was in a significantly smaller font than the other words.

A truck carrying graduating high school students drove around the square and came to a stop by the curb. The students were drunk, sweaty and soaked in bubbly. Their voices were hoarse, but they carried on screeching—mostly old hits from the 1980s: "Vill ha dig," "Sommartider." It created an odd sensation of childhood.

An empty champagne bottle smashed to the ground as a young girl in a short purple skirt climbed down from the truck on unsteady legs. Hanging around her neck was a blue and yellow ribbon with bunches of flowers that had already lost most of their petals. The girl wobbled toward Stora Nygatan, and Sara assumed she had her sights set on a door in the very corner of the square, given it was adorned with blue and yellow balloons and a sign with the name "Elsa." But the trajectory was far from being as straight as an arrow—so it wasn't easy to tell where she was heading.

It then transpired that this Elsa's heels were too high for her degree of inebriation. As her bawling classmates rolled away to the sound of "Varning på stan," she stumbled and fell to the ground.

Sara hurried forward and helped her up. She'd scraped her forehead and chin, and there was blood running from her nose and lips, but the young woman merely waved her away, her mind on partying. She needed to go home and change, she said. And then she tottered onwards, with one hand held to her face to avoid getting blood on her champagne-sodden clothes.

Sara carried on past her old regular pub from her own student days. It was still just as fascinating living here, right by Tabac—even if it was called something else these days. Once upon a time she'd commuted for more than an hour each way, a fair number of evenings a week, to hang out there. And she'd thought it was worth it. It was so important to belong when you were young. When Sara had graduated from high school, the truck had driven all the way from Vällingby into the city center, because that was where they'd wanted to show off. Stureplan, Kungsträdgården, Sveavägen, Södermalm—the entire city had been theirs. For a few hours, at any rate.

She cut across the north corner of the square and entered the narrow glass-roofed arcade. The passage continued toward Västerlånggatan, but she stopped by a solid wooden door that led up to the private flats. Most of the building was offices, but there were homes at the top. She'd been concerned when Martin had bought the flat using most of the money he'd got for his company, but just as he'd predicted, it was worth twice that today, so it had undeniably been a good investment. So long as the market didn't crash… That was all people with flats in the city center ever seemed to talk about, Sara thought to herself.

She'd never imagined living somewhere this big. It had felt strange at first, but now she'd got used to it. Some people lived like this, and she was one of them. A duplex covering almost 300 square meters with views of Slussen and Södermalm, filled with wood paneling and textures everywhere and parquet that creaked. And a gym and sauna. And at the very top, a tower with views in all directions. She usually had a glass of wine with Anna up there on the occasions they wanted to meet and didn't want to talk about work. With all the roofs, the waters of Slussen below and the German church right beside them, the tower room gave you the impression that you owned the world. It was said that a previous owner had hidden Nazis on the run up there after the end of the Second World War.

Sometimes, it felt as though she didn't have the right to call this magnificent flat her home, since she hadn't contributed a penny and would never have been able to buy a similar home by herself. But Martin had lived off Sara for fifteen years while trying to become an artist, and then when he was starting up his company. They had two children and they were married. So they were meant to share everything—in sickness and in health, as they said. But whether a huge flat in the old town was part of sickness or health, Sara wasn't sure. For her, a flat this size really meant there was just a lot more cleaning to do. She refused to get a cleaner, regardless of the fact that it was tax-deductible. Martin handled half of the maintenance, no matter how much of the martyr he played, and the kids had been made to take more responsibility for cleaning the bigger they had got. And sometimes you had to put up with things being dusty. That was how they got by.

Sara stopped at the threshold and listened for sounds from inside the flat. No one was at home.

At moments like this, pauses in life when time seemed to be standing still, she loved her home. The silence of the huge flat was majestic, as if it were set to music—and almost sacred.

Thoughts about her murdered childhood idol made Sara look for her old violin. She found it at the back of the dressing room, behind the Pilates ball, the bed of nails and the boxes of expensive boots with stiletto heels that she never wore. She hadn't played for years, but after tuning the violin she set off, playing her eternal companion and adversary, "Erbarme dich" from the

St. Matthew Passion. It had been described as the most beautiful piece of music ever written for the violin. Above all, it had been Stellan's favorite piece, and Sara had spent many hours and years of practice attempting to master it. Without success, if she was asked to judge.

Since Bach was the last thing Stellan had listened to, and since he was the one who'd given her the instrument, Sara thought it was fitting. But she felt a little ashamed when she put down the violin. Perhaps that was why it had been in the dressing room for so long.

After once overhearing a quarrel between Sara and her mother about their lack of money, Stellan and Agneta had given her the violin and paid for her lessons. And naturally, they'd chosen the best teacher available. Well, not available, exactly—given that she didn't usually accept private pupils. She'd only taken on Sara as a favor to Stellan and Agneta.

Irina Handamirov, first violinist in the Royal Stockholm Philharmonic Orchestra for four decades, professor of the violin at the Royal College of Music and grandchild of the legendary Ivana Adelenya. With three sisters who also became violinists, Handamirov had a family relationship with her instrument that had always made Sara envious.

Handamirov had frequently encouraged her to improvise when she played—to dare to get it wrong. To find new ways, new perspectives. But Sara had decided she had to master the Bach piece before she could start playing about with it. And she had never learned to master it. She'd learned to play it almost technically perfectly but, in her own view, without the soul that shone through when her teacher played the piece.

Handamirov had described different ways of getting into a piece. For Sara, there was only one. Get on with it and do it as correctly as possible. She knew that she thought more about her mistakes than the joy the music brought her, and she knew that was stupid. Holding her back.

But the piece had stuck better than she'd thought. The feelings of the bow's friction against the strings was still just as enchanting, just as tactile. The sound emerged as if by a miracle. It was amazing to think that it was Sara summoning it.

She became absorbed in the piece yet again, losing herself in it, forgetting all else. But as ever, reality returned afterward, along with its sharper edges.

She lowered the instrument and looked at it.

She knew she was talented, but she couldn't escape the sensation that her diligent practice in her teens had been more about pleasing her surroundings than herself—a way of showing gratitude for a gift she'd never really asked for.

In practice, she hadn't even wanted a violin. She'd only wanted her mother to be able to buy one for her. Just like the Bromans could buy everything for their daughters—clothes, ski equipment, musical instruments, trips. The violin had become a symbol of everything that was unattainable, and Stellan and Agneta had happened to hear of that. It had left Sara with no choice.

But the violin wasn't hers—not really. She had been given it, but she hadn't mastered it. The violin was not part of her.

And this home wasn't hers. It was Martin who had paid for it.

Perhaps that was why she'd kept her surname when they married, rather than taking Martin's. "Sara Titus" sounded feeble. Like an underconfident substitute teacher. Nowak was her name.

Otherwise, there wasn't much that was hers.

The children no longer sought her out, and in their eyes she mostly posed an obstacle on the path to everything fun that life had to offer. "Mum" was just the description of a role nowadays. And her marriage was mostly a by-numbers affair, even if that brought with it a certain sense of comfort. Like having the same things for Christmas dinner every year—not because they tasted good, but because that was how it was meant to be. Like sole and *lutfisk*.

If neither her home nor her violin were truly hers, and the kids were on the way out...

Who exactly was she?

The name that she knew belonged to her—what did it stand for?

In the absence of an answer, she turned on the television—a sixty-five-inch monstrosity that she would never have chosen. There was something unnatural about a newsreader whose face was five times the size of your own, as if giants had taken over the country and were proclaiming the new laws. Obey or be eaten.

The afternoon show was naturally about Uncle Stellan. There was always a big audience when one of the country's true icons passed away, and mourning dead celebrities seemed to have become something of a public amusement in recent years. Perhaps it was symptomatic of a narcissistic era, Sara thought to herself. As if another person's death primarily offered the opportunity to express some deep-seated thought that you could get likes for. Sara had never understood the point of Facebook posts like "RIP Whitney Houston" from ordinary Swedes.

The producer for the memorial program didn't quite seem to have decided which was most important: the brutal murder, or the nostalgic retrospective of Stellan's long career. The result was a roller coaster that segued from crime reporting to a cavalcade of memories. Even if Stellan hadn't been seen on television for many years, it was absolutely clear how much he'd helped to set the tone of Swedish TV. So they went all out and the conclusion was: "Per Albin gave us the welfare state, Ingvar Kamprad furnished it and Stellan Broman entertained it." Now all three were dead, and the welfare state with them—to the delight of certain conservative columnists.

Sara lowered the volume on the television and looked out of the window toward the water. There were usually boats down there, waiting to pass through the lock into the Saltsjön bay, but right now the whole place was a huge building site. There really ought to have been sunbathers and young couples down there enjoying the weather—or perhaps not enjoying it at all, but breaking up, or comforting each other because one of them had lost their job, or wondering why some love interest never called.

The sun was lavishing its rays on the scene even on a day like this. The weather gods were clearly above human tragedy.

But Sara couldn't let go of the mystery.

Where was Agneta?

She watched two underground trains pass each other on the railway bridge across the entrance to the bay by Riddarfjärden while she racked her brains. Had Agneta tried to escape, and had something happened to her? An accident? A heart attack? Sara's colleagues were searching as effectively as they could, and sooner or later some clue would turn up.

Might Agneta's disappearance also be connected to Stellan's work for East Germany? If so, how?

Sara considered what she knew about the Cold War. In her childhood, the term had been diffuse and vaguely frightening. A fear you could neither grasp nor understand. It was war, but there was no one shooting. You were supposed to be scared, even though you couldn't see anything to be scared of and despite no grown-up explaining why.

She remembered leafing through the thin pages of the heavy phone book. Right at the back, there had been a warning that war could happen at any moment. Everywhere—in schools, in leisure centers and in basements—there were air raid shelters with heavy iron door handles that could be turned to make the shelters safe from nuclear attacks. And inside them were table tennis tables to ensure that the kids could have some fun in the meantime, until such a time as war did break out.

The war *could* come, and that was what the Cold War was. An uninterrupted bombardment of frightening warnings, a constant fear. Things could go off at any moment. Any day now, the planet might be gone. Nothing lasted forever.

Sara went into the gym—or rather, the room in which Martin had installed a treadmill, rowing machine, exercise bike and two benches with barbells, dumbbells and weights. He'd also covered all the walls with mirrors. It was a bit nuts really, Sara thought to herself—but she put the warm-up weights on the barbell, changed, lay down and began pushing the weights up toward the ceiling and down again, over and over.

Each time she worked out, her adrenaline would skyrocket and everything she was angry about would resurface. If nothing else, it made her try harder.

After three heavy sets, she pulled out her mobile and called her mother.

"Hello. What do *you* want?" said Jane.

What a tone of voice! Was it so out of the ordinary for her to be calling? Was she such a rubbish daughter? Because that hadn't been broken Swedish—it had been reproachful. Dear God, surely she was allowed to call without wanting something? Even if that wasn't the case on this particular occasion...Sara was tempted to hang up, but she actually had a question to ask.

"You sound out of breath," said her mother.

Sara had been sitting quietly, breathing heavily while she thought.

"I'm working out."

"I am, too. I'm going to start walking. Those were some lovely walker shoes I got."

"They're called walking shoes."

"What does it matter what they're called? I'm going to walk in them—not talk to them."

"OK, OK," said Sara, pausing before getting to the point. "Stellan's dead."

"I know. I saw it on the news."

"I've been there. In the house."

"Of course. You're a policewoman."

"Not every police officer goes to every crime scene, Mum."

"What do I know?"

"But Anna's working on it. Do you remember Anna? From the police academy?"

"The hormosexual?"

She'd always pronounced it like that. The more Sara told her off, the more she exaggerated her pronunciation.

"My friend. Who is gay, yes. She called and told me—because I know the family. So I went there."

"Who was it who shot him?"

"We don't know. That was why I wanted to ask you."

"*I* don't know."

"No, but do you remember if he had any enemies? Did he quarrel with anyone? Was he ever threatened?"

"No."

"Nothing else? No crazy stalker?"

"Stork?"

"Stalker. An admirer with an obsession."

"Lots of admirers. Do you think one of them might have shot him?"

"Don't know. Perhaps not… Mum…"

"Yes?"

"He liked the DDR. East Germany."

Sara could almost hear Jane's mood switching gears.

"Yes," she said. "The idiot."

"What do you mean?"

"That he was an idiot! Praising a dictatorship! If he'd lived there, he would have spat at it!"

"Didn't you ever tell him what it had been like for you in Poland?"

"Yes. But then he said that socialism wasn't finished yet. I should have been patient. 'You think I should have stayed?' I asked him, and he said that if I had, 'I would have understood better.' Pfft… Patience. Idiot! Patience until when? Until they killed me?"

During her childhood, Sara had often wondered why Jane didn't love Stellan and Agneta as much as she and everyone else did. Sara had often accused her mother of being envious of them—because they had everything and she had nothing.

It obviously wasn't that simple, but mother and daughter had had very different perspectives on the Broman family. Perhaps Jane had been jealous that Sara always wanted to spend time with them, that she never stopped talking about them. The antagonism had grown after the move from Bromma to Vällingby, which for Sara had been an involuntary move.

But nowadays she thought she'd been sufficiently clear about her opinion of the move, even if it still stung.

From a privileged paradise to a concrete hellhole with intrigue and hormone-addled idiots. Just as she began her sensitive teenage years.

Had Jane moved so that she could have her daughter to herself? Or did she just want her own place? Her own flat, instead of living at the mercy of someone else? She had never wanted to explain—presumably because there was no explanation. Once Jane had moved, she'd remained faithful to Vällingby throughout the years.

"Could he have been a spy?"

Sara knew she really ought not to disseminate investigative details like this, but on the other hand, Anna and her colleagues hadn't taken to the spy theory—so she was technically not disclosing anything.

"Spy?" said Jane. "On what? Spying on young girls? No, he just liked being admired."

"But might he have given away information? Perhaps without realizing he was being exploited?"

"Maybe. If you flattered him, he was easy to exploit."

"Tell me more," said Sara, smiling.

"About what?"

"How you flattered and exploited him."

"Idiot," said Jane, before hanging up.

Sara didn't know any other sixty-year-old mothers who called their adult daughters idiots, but Jane was unique. She always had been.

When she was in the shower a little later, she heard the front door slam and since no one shouted "hello," she realized it was Ebba who had come home.

"Can you cook dinner?" Sara called out toward her daughter's room as she toweled off. "I think we've got macaroni and sausages."

"No time!" Ebba called out in reply. "I'm going to a party!"

A party on a Monday?

That was high school graduation season for you. Parties every night for weeks. Everyone competing to throw the best one and to go to as many as possible. And the easiest way to get invited to other people's parties was to have your own to invite them to. If you didn't go to any at all, then you were a nobody.

Ebba would be allowed a party—Martin had agreed to that, despite Sara being unsure. It would cost a fortune, and there were so many parties anyway. Was it really sensible to contribute to the frenzy? But now things were the way they were. Ebba had got what she wanted. The party had been planned for months and there were only three days left, but instead of getting everything ready, Ebba was out at other people's parties and reveling long into the night. She couldn't miss out on anything.

Macaroni and sausages. Was that *too* easygoing? Sara had never been especially ambitious when it came to food for the kids, and she had a guilty conscience about the fact that she almost always served meat in some form. Just like everyone else, she'd seen the videos of animal transporters, chicken farms and slaughterhouses. The awful treatment of the animals reminded her of what she'd seen of human trafficking, but it went even further in terms of the grimness of what was inflicted on other living, intelligent beings. Humans' indifference toward others' suffering made Sara feel sick.

She was ashamed that when it came to animals she was helping to keep the system going, just like the men buying sex whom she encountered through her job, who kept human trafficking going by demanding sex. Sara didn't want to contribute to making the world a worse place. She was going to turn vegetarian—and she was going to make the kids do it, too. Soon.

Ebba got into the shower after Sara. The flat had another shower room intended for the kids, but Ebba preferred the bigger bathroom when she was going out. There was better light by the mirror, according to her. And Mum's makeup, Sara thought to herself.

The front door slammed again and Olle came in. Sara filled a saucepan with water and put it on the stove.

"You're at home?"

She knew her son's comment wasn't meant with ill will, unlike Jane's. He was just surprised. Sara's many evening and night shifts meant she was rarely at home at dinnertime. Perhaps Olle was even happy that his mother was at home right now, but fourteen-year-olds didn't show that kind of emotion.

Just as the macaroni was ready, Ebba rushed past on the way to her bedroom, wrapped up in a towel.

While she was eating, Sara took out Ebba's peaked graduation cap and read what people had written on the lining.

"Ebba, you're the best!"

"Ebba 4-ever!"

"Life starts now"

"Who run the world? Girls!"

Decidedly traditional, Sara thought to herself as she reviewed her daughter's classmates' wisdom for life.

Life was certainly pretty strange.

Ebba was at the threshold of her life, Jane was looking back at hers and Sara was in the middle. She was in the phase where there was never time to stop and think. When you were young, you thought about how life would work out, when you were old you thought about how it had worked out, and in the long period in between you lived without thinking about it. What did she want from her life? Sara asked herself. She shrugged in reply.

She picked up Ebba's mobile, but put it back down again when Olle came and sat down at the table. He was completely engrossed in his own screen and Sara could probably have pulled up the floorboards without him noticing—but better safe than sorry. She'd recently pretended she needed to borrow Ebba's mobile to make an important call on the pretext that her own had run out of charge, and once it had been unlocked she'd gone into the settings and added her own fingerprint. Since then, she'd been checking Ebba's mobile at regular intervals while her daughter slept or was in the shower.

Ebba would have hated it if she'd found out, but there was so much that could happen to young girls these days. Sara had no intention of being so clueless that she let her own daughter run around town without keeping an eye on her. However, she'd carefully avoided pictures and messages of a more private nature.

Now Ebba wanted the new model with facial recognition, which Sara was opposing without explaining why. She knew that her daughter would get one from Martin if she asked him, so Sara had told her husband that it was very important to her that they didn't give the kids any more gadgets without discussing it with each other first. One fine day, Ebba would probably get a mobile that Sara couldn't get into—but she wanted to keep an eye on her daughter for a little longer. At least until all the high school graduation partying died down.

Sara took a sip from the Red Bull can Ebba had put down.

Laced.

Pretty heavily, too.

But Sara had no desire to lecture her daughter during the week of her graduation.

She had enough to deal with.

The whole graduation season was hell for Sara. Separation anxiety, feelings of guilt and the fear of being overprotective were all jostling for prime position. Ebba had forbidden her from planning anything to do with leaving school and receptions and student parties, since her mother was working so much and wouldn't have time to make a good job of it. Instead, Martin got the assignment—which meant completely different resources were at her disposal. Of course they had to impress their guests— why else have a party? Sara had secretly looked at the spread-sheet and seen five-figure totals. Martin had denied that it would cost very much, but Sara didn't trust him. And Martin had never understood that it didn't matter *what* he kept secret from Sara— it was *that* he kept secrets at all. Lies about unimportant triviali-ties taxed the trust between them—the tie that was supposed to hold them together.

In the living room were the small place cards for the table settings— the only part of the festivities that Sara was allowed to have an opinion about. She sighed without her son hearing.

Poor Ebba. Poor Olle.

Sara had really thought she would be a much better mother— fun, resourceful, always happy. Not like her own—tired, stressed, irritable. Angry at everything, or just silent. A martyr, as Sara had once described her during her teens. She'd had her ears boxed for that. It was the only time Jane had hit her. Sara had never struck either of her children, but she'd been absent—and probably too demanding. She often wondered whether Ebba's constant irri-tation at her was a result of how Sara had been as a mother, or whether it was just ordinary teenage behavior. She would have loved to be her daughter's best friend. Was it too late for that? She hoped it wasn't. Perhaps it would be easier to be close friends once Ebba got older.

Sara sat down in front of the giant television and went to SVT's catch-up service. She searched for "Stellan Broman" in the archive section and found multiple programs—she selected an episode of *Tivoli*.

Laughter and applause from the very beginning, the signature tune followed by a beaming Uncle Stellan welcoming the audience with his arms outspread. Taking all of Sweden into his embrace.

"I'm off!" she heard from the hall.

Sara turned off the television and went to say a few parting words, but she came to a halt when she saw Ebba.

Her nineteen-year-old daughter, her firstborn little baby, was in the hall in just a corset, hot pants, suspenders and black leather boots with stiletto heels. Her lips were flame red and her eyes charcoal black. Her graduation cap was on her head.

"What are you doing?" said Sara, aghast.

"Going to a party," said Ebba. "The theme's pimps and hoes."

"Are you out of your mind?"

"What is it now?" said Ebba, her tone one of exhaustion.

" 'Pimps and hoes'?"

"Yes?"

" '*Hoes*'?"

"For fun."

"You're dressed like victims of assault—like the poor Romanian girls who've been trafficked—for a party?"

"Mum! Stop it. It's just for fun."

"Tell that to the girls I meet at work. Raped ten times a day, assaulted, degraded, kidnapped from their home countries. And you think it's *fun*?"

"It's not for real, Mum. No one thinks there's anything glamorous about pimps and hoes—we're just using it as a cliché. Like a cowboys and Indians theme. We know the Native Americans were almost eradicated in the biggest genocide of history. But that's not what it's about!"

"What is it about, then?"

"That we're graduating from high school. You only do that once in life."

"It's exactly stuff like this that makes people look the other way when they see human trafficking. The myth about the happy hooker."

"I hear what you're saying. When I get older and wiser, perhaps I'll even agree with you and think I was an idiot for going to a pimps and hoes party. But right now I'm nineteen, and I want to have fun with my friends. If they're dressing like this then I will, too. OK?"

"No, it's not OK. Not one bit."

"You'll have to carry on shouting when I get home."

Ebba took her coat off the rack.

"It'll be too hot," Sara managed to say before she was interrupted.

"You think I should go out like this?" said Ebba, holding out her arms.

Sara had no answer to that.

"You don't need to have opinions all the time," said her daughter. "I'm moving out soon—then you won't be able to have any opinions about what I do. Perhaps you should start getting used to it?"

It was presumably just that which Sara couldn't make peace with—not sharing her life with her children any longer.

Ebba turned around and left, but just as the door closed Sara managed one more admonition.

"One at the latest, OK?"

What was she supposed to have done?

Forbidden Ebba from going?

Unlike many other mothers, she could have kept her daughter there by force, but that wasn't an option in practice. Apart from the fact that she didn't believe in using force on her children, Sara was held back by the realization that it would have led to a further deterioration in her relationship with her daughter. She remembered how angry she'd been at her own mother when she moved away from home, and how rarely she'd got in touch as a result. And she didn't want Ebba to do that—to avoid her.

At the same time, her daughter and her friends constituted a large part of the reason prostitution was able to continue—the romanticizing of this slave trade. Of course, Ebba hadn't invented pimps and hoes parties, and presumably she hadn't been the one who'd picked the theme. And no one else at the party would have listened if Ebba had protested. But they were helping to cement the structures.

For a second, Sara pictured her daughter in a flat-based brothel in some anonymous apartment block. A sweaty, much older man on her, and dozens of others waiting. She was on the verge of throwing up at the thought. She would need to speak to the parents of the girls who'd organized tonight's party. But she knew it wouldn't help one bit.

There was something titillating about pimps and hoes—something a little sexy about it nowadays. Films like *Pretty Woman* had laid the foundations for that—transforming the prostitute from an anonymous and despised person into a desirable object who was satisfied with her existence. Even a millionaire played by Richard Gere could fall in love with a whore and marry her—so surely there was nothing wrong with buying sex? You were really doing the girls a favor.

Would it have been better if Sara hadn't worked so many nights? If she'd done the school run more often, and been able to pass on her values in ways other than agitated lectures when it was really too late, when they'd already done something that Sara thought was stupid?

When the children were little, she had been obliged to work to support the family, given that Martin was busy with his shows and productions, which usually ran at a loss. But she'd tried to ensure she spent all her time with the kids when she wasn't at work. And when they'd got older, Sara had assumed they could get by on their own and that they wanted to be left to themselves more. But perhaps she'd been wrong.

And that was when Sara became annoyed at herself.

Typical that she would take responsibility. That it was the woman who sought out the fault in herself.

Martin had also worked a lot of evenings—if visiting pubs to mix with artists and agents could be described as work. Especially since he'd got the company going, which had been in parallel with Ebba's teens. Perhaps the absent father was a more significant explanation for the flirtation with the whore stereotype than the absent mother?

Sara understood that Martin needed to go out with his clients and potential business partners, and she knew that his industry was heavily based on entertainment. Opportunities for work and socializing were both to be found in the pub for many of his artists. If he wanted to have a good relationship with them, he needed to be out often. Evenings and weekends and days off. There was nothing unusual about it.

But it wasn't always fun.

It wasn't always easy when Sara worked the way she did, and her husband was often away on her few evenings off.

But she tried to be happy for his sake.

In his younger years, Martin had performed at school graduation parties and had set up his own cabarets. He'd dreamed of a life as an entertainer. When he didn't get any work as an actor or artist, he'd started doing his own productions—and after a couple he'd realized he was pretty good at it. So he'd started a company and soon enough Dunder & Brak Scenproduktion had become the biggest agency for artists and producers of stage shows in Sweden.

After a decade or so, just when Martin had almost had enough, he'd received an offer he couldn't decline: to sell his life's work to Go Live—an international giant in management and stage production—for a daft amount of money. This was on the condition that he remained and ran the company for at least ten years.

And, as the boss and with high profitability targets set by the new owners, he often ended up working late.

To Sara's irritation, Martin had spent most of the money he received for the company on buying the huge flat in the old town. And he'd carried on going to work as usual, doing the job he'd been getting sick of. The job where pub visits with guest artists and local musicians and actors was the norm. The job where most of his colleagues were young women aged eighteen to thirty.

Sara couldn't help being prejudiced against the entertainment industry. Celebrities, booze, drugs, young girls, sex. Given his position of power, Martin could naturally have as much of it as he liked. That was why she'd forced him to have photos of her and the kids on his desk at work. At first it had placated her. Everyone could see he was a family man.

Then she was ashamed for using the kids as a weapon in marking her territory.

Then she began to wonder whether he actually had the pictures on display when she wasn't there.

But tonight he wasn't working. Tonight he was rehearsing with his band CEO Speedwagon. Four blokes in management who thought they were clever. All of them were well on the way to fifty, but refused to drop the rocker dreams. They had extortionately expensive guitars but no audience—and the only gigs they played were when they persuaded their colleagues to book the band for staff parties. It was usually only once per company—apart from Martin's own company, where no one dared speak up when the same, tired old dadrock got played at the seventh party in a row. At least he let Sara make fun of his rocker dreams. That was something.

But sometimes they got in the way of more important things. If he'd been at home now, they might have been able to get Ebba to listen to the two of them together.

She turned the television on to have something else to think about, but it didn't help. She put the Prodigy on Martin's expensive stereo from McIntosh and connected his fancy headphones from Audeze. Not even "Invaders Must Die" pumping into her ears made all the thoughts about her kids, her husband and murder victims go away.

She lay down on her side and curled up. For a change, she thought about her life now, as it was happening. About how things were going for her daughter, her son, herself and Martin.

Should she change jobs?

If she couldn't hack it any longer, was she of any use to the exploited girls?

Did it help them if she gave the johns and pimps a beating—scared them, got those around them to understand what they were up to?

Her thoughts ran on, long after the album had finished.

15

Warfarin, atenolol, simvastatin, amlodipine, ramipril. Agneta couldn't remember the names of the others.

A small pellet.

Blue, yellow, mud-colored and white. For heart inflammation, diabetes and the pain in her legs.

Synjardy was a diuretic, which wasn't a problem right now—but she would have to avoid it later. And a slow-acting paracetamol for her knees and joints because of the arthritis.

She could still feel the pain from the bike ride cutting into her legs like knives. It was always worst a few hours after exertion.

Should she take a bigger dose?

No, she was far too afraid of side effects.

She hated getting old, but she hadn't liked being young either—so it didn't help to dream of going backward. She could only grit her teeth. She unscrewed the cap of the water bottle to help her swallow the pills.

The heat had her sweating buckets. And that was in addition to the insulin and the fluttering in her chest. She would have laughed at all of it, if it hadn't involved so many lives.

So far, the journey had gone fine. The car had started without any problems once the battery was charged. There had been very little air in the tires, but Agneta had fixed that at the petrol station in Träkvista. At the nearest supermarket, she'd bought more food and drink. Sunglasses and a cap were a good disguise—more than adequate provided no one was actively looking for her.

And she'd swallowed all her pills. Now things felt as if they were under control.

Getting around by car was completely different from cycling. The journey was almost peaceful. For a while, she'd forgotten both what was ahead of her and what was behind her.

From Brommaplan she needed to drive along Ulvsundaleden. It was quicker that way, she thought. What was more, she could avoid the congestion charging zone that began on the other side of the Tranebergsbron bridge. It hurt a little when she thought about how close to home she was going to be as she passed.

"Home."

Not any longer.

Had it ever been home? Or just a posting?

Now the car was her home. A comforting old Volvo. She'd been given a thorough training in how to fix the most common faults, but she really hoped she wouldn't need to open the bonnet.

Her handler had sorted out the car back then, while she'd arranged the barn. She hadn't told anyone, not even him, of its location. Agneta had always been convinced that one had to be just as careful with one's paymasters as one was with one's opponents.

Who was the car registered to? She had no idea. It wasn't registered to her, and it couldn't be in the name of her handler. Back when it had been obtained, foreign citizens hadn't been permitted to own cars in Sweden. But maybe he had false Swedish identities? It was definitely out of the question for him to have used his real name. All of a sudden she was curious about her handler's identity—perhaps because now that Stellan was dead, this person was the one who'd been part of her life for the longest, even if they hadn't been in contact for more than a quarter of a century. Despite that, the car was a physical connection between them. But whose was it?

Did the owner even know that he or she owned it? If Agneta passed a tollbooth, who would receive the bill in the post?

Curiosity got the better of her.

She got out her mobile, wrote KOA879 in a text message and sent it off to the Swedish Transport Agency helpline. The answer came back straightaway.

The car was not deregistered. It was registered to one Lennart Hagman in Sollentuna.

A collaborator, or utterly unaware?

Or a completely fake identity?

It didn't really matter.

Not now.

She slowly pulled out of the supermarket car park and then indicated right, heading for the Tappströmsbron bridge, Lovön and Bromma.

Behind her, a young man in the green uniform of the supermarket emerged from the shop with a couple of newspaper placards. "People in Ekerö earn the most" and "The best box wine for midsummer" were swapped for the new headline.

STELLAN BROMAN DEAD—MURDERED AT HOME.

16

Martin got home at around nine o'clock. It was early for a rehearsal evening, and he didn't seem all that drunk either. He propped his beloved guitar against the sofa and came over to give Sara a kiss.

"Are the kids at home?" he asked.

"Olle's in his room. Ebba is at a pimps and hoes party."

Sara looked at Martin to see how he would react.

He didn't.

"Pimps and hoes," she said again, once he'd cast himself onto the sofa in front of the television and reached for the remote. He stopped and turned his head toward Sara.

"We definitely didn't have that, back in my day."

"But, Martin, can't you hear what I'm saying? Our daughter's at a party where everyone thinks it's fun to dress up like prostitutes."

"Yes?"

"Do you know what my job entails?"

"Of course I do."

He was frozen to the spot with the remote in his hand.

"You don't see any issues with teenagers dressing up like pimps and hoes and thinking it's a lot of fun?"

"No, it's not great, I suppose. The reality is brutal."

"How fortunate that you've listened to me and can repeat everything I say."

"What? I'm not just repeating. I think it's awful. I don't know how you hack it. But you do a great job. Without you, the girls would be completely at the mercy of those perverted bastards."

"This isn't about me, this is about society as a whole. About the fact that our daughter and her friends are helping to spread an image of prostitution that allows this shit to carry on. And that they're getting the wrong impression. Who knows, perhaps someone at the party gets the idea that selling sex seems pretty cool— maybe it'd be a good way to earn some extra cash. After all, sex is fun. And they start doing it and they ruin their lives. Martin, what if your daughter were to think like that? That selling sex didn't seem so bad?"

"No. Not Ebba."

"But someone else, then? Is that better?"

"OK," said Martin, putting the remote control down. "What do you want me to do?"

"End the sex trade."

He sighed. Then he straightened up and turned toward Sara.

"About Ebba. Do you want me to talk to her?"

He placed his hand on Sara's and looked her right in the eyes.

"Do you think it'll help?" she said.

"Christ knows. But you're angry. You think I've done something wrong."

Sara pulled her hand away from Martin's.

"Not you. Don't be so self-absorbed. It's the whole world there's something wrong with. And I hate that our kids are soon going to head out into that world and we can't protect them."

"I agree with you. It's awful."

"And they don't want to be protected. They want to make it on their own. I know it's perfectly natural, but I hate it. They'll run into loads of idiots. When they're applying for jobs, when they go to the pub, when they go traveling. They've no idea how dreadful people can be. And it doesn't have to be murderers and rapists. The very thought of anyone even being unpleasant toward one of my children gets my adrenaline pumping."

"Mmm..."

They fell silent. She was getting nowhere. Perhaps he didn't feel the same.

"Put the television on," said Sara, noting that Martin was quick to do as she said. The giant screen came on and he clicked to his favorite channel.

Sport.

Dear God.

Sara lay down at the far end of the sofa and tried to filter her thoughts. On the television, there were three commentators making different guesses about what was going to happen in some tedious football league, and how long some boring player would be injured for. Martin was listening attentively.

Sara looked at her husband and wondered exactly what it was about him that she'd fallen for once upon a time.

He'd been the best-looking, most popular guy in school—so in one regard he'd been a catch. She'd won. A girl from Vällingby had got the most popular boy in Bromma. *Dirty Dancing* in reverse. But when they got together, they were no longer going to school. Sara had won, but after the fact. And what do you do with the prize once you've won it? What use is a trophy? It was like pulling a whopper of a pike into the boat after several hours' struggle, only to realize you actually fancied a salad.

He was still good looking. Very good looking, in fact, in a boyish way. Tall, dark eyes, charming smile. But it was as if somehow that charm was too boyish. He hadn't aged mentally, if Sara were to be completely honest. It was all unkempt hair, playing in a band and beer with the lads. Charming in a twenty-year-old, a little sad when it was a forty-six-year-old.

What did she actually share with Martin these days? The kids. No common interests, no sex life to speak of. Martin had said that when Sara let off steam by shouting about how disgusting all men were, he felt disgusting too. He couldn't understand that she needed to experience some good sex as a counterbalance after all the crap she saw on the streets and in those anonymous brothels.

Sara didn't want them to just be parents or friends. They were supposed to be a bloody couple, too. Who slept together. Who wanted to sleep together.

Martin claimed she'd become increasingly angry, and that didn't really leave him wanting to proposition her, he said. But in Sara's eyes, those were two completely different things. Of course she got angry. It was easy to say that you weren't going to bring work home with you—implementing it in practice was harder.

Sara noted that it was getting dark outside. A moment later she was asleep.

17

"Halbstark!"

They were off again, the Swedes. Completely hammered by
night, followed by long lie-ins so that all the agenda items in the
morning had to be postponed and Tomcat was forced to come up
with rubbish excuses on behalf of everyone who'd been stood up
by them. Toward afternoon they would arrive on unsteady legs,
shaky. But a swig of Bitburger would have them raring to go.

They had been staying with him for a week—two students from
the Södermanlands-Nerikes nation in Uppsala, one of the many
historical student associations at the town's university, hosted
by their sister nation Burschenschaft Arminia in the German
town of Marburg. A two-meter-tall military-looking type with a
shaved head and tired eyes, and a lean, hysterical joker with lots
of product in his hair.

When they eventually made it out of bed toward afternoon,
they usually wanted to hang out in the *Kneipe* and knock back a
few beers, which always ended badly. They'd organized such a wild
booze-up in the old skittle alley in the basement that it might not
be possible to renovate it.

They'd demanded to be allowed to try academic fencing and had
posted the photos on social media, which had resulted in the chair
telling Tomcat off and saying that he'd ruined the good reputation
of the student nation.

And they'd gone down to the biker club Bremsspur wearing
their student caps, so that the police had been obliged to come and
calm things down. While the Swedes laughed and joked.

The icing on the cake had been when they'd given an incomprehensible speech at the spring gala in broken German mixed

with English and Swedish. Something about youth, hospitality and *Lebensraum*, seasoned with all the foul words in German they'd learned over the course of the week. The members of the alumni club hadn't understood who these two were or what they were doing there, but they'd politely responded to the toast once the speakers were done. And then watched as the Swedes swiped a bottle of Sekt each and smashed the bottles on the stone floor.

And now they were on a tour—because the students in the Arminia nation took care of their guests. Tomcat and Peter had borrowed Peter's dad's car, and in the CD player was an old album by the punk legends Die Toten Hosen—*Never Mind the Hosen—Here's Die Roten Rosen*. A record made for fun, in which Die Toten Hosen did funny punk covers of old German folk songs. The Swedes had put it on straightaway and played it without interruption throughout the trip, screeching along with the songs.

The stench of their hangovers mixed with the smell of freshly opened beers. A third day stuck in a car with two idiots, Tomcat—alias Thomas—thought to himself.

The military-looking one just talked about concentration camps, how Rommel had actually been a first-class soldier and that the manufacturer of the ovens had been Topf & Söhne. Not that interesting if you weren't...an idiot.

After visits to other affiliated Burschenschaft student unions in Heidelberg and Bonn, they'd visited a vineyard in Trier, and now they were on their way to Tomcat's home town of Hattenbach, because when he'd planned the trip he'd thought they might appreciate meeting normal young German people. After this week, it was apparent to him that his guests would either be bored to tears or drive the whole village mad—but it was too late to change the plan now. Tomcat's mother was busy preparing dinner for them. It would be years before she forgave Thomas for the oafs that were approaching her table. And as if the Swedes' drunken bravado wasn't enough, they'd started to make jokes about the name Hattenbach as soon as they had heard it. Apparently the beginning of the name meant "hat" in Swedish, and "being in the hat" could signify being drunk. Judging by the Swedes' hysterical laughter, this was the funniest thing ever said on the planet, but Tomcat saw nothing amusing in it whatsoever.

Worst of all was the tone-deaf bellowing in broken German to the song about how all girls want to kiss.

"No more," said Tomcat in English, turning off the CD player.

Dear God. He was hung over, too. He'd been ferrying these pissed Swedes around for a week, apologizing to the Burschenschaft old boys, who were all doctors and CEOs and ministers. And he'd seen his chances of getting a job through Arminia's network of contacts go up in smoke right in front of his eyes.

Everyone seemed to think the whole spectacle was his fault.

And all he'd done was volunteer when Arminia heard it was going to have two visitors from its sister nation in Sweden. He hadn't chosen who was coming.

Now his temples were pounding.

Just one more night. Then back to the beautiful castle on the hill in Marburg for a farewell dinner, and then they would go home.

Tomcat would sleep for a fortnight.

At least.

He didn't give a shit about his exam next Thursday. He hadn't had a single spare moment to study in the last week. He had to be grateful that it hadn't caused lasting psychological damage. His studies didn't matter at this stage; all that counted was survival.

"Play 'Halbstark' again!" hair-gel guy bawled.

"No," said Tomcat. "No more Hosen."

But if he'd been hoping for some peace and quiet, he was disappointed, because in that same moment the Swedes began to screech Arminia's song instead.

"Do you know," said the two-meter-tall one, leaning forward toward Tomcat and Peter in the front seats, "in Swedish, *Heimat* sounds like *hajmat*—shark food."

When the chap let out a booming, moronic laugh, Tomcat wanted to die.

And he did.

There was only a couple of kilometers left to go to Hattenbach when the road exploded beneath the four hungover students. The blast shook the ground, burst eardrums and was audible from kilometers away.

Peter's dad's car was blown apart, and the four bodies were shredded to pieces—inexorably and brutally, as if by a careless butcher. Their skin was burned and lacerated by the wave of pressure and the heat. Fingers, toes and facial features were completely erased.

The body parts and the contorted, blackened remains of the car flew tens of meters up into the air before raining down on the ground again—asphalt, metal and blood.

On the other side of the road, two cars coming the other way were blown into the air at the same time. But they were farther from the point of detonation, and the whimpering, querulous sound of the dying could be heard for almost half an hour.

Then there was silence.

Absolute silence.

18

The white tower rose above its rural surroundings like a lighthouse—a lighthouse that was a long way inland. As if the sea had withdrawn, leaving behind a warning sign that no longer had anything to warn about.

Agneta had had no idea that there was so much in the way of forests and wilderness so close to the center of Stockholm. Despite having spent most of her life in the capital city, she'd never been to Norra Djurgården or Stora Skuggan. She'd heard the names and knew the areas were somewhere between the royal Djurgården, the university and the archipelago, but she hadn't quite settled the map in her head. She'd never understood how it worked geographically. Now that she was standing before the white tower, it also felt as though it had been taken from a story book.

But this was for real.

She felt the weight of her Makarov against her thigh as she wandered up toward the rear of the tower. She'd left the car far away in the brand-new stone-built suburb that had emerged in the space of just a few years on the edge of the Royal National City Park.

A younger murderer might have ensured she changed weapons to avoid arrest while in possession of a pistol that could be tied to multiple bodies, but it didn't matter to her how many murders she could be tied to, or whether the punishment would be any harsher. The only thing that mattered was that she managed to find and dispose of everyone.

Anything else was failure.

But if she pulled it off, then the police were welcome to arrest her. Or perhaps it would be one of the intelligence agencies.

She'd been promised help if she got into trouble, but she wasn't counting on that. Not in her line of work, and especially not after so many years.

But the thought of spending the rest of her life behind bars didn't worry her. She'd just released herself from a life sentence—being put away for another wouldn't involve a change. Unlike her younger self, she now realized quite clearly that she might fail and be arrested or killed. The sense of immortality possessed by the young was long gone. Chastened realism had taken its place.

And contrary to how it had been back then, she didn't really have a life to lose now. She was too old. What was more, unlike so many others she'd had a life's mission—a real calling. This was the life choice she'd once made and she stood by it. Now and always.

Even if she felt uncertain about whether she would actually succeed in her mission, she was glad that the phone call had eventually come. That she hadn't died before what she'd been trained for took place. Like Prince Charles dropping dead before getting his chance to be king. Or if Christer Fuglesang had never made it into space.

But now the question was—should she pry open the lock or just ring the bell? He was expecting a text message, but she didn't know whether he trusted her. If he was uncertain and planning any kind of trap, it might be worth taking him by surprise.

What if he had a dog?

She really hoped he didn't. She loved dogs, but would be left with no choice if one turned up. She would have to shoot. She didn't dare rely on the silent techniques any longer—she wasn't sure they'd ever been that effective. There was nothing to guarantee that her close combat instructor hadn't been a desk murderer. No one had ever described any assignments or missions where they'd actually made use of such skills. It wouldn't surprise her if the intelligence services and underground organizations also had their fair share of overenthusiastic habitual liars. IB had definitely been full of angry amateurs.

When she spotted that there was a stout old patent lock on the door, that decided matters. Pick it and sneak in.

It was unfair that people who lived in places this beautiful were also so protected from burglaries that they didn't need to get decent locks.

Just like many years ago, she took several minutes to open the door. Millimeter by millimeter, a staircase appeared, winding up the curved outer wall of the house. And as you went up the staircase, the various flats had their front doors on different landings, as if curling up toward heaven. An odd building.

She went up the stairs just as slowly as she'd opened the door. She placed her foot on the edge of each step and pushed it forward, slowly increasing the pressure until she could rest her body weight on the foot. Each step took thirty seconds.

The staircase continued upward, but on the first landing a warm glow shone through the crack by the threshold and classical music was audible through the door.

She leaned forward and glanced upward, but the landings above were in darkness. She should really have looked up the plans for the building at the city planning department. But her perfect cover as Stellan Broman's wife had the downside that she could be recognized almost anywhere she went if she met anyone over forty. And if some poor hollow-eyed bureaucrat happened to read that they'd found a dead body in a building whose plans she'd scrutinized, you could be certain the police would find out. She had the impression that the Security Service and counterespionage operatives were more professional these days. They would actually be able to put two and two together.

Not worth the risk.

Pressing down the handle took her three minutes. When the crack along the door widened by a few millimeters, the music got louder. Mahler, it sounded like, if she wasn't mixing them up. Once upon a time she'd had all the major composers and their most famous works down pat, as well as choice anecdotes about the conception of the works. Music, literature, art—a classical education, even if delivered mechanically—had been surprisingly effective tools in her arsenal.

She was unaccustomed to her thoughts running away like this, and it was unfortunately dangerous. As she dreamed of the past, she dropped her concentration on the present and pushed the door slightly too quickly. At the very moment she realized her mistake, she caught sight of the man in the armchair.

Kellner.

He jumped when he became aware of the uninvited guest, and to her surprise he aimed a revolver at her. In the same second, she raised her pistol in a reflex movement and fired.

She got there first, so his shot hit the ceiling. The man shouted and fell back into the chair.

That part was at least working—the reflex of shooting without thinking if her body registered danger.

But the shot from his gun had frightened her. Not because she was unused to the sound of shots—it had only been a few hours since the last time—but because she was so set on creeping about and being silent. She'd calibrated her hearing to listen for tiny, tiny sounds, which meant the sound of a pistol being fired had a tremendous effect.

She raised her arm and took aim at him while approaching the chair. She tugged the revolver from his hand and put it in her pocket. A Smith & Wesson snub-nose 38. Odd choice.

"Who sent you?" he said.

Agneta didn't answer.

"How many are dead?"

She followed his gaze to the laptop on the coffee table. The *Aftonbladet* website was on the screen. "Uncle Stellan dead—murdered at home."

News had already got out. Jesus.

She skimmed the text.

"Found by his daughter."

Bloody hell.

Did the grandchildren already know their grandfather was dead? Had Lotta and Malin already told them? It was lucky they hadn't been close to Stellan. But where did they think she was? Their beloved grandmother … It broke Agneta's heart when she thought about the fact that her grandchildren might be worried about her.

"What do you want?" said the man with the gunshot wound. "Are you …? What do you know? Or are they after you, too?"

He clearly didn't recognize her as Stellan's wife. Men didn't seem to suspect that she belonged in their world.

"I need to know," said Agneta.

"It wasn't me who shot him, if you think that," he said. But she already knew that.

"The codes," she said. "Where are you supposed to meet?"

He simply stared at her.

Well, why should he be any more feeble than she was? Same generation, same ideological motivation, same commitment.

Behind him there were CDs along all the walls on what must have been custom-built shelves. Hundreds, if not thousands of hours of classical music.

Who even listened to CDs nowadays?

She looked at him again. He was clearly in pain as a result of the gunshot wound, but there was nothing in his face to suggest he'd given up.

Kellner.

For decades, it had been one of the key cover names, but now there was a face to go with the seven letters. An aged face. Weather-beaten but mild. A bald crown with a completely white mane of hair beneath it. Watery blue eyes that blinked with irritating frequency. The slightly bowed body of old age, and trousers too high around the waist. A short-sleeved check shirt and well-trimmed nails.

144

An old man.

Once upon a time, when he'd moved into this white tower, had he thought that someone like her would be here one day, holding a pistol?

Agneta Broman. A completely peripheral figure to him. But with the power to decide how his life proceeded. His nemesis, summoned by tragic wrong choices in the past.

"What are your instructions?" she said.

"For what?"

"If the ring is to be activated."

"None at all."

She struck his nose with the butt of the gun. She wasn't all that strong anymore, but the butt of a pistol hurt a lot anyway.

He cried out.

Blood poured out of his mouth and down his chin, some of it dripping onto the check shirt. He looked both angry and surprised.

"I was to await orders," he said, once the pain had subsided. "Stand by."

"For what?"

"Don't know."

She hit him again. He cried out again.

"Where are you supposed to meet Suleiman?"

"Who?"

"Abu Rasil."

"I don't know. I was simply to await instructions."

Now he was off, talking. He would probably have dropped his guard by now.

"Where are the codes?" said Agneta.

"Which codes?"

She gripped the pistol, took aim and fired a shot into his right knee. He bellowed with pain, wheezing for a long time and writhing on the armchair. In the meantime, she went over and turned on the television and zapped through the channels until she found an action movie with weapons and lots of shouting. She turned up the volume as high as she could. She hoped no one would call the police. Then she went back to Kellner and clipped him around the ear.

"Which codes?" he cried out in despair. "I don't know which codes you mean!"

"One more chance," she said, pressing the barrel of the gun to his other knee.

"No, no, no! I said I don't know! I don't know! You can have my money. I've got a hundred thousand in the bank. Take that."

She looked deep into his eyes and saw only panic. No secrets. While she took the only possible decision, she put her hand in her pocket and checked.

Should she show him what she had there?

Was he supposed to find out why she was doing what she was doing—why he had to die?

No.

She was building a world that he would never get to see.

She moved the pistol from his knee to his forehead and pulled the trigger. His head jerked, but his body was held in place by the armchair. Then she put another bullet into his head to be sure, and he barely moved at all.

No, he didn't know anything about the codes.

Jesus.

But she couldn't have let him live.

She consoled herself that what she'd done was nothing compared with the treatment he would have received if the others had got hold of him.

At any rate, there was one person fewer who knew the truth.

Two down, two to go.

At that moment, flashes of blue light penetrated into the room. She hurried to the window and peered out. She feared the worst, and her fears were borne out. A police car with lights flashing. The sound of footsteps on the gravel, a door opening and voices. Then new footsteps, and the sound of the downstairs doorbell.

What should she do?

Just sit and wait?

She hadn't done any reconnaissance on escape routes—she hadn't thought that far ahead.

Idiot. Stupid, decrepit idiot.

Were they leaving again? The sound from the television could explain the first shot. She assumed that the neighbors had called it in right away, given that the police were already here. But if they could hear that the television was on and no one opened up when they rang the bell, perhaps they would have to force their way in. And no matter how well trained she'd once been, it was by no means tempting to contemplate a firefight at her age with young police officers in a confined space.

But she didn't have much choice.

Best to try and gain the element of surprise.

She crept down the steps again, stopping inside the door on the ground floor, where she raised the pistol and aimed it right at the door at chest height.

The police rang the bell again. The sound of the television was audible from upstairs. Would they try to get in or leave?

Her exit was unclear, but she couldn't risk her mission. Then she had an idea.

She crept back up the stairs again and saw that Kellner had also kept a landline. It was probably only old spooks who still did.

She dialed 112 and explained in a jittery whisper that someone was ringing her doorbell, crying out that she was afraid because her brother whom she was visiting was not at home. She didn't know anyone in Stockholm, and now she thought there were burglars trying to get in. She gave the address, and after a while the operator was able to confirm there was a police patrol vehicle on the scene and that it was probably the officers ringing the bell. Agneta said in a frightened voice that she wasn't going to open up to anyone, no matter who they were. She made sure to stand right by the television when she called, so that the operator eventually asked her what the noise was, and Agneta explained it was the television.

The maneuver seemed to work, because after a few minutes the police car departed, the officers probably cursing bumbling old hags who wasted their time when they had proper crimes to solve.

Once the police had gone, she changed channel from the action film to the news, and it didn't take more than a few minutes for Stellan's death to be covered. His career, his violent end, the rise in violence. Sweden's lost innocence, the crumbling welfare state.

She turned the television off.

She'd thought she would have several days before anyone found Stellan, but she would now have to anticipate that she would draw significantly more attention. They hadn't mentioned her on the news, so the police must have kept her disappearance a secret. The question was what they thought had happened to her.

She went into the kitchen and found a pair of scissors. She stood in front of the bathroom mirror and washed the makeup off her face. Kellner had nothing but soap, but it would have to do. Then she took the scissors, leaned over the basin and cut off her hair—lock by lock—until there was just a white stubble remaining.

A completely different person met her gaze in the mirror.

Older, tougher.

Good. She needed to be someone else.

She had really always been someone else.

She collected the hair cuttings, flushed them down the toilet and then rinsed the final strands from the sink.

She went to the front door and glanced back at the body.

Kellner was out of the way, but she now had far less time to act freely.

It was imperative she find Ober quickly.

19

Sara woke up at three o'clock in the morning. Martin had placed a blanket over her and she'd been sweating like a pig in the warm summer night, but she still appreciated the gesture. Perhaps he'd tried to wake her up so that they could go to bed together. Sara knew that she was almost impossible to rouse once she'd nodded off on the sofa. Long ago, Martin used to sit there and wait for her to come to enough that she could come with him to the bedroom. But he'd learned that it sometimes took hours—so nowadays he would let her sleep.

She sat up and tried to interpret the strong sense of unease she was feeling.

Ebba.

When she spotted that it was three o'clock on the display of her phone, and that there was no message from her nineteen-year-old daughter who'd vanished off into town in not much more than her underwear, she panicked. At the same time, she didn't want to seem too worried in case Ebba was simply still at the party and everything was fine. And she didn't want to make her daughter think that she didn't trust her.

But what kind of student party carried on until three o'clock in the morning on a Monday night?

She sent a text message.

How's it going?

Then she waited.

She went upstairs and brushed her teeth so that she had something to do.

No reply.

She peed, removed her makeup and brushed her hair.

No reply.

Another text message. More direct this time.

Where are you?

No reply after three minutes.

Sara tried calling. There was no answer.

Now she was worried.

She called emergency dispatch and gave her credentials before asking whether there had been any reports of attacks on young girls.

Nothing like that.

Stabbings of young men. Drunken brawls. Careless driving.

No rapes or assaults of girls.

Jesus.

If it was just that Ebba was too pissed to hear her mobile, she would...

Sara stopped herself. She shouldn't start threatening Ebba in her inner monologue, not until she knew that everything was OK. But wearing those clothes...She should have stopped her.

She tried calling again.

This time her daughter rejected the call.

Sara was furious and sent a text in all caps.

PICK UP WHEN I CALL!

Then it occurred to her that it might not even be Ebba who'd rejected her call. And then she felt really sick.

The best-case scenario was that someone had stolen her mobile and that she was stuck somewhere, angry and unable to call home or for a cab precisely because her phone was missing. But the worst-case scenario was that the person who'd taken the phone had also done something to Ebba.

Sara needed to go out. She had to find her daughter.

Where had that party been? Hadn't Ebba had an invitation on her desk?

Sara tried calling her daughter yet again while she headed toward her bedroom and once again Ebba rejected her call. Or perhaps it was someone else doing it.

At the very moment Sara opened the door to Ebba's room, she saw her daughter put her mobile back on the bedside table, turn over in bed and start snoring. Ebba had rejected Sara's call because she was sleeping. And she hadn't even been woken by the first call.

She was at home.

The room reeked of smoke and booze, but right now that didn't matter. Not one bit. Because Ebba was lying there in her pink nightgown, asleep. Home. Safe.

Sara looked at the corset that had been dumped on the floor alongside the fishnets and the hot pants.

Was it really her little Ebba who'd been wearing them? Even if it had only been for fun, it still felt very peculiar. Regardless of what you thought of the pimps and hoes theme.

Her daughter was grown up.

She was making her own choices.

20

"The parties."

He smiled to himself.

"It's the parties I remember. And all the attention you got when you were traveling around the country with Stellan. There would be thousands of them jostling to catch a glimpse of him—and maybe even speak to him or shake his hand."

After that final remark, he laughed—a croaking, hoarse laugh that triggered a new coughing fit. He put the tube to his mouth and inhaled.

Lelle Rydell, a faithful old henchman, ideas guy and scriptwriter. Stellan Broman's loyal companion through thick and thin for a couple of decades. He must have been significantly younger than Broman, and it was still possible to discern the novice's admiration in the voice of the now-retired television man on his deathbed whenever his older mentor was mentioned.

They were in a one-bed apartment in one of the functional design buildings between Ladugårdsgärdet and Tessinparken. Sara got the impression that he'd lived there more or less his whole working life. She'd been led to believe that the entire Gärdet and Östermalm neighborhoods were crawling with old SVT personnel—everyone who'd been on Swedish telly in the 1960s and 1970s. Nowadays, everyone at SVT lived in Södermalm and in the southern suburbs. They would be bussed in to work on the number 76 in the same way school pupils had been bussed around the USA in the 1960s.

"Did you know that Kissinger's uncle lived in this building?" Rydell said. He looked at her. "Right up until the 2000s. It said 'Kissinger' down by the main door next to the buzzers. And once when he was visiting Sweden—the nephew, you know—when he was secretary of state, there was a whole bloody motorcade of limos and police cars and motorbikes that came round here so that he could visit his uncle. The place was teeming with Secret Service operatives on the stairs and in the courtyard round at the back. I had to show them some ID just to get in the lift."

Yes, he'd clearly lived in the building for a long time.

"I didn't know that," said Sara, who was unable to fully recollect what it was that had been so special about Kissinger. Something to do with Nixon or the Vietnam War. Or was it both? At any rate, she recognized the name.

But it was Uncle Stellan she wanted to hear about.

After some online searches and a few phone calls, she'd found this bloke Lelle, who'd been at Stellan's side for so many years. Until now, he hadn't said anything that might help her solve the murder. But he'd talked about ratings, letters from admirers and hypersensitive complaints to the TV ombudsman that never led to findings in favor of the complainant. She now knew a great deal about these subjects.

And the partying.

"Tell me more," said Sara.

Rydell grinned.

"Once, he rented the entire theme park at Gröna Lund for a wrap party. And the next year he rented the whole open-air museum at Skansen. And they once let him hire the Vasa Museum for a 'sea battle.' Everyone was dressed up as pirates and beer was being served out of casks. I seem to recall that the king himself was there. I suppose that was before he had kids."

"Were there a lot of influential people at these parties? Politicians, executives?"

"Anyone who was anyone. And there was us—the production team. He always took good care of his colleagues—he was truly amazing like that. Often, people who become celebrities quickly forget about their old friends and only hang out with other celebrities.

But not Stellan. Jesus—he'd be standing there with some billionaire and if you walked by he'd call you over and introduce you as if you were some kind of genius."

Rydell looked almost teary-eyed.

"It was pretty fantastic. I might be sitting there on the sofa with a government minister and some star athlete, and we'd be discussing sex positions."

He laughed, causing another attack of coughing before he breathed in again through the mouthpiece.

"I think it was a draw," he added. "One vote for doggy style, one for missionary and one for 69. If I remember correctly."

Rydell was once again lost in his own memories.

"Stellan basically offered you a safe place. It was awesome to see elected politicians, major artists and famous directors truly let loose. But he never lost control himself, did Stellan. Never. He was always in charge, he talked to everyone and he helped the ones who got too drunk into their taxis."

"Was his wife present?"

"Agneta? Absolutely. She was an incredible host. She would introduce people to each other and made sure you always had something to drink. She would roam around smiling and making everyone feel welcome. Both Stellan and Agneta always remembered all sorts of minor details about everyone. They were able to ask after kids and grandkids, and inquire about sick wives and cabins that needed paint jobs."

"East Germany?"

"Beg your pardon?"

"Did Stellan ever talk about East Germany?"

"No."

Rydell sounded surprised.

"Never?" said Sara. "He didn't love or hate it? There's nothing else that springs to mind when I say East Germany? Or the DDR?"

"We had East German guests on the show sometimes. Singers. Maybe some songwriter. Oh, and there was an author that Stellan said ought to be awarded the Nobel Prize. I can't remember his name, so I guess he didn't get it."

"And at his parties?"

"East Germans? Maybe. Don't know. It was mostly Swedes. Celebrities and hot women."

"Was he political?"

"Not one bit. I mean, he was engaged. He cared about the little person. He would get worked up about injustices. And…Oh, yes. Peace. He was committed to peace. If you'd call that political."

"Peace?"

"Yes. Stopping nuclear war."

"Yes, he was certainly a draw. He did a lot to get people on board."

Marks Olle Boo was well over eighty, but his bright blue eyes gleamed with energy even if they were rather teary. He was short and hunchbacked, but he looked as if he was fighting valiantly against the onslaught of the aging process. His hair was bushy and white and had begun to thin, but must once have been akin to a lion's mane; what still remained of it flowed in large waves down toward his shoulders. He was wearing khaki-colored trousers with lots of pockets stitched down the legs—pockets that appeared to be filled with bits and bobs. And he was wearing a blue and white striped collarless shirt. His fingers were bony, but he often stretched them out in emphatic gestures. Sara had read around and discovered that Boo had been a prominent figure in the Swedish peace movement. A driving force and inspiration who'd led hundreds of protests and demonstrations, he'd been arrested by the police dozens of times and had been an invited speaker in countless television debates and current affairs shows. He showed no signs of needing to leave his tidy little flat close to Stockholm's south station in order to move into an old people's home any time soon. Hundreds of files and thousands of books lined the walls. There was an armchair with another stack of books beside it on the floor.

Sara got the impression that Boo wasn't just hanging on to the files as mementos—he seemed to be actively working with them. And that he would continue to do so for as long as he could.

"We had a lot of so-called celebrities join us," he carried on. "Hasse and Tage. Sara Lidman. All sorts. And the warmongers tried to play down the peace movement precisely through dismissing us as a bunch of celebrities. As if the matter at hand was affected by the fact that you were known to the public."

Boo tapped his gnarled index finger on his temple to show how stupid the idea was.

Sara was reminded of occasions when she'd seen celebrities like the ones that Boo had just mentioned at the Bromans' home, even though there hadn't been parties going on. They'd been serious, but exhilarated. The peace activists had almost certainly met at Stellan's every now and then, and it was as if a piece of a jigsaw had fallen into place. As a child, she'd never understood what they were doing. They'd behaved differently compared with when they were on show.

In fact, she was sure she recollected that even Olof Palme had been there at some time for one of those unfestive meetings...If so, was it a declaration of sympathy, or an informal gathering to placate the almost uncontrollable peace movement?

"Do you know Eva Hedin?" said Sara. "The researcher?"

"I've got her books just over there."

Boo pointed toward the bookcase.

"All a bit of a witch hunt, I'm afraid," he said. "She seems to have some fixed idea that it's up to her to hold criminals accountable even though no crime has been committed. A Swedish Simon Wiesenthal, but without a Holocaust."

"She's identified Stellan Broman as a Stasi informer."

"Yes, she even goes so far as to say he's a spy. Or at least, that's the impression one gets."

"Did the rest of you know about that?"

"What?"

"That he was helping East Germany?"

"His engagement with German culture was hardly something he kept quiet. He often went there to participate in festivals and ceremonies and all sorts of official things. He was awarded medals and the like, and I think he appreciated it. But even if you have views on his somewhat vain nature, I have to emphasize that it was *all* German culture that he loved. He didn't distinguish between East and West—to him they were the same people. And it was this particular issue—that he didn't make a stand against the DDR—that some people got hung up about. The sixties and seventies—not to mention the eighties—were a very single-minded time. The Eastern Bloc was evil, and any dealings with it were evil in themselves. But nowadays, the same capitalists have a completely different perspective on China. They're just as communist as the Soviets or the DDR, but now you can make money off the dictatorship. Big money. So suddenly it's a good thing for democracy and transparency to trade with regimes like that. And just look at the USA—soldiers from private corporations, vice presidents who are shareholders in weapons manufacturers, presidents who are oil tycoons. We were praised by Chelsea Manning—the whistleblower—because here in Sweden we showed the world that it's actually possible to cut military spending significantly without anything happening. But that's not a popular view with everyone. Do you think it's a coincidence that there are suddenly so many books coming out about the threat currently posed to us by Russia? They can't afford to pay state pensions, but they're planning to occupy Gotland. At the same time, we're doing business with both China and Saudi Arabia. Not to earn money—oh, no—but to spread democracy and openness. Well, you can certainly see how well that's gone. China hasn't been this totalitarian since back in the days of Chairman Mao, and in Saudi they've got a conveyor belt of women running straight into their jails. They flog the homosexuals. More tea?"

"No thanks."

Herbal tea wasn't Sara's thing. She had only finished her cup out of politeness.

"To go back to Stellan," she continued. It wasn't easy to get Boo to stay on topic. "You don't think, then, that he passed information to East Germany?"

"What information? If an East German had asked him what the time was and he'd given them an answer, there would have been a bunch of right-wing warmongers who would have cried out 'traitor.' He probably said all sorts of things, given what a good host he was. He knew everyone and was interested in everything, so of course he may have shared information that might have been purely, technically, considered classified. He would never have said anything that would cause harm to the country. He wasn't naive. But he wanted to treat everyone equally. Anything that he might have told people from the East he would just as happily have told to people from the West. And I'm sure he did, but back then there was no one who cared about it. Such was our precious neutrality. We were sitting on America's lap and were terrified of contact with all other countries. Africa, Asia, the Eastern Bloc. Everyone was evil except for Uncle Sam. All *we* wanted was to treat everyone equally. That's why we gave our wholehearted support to peace activists in all countries—even behind the Iron Curtain."

"So he wasn't a spy?"

Boo shook his head. Then he took a gulp of tea.

"It was all about peace for him. I don't think he was in favor of the system in East Germany. Not at all. I imagine he said whatever it took to win the ear of the powerful. So that he could then exert influence. He considered nuclear weapons to be a terrible threat toward all of humanity, and he thought he could do something to help. By giving East Germany more attention, getting them to be accepted as an equal partner in dialogue, we could avoid war. Stellan was the least pugnacious of the lot of us. All he wanted was for everyone to be happy."

Sara processed her thoughts. This happy Stellan was someone she remembered. It was the official Uncle Stellan, the one seen by the Swedish people. And at home he had been an absorbed, often absentminded father. But political Stellan had passed her by.

"Did you receive any funding from East Germany?"

Boo screwed up his eyes and almost squinted at her.

"No, we never received any funding," he said with a shake of his head. "We might have been invited on the odd trip, but it was always to events we would have gone to anyway. Festivals, demonstrations, seminars. We barely had any money at all in the peace movement, and every penny we saved was a blessing. If we'd gone to the USA for a demonstration, we would happily have let the Yanks pay. But our beliefs weren't for sale. We never let ourselves be bought."

"Just travel?"

"And maybe a grant for the odd demonstration here or there. If we needed to rent the park at Kungsträdgården or anything like that. Lighting and sound costs. Paying the travel costs for some big name from overseas. Anything that brought us attention was a good thing. Well, positive attention. We didn't seek out scandal."

"Grants for the odd demonstration?"

"Yes. We wanted to reach the people. It was five to twelve on the Doomsday Clock and we wanted to save as many as we could."

"And those grants weren't in cash?"

"No." Boo now looked irritated. "Not cash we could pocket. Not cash we could do whatever we liked with. It was to cover specific expenses, and we made it clear that they could expect nothing in return, because otherwise we wouldn't have accepted so much as a penny."

"But you accepted quite a lot of pennies."

"I don't know how old you are or what age you were when the Wall fell. But it wasn't Reagan and his Star Wars program that brought the Wall down. It was our friends. The dissidents. The people protesting against nuclear weapons on the other side of the Iron Curtain. Normal, peace-loving Germans."

"And you happened to accept funding from just those particular oppressors?"

Fred Dörner was almost six foot six, had curly white hair and wore small spectacles. He had big bags under his eyes. He lived in a one-bed ground floor flat in Farsta. He had a chunky old-style TV and an old IKEA sofa and his bookcase was stuffed with biographies. When he spoke about Stellan Broman, there was something that came alive in his gaze.

"He invited me to one of his parties. At first I wondered why, but there were other people there from the public sector—senior civil servants and political types—so I assumed I was there as a representative of the more... academic species of civil servant. He liked to have a real mix."

"What did you work on?"

"FMV. The Defense Materiel Administration. I worked on major weapons systems."

"Wasn't that classified?"

"Yes, but since I was a refugee from the DDR and a committed anti-communist, I was probably considered reliable. During the Cold War, it was often all about mutual enemies."

"What happened?"

"It was a...honeytrap. I gather that's what it's called. You're tempted with sex and then you're blackmailed."

"You were propositioned?"

Dörner nodded.

"So Stellan had hired a young girl?"

"A guy."

"OK. And then he blackmailed you?"

"Not him. It was someone else who sought me out and explained what would happen to the tape if I didn't start passing information to them. Back then homosexuality was a touchy subject. Precisely because you could be extorted. And I still walked straight into the trap…"

"What about Stellan?"

"Well, what do you think? He arranged the whole thing. Invited me to the party, rustled up the boy and got him to take me to a room where he'd…rigged a camera."

"So you passed them the information?"

"No. I refused."

"And did they send the tapes to anyone?"

"To my bosses. The young man was from the Stasi, so I lost my job. *Ohne Abfindung.* No severance package, since I hadn't told them about my sexual orientation. The thing that had got me into this…exposed position."

"What did you do then? Did you find another job?"

"Taxi driver."

"Were you angry at Stellan Broman?"

"Am. I'm *still* angry at him. Even now he's dead. Once they've buried him, I'm going to go and spit on his grave. He was a bastard. Do you know the worst thing about it?"

"No."

"For a brief moment, that young man made me think I was loved."

21

"There's no need to worry," said Sara. "I'm not in the middle of a breakdown."

"You kicked him. While he was lying on the ground."

"He used a knife on me."

"But you're a police officer."

"And police officers stick together, right?"

David sat there with his eyes staring straight ahead. They were carrying out surveillance on a brothel in a residential flat in a shabby, sad-looking high-rise that the inhabitants referred to as "the Projects," having been inspired by American cinema.

The buildings were pale blue, dilapidated monsters—depressing in a way that made you think the architect's vision had from the very beginning included drug dealing and suicide. The kinds of things you never saw in the idyllic plans that were put on display in the public library in order to convince skeptical locals.

"And I'm not pissed off that you talked to Lindblad," Sara said. "But you know how manipulative she is."

"I didn't talk to her. She weaseled it out of me."

"I can imagine."

David continued to stare straight ahead.

"But you can be pissed off if you want to be," he added. "I'm used to it."

Sara glanced at her colleague. He seemed to be fully preoccupied with playing the martyr, she thought to herself. And then she remembered that she'd heard something about David testifying against a colleague when he was a beat cop. A colleague who'd shot a man running away from him in the back. And who'd then been fired.

"What's most important to you?" asked Sara. "Putting away dirt-bags or putting away your colleagues?"

David turned to Sara.

"I'm never going to lie to protect a colleague who carries out an assault. And after all the hassle I got in Malmö, I've decided to always speak my mind."

"That's fantastic, David. Believe me. Just imagine if you could be that direct and honest with your family, too."

"Stop it!"

Sara shrugged.

"OK. But it affects me, too. You're worried about how I'm doing and I'm worried about how you're doing. You realize that it does more harm to suppress your emotions than it does to let them out like I do."

"Stop assaulting people in custody and I promise to tell my family."

"Perfect. Just think what a beautiful world we'll live in then."

At that moment, Sara caught sight of an old acquaintance.

"Fuck me, it's the Baron."

David followed Sara's gaze and spotted the same thing she had.

Thorvald Tegnér, former justice of the Supreme Court, was still a diligent client of the city's prostitutes at the ripe old age of eighty-nine. He had a taste for young girls. He was a regular who never tried to apologize, never pleaded with the police who arrested him, nor became angry or tried to escape. He always confessed on the spot, accepted his order to pay a fine and coughed up. And then he would turn up again a few weeks later at another brothel, or in the apartment of another escort. If they caught him in the act, then he simply withdrew and would stand there completely unembarrassed, talking to the police while stark naked. Sara wasn't looking forward to Martin getting old. Droopy balls and sparse white pubic hair was not a pretty sight. But perhaps she would like it then.

The Baron was no nobleman—he'd been given the nickname as a result of his haughty manner. On this particular day, the Baron had an H&M shopping bag in his hand, which was unusually relatable for a fastidious snob like him.

"Let's arrest him. Who cares if he just carries on? He can't be allowed to think we've given up."

"OK," David said. "Ten minutes until take-off."

After they'd been waiting for a little while, Sara's mobile rang.

"Yes?" The ringtone had divulged that it was Anna.

"Update." Her friend didn't offer any greeting either. "No trace of the burglars at the Bromans' house. No blood, no fingerprints, no hairs. The masts being used by their mobiles also suggest it's not them."

"Doesn't surprise me."

"How much have you actually got on this Cold War trail?"

That explained it. Sara had been wondering why Anna had called to report to her, given that she wasn't part of the investigation, but now she got it. Anna had realized she'd been wrong and wanted to try out Sara's theory. She felt flattered, at any rate.

"Lots. I can show you. But not now. See you in a couple of hours?"

"OK. Call me."

"Yes."

They hung up, as it was still known—despite the fact that no one actually hung a receiver back on to a telephone any longer. These days, you tapped the call away.

"What do you think? Time to go in?"

David checked his watch.

"Roger that."

David pulled out one of the team's unregistered mobiles and called the number they'd found online.

"Natasha," said a young girl with an Eastern European accent.

"Hi," said David. "How much? I'm outside. I've only got ten minutes."

"Twelve hundred for half an hour."

"OK. Which floor?"

"Four. Hallman on the door. Code is 2121."

They got out of the car, ambled over to the main door and entered the code. They took the lift up to the fourth floor. It was customary for a pimp to sublet a flat from a subletter, or even from the subletter of a subletter, for a rent of up to five times the original price, without the actual tenant having a clue about what was going on. Then the pimp would pack as many girls as he could into the flat and turn it into a brothel.

Nowadays, there weren't any big guns or muscle guarding the girls. The human trafficking gangs controlled them by threatening their families. They would say they'd either kill their mothers or kidnap their sisters, and do the same to them as the girls were experiencing. And the girls usually gave in at that point. That was part of the reason they so rarely wanted to cooperate with the police—out of fear that something might happen to their families back in their home countries. And the Swedish police couldn't protect them there.

Sara hated that she didn't have a ready answer when the girls explained why they didn't want to report their pimps or testify against their customers.

She lingered a few meters away from David as he rang the doorbell since there was a peephole in the door. But when the door opened, she quickly stepped forward at the same moment as David grabbed the door handle, stuck a foot inside the door and flashed his police badge.

"Police," he said in a low voice. "We're coming in."

And then he signaled to the girl to be quiet.

The girl who'd opened the door was clearly on drugs, and looked frightened. She couldn't have been more than eighteen years old. Perhaps she was a recent arrival and thought the police in Sweden were like the ones in her home country. That she was at risk not only of being raped, but having her income stolen.

"Where is he?" Sara whispered. She repeated herself in English when she got no reply.

The girl pointed toward a closed door along the hall. Sara positioned herself and then David opened the door. Inside was an empty room with the blinds pulled down and nothing apart from two mattresses on the floor. In front of them was a girl who was far too young, kneeling while she gave the wrinkly old Tegnér a blow job. He had a firm grip on her hair and had his other hand just a couple of centimeters above her head, as if he was ready to slap her at any moment. The girl was no more than fifteen or sixteen. Her hair was tied up in pigtails and she was wearing pink tights and a pink T-shirt emblazoned with the words "Daddy's girl." Lying on the floor beside her was a big teddy bear, the H&M carrier bag and a receipt.

"Police," said Sara to the young girl, who interrupted her blow job and looked at Sara and David with a vacant stare. She looked uncertain for a couple of seconds, but then she turned her head away again and carried on sucking. She received an encouraging pat on the head from the Baron, who looked Sara in the eye with a smile.

She went up to them and pulled the girl away. There was a plopping sound as his penis slipped out of her mouth. Then Sara pushed the girl over to David and turned to look at Tegnér.

"How many times does that make it? A hundred?"

"Isn't she pretty?"

"If she's under fifteen, then you're in real trouble."

"She's eighteen. I've got it in writing."

"Surely you can see she's not."

"At my age, you can't tell the difference between fourteen and eighteen. You must realize that."

And then he smiled.

He was in all likelihood right. He would probably get away with that excuse. Especially if the judge was someone like him—older white heterosexual male with an inflated ego. They always showed each other a great deal of understanding for their excuses and apologies.

Tegnér could probably provide a text message in which the girl stated she was over eighteen, and at his age it could be difficult to tell the difference between a fourteen- and an eighteen-year-old. Theoretically.

This was what bothered Sara most of all. That the ones who committed these outrages just carried on. No matter how often Sara and her colleagues caught them out.

They just turned up again. Cheerily smirking.

David called their contact at social services to get the girl taken care of. Sara knew they aimed high and did a good job, just as long as the girls were willing to accept help. David helped the girl to her feet.

"Wait," said Tegnér. "Don't take her away. I need to finish first."

Sara turned toward him and saw him looking at the girl and smiling while slowly pulling his foreskin back and forth over his glans.

It took a second for her to realize what he was doing—it was so awful she couldn't interpret it at first. Then, purely on reflex, she struck him down. She hit Tegnér right on the chin, and she heard the crash when her fist made contact.

22

Her knuckles were tender, and David refused to speak to her on the way back into the city, so Sara had plenty of time to think about what had just happened. Twice in such quick succession. But she couldn't honestly bring herself to say she had any regrets. Both Vestlund and the Baron had got what they deserved. No one else was going to fight the victims' cause, so how on earth was it wrong that she had? She fully understood the argument that police officers couldn't exercise their own personal justice, and assume responsibility for the punishment of criminals, but when nothing else stopped them, how could it be wrong to at least try doing something?

Was David going to tell Lindblad about this? Maybe. And what would happen then? It was hard to say. But were the work-related consequences for her personally the important thing here? Wasn't the issue that society was in the state it was in? That, if anything, it was moving backward from the progress that had been made by past generations?

As her anger at the Baron slowly dissipated, the murder of Stellan surfaced in her thoughts once again.

Mad stalker, burglar disturbed mid-crime, or former East German who'd had their life ruined? Or was there someone completely different behind it?

Regardless of who the murderer was, the motive was in all likelihood connected to Stellan's apparent espionage. That was the only part of his life that provided an explanation for such a violent act. TV fans and housebreakers didn't shoot eighty-year-old legends in the head. It had to be the espionage angle.

Sara's mind was made up about it.

The excerpts from the records that she'd seen with Hedin's help had been annotated with the names of three informants for the Eastern Bloc who'd never been punished: hiding behind the code names Geiger, Koch and Kellner were Stellan, plus one Stiller and one Schulze. Since David was driving, Sara could search online on her mobile. There were around twenty people in the right age group. Who were the right ones? And did they know who Ober was? The ringleader Hedin had lacked a name for...If the spy ring had been activated, wouldn't it be Ober who'd performed the activation? Was it one of the other three who'd killed Stellan? Was it to protect some secret from the past? Had Stellan threatened to reveal something? How would she find the other three?

It would take too long to search for the answers by herself—especially if she had to do it alongside her day job. She glanced at David, who was still sulking, and then she called Hedin.

"Which Stiller and Schulze are they?" Sara said as soon as Hedin picked up.

"What?"

"Kellner and Koch. You'd noted that their real names were Schulze and Stiller, but there are dozens of them who are the right age. Which ones are the ones we're looking for?"

"You know I can't say that."

"Give me two first names, then—any that you like."

There was no reply from Hedin, but she seemed at any rate to be thinking it over given that she hadn't refused point-blank.

"If I find the right people, it's possible I might find out something about them that could be of interest to your research. I promise to share it with you if I do."

A longer silence. Now Sara could tell that she'd got Hedin hooked.

"Just give me two names. Any names. It's not a crime."

"Hans," said Hedin. "And Jürgen."

"Give me the name of a town, too. Any town you like."

"Stockholm. The Stora Skuggan neighborhood. And Tranås."

"Do you know what they do now?"

"The one in Tranås is a priest. The other one is retired—he was an economist for the county council, I think."

Sara hung up without thanking Hedin and called Anna. She'd shown some interest in the DDR trail. David glanced at Sara. He must be wondering what she was up to, but if he didn't want to talk to her then she could do whatever she liked.

"Yes?"

Anna answered the phone as curtly as ever.

"I know the names of two of the IMs. The person who shot Broman might be after them, too. Or perhaps it was one of them who did it. Otherwise they might know something important about the murder."

"OK, what are their names?"

"The first one's called Hans Schulze. He lives here in Stockholm—in Stora Skuggan. The second one—"

"Hans Schulze?"

"Yes," said Sara, who could tell from Anna's voice that the name rang a bell.

"Hang on a sec." There was the sound of keys being tapped. "Yes, I thought I recognized the name. I've been going through lots of reports to see whether it sparks any ideas—there was a patrol called out to one Hans Schulze yesterday."

"Yesterday?"

"Yes, exactly. Yesterday evening. Someone reported a noisy disturbance—said it sounded like shots being fired. So a patrol went out there, but it was just some old woman whose TV was on too loud."

"Did they speak to anyone?"

"Wait a sec…Only to Schulze's sister, who refused to open the door. She was scared. So they left again before she panicked."

"Anna—get there as fast as you can. See you there."

Sara hung up and looked at David.

"I'll drop you off," he said without looking at her.

He still sounded angry, but there was apparently still a certain degree of loyalty between them.

When no one opened the door, they summoned a locksmith. Sara wanted to try climbing in through a window, but Anna stopped her. Either something had happened, or it hadn't. It made no odds if they had to wait a little longer.

Sara reluctantly agreed. It went without saying that the locksmith took an hour to arrive and didn't have the professional pride to apologize.

The postman arrived while the man was working on the door, and she had to flash her police ID to calm him down. Then he wanted to take photos and post them on Instagram, but Sara quickly managed to change his mind about that.

Once they got inside the flat, they found what they assumed to be Schulze, dead in an armchair.

Shot.

Whether it was a generational thing or a personality thing was unclear, but Schulze had no PIN on his mobile so Sara could check his call history right away. There had been one single call the day before, and before that a couple of calls a week. He wasn't a chatty phone calls type of guy. Sara asked Anna to check out the numbers and got a tired look in reply.

"Don't you think we'd have thought of that?" she said.

Then she called Brundin at the Security Service again. A second victim from among the old informants—surely now they had to say what they had. But Brundin refused. She could neither confirm nor deny that they held any information pertaining to one Hans Schulze, and she had no other comment to make.

Jürgen Stiller, the priest, did indeed live just outside Tranås in Småland, although it transpired that he was based in Östergötland county, since his church was in Ydre just across the county boundary. Anna got the Linköping police to dispatch a patrol car—sirens and all—to provide police protection until the murderer was found. Following Schulze, the threat against Stiller was being taken seriously.

Then Anna and Sara waited for Forensics.

"Stellan and this Schulze guy have both been fingered as spies for the DDR in Hedin's book," said Sara, gesturing toward the corpse. What do you make of it? Do you think there's something to the spy angle now?"

Anna remained silent—which indicated that she thought Sara was right. While they waited for their colleagues to arrive and the usual procedures to get started, they looked around the flat.

It was an odd home—located in an old tower. Plaster walls and wooden floors. There appeared to be three or four flats within the building, each with their own front door on different sides of the tower and rooms over several floors. The bedrooms and bathroom were upstairs, while the kitchen and living room were downstairs. In the bedroom was a single bed, neatly made. There was a clock radio on the bedside table. The kitchen was spacious, with a wooden dining table. Judging by the fridge and shelves, the inhabitant had been no gourmet chef. Blood pudding, porridge, potatoes and sausages.

In the living room, the walls were completely covered in shelves with classical music CDs. The stereo was still on. Linn, Sara noted to herself. Martin was an audiophile, and she had even gone with him to the HiFi expo on a few occasions, so she knew her stuff. Linn was a connoisseur's brand. Expensive. But nothing else in the flat was at all indulgent, so music and sound appeared to have been the deceased's only vices. There was a lot of Deutsche Grammophon—all the major composers, and plenty that Sara had never heard of. In any case, what was in evidence was the same love of classical music that Stellan had had. There weren't many of Sara's generation who had the same interests.

Schulze, the music lover, had been shot in the knee—in addition to the fatal headshot. The knee injury was different from the murder of Stellan. As if the murderer had tried to extort information from Schulze. Had he succeeded? Who wanted to see these old men dead so long after the fact? And why?

Or was it not actually "after the fact," Sara thought to herself. Were these executions the consequence of something that had been going on all along? Had the Cold War never really ended? Hadn't Hedin said something about that?

With both the Soviet Union and East Germany gone, who might be behind it?

Sara turned to Anna.

"Where does Agneta come into this?"

"She might have seen something she shouldn't have and been abducted?"

"Like the murderer? But why take her with them? Why not just shoot her and dump the body—like they did with Stellan and Schulze?"

"Maybe she knows something? Do you think she knew that Stellan was a spy?"

"No. Not Agneta."

Anna's mobile rang.

"Yes? In Stora Skuggan. Another murder—victim had been identified as a Stasi spy... Thanks to Sara... She's here with me now."

Anna listened for a minute, then she hung up and turned to Sara.

"We need to get over to the campsite in Ängby."

23

Despite the fact that no one had told them to hurry, Anna was doing one hundred and ten kilometers an hour down the long straight on Drottningholmsvägen. As they approached the campsite, they spotted the head of the preliminary investigation, Bielke, standing waiting for them outside the barrier across the road.

Had they found another victim?

Or had they located Agneta?

They were hardly throwing a surprise party in Sara's honor. So why did she have to be here?

They got out of the car and followed Bielke past the red wooden cabins by the site entrance to a large motorhome surrounded by similar vehicles from a variety of countries. This one happened to have German registration plates, a tent porch and sun loungers, but the curtains were drawn. German Schlager music was audible inside.

Bielke knocked on the door, and a burly man opened it with his hand behind his back. He was wearing what Sara was certain was a bulletproof vest under his tracksuit top. Inside the door there was a metal detector that beeped when the three of them stepped inside, and they were obliged to hand over their service weapons before the inner door, made from a huge chunk of metal, was opened.

The inside of the motorhome was most definitely not a holiday home.

Running along the sides were tables bolted to the wall, groaning with radio equipment, a plethora of displays and rows of computers. There were filing cabinets and what looked like a miniature laboratory. In the center of the room, there was a boardroom table—perhaps it doubled up as a dining table, too. A bijou kitchen and a couple of sleeping berths were the only reminders of the vehicle's original function. The outer walls were so thick that Sara had to assume they were substantially reinforced—possibly with armor-plating. A motorhome for war zones, Sara thought to herself. It wouldn't have looked out of place in a *Mad Max* movie.

Seated at the table in the center were two women in their sixties and a man who was slightly younger. The latter was rotund and looked like he weighed at least 150 kilos. One of the women was white-haired and dressed all in white. The other had short gray hair, and was wearing jeans and a very badly fitting jacket. The white-haired one nodded at Sara to indicate she should sit down. The other scrutinized her in silence. Sara noticed that they didn't seem at all interested in Anna.

"Sara Nowak?" said the white-haired woman.

"That's me," she replied in her overly diligent schoolgirl English, characterized by an almost over-the-top British accent.

"I'm Doctor Breuer and this is Doctor Strauss," said the white-haired woman in heavily accented English. "We're from the BND—the Bundesnachrichtendienst. This is Frau Brundin from your Säpo—the Security Service."

The word "Säpo" sounded funny in German-accented English, Sara reflected before noting that Brundin looked more or less as she'd imagined.

Sour and suspicious.

A remnant of a more bureaucratic era at Säpo.

"You knew the family?" said Breuer.

"Yes," said Sara.

"Played with the daughters?" She nodded in reply. "What were they like?"

"Like all children. Sometimes kind, sometimes mean. But I think it was special for them, being part of Stellan Broman's family. He was the most famous person in Sweden for many years."

"But you didn't notice anything strange?"

"Spies and mysterious strangers? No. There were always lots of new acquaintances in the house. Lots of guests and parties when he wasn't working. Can I ask you something?"

"No," said Brundin.

"What?" said Breuer.

"Why are you here? Was he a spy?"

To Sara's surprise, the burly policeman in the tracksuit top began to lay out a picnic on the table in front of them. Sausages and cheese. But Strauss was the only one to help himself.

"Your friend Anna told her boss you have a theory that the murder may be connected with the Cold War," said Breuer.

"It's *a* theory," said Sara, although to her eyes it was the only reasonable one—especially given this visit.

"Where did you get that theory from?"

"A book by Eva Hedin."

Brundin rolled her eyes in an exaggerated fashion that would have looked overdramatic even in a pantomime.

"Hedin..." said Brundin.

"And what did she say?" said Breuer, ignoring Brundin's interjection.

"Tell me what you know first," said Sara.

"Secret," said Strauss, shoving a toothpick around his mouth.

"OK," said Sara, deciding to keep quiet.

For a long time.

"Remember that you're a police officer," said Breuer.

Sara still stayed quiet.

"Nowak, please answer the question," said Bielke. But that didn't help either. Sara stayed quiet.

Until Breuer gave up.

"OK. I guess that your profession is in possession of the same information that we are," she said. "So I can tell you. Stellan Broman is listed in the Stasi archives as an IM—an informal collaborator. Code name Geiger. There are hundreds of old informants and spies all over the world who've never been brought to justice, but the vast majority are inactive. We thought Stellan Broman was inactive, too."

"Why were you watching him, then?"

"We weren't."

"You just *happened* to be passing right now?"

"We were monitoring a phone number in another country," said Breuer.

"A number that made an unexpected call to the Bromans," said Strauss.

"We didn't know he'd been shot when we arrived," said Breuer. "When we drove past the house, we saw the police tape."

"And who called Stellan?"

"That's not something we can go into," said Breuer. "But we've reason to believe that they've activated another old player from back in the day—a terrorist with many lives on his conscience. And we believe he may be on his way here right now. So we need to know more about Broman. We need to understand the connection between the people we're monitoring and an old IM here in Sweden."

"And that's why we need to know why he was shot," Strauss added. "And by whom."

There was silence inside the mobile command center. Sara looked around. Did the Swedish Security Service have equipment this cutting-edge?

Her gaze fell on a computer display with several open tabs. They appeared to include both Swedish and German newspapers, and all the articles were about an explosion in Germany the day before. Five Germans and two Swedes had died when a road was blown up. EXPLOSION A MYSTERY, SEVEN DEAD ON AUTOBAHN, GAS EXPLOSION OR BOMB? TERRORIST CONNECTIONS UNDER INVESTIGATION were just some of the headlines.

"Is this to do with Stellan's murder?" said Sara, pointing at the screen with the articles and looking at Breuer, whom she perceived to be the leader.

"Why would it be?" asked the woman in white.

"German–Swedish connection. Might be a terrorist act, and you just said that the terrorists you've got eyes on have started to move."

"No comment," said Strauss.

"As we said, they're here because of the call to Stellan," said Bielke. "But when we checked the Bromans' call logs we didn't find any incoming calls at all for yesterday, despite the daughter's statement and our German friends. So we compared phone numbers."

"Count Bielke's inspired idea," said Breuer generously.

"And they had two lines," he continued. "One number that friends knew about, and a secret one that they've never been called on, going back as far as Telia can see. The phone in the study had a different number from the other phones in the house."

"What do Säpo say?" said Sara. "I tried to find out whether they had a file on Stellan, but Brundin refused to answer. Maybe she was more impressed by you?"

"Frau Brundin is highly knowledgeable with regards to the Cold War and counterespionage in that era, and has been most helpful," said Breuer. "But it goes without saying that I cannot comment on what materials Säpo may or may not have."

"But thanks to our information, Säpo and the Swedish police will keep an eye on ports, railway stations and airports," said Strauss.

"He'll get in anyway," Breuer muttered.

"You do know that another old spy has been shot, right?" said Sara. "Kellner. Yesterday. He was part of the same ring—I think that's what you'd call it?"

"Bielke told us," Breuer confirmed with a nod.

"Hedin says that the spy ring was led by someone called Ober," said Sara. "But she doesn't have a name for him. Do you?"

She looked from Breuer to Strauss and then to Brundin, examining their faces carefully to see whether she could make out anything in their expressions. A small tremble, a quick glance, a brief hesitation. It was almost like playing poker and looking for any signs in the gestures and expressions of your opponents. Sara had realized that information was hard currency in this world, and that it wasn't to be shared unless absolutely necessary. This was completely contrary to how she usually worked with her colleagues.

"No," said Breuer. "A lot of files were destroyed when the Wall came down."

"Do you know anything about Ober?"

"We know that he recruited Geiger, and that they met in Geiger's home to hand over information and for ideological education."

"His home?"

"Regularly."

"So I may have seen Ober?"

"Very possibly," said Breuer. "That was why we asked you to come here. To help us identify him."

"Do you know anything else? What kind of person are we talking about?"

"He was radical. He handled contacts with certain Palestinian groups at that time. He helped European terrorists to access training camps with them. And we believe that he supported West German terrorists by providing them with accommodation and money here in Sweden. Your country was something of a refuge for the world's extremists back in the seventies."

"We had them under surveillance," said Brundin.

"Are these terrorists still active?" said Sara, pointing at the articles on the display.

There was a nod from Strauss.

"We assume the call was a signal to Geiger to be prepared," he said. "But what were Geiger's other instructions? Why was he shot?"

Sara remembered the meeting with Lelle Rydell, but couldn't imagine him as an East German spy. Which was possibly the perfect cover. Seemingly harmless and uninterested in politics...

"Is Ober next on the list?" said Sara. "Is this urgent?"

"Maybe Ober is the one getting rid of everyone else," said Breuer.

"If so, then the question is why," said Strauss, looking at Breuer as if he was hoping she would evaluate his contribution.

Sara glanced at Bielke, who was sitting peering at the acerbic Brundin. He would probably have preferred the main line of inquiry to have been a different one. He was always so careful to avoid treading on the Security Service's toes.

"That phone number abroad," said Sara. "You mentioned Palestinian groups—you mean Black September and others like them?"

"And others like the IRA and ETA. And the Red Army Faction. With a focus in the Middle East. And some of the people who were active back then have carried on freelancing for various clients. Today there are new players who have joined the old activists. You might say they have interests in common. Hatred of Israel, the USA and the West."

"Al-Qaida and Islamic State?"

"Those kinds of organizations."

There was a knock on the door. Sara jumped and all the Germans' eyes turned to a screen that was obviously connected to a CCTV camera.

Standing outside the motorhome was a man in Adidas shorts with his torso bare, together with a boy of around twelve. The burly policeman drew his weapon and concealed it behind his back before going out of the security door and closing it, and then opening the outside door.

"Do you want to play volleyball with us?" said a voice with a strong Västgöta accent.

"*Ich spreche kein Schwedisch*," said the policeman.

"*Der Volleyball?*" said the man with the accent.

"No. Sorry. Wife sick," said the policeman.

"OK. Sorry. *Gesundheit*," said the eager sports fan.

Then the door closed and the policeman returned inside.

Sara turned toward Breuer.

"I need to ask something. What exactly was Stellan spying on? What information was he able to provide to East Germany? He was just a television presenter."

"The DDR loved cultural personalities," the older woman replied. "They provided an air of credibility and could 'lead the masses' in whichever direction the Stasi told them to. And men like Broman, who socialized with the upper crust of society, were in a position to make those people more positively disposed toward the DDR and to gather information about high-ranking Swedes and their weak points. Politics, sexuality, substance abuse, and so on."

"Let me read a couple of lines to you," said Strauss, pulling out a folder from the filing cabinet. When he'd found the right page, he translated the contents into English. "Assessment of IM Geiger: 'G is completely faithful to our cause, a devoted sympathizer, bordering on fanatical. Does not hesitate to carry out drastic action in the name of peace and socialism.'"

"That wasn't my impression of Stellan. To Swedes, he was a playful uncle and I mostly viewed him as a workaholic."

"When a spy is uncovered, his nearest and dearest are always just as surprised as everyone else," said Strauss.

"The wife is missing." Breuer turned to Anna.

"Yes."

"No trace?"

Anna shook her head.

"And what does your source say about that?" said Breuer to Sara. "The professor?"

"Nothing. She only cares about Stasi spies."

Breuer looked at Sara for a long time.

"What?" said Sara. "Was Agneta a Stasi spy, too?"

"No, we don't think so."

"Well?"

"It's a little unclear."

"Is she dead?"

"Or she's fled the country. When everything began to heat up again."

"There was one thing you didn't answer."

"What?"

"What does them calling Stellan actually mean?"

"That something very dangerous is happening."

24

Sea-green tiling with an air of the Mediterranean, Schlossberg towels, a steam room with plenty of space for four people and an enormous bath from Duravit offering magnificent views of Vasaparken. The whole lawn and sports pitch at your feet. Life on the street unfolding right before the eyes of the landed gentry, as if they were seated in an amphitheater.

And that was just one of the bathrooms—the en suite in the biggest of the bedrooms. The "master bedroom," the Anglicism it had become known by in Swedish of late. Featuring a "walk-in closet," as the new bourgeoisie put it. With an enormous double bed from Dux. Or it might have been Hästens... Shiny silk sheets in pale pastels.

There was a small bathroom off the hall, and probably a separate WC somewhere else. An orangery and a couple of smaller bedrooms for the kids in the rear portions of the apartment.

The walls were adorned with photographic art—as people liked to call it when ordinary photos were signed, framed and cost a bloody fortune. Art for the uncertain, Sara thought to herself. She recognized a few of the pictures, while others she could at least tell had been well composed—or whatever you were supposed to say.

There were guitars on one of the smaller walls. They were no doubt expensive. They were probably a mausoleum for the husband's atrophied dreams of rock stardom. There was no trace of Lotta's old musical ambitions. Sara remembered how she'd always got to play at the end-of-year school assemblies. She'd been so vapidly talented in a way that left all the adults completely blown away, while the kids would sit there bored and jealous of the attention.

The apartment must have been heading for 200 square meters, of which the lion's share comprised a gigantic open-plan kitchen, living room and study all in one. Outside, there was a balcony running the length of the wall that faced the park. Although it was a rather narrow one, Sara thought to herself with a note of malicious delight. It wasn't as deep or secluded as her own terrace, but perhaps that was the point of somewhere like this. To see and be seen. Show your place in the pecking order.

When Sara had called, Lotta had invited her round together with Malin. A lot of people with beautiful homes seemed to be terribly eager to invite people round, or so Sara had noticed. Perhaps because they were so thrilled to show off what they had.

Sara never invited anyone around except Anna, yet she lived a grander existence than any person whom she'd ever visited. She wasn't shy; she simply found people difficult.

Naturally, Lotta had an espresso machine in her home—a proper, professional machine that she used to make a perfect flat white. Like a latte, but with less milk. It tasted amazing. Sara had never managed to make a latte without ending up with a bitter aftertaste. *Fucking Lotta.*

Even if her childhood friend had known that Sara lived even more luxuriously than she did, she probably wouldn't have cared. That was just what the privileged were like. It was impossible to break them. They were never envious—and wasn't that what was worst about them?

Lying on the coffee table were papers from a funeral director— brochures with different types of coffins and flower arrangements. There were also printouts with poems and hymns, photos of Stellan and a pad of paper with a long list of names on it. Probably guests to be invited to the funeral. A reminder of life's finite nature—in the midst of all the material success that surrounded them.

"I've had it confirmed," said Sara. "By German intelligence. Your dad really was a Stasi informant. When you heard the phone ringing, Malin, it was a call from abroad. From people with terrorist connections. A call that triggered all of this."

"Sara," said Lotta. "You came round loads. You practically lived with us for a bunch of summers. Does it sound reasonable to *you*?"

"Don't know. But the BND think it might be connected to this car that was blown up in Germany. Have you read about it? There was a bomb under the road."

Lotta shook her head, and Sara wasn't sure whether it was because she hadn't read about it or because she didn't believe it could be connected with the death of her father.

"They're looking for the person who recruited Stellan," said Sara. "But they only have his code name. They think there's some sort of meeting taking place."

"I have real difficulty believing this. It's possible they got him to work for them somehow. But he won't have seen it as spying—I promise you that. Dad was a bit naive. Always saw the best in people. Perhaps they made him feel important, stroked his ego, made him think he was making the world a better place."

"The important thing right now is for us to find the other members of the spy ring. Above all, its leader. He had the code name 'Ober.' Does that ring any bells for you? Ober?"

"No," said Malin.

Lotta stared straight ahead—seemingly both concentrating and absent at the same time. A couple of seconds passed and then she shook her head.

"Apparently it was someone who visited your dad at home. That was where Stellan was recruited, indoctrinated and then reported back. Can you think of anyone who came round a lot? Someone who must have talked to your father one-to-one. It's quite possible he would have been there in the evening after you'd gone to bed, but this went on for many years. It can hardly be a complete stranger. Are there any recurring faces?"

"There were always loads of people in and out of the house. New faces all the time."

"Of course, some were there more often than others. TV bosses, Dad's colleagues, cultural personalities, the odd government minister, a few CEOs. But that was when he and Mum had guests. Otherwise he mostly kept himself to himself."

"No one you remember talking politics?"

"No. Not that I recollect," said Malin.

"Everyone talked politics back then," said Lotta. "Don't you remember the shows on kids' TV? It was straight-up indoctrination."

"Could you write me a list of names of people who visited the house a lot?"

"Is this your investigation now?" said Lotta, looking at her challengingly.

Sara stumbled slightly. Lotta clearly didn't like being bossed around, but she couldn't very well lie to her.

"No," said Sara. "Not formally. But I'm helping out—since I knew Stellan."

"We've got a lot to deal with around Dad's funeral right now. If the people leading the investigation ask us for help then we'll do it, but we can't spend lots of time on random tasks."

"It'll take no time," said Sara, almost pleading in tone, but Lotta had made up her mind.

Sara didn't know what to say. She had no mandate to demand anything from them in a police capacity, and she'd apparently failed to acquire enough personal authority during her lifetime to assert herself against her childhood friend.

"Have you watched the videos?" said Malin, possibly just to break the silence. "Dad filmed everything."

"He probably didn't film secret meetings with a spy," said Lotta acidly. "If he even had them."

But Sara wasn't as skeptical.

The videos...Malin could sometimes be pretty sharp.

If Ober had been such a frequent visitor to the Bromans' as the Germans thought, it wasn't at all improbable that he'd been caught on film.

He must have had some other reason for being there—he would have needed to display an innocent facade. It would have been strange if Stellan had refrained from filming one single person when he filmed everyone else. Ober had probably done his best to blend in among all the friends, colleagues and partygoers.

Stellan's videos...

25

Sara stepped across the police tape and approached the house. She tried to take in the scene in front of her eyes, but it was still not quite possible to see the Bromans' home as a crime scene.

A glance down toward the water made her stop in her tracks. Once again, her mind was drawn to the memory of the three girls on the jetty, chucking sandwiches in the water and laughing.

Loud, happy laughs.

One reason for Sara's joy was that she hadn't had to swim, she now remembered. As a child, she'd been frightened of the water and what might be below the surface: fish, eels, water snakes, seaweed, junk, sharp sticks and the like.

Sara had felt anxiety at the mere smell of sun cream, and it lingered on in her, even now in adulthood—because she still associated it with swimming, she assumed. Although they never had swum when they were hanging out on the jetty. Not so far as she could remember.

She'd never told the sisters about her fear, because she knew that it would have led to constant encouragement to jump into the water, hold her breath beneath the surface and swim among the reeds.

Now she remembered how hungry she'd been when they'd been lobbing their sandwiches in. But the laughter and the solidarity with the sisters had taken priority over the needs of her body.

It was stupid, but Sara still smiled at the memories.

Then her gaze settled on the fisherman's hut, the small building down by the water's edge that doubled up as a visitor's cottage with its bunks screwed into the walls, its compost toilet and its kitchenette.

The fisherman's hut that Sara and her mother had lived in. As if on the Bromans' charity.

So close to the happy family, while simultaneously so separated from it.

Like staying in the hall throughout the duration of a party.

The cramped little hut that she'd been so upset at being forced to leave.

She went up to it and peeked through the window. The sunlight made it hard to see anything inside, but it was still possible to make out the table in the main room as well as an armchair. Had they even had a TV? Sara wasn't sure.

She left the small building and all its memories of crampedness and rows with her mother, Jane. She went round to the back of the Bromans' house and picked up a lobelia. Lying in the cracked white pot containing the flower was the spare key to the house. Just as usual. Sara went back round to the front and stepped across the threshold.

In the hallway she came to a halt and took in the scents once again—just as she'd done the day before. It really did smell just like it had back in the day. This time she spotted Malin's old pink baseball cap on the hat rack. It was tatty and a little grimy with earth. Perhaps Agneta had taken it over from her daughter, who'd probably owned dozens of hats since then.

The sisters had always got as many clothes as they wanted. Expensive clothes, designer gear. Sara remembered her shame in the presence of the stylish sisters. It had got even worse when she'd started to inherit Malin's and Lotta's discarded garments. The finest clothes from last season—something that others at school had naturally commented on. Beautiful, expensive clothes. But clothes that she'd been given secondhand. Sara had been both ashamed and proud.

It was probably Agneta who'd had the idea, and thought she was doing a good deed. That she was making the three friends more equal.

Autumns had not just been about comments from her classmates about her inherited wardrobe. They had also been about Malin and

Lotta going back to their usual friends—the ones who'd all been in Torekov or Båstad or the French Riviera for the summer.

Was it really just the summers that had been so enchanting? All her positive memories were from that season, at any rate. Bathed in constant sunshine. In pure weather terms, the uninterrupted heat of this year's summer was reminiscent of her childhood—at least the way Sara remembered it. But given the knowledge of climate change at the back of her mind, it was a pretty alarming insight.

Stellan's murder felt like an incomprehensible tragedy in the promised land. It had set the innocence and happiness of childhood against the shitty world in which they now lived. A world where Sweden's playful uncle could be murdered.

It was like someone murdering Santa Claus.

Hasty, unexpected endings had been a common feature of her entire childhood.

Like the day when Jane had suddenly said they were moving, and had shoved Sara and their possessions into a taxi and left. Without any prior warning.

In the morning, Sara had lived in a fisherman's hut in a land of fairy tales, and by evening she'd been resident in a cramped rented flat in a concrete-clad suburb. She'd quickly realized at her new school that her ties to the Broman family were nothing to boast about. On the contrary, each reference she made to her old world had been severely punished.

It had been a new reality that had shaped her into the person she was today, in many more ways than her previous existence had ever done.

The years had gone by and Sara had been invited to Malin's high school graduation party—completely unexpectedly. She assumed that it was Agneta who had added her name to the list, but she'd gladly accepted the invitation. Perhaps everything would be like it had been in the past...

It hadn't been.

Malin hadn't spoken to Sara, and the other guests had smirked at her peaked graduation cap with the name of a school so far out in the suburban wilderness. Eventually, she'd got hammered and faceplanted on the floor.

A total disaster.

But that had been then. She came back to the present.

Or, rather, she didn't. She was there to dig around in the past. Not just her own past, though, even if there was some connection.

So what might be left? Pictures, photos, videos, articles?

A man like Stellan would surely have documented his life in the limelight. Sara remembered how important it had been for him to emphasize how ordinary all the great men and women he spent time with were. How rarely he thought about the fact that the people around him were idols and global stars.

As ever, the vanity became clearer the more one attempted to conceal it.

She'd known since childhood that the walls of Stellan's study were covered in photos of him with various celebrities. She could make a start there.

And back then, almost every family had kept a detailed photo album. The Bromans must have done that too. In fact, *especially* the Bromans.

And as the sisters had told her, Stellan had recorded a lot of film.

Were the films still around?

Where would they be?

Sara quickly rifled through drawers and cabinets in the study, the living room and the kitchen before climbing the stairs to the upper floor.

But then she stopped herself and retraced her steps to the kitchen. Something had caught her attention.

Was it related to the investigation?

She opened the cleaning cupboard again.

Vacuum cleaner, duster, pail, mop. And lying on the bucket were a pair of green washing-up gloves with a name written on them.

"Jane."

Her mother's old washing-up gloves were still there. The Bromans probably used a cleaning company these days.

What had it felt like for Jane to cook and clean in a house where her own daughter was running around and playing with the kids? With the upper classes. Wasn't it rather strange for Jane and Sara to have lived on site?

Having your domestic help living in had a rather nineteenth-century British vibe about it. Like *Downton Abbey*, but without the reassuring drama.

Or was it more honest?

Nowadays, domestic help would vanish when they were done, since the servants worked for their own companies and stayed out of the way. There was no need to hang around, looking the class divide in the whites of its eyes.

But perhaps that was exactly what the Bromans had wanted to do?

Sara felt like the servant girl's daughter—the cleaner's bastard child. And she realized this was a feeling she'd had many times before. She tried to be proud of it.

When she didn't succeed, she focused instead on the upstairs bedrooms.

In Malin's old room, she found the school yearbook from her first year at sixth form. Bromma Sixth Form—the one that Sara had never got the chance to go to.

Unlike Sara, Malin had left her old yearbooks at her parents'. She presumably had no interest in digging through the past. Not yet, anyway. But before long, external influences would take hold and the flight into the memories of her youth would begin.

Yet again, Sara had a guilty conscience at her own malicious joy in all of this. She had nothing against the grown-up Broman sisters. They were strangers, and in that regard completely uninteresting to her. She would dearly have loved to see cracks in the facade of the sisters as children. A glimpse into the teenage soul of Malin might be caught through her reviews of the other pupils in the yearbook.

"Ugly," "bimbo," "loser," or a red or purple heart. A difficult-to-interpret line under a name, or simply a black cross over a face.

There weren't many who got a good write-up from Malin.

There's no harsher judge than a teenager, Sara reflected. And it actually softened her guilty conscience in relation to Ebba just a little when she was reminded of quite how complicated teenagers had always been. It was probably not just Sara's fault that things were the way they were between the two of them.

Toward the back of the yearbook, she found one of the graduating classes and she felt her stomach flip when she was met with a pair of warm brown eyes.

Martin in his late teens, before they got together. When all the girls at school were still competing for him.

Even Malin had been infatuated with Martin. And Lotta had done what she could. But it had been Sara who had got him in the end.

She leafed to the back of the yearbook, where all the associations and clubs were listed. She saw Martin listed against the am-dram group, the student council and the literary society, *Nemo saltat sobrius*. What on earth had he been doing there? He'd surely never been interested in books. He had probably only been in it because "Nemo" had been exclusive and had used selections and secret rituals. An Olympus for the most popular. Books weren't all that important in a literary society. Not in sixth form.

Sara put down the yearbooks and headed down to the rec room in the basement.

This was yet another phenomenon that seemed to have died out with the arrival of the 1980s—the general need for a rec room at home. Down in the basement—without the slightest concern about mold or radon.

That was where she found what she was looking for.

Not only were there about ten photo albums, but she also found several dozen cases of film roll, an old Super 8 cine camera, a projector and a screen.

There was also a rickety old-school TV that had been broken even back when Sara was a child. Had Stellan kept it as a reminder of his forgotten greatness? Peculiar.

The sight of the projector opened the door to a long-forgotten room in Sara's mind.

Now she could picture Stellan with the camera, filming everything that happened in the family, and how Malin and Lotta had looked uncomfortable during the long film screenings in the evenings. Screenings that Sara had loved. She loved getting to participate in the fairytale family's life in detail, to share their journeys, see more of the world through Stellan's camera lens and fantasize about how she would shyly avoid questions from envious friends about why she got to hang out with the famous Uncle Stellan.

Sara didn't imagine that Stellan had got out the cine camera in connection with his secret talks—that he would have documented every single aspect of his life, no matter how private, like a present-day video blogger.

But perhaps it was worth starting by checking out who had been a presence in the Broman residence in the 1970s and 1980s. If Ober had met Geiger that often, then he could definitely be there. But how would she know who he was? Sara had no idea.

She rigged the projector and screen. She'd spent so many hours lying there and listening to the rattle of the faded film as it was fed forward. Sometimes she'd fallen asleep while Stellan was talking. When she woke, she was sometimes alone with him, and he would either have carried on talking without noticing that she'd drifted off, or the film was over and he would be sitting there looking at her with a friendly smile.

She loaded the first roll of film into the forward mount, which was on an arm that had to be angled upward. Then she carefully fed the strip of film through the slots and all the small wheels that ran the film. She inserted it behind the lens and up onto the empty reel that she'd attached to the rear mount.

Then she drew the curtains over the windows of the rec room. They were just below the ceiling. The room was below ground level—something of a symbolic grave, it struck her. Complete with flowers visible in the beds outside. Two meters below—what on earth was she going to encounter?

The first roll began to turn, and on the white canvas she saw a square image in faded colors depicting the Bromans next to the Ölandsbron bridge.

They had clearly rented a cabin from a farmer on Öland, and Stellan had deemed him and his wife sufficiently exotic to merit several minutes of footage—the farmer in the barn, the farmer driving his tractor, his wife milking the cows. The picture shook slightly when Malin reached forward with her hand toward the muzzle of a calf, and cried out with fright as the big pink tongue shot out and drowned her tiny hand in saliva. Sara assumed that Stellan had laughed at the terrified child, hence the slight tremble. Was that what he'd been like? The jovial father of past times, who derived malicious pleasure from his duties? To whom children were more entertainment than responsibility?

Sara realized that farmers on Öland were probably not the prime suspects when it came to espionage on behalf of East Germany, and she switched to a new roll of film.

It was an ordinary summer's day in the Bromans' home. Agneta was in the kitchen; Jane was in the background with the vacuum cleaner. Then Stellan went into the garden. Malin and Lotta were in the hammock. Sara was on the lawn with her arms pointing straight in front of her, walking jerkily.

"Robot."

A popular game when they had been little.

Sara had been tasked with walking like a robot and obeying the sisters, no matter what they said. Fetching toys, stealing sweets from the kitchen or just walking around and sounding mechanical until Lotta came up with another order.

A strange game.

Neither of the sisters had ever been the robot.

Sara put the roll of film back in its case. Was it possible to copy these films? Was that something she wanted to do?

Would her kids want to watch them? No matter how you interpreted the films and what they depicted of children's play, they were an important part of her childhood.

Then there was a roll of film showing Midsummer festivities and a string of faces. Agneta, the daughters, a young Lelle Rydell together with the merry sextet Tage Danielsson, Monica Zetterlund, Lena Nyman, Magnus Härenstam, Brasse Brännström and Eva Remaeus. And three unknown guests. But when Sara took photos of them on her phone and sent them to Lelle Rydell, he was quickly able to identify them.

It turned out the unfamiliar faces belonged to Netan Stenberg, the legendary producer in SVT's entertainment division; Luna de Lyon, the queen of Swedish private theater for decades; and Lasse Warg, the biggest entertainment producer in Sweden in the 1970s and 1980s.

Midsummer with the entertainment elite of Sweden, then.

"Summer party '85" offered a more mixed crowd: Lennart Bodström, the foreign minister fired for refusing to accuse the Russians of operating submarines in Swedish waters, Ebbe Carlsson and Harry Schein. Anders "Lillen" Eklund, the recent European heavyweight boxing champion. He seemed palpably uncomfortable in the assorted company. Then Lill Lindfors made an entrance, and to the delight of the guests she offered up a version of the skirt-removal move that she'd pulled off at the Eurovision Song Contest earlier that spring. Her skirt fell down, and when the penny dropped with the other guests, there was an outburst of vociferous applause. Sara could see the eagerness in the silent clapping, the open mouths as she brought the house down.

So many faces, so many people, so long ago.

Thrilled to be there, to be a part of it all, to belong.

They were all gone now.

Sara looked up 1985 on Wikipedia.

Chernenko had died in the USSR after just fourteen months in post as General Secretary and was succeeded by Gorbachev. It had been the middle of the Treholt espionage trial in Norway. The Bofors scandal was in full swing. A bomb at Frankfurt Airport had killed three and hurt forty-two. Islamic Jihad had taken responsibility. Greenpeace's *Rainbow Warrior* was sunk by the French secret service with one fatality. In December 1985, Palme had announced that he was to undertake an official visit to the Soviet Union in the spring of 1986. There was outcry among the country's military officers. Palestinian terrorist attacks at airports in Rome and Vienna.

What had Sara been doing then?

She had been alive, but in another world. In 1985, Sara and Malin had been ten years old, Lotta had been twelve.

In the films, the fashion of the era was reflected clearly in the sisters' hairdos and clothing. Backcombed hair, pastel colors, loads of bracelets.

Then parades in East Berlin. Street scenes. Sights.

The old films lacked sound, and it occurred to Sara that it had been at the Bromans' that she'd first become interested in silent films. She still loved the dramatic expressions in old silent movies. Faded tints, jerky movements and the odd feeling of seeing people talking without there being any sound.

A big park, a TV broadcast tower, a large monument. It seemed to be Berlin, just like it said on the case. Then a reception. A large children's choir, the audience with Swedish and East German pennants. Stellan receiving some prize. Agneta beside him, but two steps back, as ever. Malin, however, was at her father's side. So it was presumably Lotta filming.

A dinner in a large room with a giant painting depicting the heroes of the revolutions and huge East German flags. Once again, Lotta seemed to be filming. The division of labor seemed to be this—when it was important for Stellan himself to be on film, his daughter was handed the camera.

Who were the other guests? Some form of East German potentates, yes, but were they just cultural figures or were there secret service people there too? In the DDR, they often seemed to have been one and the same thing.

Perhaps Hedin would be able to identify some of them?

The hours passed and Sara was lost in a past that felt increasingly mysterious, despite the fact that she herself had been there.

Clothes, glasses and haircuts from another era. It wasn't that cult nostalgia that hit home whenever you watched films from the 1970s and 1980s. It was more frightening—with an ominous undertone.

Even the patterns of movement and postures were different, and Sara found herself thinking of Swedish cinema from this period, in which the way the characters spoke had more in common with movie actors of the 1940s than people in 2020s Stockholm.

How odd to go back to that time with all the answers in hand—to know how different everything would become. That the Cold War would end. The internet. September 11, 2001.

Had something that had taken place then changed the course of history?

Stellan and his friends had obviously wanted to prevent the collapse of East Germany. If the authorities in the DDR had known what was going to happen, would they have taken a tougher line?

The next film transported Sara to a big party at the Bromans' home. There was some sort of *Great Gatsby* theme. White tie, big band, cocktails. The film cases contained handwritten lists of names that Sara assumed were the invited guests, line upon line of names and places of work: Ministry of Defence, Ministry of Foreign Affairs, Ministry of Finance, Bofors, Ericsson, ASEA, Stockholm University, Uppsala University, SVT, Swedish Radio, SAS, army, F 13 and F 16 Air Force stations. Not just celebrities, then. Sara assumed that it was Agneta who'd been assigned to preparing the lists, since they were written in a woman's handwriting. Perhaps she'd had no idea of their double purpose.

Sara spotted Martin's father Eric among the listed guests. Of course. A successful CEO who lived in the same neighborhood. She wondered what Eric Titus would say if he found out he'd been tricked by a Stasi collaborator...

Then she watched a film from New Year's Eve, in which all the rooms in the house were filled with fake snow and everyone was dressed in winter sports gear. Parties that lived long in the popular memory.

And then other films with less striking events.

There were games of cards, dinners, events with fewer entertainment personalities and men with more businesslike appearances—pipe smoking, discussions, sweaty atmospheres—some of them firmly gripping their drinks. People passing by in the background or parked with young blonde women in various corners. Middle-aged men in ill-fitting suits with unfiltered cigarettes and weird haircuts. Eastern European in appearance, was Sara's prejudiced evaluation. And she trusted her prejudices.

She stared at the men and realized that she needed help.

There was really only one person she could call: Eva Hedin.

The retired professor was helpful—she was clearly finished with her work for the day. She said she couldn't receive picture messages, but emails were fine. So Sara took photos of the projector screen and sent the images to Hedin. Maybe it wasn't so secure sending them online, but it was a quick way to get help.

Three faces were given names: Alexei Grigorin, Yuri Dmitri and Jerzy Dudek. All had later been deported and declared persona non grata, and prior to that they'd all worked for Eastern state embassies with various cover stories. Grigorin had been first secretary to the legation, but had in fact been the KGB number two. Dmitri had been a naval attaché, but had actually served as the GRU military intelligence chief in their Stockholm bureau. Dudek had been secretary to the ambassador at the Czechoslovak embassy.

Contacts with diplomats from the East were nothing out of the ordinary at the time, Hedin explained. Firstly, Sweden's official stance was one of neutrality—freedom of alliance in peace times, with the aim of maintaining neutrality in times of war. The plan was to avoid taking a position in the ideological struggle between communism and capitalism, which meant it was no stranger to socialize with Russians, Czechs and East Germans than it was to socialize with Americans and British people.

Naturally, it also helped that the Russians and Poles were good drinking buddies. They were generous with the vodka, entertaining when they sang their melancholy songs and impressive in terms of their tolerance for alcohol. Merely seeing a second secretary from an embassy drain two whole bottles of booze by himself was reason enough to invite him.

Sara sent photos of all the participants to Hedin, and received a string of names and positions in reply. Undersecretaries of state, director generals, cabinet ministers, officers, desk officers, pundits, editors, authors, publishers, artists. Anyone who could be involved in helping to shape perceptions of the East, according to the professor.

A more crass description was that at Uncle Stellan's, the Stasi, KGB and GRU could let their hair down and party while getting on good terms with Social Democratic Party bigwigs.

Before Hedin could carry on, Sara's mobile beeped to mark the arrival of a text message. After apologizing, she took the phone from her ear and read it.

It was from Anna.

We're going to announce that Agneta Broman's missing.

OK.

Perhaps it would help. If Agneta had been kidnapped, then the kidnappers really ought to have been in touch by now. It was probably just as well the story went to the media.

Sara remembered that Hedin was waiting for her and put the phone back to her ear.

"Sorry, I received a text message…Hello?"

Hedin seemed to have hung up.

Understandable.

At any rate, Sara had found out much more about the guests at Stellan's parties, and the thinking behind who was invited. It wasn't as straightforward as anyone who was successful being allowed in. There had been a clear agenda.

Sara put away her mobile and pulled the stack of photo albums toward her. These contained the same mixture of politicians, celebrities and family holidays. Paris, London, Berlin.

In addition to the very biggest artists and quite a few foreign celebrities, all of Sweden's prime ministers appeared to have visited the Bromans' home—for parties, dinners, lunch or coffee. The visits had been carefully documented: Erlander, Palme, Fälldin, Ullsten, Carlsson and Bildt. Only Göran Persson was missing. And after his stint, there didn't seem to have been any social gatherings of that kind at Uncle Stellan's.

And there was a real showstopper: Mikhail Gorbachev. Accompanied by Ingvar Carlsson.

In an album from 1991 there were a dozen photos depicting the meeting. First, Mr. and Mrs. Broman met the Swedish prime minister and the Soviet president in front of the house. Then there were photos of Stellan showing them around the garden, and after that dinner, which seemed to have carried on fairly late into the evening. The table was decorated with Swedish and Soviet flags, as well as blue and yellow garlands. There was plenty of schnapps. But following the main course, there was nothing further documented.

Well, even the world's leaders needed to unwind on occasion...

Sara remembered Gorbachev's visit to Stockholm. It had been the National Day, and she'd gone into the city, just like thousands of others, to catch a glimpse of the president and Nobel Peace Prize laureate. At the time, she'd had no idea that the legendary leader was going to the Bromans' that evening. The house where Sara had played so many times. It was strange that he didn't dine with the king. But Sara googled it and found out that it hadn't been a formal state visit, so perhaps that explained it.

Just a few months after the visit to the Bromans', both Gorbachev and Ingvar Carlsson had fallen out of power.

The next album that Sara opened was labeled "Bromma 1982."

A young Agneta Broman in a summer dress was serving food in the garden, her face almost completely hidden by her huge glasses—1970s spectacles. The 1980s hadn't yet arrived on her face.

Did she know what Stellan was up to?

Did she care?

Where was she now?

Would the public appeal turn anything up?

Agneta was the piece of the jigsaw that Sara couldn't find a space for. If she'd been shot, too, then where was her body? If she'd fled from the murderer, why hadn't she made contact? If the murderer had kidnapped her, then why?

What was she doing right now?

26

STELLAN'S WIFE MISSING.

"Where is Aunt Agneta?"

"Murdered?"

The final headline had her old driving license photo underneath it. The evening news placards outside the 7-Eleven on Hornsgatan were all about her, just like the front pages of the morning papers that people were reading in the sunshine.

Agneta felt the contours of the pistol against her thigh. It might be necessary in the unlikely event that anyone recognized her, and it was close to hand in her coat pocket.

An old woman wearing a coat in the heat of summer was hardly worthy of notice by anyone else. The surrounding world's lack of interest was to her advantage, Agneta had come to realize. Without doubt, she preferred anonymity—and not just for the sake of her mission.

"Aunt Agneta" was all over the place.

She'd suddenly found herself at the center of the news cycle. For the first time in her life.

And it was, unfortunately, extremely poor timing.

Right when she needed her invisibility most of all, the country was wallpapered with striking yellow placards bellowing at the public to keep their eye out for her.

It was all meant with the best of intentions, of course. Let's all pitch in to find the father of the nation's wife. The entire country's second mother.

She'd never been that, throughout all those years when her husband had dominated the media scene. Instead, she'd blended into the background—it had all been about him. And all the reports that had been done on the family had focused on their daughters and shown them together with their father.

But now the sensation-hungry hacks were taking the opportunity to depict Agneta as a mother figure to anyone who'd grown up between the years 1965 and 1990.

She didn't dare buy any copies of the papers, even if it would be good to know which other photos of her they had. She hoped that her new appearance was sufficient disguise.

Hoped, but she needed to be certain.

A gray crew cut, no makeup and a pair of thick-rimmed reading glasses. A new coat—a cheap one from H&M, so that she used as little of her war kitty as possible.

The haircut felt good. It was a bit like being young again. Her schooling, the training camp, the constant state of readiness. The restlessness and the commitment. The same haircut that she'd had back then, when she'd been passionate about something. When she'd made the choices that were governing her actions today.

She wondered what her daughters would say if they could see her now. Now that the groundskeeper and housewife had been peeled away. Would they be able to understand who she was? What she was?

What would her daughters think? What would they make of their own childhood when the truth about their parents eventually emerged? That the girls had simply been—in one way—part of a facade? Pawns in Agneta's game. Did that change anything? Would they view their childhoods differently? She supposed they would, but how?

She knew that when that big Russian spy ring in the USA had been uncovered in 2010, and the spies had been deported after spending almost twenty years living under false identities, at least one child of the various couples had remained in the USA and continued his career as a pianist. He'd opted to transform his fictitious life into his real one, because that was what he had believed in.

But which parts of Agneta's life were real?

Well, that was surely what all this was about. All the secret loyalties and hidden agendas meant that it wasn't easy to know what was true.

If anything was.

She could only hope that her children would continue to live their lives on their own terms—that they wouldn't assume and perpetuate their parents' poor choices. Agneta was ready to do everything she could to protect her grandchildren. To bring an end to the damnation. The traitor's original sin.

She'd had her daughters when she was still absorbed by the mission—the struggle for peace. She'd had them as part of her cover; she was aware of that.

It was unfair on them. She was also aware of that. But the grandchildren had come into the world when it had all been over. Or when she'd *believed* it was all over. When she'd dared to become Agneta Broman for real.

She didn't want to lose them in the way she felt she'd lost her daughters—or, at least, lost the right to call herself their mother. Since she'd had them for a purpose, rather than for their own sake. Not even for her own sake.

The grandchildren were the proof that normal life was the victor over ideology in the long run. They had grown up completely ignorant of the threats and dark alliances that had marked Agneta's own life. The Cold War and all the old enemies were completely alien to them. They were a symbol of real life. The life that even she had begun to believe in after all those years.

The square at Mariatorget was full of people. Tourists from Asia, young girls with dyed hair and nose rings, fifty-year-old beardy guys you only found in the Söder neighborhood, with flat backsides and T-shirts emblazoned with the names of guitar manufacturers. She'd been lucky to find a spare seat on one of the park benches, and had taken the chance to enjoy the sun and rest for a while. But now it was time.

A ball came rolling toward her. She stood and picked it up before walking over to Hugo.

"Does this belong to you?"

"Thank you."

There was no credit due to Malin that Hugo had said "thank you." Her daughter hadn't much cared about the raising of her children. It had been Agneta who'd taken care to ensure they said "please" and "thank you." And asked whether they could leave the table.

However, the important thing was that Hugo hadn't recognized her. Despite the fact that he'd just spent an entire week in her company.

Agneta remained where she was until her grandson had gone back to Malin. She put her hand in her coat pocket and ran her fingers over the object she'd taken with her from home—the secret weapon that was going to help her if she encountered any obstacles. She felt immediately reinforced by the power of it. Then she pushed the object to one side and caressed the barrel of the Makarov in her pocket. In her other pocket she had Kellner's Smith & Wesson. If the test didn't go according to plan, then she would need to make her getaway—and fast. A shot in the air ought to be enough. Or into someone's leg, so that there was also a real shriek of fear.

Predictably enough, her daughter was holding a latte in her well-manicured hand and chatting to a friend. Next to her was a handbag that had cost the same as two washing machines.

Hugo pointed at Agneta, and her daughter looked at her distractedly but didn't respond. Perfect.

She went over the checklist:

Meet her grandchildren and remind herself why she was doing this—check.

Test her new appearance in a tight spot—check. Her nearest and dearest hadn't recognized her.

She was no one now. She was invisible.

For safety's sake, she strolled past Malin and the friend as she left. From the corner of her eye, she saw her daughter looking straight at her without recognizing her. Agneta let go of the pistol, removed her hand from her pocket and closed the zip.

Now she didn't have to be so worried that someone might recognize her. She was free to act.

Now she could concentrate on the meeting that was to come.

27

The entire apartment was dark when Sara got home. There was light visible in the crack at the bottom of Olle's door, but otherwise everywhere was dark. He was often up late playing computer games unless someone told him to stop. Sara hadn't been able to make up her mind what she thought about his gaming. She'd forbidden him from playing the most violent releases, and had had to be clear with Martin that he was not to buy those games for himself either. They had to set a good example. But what was she supposed to make of all the hours spent gaming, if the games themselves were harmless? Wasn't it just a hobby like any other? Would they have imposed any equivalent of their screen time limits on Olle if he'd been interested in stamp collecting as an alternative? Or football? Wasn't it the countless hours of training that had turned Zlatan Ibrahimovic into the player he was? Or Björn Borg, back in the day—he'd hit tennis balls against a garage door in Södertälje hour after hour, day after day. How exactly did computer gaming differ from other interests? Sara carried on through the apartment while she turned this over in her head. Even though the evenings were light, the apartment was so big that it was still necessary to turn on the odd light here and there.

Sara remembered that Ebba was at another party. There really were parties every single evening at the moment. And it felt as if they were much wilder than they'd been back in Sara's day. More alcohol, more sex—maybe there were drugs, too.

Sara found her husband asleep on the living-room sofa, his beloved Martin guitar in his arms. The same name as its owner—that had to mean something, surely, Martin used to say.

Was this how he spent his evenings when she was gone?

Striking chords? Keeping his dreams of rock stardom alive? The guitar had cost over 40,000 kronor, so Sara was careful as she pried it free from his grasp so that he wouldn't drop it on the floor or roll over onto it.

Paying 43,000 kronor for a guitar that he was almost incapable of playing, she thought to herself. Like hiring the biggest stage at the national theater to tell a joke.

Martin let out a snore, and Sara looked at him. There was drool all over his chin. It wasn't a pretty sight.

Her catch.

Would she have gone to the lengths she had to get him, if Lotta hadn't tried to take him from her?

If she was being honest, she wasn't sure. The decision to win him over had undeniably had an impact on Sara's whole life.

Ebba and Olle.

The years when Martin had been trying to break through as an artist, and they'd lived on her salary.

When he'd sold his company and they'd been able to move into this gigantic apartment.

Spending time with his parents.

Without Martin, none of that would have been a part of Sara's life.

Suddenly she felt ashamed. She tried to shake off the feeling that Martin was, more than anything, proof that she'd won against the sisters. Revenge for a childhood spent under their heel. She'd got the guy that Malin had been infatuated with, and Lotta had tried to snare.

Was Martin just a symbol for the fact that Sara always had to win?

And if that was true, once she'd won, what was she supposed to hang around for?

Martin had been part of the idyll in Bromma. He'd lived just a couple of blocks away and had often passed by with his mates on a bicycle, later to be replaced by a moped and then a motorbike, before eventually ending up with a car. They'd been checking out Lotta while Malin and Sara had been checking them out. Older boys. Martin had been in eighth grade and Malin and Sara had been in sixth grade when Jane had suddenly quit at the Bromans and taken her daughter to Vällingby, just a week before the schools broke up for the summer holidays. When her classmates had sung "Now Comes the Time for Flowers," Sara had been alone in an echoey, empty flat with a bowl of Sugar Puffs. Back then, she'd thought she would never see her idol again—but the move had merely delayed her plans for love a few years, rather than crushing them entirely.

Sara remembered how jealous she'd been when she'd heard the rumor that Martin had slept with Lotta. It had been at Malin's graduation party—the same party at which she'd hit rock bottom. There had been something going on with Martin, but if it had ended up with them being together that night, then it might just have been a passing teenage infatuation that lasted a year or so before they went their separate ways. When Lotta had got involved, things had turned serious in a completely different way.

Now that she'd been allowed back into the sisters' lives, she didn't intend to give him up. Martin was hers.

Sara had spent the whole summer feeling sorry for herself because she'd been cut out by Lotta, until one day she'd been taking off her makeup after attending a fashion show at the NK department store. She'd looked in the mirror and thought to herself that if she was good enough to be a model at Stockholm's hottest agency, then perhaps she didn't have to be so underconfident.

She'd simply called Martin and asked him whether he wanted a coffee. And he did. To begin with, there had been a slightly weird, hesitant atmosphere—probably as a result of what had happened at Malin's party. But it seemed as if neither of them wanted to leave the other—that they were both hoping for something.

And after an hour or so, they'd both loosened up and they'd carried on seeing each other.

The realization that she had the power to control her own life had been decisive for Sara. It had induced her to quit modeling after a couple of years. She'd started martial arts training, and read lots of rambling self-help books about taking command of your own existence. She'd jumped between different jobs in cafes, domestic care, working as a courier and as a caretaker—until she'd finally settled on the idea of being a police officer. By then, she and Martin had moved in together and he was getting by in the entertainment industry. The most common fee he received was free beer, so their rent had been paid with Sara's salary.

Over those years, Sara had had almost no contact with her mother. It was only really after the kids had been born that she rekindled the relationship—with decided reluctance. She realized now that the reason she'd broken away from her mother was to do with her own personality, and how ashamed she'd been at the anger she felt toward Jane.

But she'd never understood the point of the move away from Bromma. Instead of cooking and cleaning in Stellan and Agneta's home, Jane had cleaned schools for the rest of Sara's childhood. Was that better? Had she felt inferior to the Bromans because she dealt with their dirty laundry—because she was dependent on them? It was thanks to them she'd found a job as a young, pregnant, recently arrived woman escaping the Polish dictatorship.

Sara picked up her laptop and went online to search for the sisters' names. She convinced herself that it was connected to the investigation, but she knew in her heart of hearts that wasn't true. Lotta and Malin had begun to eat away at her brain again, and she wanted to find a way to put some distance between them. She wanted to free herself from their influence.

By the time she'd reached the second page of links about Malin, she'd found articles, blogs and forum posts about her stint presenting

Sommarbubbel. Sara read everything carefully. Malin had been a disaster—she'd turned to the wrong camera, asked the guests daft questions and not understood their answers. Most of the other links were about shows where she'd worked behind the camera, and the reviews in that regard were much more mixed. And there were lots of crowd photos from celebrity and TV parties. Plus the mandatory thread on a major online forum where lonely men shared their gossip and fantasies about famous women who were out of reach, in terms that were awful. In this case, Malin Broman was listed under the heading "Where are they now?"

Lotta's appearances in crowds were only at serious events—if a party could be described as serious. Parties at the development agency, those thrown by other aid organizations, Almedalen Week, some TV gala with a touching purpose. The Guldbagge film awards gala. Otherwise, there were lots of links to the Swedish International Development Cooperation Agency's work, to committees she'd been on, her career in the athletics movement and much more. The only actually negative things Sara could find were a few articles about aid to organizations that the writers argued were supporting terrorism, where Lotta was made the scapegoat, given that she was the boss.

Her browsing was interrupted by a strange hissing. Sara left the computer and headed toward the sound. In the kitchen, their cat Walter was skittering about. He was scratching his claws along the floor, jumping up, wandering around and then returning to the same spot. He would lie there, still and waiting, then shoot out a paw and strike again before resuming his dance. Then Sara saw that he'd caught a mouse. That was how it was in Stockholm's old town—there were rodents all over the place, in the pipes and walls. It was a relief that it wasn't one of the big sewer rats, but if it had been one of those, it would probably have got the better of Walter.

Then the game stopped. The cat abandoned the mouse, went over to his food bowl and ate hungrily after the physical exertion.

Sara went over to look. The mouse had been bitten on the body several times and it was now in pain. Dying and suffering. It might be drawn-out. Walter no longer cared. She sighed. She really didn't want to do it, but she fetched a small plastic bag and a hammer. She wrapped the bag around her hand, picked up the mouse and turned the bag inside out. Then she put it on the floor and crushed the mouse with a hammer blow. She hated doing it, but she didn't want it to die slowly and painfully, and she didn't want to ask her husband to do it either—it seemed too nineteenth-century.

Walter didn't react to the blow. He merely wandered out of the kitchen without looking back.

Sara found it hard to make head or tail of his various character traits. On the one hand, he was a cuddly cat—the world's friendliest; he loved being stroked and never bit anyone. He didn't jump down to the floor if you put him on your lap. On the other hand, he was a sadistic murderer and mouse torturer.

She flushed the mouse corpse down the toilet and threw the bloody bag in the bin. On the way down the hall, she saw that the light was still on in Olle's room. Had he fallen asleep and forgotten to turn off the light?

Sara opened the door and saw Olle at his computer. Over his shoulder, the screen was showing two busty naked girls taking turns to suck a huge black penis. Olle slammed the laptop shut as soon as he heard the door open.

"What is it?" he said in a stressed tone of voice.

"I was just coming to turn off the light." Sara was shaken. "Were you watching porn?"

"No."

"But don't you know that they exploit people?"

"Go away!"

"There are better depictions of sex, if you want to watch that kind of thing. But that's just downright degradation of women."

"Out!"

Her son leaped up from his chair and shoved Sara out of the room. She shouted through the closed door.

"I'm not angry," she attempted to say.

There was no answer. It was as if there were an invisible wall between them. If they didn't discuss this now, the wall might always be there.

"Olle, we really could do with talking about this." She paused briefly to wait for a reply. It didn't come. "It's nothing to be ashamed of. But it's really a dreadful industry."

Still no reply.

Jesus.

Perhaps she was just making the wall even higher now.

Of course he was ashamed. And angry. Your own mother discovering you doing something sexual—it didn't get worse than that. Plus the fact that you know what you're doing is wrong. Olle was fully aware of Sara's views on the porn industry. But it was so easily accessible—so easy to find. And those interests in the younger teenage years could be extensive. Guiding her son to "good" porn felt weird—a mother shouldn't get involved in her children's sex lives. Unless they had questions, of course. Normal questions. Not questions about where to find good porn films.

Sara was convinced that it was all connected—porn and prostitution. It was as if Olle was nudging open the door to a world that she knew was incredibly dirty and depressing. A world she really wished didn't exist.

She ought to speak to Martin about this, she realized. So that he could have a chat with their son about it—right away, while it was still a hot topic. Martin was a guy, too, and probably knew more about how boys of that age worked. If they threatened a total ban, then it would probably just make it more appealing.

When Sara went toward the sofa to wake her husband, his mobile was flashing on the coffee table. Sara thought it might be Ebba looking for a lift—she usually contacted Martin when that was the case. Partly because Sara usually worked late, partly because it was much easier to persuade her dad to chauffeur her around.

She picked up Martin's mobile and pressed on the screen. There was a new message. She entered his PIN and opened the messaging app to select the most recent one. It was from an unregistered number.

It was a picture message.

A close-up of a female sexual organ with a piercing. And a hand with some long nails covered in turquoise nail polish holding open the labia to give a full view.

Sara didn't know what to think.

She scrolled up. It wasn't the first picture of a pussy Martin had received. There were five from the same number over the last few weeks.

Sara googled the mobile number. It wasn't in the phone book, but it turned up on a website for "Nikki X—Luxury Escort."

Sara looked at her husband and then back at the pictures of the pussy again. And then back to Martin.

An escort.

Her head felt entirely empty. She tried to think, but she got completely stuck.

She carefully put down the mobile on the coffee table. Then she picked up Martin's beloved guitar and struck it against the table so that it smashed.

Her husband leaped up, but Sara was already in the hallway, keys in hand.

Martin.

With a prostitute.

With a whore.

Sara never used that word about the girls she met while working.

But Nikki X was a whore.

A real fucking whore.

This was all Martin's fault. He was the one who was married with kids. He was the one paying a girl for sexual services.

But Nikki X was still a whore.

Sara felt stupid. So horribly stupid.

Easily deceived, dumb, stupid.

Conceited, righteous Sara Nowak, who condemned all the men who paid for sex, and pitied their wives and families, but who deep down felt that it was their own fault. The wives had picked the wrong men to share their lives with. Sara had always known that she would prefer to live alone than to be married to a man who would even contemplate paying for sex.

Now she realized it wasn't about morals—it was about self-delusion.

Sara ran outside into Kornhamnstorg.

She had no idea where she was going.

To work?

Should she call David? Was he willing to listen to her without judging her? Without making Sara feel like she'd lost? Jane was out of the question.

Where should she go? She didn't want to wander around amid strangers—whether they were pissed or happily in love.

She wanted to be left in peace. There was a hotel on Lilla Nygatan. *Good.* She needed to go somewhere.

Sara turned the corner into Lilla Nygatan. She checked in her pocket to make sure she'd brought her wallet with her, so that she could pay for a room. She was also afraid she would smash it to pieces.

"Get lost!"

Sara recognized Ebba's voice right away. It was coming from the square behind her, and she turned around and hurried back. When she emerged back into Kornhamnstorg again, she caught sight of her daughter. She'd just come out of the underground station and had two burly lads following her.

"Whore, whore, whore!" one of them taunted her, clapping his hands like a grotesque, solitary cheerleader.

"Hold up, stop!" the other one shouted.

"Get lost!" Ebba shouted again.

Then the cheerleader guy caught up with her and grabbed her hair. "Fucking cocktease! Come here!"

A second later, he landed on his back, screaming with pain. Sara had flown at him with her arm bent, crouched and inserted it between his legs before standing up. She'd lifted him up at the same time as she tipped him forward. It was a krav maga move she'd never tested outside the practice room before, but it seemed to work well. The man cried out as he lost control of his body, flying through the air and hitting the ground hard.

She couldn't resist kicking him in the stomach while he was lying there, so that he wouldn't be tempted to fight back. Before the other lad had time to realize what was happening, Sara grabbed him by the collar and shoved a knee into his solar plexus. She pushed her hip forward as much as she could to give it extra force, and he crumpled at her feet.

"Don't you fucking dare harass girls like that!" Sara shouted, her face just millimeters from the closest of the two lads.

"Mum!" said Ebba. "What are you doing? Why are you here? Are you following me?"

"No, I came from over there," said Sara, waving toward Lilla Nygatan. "I heard you cry out."

"But you can't knock people to the ground!"

"Would you have preferred it if they'd attacked you? You've no idea what scum like this are capable of—how much shit I've seen."

"Well, why don't you change jobs if it's so awful? That way you won't have to assault people! You clearly can't handle it!"

Ebba stormed off. Homeward, Sara noted with relief. And this time she was pretty certain that her daughter's anger toward her had been exacerbated by the shock of being ambushed. It was just as Sara had suspected—Ebba hadn't fully realized how vulnerable she was as a young girl.

She turned back to the two guys on the ground. The one she'd thrown to the floor was at least sitting up, and the other one had

GUSTAF SKÖRDEMAN

got to his feet, although he was still clutching his stomach. The one on the ground was bleeding from his forehead and nose.

"I was protecting my child," said Sara. "You were behaving like bastards. But if you want to report it, then I'll help you."

"No, it's fine."

"I'm bleeding."

"Let's sort that out," said his friend. "They have plasters at 7-Eleven."

"OK," said Sara, making her way back home. She had to go back. It felt like the whole world was caving in and that it was up to her to try and stop it.

First there had been Stellan's murder, and now Olle was watching porn, Martin was cheating on her and two young guys had harassed her daughter.

What the hell was going on?

The moment she opened the door to the apartment, Ebba came out of the bathroom and went into her bedroom, slamming the door behind her.

"What on earth are you doing?"

Martin came out of the living room with what remained of the guitar in his hand. He looked completely devastated, but Sara found it difficult to feel any sympathy toward him.

"Ask Nikki X."

"Who?"

"The one sending you photos of her pussy."

He reacted to those words.

"What do you mean?"

"I thought it was Ebba messaging, so I checked your phone and instead I got a close-up gynecological exam. And it wasn't the first, either."

No reply from Martin.

"How long has this been going on? Where did you meet her? And how the hell can you pay for sex when you know what I see day in, day out?"

218

"Stop it! I haven't paid for sex. I haven't had sex with anyone else since we got together."

"That's not what the pictures say. Even if you haven't put it in there, you've clearly had phone sex."

"No, we haven't. It's a girl who's trying to get a contract with Go Live and thinks that's what she should be doing."

"Contract? She's an escort!"

"That's entirely possible. But she's also a singer and records her own tracks."

"And she sends photos of her genitals to secure a contract with your company?"

"Yes—I suppose she thinks that how it's done."

"And where did she get that idea?"

"From her experiences of men, I don't suppose it's surprising if she's got the impression that all men think with their dicks."

"You do."

"I've never encouraged her. You can see for yourself. I've never answered."

Martin held the mobile up facing Sara and scrolled upward. There were only incoming messages from Nikki X—none to her.

"So you're just an innocent victim receiving photos against your will?"

"Yes."

"Why the hell are you saving them, then? No, there's no need to say anything—I understand."

"No, I'll say something, because you're fabricating your own reality. I've saved the photos in case she goes off the rails and ends up being dangerous and I have to report her to the police. If that happens, I want evidence of the stalking."

"And why haven't you discussed this with your wife? Your wife who is a police officer."

"Because you would react just like this and think that I liked it."

"But then I would listen to you, just like I'm doing now."

"Show that you're listening and you believe me."

"Show me your phone."

Martin handed over his mobile. There were no calls to or from the number anywhere in the call history. And the messages had only come from her.

Sara chose to believe him, but remained skeptical about the decision to keep the photos. Martin was acquitted—at least for the moment.

"I loved this," said her husband, holding up the remains of his guitar.

A crushed Martin and a crushed Martin.

28

It was really the middle of the night, but dawn had already begun to illuminate the flat. Agneta had hoped to surprise him, and had been prepared for strong resistance.

But all she had encountered was an abandoned home.

He had lived here.

Ober.

Above a branch of the state-owned off-license sandwiched between a petrol station and a Thai restaurant, in an unassuming one-bed flat. With fine views toward the water.

Out there on the water was where the small yellow car ferries ran their constant shuttle between Vaxholm and the surrounding islands. Right now all was calm. The sea was tranquil, but Agneta assumed that the waves rolled forcefully into the harbor during autumn storms.

This place was in the archipelago, even though it was on the mainland. She could really see why people wanted to live here. In the past, she'd merely considered Vaxholm to be a long way out of town. They had views of the water back home in Bromma, too. But this place had a different feeling to it—a different sense of calm.

Agneta had been prepared to climb up onto the balcony and get in that way, but the lock on the door had turned out to be easy to pry open. Holding the pistol in one hand, she'd slowly opened the door. Ready for an attack.

But nothing had happened.

And when she went inside, she encountered echoing silence. Given the unfortunate spread of news about Stellan's death, Ober had probably fled and hidden at a secure address. The alternative was that he had gone to meet Abu Rasil, and that everything was already underway.

Agneta hoped that wasn't the case.

Now she was standing here, feeling astonished by how commonplace daily life as a spy could be. She went through the fridge and larder. Yogurt and coffee cream. Goat's cheese. Lots of cereal and muesli.

Then the bathroom. Medication for stomach ulcers and denture cleaning fluid in the bathroom cabinet. A bath towel with Sunwing package holiday branding and the date 1991, and a small red towel hanging on a hook beneath a sticker with the word "bottom" written on it. In the bedroom there was a neatly made bed with a burgundy throw spread across it. Being a single bed, it indicated that all hope of one day sharing his existence with someone had evaporated.

In the living room she found the remote controls for the TV and VCR lying on a crocheted white cloth spread across the coffee table. There was a two-seater sofa and an armchair in matching drab brown upholstery. He had allowed for guests in his plans, at least. There was a bookcase filled with crime fiction, biographies and books about animals and nature.

Agneta searched the flat yet again for anything that might be linked to Geiger and the spy ring. There were no hidden compartments or hollows behind the tiling—or so it seemed. But Ober had left a box wrapped in a black bin liner beneath the floor of the cupboard under the kitchen sink, and inside that she found an aged radio transmitter. It was made of green metal and had knobs and dials on it.

How long had he used this for?

And why had he kept it?

Was he still active after all these years, or had he just been hoping? Whatever the case, the transmitter was compromising evidence, so Agneta took it with her. Others might follow his trail.

She had to find Ober before anyone else did.

What exactly did Stellan's death being public knowledge mean?

What did they make of her own disappearance?

And if they connected the murder with the spy ring, would they manage to find Ober—and would Ober talk?

Or was Ober keeping out of the way because he was determined at all costs to complete the mission he'd once sworn he would—the devastation of the decadent West?

29

Sara woke up early, restless. The events of the day before had shaken her. In practice, everything had ended well, if she was to believe Martin. Ebba was home safe and sound, saved from potential assault. And new guitars could be bought.

It wasn't even six o'clock, but she couldn't sleep, so she pulled on her workout clothes and headed out for a run. She was wearing Ebba's old, abandoned three-quarter length trousers with Elsa from *Frozen* on them, and a T-shirt with a "CEO Speedwagon" print on it. Even a hobby band needed merchandise. At this early hour, the only people up were other joggers, so Sara didn't care what she was wearing.

She ran a lap of the island of Kungsholmen, choosing to go anticlockwise for a change. Around an hour later, she stopped to sit down by the pier next to City Hall and stared out across the glittering water at the white boats that had their sights set on the islands of Mälaren, Mariefred and Strängnäs. She thought about Breuer and Strauss. And the blown-up road in Germany that they were so interested in.

Was it connected to the murder of Stellan? If so, how?

Who could know that? Was she in possession of information that someone could help her interpret? Stellan's death was plausibly linked to his past.

Who could help her when Brundin from the Security Service refused?

There was only one person she could think of.

Since she was wearing her running gear and was by City Hall, she simply jogged through the old town and past Slussen onto Södermalm. She felt her top getting soaked through with sweat again. When she spotted Hedin's door, it occurred to her that the researcher might not be awake at this hour. When the time came for her to retire, Sara had no intention of ever getting up before eleven. The street was deserted, so no one reacted when she leaned her forehead against the window and stared through the pane of glass into Hedin's flat.

She was most certainly awake.

Through the window of that room, Sarah could see her sitting in the kitchen and writing. The retired professor didn't react when Sara tapped on the window, but she didn't give up. She began knocking instead. Harder and harder until Hedin came over and opened it from inside.

"I'm working," said Hedin, making a motion to close the window again, but Sara stopped her.

"This is more important," she said.

She grabbed hold of the window frame, jumped up and heaved herself in. She ended up on her belly on top of the windowsill before slithering down onto the floor. It wasn't the most dignified of entrances. Then she got up and looked at Hedin.

"The explosion in Germany—"

"Yes?"

"What's it got to do with Stellan?"

"I don't know."

Hedin turned around and went back to the kitchen.

"You've heard about the explosion, right?"

"No."

Hedin was staring down at an open book full of underlinings while her fingers tapped away at the keys. The text was in German. Lying around her were photocopies of various archival documents, and dozens of scraps from various bits of cardboard packaging— rice, oats, muesli—that had been cut up so that the blank sides could be used as index cards. The computer was easily ten years old, and the printer was a dot matrix model perched on the other table. Sara couldn't help thinking how few expenses Hedin must have.

"Hattenbach was the name of the place," Sara said. "The whole road is just a crater. Six dead, I think."

"Hattenbach?"

Hedin pulled out an old atlas and leafed through it.

"*Fulda-Lücke*," she said, before putting down the book. "The Fulda Gap. Fukuyama was very wrong."

"What does that mean?"

Sara recognized the term—Fulda Gap—but couldn't remember what it meant.

"It was in the Fulda Gap that everyone thought the Third World War would start," said Hedin. "East of Frankfurt, on the border between East and West. There's a couple of valleys there that are practically made for a tank-borne invasion. Corridors straight into the heart of West Germany, into the Rhine where the Americans' key NATO bases were located. There have been a lot of books about it, movies, even a board game. Don't they teach anything in schools these days?"

Sara didn't know whether Hedin was lumping her in with the school pupils of the day, but she chose to ignore the question.

"Could it be connected to Stellan Broman?" she said. "It happened right at the same time, and in both cases there are ties to the Cold War."

Hedin was silent.

"Why would anyone blow that place up today?" Sara added.

"There could be any number of reasons." said Hedin. "Loyalties shift over time, and yesterday's enemy is today's friend. Did you know that the German security service's headquarters in Pullach belonged to the Waffen-SS? And their commander-in-chief, Gehlen, was a dedicated Nazi and spy chief during the war. The USSR was his area of expertise, and they thought that was the perfect fit in postwar West Germany. The Nazi past didn't matter so much then."

"I had no idea."

"There's a lot you don't know."

Sara didn't know whether "you" referred to the police, the school pupils of the day or all of humanity, as far as Hedin was concerned.

"Do you want to know what you should do?" said Hedin. "You should talk to someone who has more of a military interest—someone more international. My research is about Sweden."

Sara was a little surprised when Hedin pulled out a mobile. She'd almost been expecting an old Ericsson Dialog with a dial.

"Good morning, it's Eva Hedin. You've someone specializing in Fulda and Germany with you, don't you?" She listened and nodded. "Yes, that sounds good."

She grabbed the back of a cut-up tea packet and took notes.

"And you think he'll answer?" she said on the phone. "Good. A police officer is going to call. I don't think she wants to say much about why, but I guess that's something you're used to?"

For the first time since Sara had met Hedin, she saw her smile.

"Thanks for your help, and thanks for the annual conference, by the way. Such a fascinating lecture. What a pity Theutenberg couldn't make it. Goodbye."

Hedin ended the call and looked at Sara.

"Tore Thörnell. Retired colonel. He may be able to help you."

"Who did you call?"

"Christer Hansén."

"Military?"

"Chairman of Sweden's Eyes and Ears."

"Which is?"

"A society for people who've worked in or are interested in intelligence services—primarily the historical side."

"And you're a member of this society?"

"Yes," said Hedin, sounding rather taken aback, as if Sara had asked whether she customarily engaged in breathing. "I've given several papers to them. Here are the numbers. Now it's time for you to leave."

Hedin handed over the piece of card with the phone number, then sat back and began to rattle away at her keyboard. She didn't even reply when Sara said goodbye.

Out in the street, Sara began by checking whether the number was registered. It wasn't. Only four other people had searched for it, according to her app, so it was clearly not a well-used number. Then she called.

"Thörnell," said a grave elderly voice on the other end of the line.

Sara introduced herself, said she'd been given his number by one Christer Hansén, and that she hoped Thörnell would be able to answer a few questions about the Cold War and the Fulda Gap. He promised to do his best and asked her to come to his home an hour later. Bergsgatan 16; the door code was 1814.

"1814?" said Sara. "The last year Sweden was at war."

"At least officially," said Thörnell, before hanging up.

An hour gave her enough time to run home again and shower before taking the number 3 bus to Kungsholmen. Everyone had left for school and work, so she had the apartment to herself. As she turned on the water and pulled off her running clothes, she thought back to the evening before, and how dramatic it had been for her and her family. The others probably all thought she'd overreacted and stuck her nose in things that weren't her business. Personally, Sara wanted just wanted to protect her family—both the individual members of it and the family as a unit. But did that have to be on her terms? Was she struggling to accept that the others had their own wills? She just wanted the best for them.

Sara turned off the shower, toweled off and then stood for a long time in front of the bathroom mirror, examining herself. This was who she was. Sara Nowak. Mother of two, police officer, resident of Stockholm's old town. When she was a child, she wouldn't have been able to guess much of what would happen during her life. Was she satisfied with her life? Was there anything she regretted? Anything she felt she ought to have done? A dream she still hoped to realize? She'd probably had loads of dreams in her childhood and teens, but by and large she felt that her dreams changed as her life went on. They were no longer about glamorous jobs or fame. Now she dreamed of success on behalf of her children, retaining her health, someone tackling the world so that it started going in the right direction again.

Her meditation in front of the bathroom mirror had left her short of time. When she saw how late it was, she'd to pull on whatever she could find, skip her makeup and run down to the bus stop at Mälartorget. She had to be there on time.

After six minutes on the bus and two minutes' walk, Sara reached Bergsgatan 16. It was a grand old salmon-pink stone building with bay windows and balconies, beautifully situated opposite the Kungsholms Church. She entered 1814 and the door opened.

At least officially, she thought to herself.

And then: *Voi ch'entrate…*

The stairwell echoed in that fine old way. A warm, dark echo. It wasn't at all cold and hard, like the stairwells in the social housing blocks from the 1960s.

The building had clearly been constructed with the well-heeled in mind. There were three doors on each landing—one large set of double doors and two singles. On several floors, one of the single doors was just a side entrance to the double doors, and had probably been used as the way in for the kitchen and domestic staff from the beginning. Sara got the impression that the building had been designed to house one large apartment and one smaller flat on each story. One for the landed merchants and important dignitaries, and one for the more anonymous civil servants, who still benefitted from a central location with beautiful views beyond the church toward Norr Mälarstrand.

When Colonel Thörnell opened his door, Sara's theories were confirmed. Behind him, there opened up a vast expanse of apartment with wooden paneling on the walls and plaster on the ceiling.

"Sara Nowak," she said, proffering a hand.

Thörnell shook it and showed her inside.

The retired colonel was a gentleman of around seventy years old, with his white hair slicked back, a small mustache, a moss-green cardigan and a white shirt and tie. And shoes indoors. He was properly turned out, even in the midst of a heatwave. He looked a little like an aged movie star from the 1940s. A white-haired Cary Grant.

"Coffee? I've laid the table in the drawing room."

Sara stepped inside and jumped when she saw a movement from the corner of her eye, but she quickly realized it was just a huge floor-to-ceiling mirror in the hallway. A sign of vanity that didn't quite fit in with Thörnell's rather stern image.

They entered a living room with a bay window looking out over the trees of the cemetery. There were five windows in a gentle outward curve. The sun was shining, and Thörnell went over to draw the curtains.

There was a sofa, armchairs and a table—all in neoclassical style. Sara couldn't determine whether the furniture was all genuine antiques or just made to look that way. Hanging on the walls were oils of grim-looking men, some in uniform, others civilians, even the odd priest's cassock. There were a couple of framed diplomas and a telegram—in English and French, so it seemed.

"The Fulda Gap," said Thörnell, apparently accustomed to coming straight to the point. He didn't seem to be in any rush, anyway. The calm in the stately apartment was palpable—almost physical.

"Yes," said Sara. "I gather that was where they were expecting the Third World War to break out."

"Correct. There were several plausible scenarios, but Fulda was deemed the most likely by, among others, NATO. That was why they put extra reinforcements on the border, just in case—and that's putting it mildly. There were even nuclear weapons. Germany risked being the stage for a completely devastating war."

"Does the explosion the day before yesterday have anything to do with the Cold War? It happened in that area."

"But the Soviet Union and the DDR are long gone, as you know."

"Russia is no less aggressive," Sara said tentatively.

Thörnell leaned back in his armchair, coffee cup in hand.

"What happened in Germany happened on historic land—but that doesn't have to mean it has ties to history. In mainland Europe, more or less all land is historic. Two world wars and a string of bloody dictatorships—both left- and right-wing. No matter which stone you turn over, you risk finding a body underneath it."

Silence descended on the room, and it struck Sara that no sound was penetrating from the outside world. The traffic was probably not all that busy up here by the church, but there was no sound of cars, children or sirens to be heard. It was well insulated.

"You may have read about the former television presenter Stellan Broman being murdered," said Sara.

"Shot in his own home," said Thörnell, casting a glance over his shoulder as if he was considering the possibility that the same thing might happen to him.

"It's emerged that he was supposedly an informant for the DDR," said Sara, awaiting the colonel's reaction.

"Continue," Thörnell said calmly.

"I wonder whether this explosion in Germany might be related to Stellan's murder in any way? Both are acts of violence that can be tied to the Cold War."

"And what does this have to do with me?"

"Do you see any connection? Why did Hedin and Hansén send me to you?"

Thörnell looked at her like a teacher scrutinizing their favorite pupil when they couldn't answer a question. Surprised, disappointed, almost wounded.

"I confess," said Sara. "I don't know what you've done—merely that you're a colonel. How is it that you know so much about Fulda and the Cold War?"

"I'm not in the habit of speculating about the motives of others, but it's not unreasonable to assume that Hansén had my rather specific specialism in mind. I shouldn't think Hedin's aware of it—we're not so public in my line of work. But I should think that's why she rang Hansén."

"And what is your line of work?"

"Let's just say that for many years I worked on...certain international matters."

"Which means?"

Thörnell smiled. He seemed to appreciate Sara's frankness.

"Liaison officer in military intelligence on secondment to NATO headquarters in Brussels. Look at you—now you know something that only half a dozen other people in Sweden are aware of."

"And why are you telling me?"

Sara couldn't help but feel a small twinge of suspicion. Hedin had been so helpful from the off, and now this secretive colonel had received her without hesitation into his home and answered her questions. Did they have motives other than helping her, or was Sara just so used to encountering resistance and refusals to co-operate in her usual work that she'd forgotten what normal people were like? Or had she just struck lucky when she found Hedin? Perhaps Sara could have made use of Hedin's dedication to old Stasi informants. Sometimes you really did get lucky.

"Because it's been fifteen years since I retired," said Thörnell. "And as a favor to my good friend Hansén. If he asks me a favor like this, I deliver—usually I wouldn't even admit I'd been abroad. Well, except to Majorca."

Thörnell indulged himself in a smile.

"I'm a childhood friend of Stellan's daughters," Sara said, "and I remember that there were sometimes big parties at their home with lots of people. Plenty of them were recognizable even to a child—people off TV, celebrities. But I now gather that there were other important people there. Politicians all the way up to cabinet level, business leaders, researchers, sometimes even people from the military. And spies from the East."

"He did indeed have a wide network of contacts."

"Did you ever go yourself?"

Thörnell looked slightly taken aback, Sara thought to herself.

"Good question," he said. "I thought we were going to discuss the Fulda Gap, but by all means... Yes. I met Stellan Broman at his home a couple of times. Socially. He was an incredibly hospitable person."

"Just a couple of times?"

"Yes, I've never been madly keen on festivities. And even back then, I got the impression there was some sort of underlying motive to it all."

"So you reported it?" Sara asked.

"If I did, then the files are still classified as secret, and I can't confirm or deny."

"Then what would an East German informant have wanted to find out that you knew about?"

"Good question. What did the DDR want to know, full stop." Thörnell thought for a bit. "Sweden's attitudes toward NATO, of course," he said.

"Whether we were going to join?"

"More to what extent we were already in it."

Sara remembered reading about Sweden's far-advanced co-operation with NATO—an alliance that was kept secret from the Swedish people, and that the USSR obviously knew about. Some journalist had uncovered it. An alliance that had been top secret for decades, and had led to heated debate when it had been disclosed, but which had then been pretty quickly forgotten about again. The issue of neutrality was obsolete—as Sara assumed the colonel would have put it.

It felt as if the murder of Stellan was growing into something much bigger than she could have guessed—so big that she wouldn't be able to keep a grip on it. Especially not given that she had her day job to think of. Everyone needed her help there, and everyone would get angry with her for meddling in an investigation that wasn't hers. It was gross malpractice, when you thought about it, but she assuaged her conscience by pointing out to herself that she wasn't on the clock right now. She was asking questions of an old friend of the family in her spare time. And the more she found out, the more worried she was that her colleagues wouldn't manage to find the truth. She didn't know what to do. Let go of it all, or carry on against her better judgment.

"Was that all?" said Sara, feeling as if she'd found out more than she could handle.

"That was the overarching aspect," said Thörnell. "But the more detailed the information was, the better. NATO exercises, how they were planned and by whom. Whether the West had plans to attack under cover of an exercise. And then, of course, there was the matter of NATO's actual capabilities. Were the West's statistics about its own resources reliable, or were they exaggerating, just like we suspected the East did? Or were we hiding our strength in order to mislead them? Then I should imagine they wanted to know what the West's plans for responding to an invasion were—that had a significant impact on their war planning. All told, everything to do with NATO's top secret strategies and defenses was of interest to the DDR—things like Stay-Put and so on."

"Stay-Put?"

"Now I've said too much."

For a man of Thörnell's calm and controlled demeanor, the light stress in his voice was almost akin to the desperate cry of anxiety emitted by a normal person.

"Not at all. Tell me more."

"I'm afraid I can't."

"I'm a police officer."

"But you're not military."

Thörnell thanked Sara for her interest in what an old soldier might know, and he led her back into the hall. There he stopped and looked her in the eye.

"You know you're treading upon historic ground?" he said.

Before Sara had time to say anything, Thörnell stuck a couple of fingers inside the frame of the big mirror in the hallway and pushed. Sara saw her reflection vanish as the old colonel gently swung the glass to one side. Inside were a couple of rooms with bookcases and desks and old black Bakelite phones.

"This was where the leaders of the Swedish Stay-Behind network were based," said Thörnell, gesturing toward the hidden rooms.

"The ones who murdered Palme?"

"No, they didn't do that. They were burdened with organizing defenses behind enemy lines in the event that the country was occupied."

"Was that all people thought about back in the day? That the country might be invaded?"

"First came Denmark, Norway, Belgium and Holland during the war. Poland and Czechoslovakia during the Cold War. And Hungary and East Germany. All countries behind the Iron Curtain had Soviet troops based in them. So yes, invasion was a real threat."

"And what were Stay-Behind supposed to do in the event of Sweden being invaded?" said Sara, peering at the old equipment.

"Organize a resistance. Sabotage."

"Isn't this also top secret?"

"I'm merely telling you things that are in the public domain."

"Have you kept this room because it might be used again in future?"

"If so, I'm not sure that old typewriters will be much use. This is a reminder that history is always present. Perhaps it's thanks to what happened in this room that we were never pulled behind the Iron Curtain, and were able to continue living in freedom."

"Wasn't Stay-Behind something that was meant to be initiated if Sweden was occupied?"

"It was vital to make sure the stakes were high. The Russians knew that every country was making preparations like this, but for as long as we could keep secret who was organizing it and what resources they had at their disposal, we still had the trump card in our hand. And it worked, despite the best efforts of the likes of Stig Wennerström and Stig Bergling."

"What was the difference between Stay-Behind and Stay-Put?"

"Don't even try," said Thörnell, with a smile.

They stepped back into the hallway. The colonel pushed the mirror into place and Sara once again saw her own face.

Her eyes were focused.

As if she'd thought of something.

And she had.

30

She was on the E18 motorway heading toward Norrtälje, but instead of taking the exit for the small town, Agneta carried on toward Kapellskär. Then she turned left onto Rådmansövägen, heading to Räfsnäs. Of course, it was just on the off chance—but she reflected that Ober had probably not acquired a new refuge in the years that had passed, given that everything that had once seemed alarming had quickly faded away. How quickly some people began to think they could live ordinary lives and forget about their true existences! Forget who they really were...

Also, Ober had no reason to believe she knew of his hideout. On one occasion he'd used it for a meeting with Geiger, and she'd heard them agree to meet at his sister's summer house—in Räfsnäs. Later on, she'd made sure to ask for the sister's name—in entirely different circumstances—and then it had been easy to put together the pieces of the puzzle.

It had been over thirty years, but she still retained a lot of information from back then. Names, places, appearances, anecdotes, family relationships, personal preferences. The only question was which bits of it would be put to use.

She parked by the harbor in Räfsnäs, where the boats for Tjockö and Lidö and Fejan all departed and where there was a lifeboat stationed. There was a small kiosk targeting sweet-toothed holidaymakers, and beyond that there were small red fishermen's huts. Just above the car park was the bus stop and the community gathering point. It seemed Ober was faithful to the archipelago.

She stayed in the car while she checked the old A–Z map she'd had in the car since long before the advent of mapping applications.

Karlsrovägen 5. It ought to be a house diagonally across the narrow lane running along the water's edge. There was one larger house and a few smaller ones. Agneta used the rearview mirror to continue examining the houses without having to turn to face them. Perhaps it was best to sneak in from the back. Was that unduly cautious? If anyone saw her, it would seem suspicious—there were people all over the place here.

She examined her reflection in the mirror. No, he wouldn't recognize her. She'd changed too much, what with her shorn hair and lack of makeup. So—it would be better to enter from the road and just knock on the front door. There were lots of people around during the summer—holidaymakers who were there to catch boats, friends visiting, people renting houses for a week or two. She might just be a visitor who'd gone astray, an older lady who desperately needed to use the toilet, or a tourist who'd fallen in love with the place and wanted to buy a house. There was no reason for Ober to be suspicious. On the contrary, he had every reason to act normally since he was likely to be a familiar face in these parts and wouldn't want to draw attention to himself.

He'd been to their home so many times. He'd spent so many hours with her husband. He'd spent so much time on his pupil, Geiger. Indoctrinating, enlisting and educating his novice.

Was it all his fault? What would her life have been like if Ober hadn't managed to recruit his devoted Geiger?

She stepped up onto the cracked, unpainted porch steps of the house. It would be best if she knocked hard on the door—like someone with nothing to hide. A proper knock.

Before long she heard footsteps from the other side of the door.

A woman.

The sister.

There were similarities between them, in that sibling fashion. No matter how different siblings were, the shape of the nose or a certain angle to the mouth always divulged the truth about the familial connection. Two individuals who'd been manufactured by the same people—even if the creators were long gone.

"Sorry, do you possibly have a phone I could borrow? Mine's died and I was supposed to meet my daughter in the harbor, but I've no idea where she is."

"Of course, come inside."

The sister turned around and went back into the house. Agneta followed her.

There was a small hallway and then they entered the kitchen, which seemed to serve as a common room. The decor was dated and the worse for wear, as was so often the case in summer houses. Furniture and textiles left behind for the winter, to be subjected to the cold and damp. Things that hadn't been used for decades but were left where they were, because that was where they'd always been. Fly feces and spiderwebs. Cracked and stained porcelain, odd sets of cutlery, glasses that could never be quite fully cleaned. In the center of the room was a large dining table with stacks of magazines and books on it. There was an armchair with a footstool next to it, and a window looking out on to the garden.

Agneta looked around.

The frying pan would do nicely.

Before the sister had time to turn around, Agneta slammed the frying pan into the back of her head. The woman collapsed, and Agneta immediately began to wonder how much violence old people could cope with. Could a blow that hard have finished the sister off?

She tied the woman to a chair for safety's sake, and then she checked for a pulse and listened for her breathing. Yep—she was still alive.

Summer houses had thin walls and there were a lot of people on the move around Räfsnäs. Agneta found a top and cut it into strips using the kitchen scissors. Then she pulled out her pistol and pressed it against the sister's temple in case she came to, before filling her mouth with the rags. Then she took a longer strip of fabric and tied it across her mouth and around her head.

It took a long time for the sister to regain consciousness. Almost an hour.

While she waited, Agneta stayed out of the way in a small bedroom. In the unlikely event that any visitor called, the woman was positioned so that Agneta could sneak up behind the interloper and use the frying pan again. Or her pistol.

In the meantime, she contemplated what to do next. She didn't remember much of her training, and really didn't feel tempted by the prospect of torture. Perhaps threats would suffice? She hoped so.

"Where is he?" said Agneta, when the sister finally came to.

The woman didn't answer, and Agneta tried to remember her name. Lisbeth? Berit? Betty? Details like that usually helped, but her mind was completely blank. Why had they never been trained how to deal with forgetfulness? It wasn't just her body that was failing. Her brain was also slowly but surely packing up.

"Where is he?" she asked again.

The sister merely shook her head.

Agneta looked around and had an idea. This particular method of torture was one they'd never used back in her day, but it seemed to be very popular nowadays. She went over to the wood burner, picked up the bucket of water standing beside it and grabbed a tea towel. She carried the bucket over to the bound woman and pulled her head back with a firm grip on her hair. Then she put the towel over her face and poured a scoop of water over her.

She had no idea whether she was doing it right, but water boarding was water boarding, she thought to herself. It was unlikely to be a pleasant experience, at any rate.

When she paused, the sister mumbled something through the fabric.

"Are you trying to tell me where he is?" said Agneta, and at that moment she remembered the sister's name. Elisabeth.

Elisabeth shook her head and gave her a rancorous look. Agneta shrugged her shoulders and carried on. More water, longer periods, shorter breaks.

When the sister was snorting enough that Agneta was concerned she really might keel over, she stopped for a longer break.

While Elisabeth tried to recover, Agneta went to search the kitchen drawers. Some of the knives looked pretty scary. She laid them out on the dining table, and then looked at Elisabeth for a long time. Elisabeth stared back at her pugnaciously.

Agneta was about to pick up one of the knives when the other woman began to waggle her head and move her mouth to show she wanted to talk.

Agneta went and removed the strips of fabric from her mouth.

"*Pass auf!*" Elisabeth shouted as soon as she could, and at that moment Agneta heard a sound behind her. She turned quickly and caught a glimpse of a figure disappearing.

Shit.

The cow had tricked her. She'd heard her brother's footsteps and pretended she wanted to talk, but only so she could warn him.

She ought to stick a knife in her, but it was more important to get hold of Ober.

Agneta struck the bound woman with the pistol handle, then ran out of the door and around the corner of the house outside. She saw Ober ahead of her, on his way toward the harbor.

She followed him, wondering whether he had a car parked there or whether he would leap onto one of the boats.

But he did neither.

When he reached the asphalt between the kiosk and the boats, he stopped and turned toward her with a smile. She fumbled for the pistol, but he simply looked at her.

"What are you going to do? Shoot me? With all these people around?"

Agneta looked around her. Families with children, pensioners, youths. People everywhere.

He was right.

She pushed the pistol back into her pocket again. At that moment, he recognized her, despite her new appearance.

"It's you," he said. Shocked.

Of course he'd always known that people like her were part of the game—that they might be after him. But he'd apparently never guessed that she was one of them.

"Who do you work for?" he said.

She didn't answer.

"Have you always...?"

She turned around and headed toward the car. He remained rooted to the spot. Safe but disconcerted. His sense of composure gone.

She got into the car again. How the hell was she going to deal with this?

Now he knew who she was. He would either talk to the police, or he would contact his handlers. The ones who'd activated the old spy ring again. In all likelihood, they were tough people who would go after her family.

In the rearview mirror, she saw him take a couple of cautious steps back toward the house—probably fully preoccupied with processing what this meant. That he'd got away. That she was the one who was after him. That everything had kicked off.

Did he know what their mission was? Did he know what he and the others were to be used for?

He would never confess now. But it was that possibility she had to remove.

So she made up her mind.

She turned the key in the ignition.

Shifted into reverse.

Put her foot down.

All the time, she had Ober in her sights and not until the last inch did he turn in response to the sound of the engine.

He probably had no idea what was happening.

She reached over 60 kilometers an hour before she hit him. That ought to be enough. There was a dull thud, and then the car shuddered as the back wheels went over the body.

She braked and heard the first hysterical screams as she got out, and saw the blood trickling from beneath the car.

She quickly pretended to be distraught, assuming the role of a confused old woman who'd lost control of her car.

"Oh, my God! Oh, God! How could it happen? How could it? The car just went out of control!"

Then she turned to the crowd that had gathered, continuing in the same pleading tone.

"The car just went out of control…"

It worked. A young girl even began to comfort her.

"It wasn't your fault."

A middle-aged man in shorts and a polo shirt was already on his knees, looking under the car. Over by the lifeboat, she could see two men running toward them. The man in shorts backed up and Agneta bent down and crawled under the car.

She wriggled in so that she got her mouth right to his ear.

"Where are you meeting?"

He glanced at her with bloodshot eyes. His breathing was labored and rattling.

"I have your sister tied up in the house. Do you want to save her?"

And then he talked.

When he was done, she pressed her fingers against his throat so that the blood supply to the brain was stopped. She pressed as hard as she could, so that her knuckles went white. And Ober was too weak to offer up any resistance.

"He's dying!" she cried out, with as much panic in her voice as she could muster.

And once he was completely still, she scrambled out from under the car and got back to her feet.

"Call an ambulance!" she shouted at the crowd standing around her. "I'll go and meet it. The car just went out of control…"

Following her exercise in improvised disinformation, she left the harbor but then turned right toward the house instead of waiting for the ambulance. It wouldn't be there for another half an hour anyway.

She would have to abandon the car, and she coolly assumed that the name of the owner was unlikely to help the police anyway. She needed to get away.

Fast.

She'd been ready to use the pistol to get away, but it hadn't been needed.

As she left, she'd looked through the side windows of the estate's boot. Lying there under the blanket was her Kalashnikov. She would probably have found a use for it, but she didn't dare retrieve it. It would have to be a mystery for the police, just like the owner of the car.

She put all her energy into walking in a calm and controlled fashion. Everyone in the harbor was stunned by the blood and the body under the car, and no one shouted or came after her.

Inside the house, the sister was still there, tied up but conscious. Agneta thought to herself that she personally would have made an attempt to free herself. Perhaps this Elisabeth woman was in shock? Perhaps she was counting on her brother coming to her rescue? It was unclear. But Ober would never save anyone again.

"Car keys?" said Agneta, and the sister nodded toward the kitchen counter. She appeared to admit defeat.

Hanging on a hook above the counter was a keyring with an old BP mascot made from plastic on it. A Renault. Agneta was a skeptic when it came to French cars, but it would have to do.

She pulled down the keys, and suddenly she wasn't sure about the sister's name any longer. Maybe it was Elsie?

Then she pulled out the pistol, pressed the muzzle to Elisabeth's forehead—or whatever her name was—and pulled the trigger.

If she hadn't been thinking so much about what would have happened if Ober had escaped, she probably wouldn't have bothered getting the sister out of the way. And she would probably have caused herself a whole lot of trouble.

The sister appeared to have helped the brother in his activities. Perhaps she even knew what was going on. Perhaps she would have helped to carry it out.

She'd been tough enough to keep quiet during the water boarding, and smart enough to manage to warn him when the opportunity presented itself.

A soldier.

Zealous and dedicated.

What kind of sick parents had brought two children like that into the world?

By the edge of the garden, she found an old beige Renault 5.

She unlocked the door, checked the gearstick and the controls. Hanging from the rearview mirror was a pennant with green bobbles hanging off it and the word Kåseberga.

The little car started without any trouble.

She would need to dump it within an hour or so to be safe, but first she wanted to get back into Stockholm.

She finally knew where the meeting was to take place, but she didn't have much time.

31

Ebba had, with the utmost reluctance, agreed to meet her mother at the Caffè Nero across the street from her school. She was in the final days of her school years, so Sara didn't bother to check whether Ebba really had a free period. The Cold War, Stellan's murder and potential terrorist acts—none of it could hold back thoughts of the night before. With Olle, she thought things would just get worse if she tried to talk to him, and she'd chosen to believe Martin, but she felt as if she needed to try and get through to Ebba. Sometimes relationships improved when mother and daughter went their separate ways and led their own independent lives—but Sara didn't want them to be separated by such a tremendous distance. The better the relationship between them when Ebba moved out, the stronger the ties between them would remain. Or so she thought.

Sara ordered a latte, but Ebba didn't want anything when she eventually cruised in and sat down opposite her mother, looking surly and dismissive.

"What is it?" said Ebba, when she finally opened her mouth after staring out of the window for a while. In the meantime, Sara had been scrutinizing her daughter in silence. She was a beautiful young woman, illuminated by the early summer sun in Vasastan, on the starting blocks for her own life, where she would make her own decisions. What were her goals and dreams? Her daughter had talked about law school, business school, studying abroad. Were those her own thoughts, or had she acquired them from her friends? The school you went to and the friends you had during your youth could affect your trajectory through life more than your parents, sometimes. And that felt wrong to Sara, but right now she didn't think anything she said would be taken well by Ebba.

"I just wanted to talk to you about last night. To explain that I'm not spying on you, that I trust you, and that I only took down those guys because I wanted to protect you. I told them afterward that they could report me if they wanted to, but they didn't."

"I don't care about them. But you didn't need to hit them like that. I can look after myself. Don't you think I've had to deal with disgusting guys before?"

"Well, of course—"

"I don't know what kind of world you grew up in," Ebba said, interrupting her mother. "But nowadays, you can't do anything without disgusting guys trying to hit on you and evil bitches calling you a whore."

"But don't you understand that I just wanted to help you?"

"I don't want that. How am I supposed to manage later on?"

"You don't have to—manage by yourself, that is."

"You're going to follow me around my whole life?"

"You're only nineteen."

"I've been managing by myself since I was twelve. I want a coffee."

Ebba got up and went to the counter to order a white coffee. Lots of milk. Then she returned with the pale brown drink and sat back down.

"All those nights when you were working and Dad was out entertaining, did you think I was just at home?"

It cut into Sara's heart. She pictured a fourteen-year-old Ebba in the nightclubs of Stureplan. Ebba saw the anxiety in her mother's eyes.

"Relax. You've taught me exactly how guys operate. I hung out around town, but I was always with friends, and always on my guard."

"Friends? But surely they were young girls, too?"

"That was enough. Young girls can scream very loudly."

"Do you think I've been a bad mother?"

"No," said Ebba, laughing. "No worse than anyone else. We often compare our mums and I've come to realize that there are some

247

who are worse. Much worse. What's more, I think people find their own mums more annoying the more alike they are."

When had Ebba become this wise? Contrarian, teenage Ebba. Sara didn't know what to say. In the middle of her surprise, Sara suddenly felt a new sense of security emerging. Perhaps it was all going to be okay after all.

"What happened to Dad's guitar?" said Ebba, interrupting her mother's ponderings.

Sara looked at her daughter and didn't know what to say.

"It was completely smashed to bits," said Ebba. "And Dad didn't want to say anything. He said he'd dropped it on the floor, but that wouldn't leave it that smashed. And then when you weren't at home this morning, I thought you might have had a row."

"I was out running."

"And the guitar?"

"It broke."

"Hmm, yes, I saw that much. But I thought Dad would have been devastated. He loved that guitar."

Sara couldn't find anything to say. She simply let the words die away. They finished their coffees and then Ebba said she had to go back to school, and Sara suspected that it wasn't her classes that were drawing her back. The final week of sixth form was a time when you didn't want to miss a single second of what felt like the high point in your life. It was probably one reason to be particularly pleased that Ebba had granted her this audience.

Sara was permitted to give her daughter a hug, and as she stood there on the pavement watching her cross Roslagsgatan, she thought to herself that she had at least got slightly—just slightly— closer to her daughter.

At the same time, there was something at the back of her mind bothering her.

"I thought Dad would have been devastated."

Ebba was right.

Why hadn't Martin been more upset or angry when she smashed up his guitar?

Because he had a guilty conscience?

Sara did what she could to push away the doubt. She tried to focus on work, but instead it was Uncle Stellan who filled her mind, along with everything she'd found out from the retired colonel. She needed to talk it through with someone.

This time, Hedin opened up for Sara. Either she was finished with her work for the day, or she was curious about what Thörnell had told her.

"What did he say?" was in fact the first thing she said, once they'd sat down in her combined bedroom and lounge. She was on the edge of the bed, while Sara was seated in the only armchair. Hedin didn't seem to entertain at home very often.

"Not that much, to be honest," Sara said. "He was able to confirm that Stellan Broman had an intensive social life and that he'd visited him a couple of times, but then refrained from going."

"He must have guessed the purpose of the parties, given his position."

"But he mentioned something that he regretted, and that made me curious. 'Stay-Put.'"

"What's that?"

"Something to do with NATO's secret defense plans, if I understood correctly. But he refused to say anything else. That was the only thing he was secretive about."

"Apart from everything he didn't even mention," said Hedin, and of course she was right.

"What is Stay-Put?" said Sara.

"No idea. Wait a second."

Hedin went into the kitchen and began to search cupboards and drawers. Sara realized there was nothing she could do to help, and she stayed in the armchair. Hedin's system was presumably beyond comprehension by anyone except her. Sara hoped she'd written some instructions, so that someone else could take over her research when she was gone.

She looked around the room. Hanging on the walls were a couple of paintings that Sara thought were heirlooms—a field and a monk blowing a horn. There were two small oval frames containing photos of young children. Perhaps they were nieces and nephews—she hadn't got the impression Hedin had any of her own. A noticeboard with letters from the council, newspaper clippings and statutes from the tenants' association. A bed with a stripy throw over it, a wall-mounted bed light, a bedside table with a large stack of books—and a few more on the floor next to it.

Sara felt like more coffee, but she didn't want to interrupt Hedin. Instead, she nodded off in the armchair, her head at an angle— the sort of pose that meant she woke up every two or three minutes because it hurt, turned her head the other way and carried on sleeping. The morning run and the emotional outbursts of the night before had taken their toll.

After an hour, the researcher called out from the kitchen.

"Here it is!"

It took Sara a few seconds to remember where she was. Then she got up, took a step in the wrong direction, turned around and went into the kitchen, feeling slightly groggy.

Hedin was sitting at her computer and nodded toward the screen, where the browser was showing an article from the *Dagens Nyheter* archives. Sara leaned in and looked at it. The article was from Thursday 13 March 1986, and had the headline BOMBS EVEN IF WE COMPLAIN. Hedin pointed at a picture in the bottom right-hand corner, of a man on a road who was showing a drain cover to the reporter.

"The caption," she said.

Sara read it aloud.

"According to the 'Stay-Put' program, civilians will be kept in their villages in the event war breaks out, to avoid disrupting military traffic. Thus, bombs will be positioned under the round drain covers on the access roads to all villages."

She turned to Hedin.

"Are those bombs still there? Why?"

"And up there," she got as her reply. "Look under the subheading 'The Fulda Gap.'"

Sara read on.

"High above the plains, the khaki helicopters of the USA sweep past on their way toward the East German–West German border approximately twenty kilometers to the east. To the north and the south, the mountains rise around a thirty kilometer wide valley—known in military parlance as 'The Fulda Gap.' Here, right in the heart of divided Germany, is Hattenbach—home to farms, small lanes, and ancient half-timbered houses. A comforting dollhouse idyll like thousands of others in West Germany."

Sara turned back to Hedin.

"Hattenbach—that's where the bomb went off the day before yesterday."

Then she carried on reading.

"Strategists in the East and West believe that the Fulda Gap is where the first devastating blows will be struck if a third world war breaks out. 'It came as a shock,' says Hans Schäfer of Hattenbach, speaking of the day around three years ago when he realized the fate planned for him and his neighbors in any eventual war. On his television, American generals were speaking about the importance of making the enemy's advance more difficult immediately after the outbreak of war. American officers practiced using atom bombs on a sandbox model in Texas to transform a West German village into a radioactive obstacle. These images would shock millions of West Germans, but among the villagers in Hattenbach, they had a particularly ominous resonance. The model showed that their village in particular was designated to be wiped out."

"Here's a good summary," said Hedin. "'In 1983 and 1984, the Fulda Gap was often discussed and written about in West Germany. Leaked military documents indicated that this particular area was one in which the civilian population ran a high risk of being sacrificed by troops on their own side.'"

"And they lived with this," said Sara. "Every single day."

"They didn't want to be reminded," said Hedin. "It says here, 'The only way to live with the fear is to deny it.' And read this…"

Sara squinted at the screen.

"'They became angry, explains Hans Schäfer, referring to his neighbors. Not at the tactic, not at the American military chiefs, but at the fact that they'd been allowed to find out themselves.'"

"There's a documentary that was shown by CBS in the USA too— *The Nuclear Battlefield*. Apparently they talk about Hattenbach in it, as the ground zero for a nuclear war. Stay-Put became common knowledge in the mid-eighties, but it seems as if all parties agreed to forget about it again. Almost nothing has been written about it since 1986."

"But the bomb in Hattenbach wasn't an atom bomb. It didn't destroy the whole village—just part of the road."

"That was probably just a taster," said Hedin. "Someone wants to demonstrate that the threats of old still exist."

"Do the atom bombs still exist? Could they also be set off? And how many of them are there?"

"We don't know."

32

Sara had called and explained what she'd found out, but Anna had told her she was busy and asked whether they could discuss it later. They were searching for Stellan's old stalkers, and had received in excess of two hundred tips from people who claimed to have seen Agneta—everywhere from Boden to Bangkok. Bielke was probably quite happy to let the Germans handle the more dramatic aspects of the investigation.

Sara had wanted to hand over the information and push everything to do with the murder and the Cold War out of her skull, with the assurance that Anna and her colleagues would get to the bottom of it all. However, she could tell from her friend's tone of voice that buried bombs in Germany were a little bit too imaginative for her tastes. If there was anything in the espionage angle, she would have to deal with it by herself, Sara thought. She'd already gone way over the line in her private investigative endeavors. But what if she was on the right track? Was she prepared to take responsibility for letting Stellan's death remain unsolved?

Sara's thoughts wandered from Stellan to the house in Bromma, and to her own childhood, and to Martin, who hadn't been crushed by the fact that Sara had smashed his guitar to pieces. In her mind's eye, Sara pictured Martin with hordes of girls who wanted to become pop stars and sent him photos of their naked bodies. And how was Martin supposed to resist? Girls who were offering themselves up to him with their young, beautiful bodies. Girls who listened and were understanding. Nothing like Sara.

She knew that her thoughts weren't especially constructive, and that they had little relationship to reality. Even if there was some basis to them, it didn't help her one bit to torture herself like this.

She considered going into work earlier, just to have something else to think about, but she realized that it would do nothing to divert her thoughts if she sat in the office on her own for hours, drinking coffee while she waited for David to arrive.

What could she do?

Sara thought about what she and Hedin had talked about, and realized that she had to find out more. If nothing else, she owed it to Agneta to try and uncover the truth about Stellan's death.

The motorhome was still in the same spot. She went up to it and knocked on the door. When Sara got no answer, she knocked again and called out in English.

"Police! Open up!"

It didn't take more than a few seconds for the burly German police officer to open the door. They must have been in a rush to shut her up, because the man had forgotten to close the internal door behind him. Careless, Sara thought to herself. She pushed past him and he stepped aside. These particular campers had no desire to draw any attention to themselves.

Inside the mobile command center, Breuer and Strauss were sitting at a computer screen each. Strauss seemed to be reviewing passenger lists from airlines, while Breuer was checking CCTV images that had clearly been pulled from airports. Both turned around when Sara entered.

"*Ruhe, bitte*," said Breuer, getting up and waving her arms deprecatingly. Then she switched into her heavily accented English. "What are you doing here? You shouldn't be here."

"I know what Stay-Put is," said Sara. "I know the bomb in Germany is to do with Stay-Put."

"And?"

"The people investigating the case don't believe it's to do with the DDR and the Cold War. They're going through old stalkers—so they won't help you. But I can help."

Breuer remained standing with one prohibitive hand still extended.

"We're used to getting by on our own," she said.

"Remember that I know the family. I was there all the time. I may have seen things."

Breuer gave Strauss a look.

"Sit down," she said curtly, looking at Sara, who nodded and took a seat at the conference table opposite Breuer. The big guard dog of a policeman went to take his seat by the door.

Strauss came over with a beige folder that he placed on the table in front of Sara.

"Sign first," said Breuer, crossing her arms and leaning back.

"What is it?" said Sara, looking at the German text.

"Confidentiality papers."

Confidentiality papers.

Sara wondered whether that was the correct term, but she grasped what they meant.

"I don't understand what it says," she said.

"It says you can't tell anyone about what we've discussed without going to prison."

"That's not up to you."

"In this case, it is. Sign or leave."

Sara hesitated. There was probably only one way to obtain the truth about her childhood idol and her friends' father. So she signed and slid the paper back across the table.

"Stay-Put is no secret," said Breuer, as soon as the paper with Sara's signature had been deposited in the filing cabinet. "It's been common knowledge since the eighties."

That might be true, Sara thought to herself. The *Dagens Nyheter* article had been from 1986.

"But no one's connected it with the bomb that recently detonated in Germany," she said. "And you'd prefer that no one did, wouldn't you?"

No answer.

"Was it one of those bombs that blew up?" said Sara. "Are there more of them?"

"Don't know."

"Are there nuclear explosives still in the ground?"

"Don't know."

"And what does Stellan Broman have to do with the bombs?"

"Don't know."

"What's the point of signing confidentiality papers if you just say 'don't know'?"

Breuer merely stared at her, completely unmoving. Sara got up to leave.

"OK," said Breuer, signaling that she should sit down again. "What we do know is that the people who called Geiger have come across information about old defense systems from the days of the Iron Curtain."

"How?"

"It's to do with old revolutionary groups who used to receive assistance from East Germany in the old days, and who always had strong ties with revolutionaries in the Middle East."

"Why are you telling her this?" Strauss said to Breuer. He spoke in German, so Sara wasn't completely certain of his meaning.

"If she's going to help us, then…" Breuer replied, also in German. Sara didn't catch the end of the sentence.

Strauss was silent for a moment, but seemed to accept the explanation.

"Are Palestinians behind the bombs?" said Sara, thinking about the Palestinian groups that had been active during her own childhood. Terrorists in the eyes of some, freedom fighters in the eyes of others. At any rate, they killed people. And what you saw on the news was destined to be talked about at breaktimes. Sara even dimly remembered playing airplane hijack in the school playground, when those acts had been at their most common. They'd demanded the release of prisoners without really understanding what that meant.

"No," said Breuer. "We don't think so—but we think they first received the information in the eighties, and that someone there has now sold it on to militant Islamists. Probably to raise money for their own cause or for personal enrichment. Or perhaps someone's been radicalized, and realizes that this is a powerful weapon against the West."

"East Germany was tremendously successful at infiltrating West Germany and NATO—right up to the top," said Strauss. "You might have read about Rupp and Guillaume. Only the CIA, who have the Rosenholz files, have any idea how much information the Stasi obtained. A lot of this information—especially about weapons systems—was put up for sale when the Wall fell. And there was even more when the Soviet Union collapsed. The revolutionary groups may have been given a slice of the action as a form of revenge. The PLO, the PFLP, Black September and so on."

"And Stellan?"

"We think that the East German spy ring here in Sweden was somehow in possession of key information about the explosives," said Strauss. "Their locations, or how to activate them, or something like that. They needed to hide in a neutral country—wherever that was. During the Cold War, Sweden was a meeting spot for all sorts of terrorist groups—especially West Germans and Palestinians—but in their wake you also had Italians, French, Spaniards and Japanese who came here to coordinate their own terrorist activities. They could meet here undisturbed, thanks to your somewhat naive police force."

Sara recollected the disobliging Brundin from the Security Service, and was amused by the Germans' perspective on her generation of operatives.

"And most IMs have been living here in perfect safety following the fall of the Wall," said Breuer. "Very few have been uncovered, none have been punished, and their files have been classified as top secret by your Security Service. It's possible that some of them have retained their political convictions and want to teach the decadent West a lesson."

"A lot of old friends of the DDR are filled with the thirst for revenge," said Strauss. "They think their dream country was betrayed. That it was dissolved following a huge desertion. Very much a stab in the back."

"Your Security Service classify everything in order to conceal what they missed back in the day," Breuer interjected.

"But why are you here?" said Sara, suddenly hit by a realization. "You set off before you knew that Stellan was dead, so it's not the murderer you're after. And you've stayed on despite him being dead, so you weren't after Stellan either. Who are you looking for? The person who made the call?"

Sara could feel that she'd struck the bullseye. There was no better feeling than that, when intuition worked hand in hand with intellect.

Breuer was silent for a long time before speaking.

"I don't know how much you know about this world. Terrorist networks, international operations, collaboration between groups across different parts of the world. Everything is about personal ties. You only trust the people you know. We think that the buyers of the information about the explosives have sent someone that the contact in your country knows personally, in order to set the ball rolling. Thirty-year-old information requires thirty-year-old ties."

Sara was startled when a cup of coffee was placed in front of her. The cup was remarkably small in the hand of the burly policeman, who, despite his bulkiness, had still managed to brew coffee without her noticing. She wondered whether the others had noticed. Of course they had. They were police officers. Sara bent forward to take a sip of the hot liquid.

"You stay loyal to your old friends," Breuer continued. "You don't do anything for another country, for an ideology, but you do for a friend you trained with, saved the life of, were saved by. Someone that you know you've depended on completely in the past—perhaps you still do. It's the secrets you share that bind you together."

"And Stellan was the one who was supposed to hand over that information? But why are you still here if he's dead?"

"Someone is still coming to collect the information."

Sara let those words sink in.

"And you want to arrest the person they send?"

"*Genau.*"

"Who is it?"

Once again, the two Germans quickly exchanged glances. They were apparently in agreement.

"Abu Rasil," said Breuer. "At least, that's one of his names. Abu Omar, Doctor el-Azzeh, Abu Hussein. The man was behind more than ten spectacular terrorist attacks in the seventies and eighties. He has the lives of more than one hundred people on his conscience. He's been lying low for years, but we think that he's suddenly been activated. Tempted in by the person who sold the information, because he's the only person that Geiger and Ober would trust and hand the information over to.

"He was a frequent visitor to East Germany at the invitation of the Communist Party, and he took East Germans and their sympathizers from other countries to training camps that he organized in the Middle East."

"Or so the rumors say," said Strauss, who received a somewhat unhappy look from Breuer in response.

"Including Swedes?" said Sara. "Did Stellan go to a training camp? What about Ober?"

"One of them. Perhaps both. And that's where they formed the personal ties. Abu Rasil is the only person who can extract the information, so they have to send him. Which I'm sure he'll be richly rewarded for."

"And you're after him?"

"Yes. Four terrorist attacks on German soil. Not including the current bombs."

"Breuer was tracking him in the eighties, and was close to catching him," said Strauss. "Since then he's been lying low."

"But at least his plan was stopped," said Breuer. "We believe he was planning a huge attack in protest at German reunification."

"And now it seems as if he's out for revenge. Stay-Put is the perfect reminder of the old contradictions, and of how the USA treated the German population as insignificant pawns in their political games. There are many who would like to see a schism like that between the USA and Europe."

"But how can you be so certain that he'll come? Stellan's dead."

"There may be someone else in the network who can pass the information to him. You haven't been able to find Ober, for instance."

No, they hadn't. Sara took it to heart, even though it wasn't her responsibility.

"But it may be fortunate," said Strauss. "Ober might lead us to Abu Rasil."

"I've got one question," said Sara. "They seem to be able to detonate bombs anyway. Why do they need this?"

Breuer looked at her for a long time.

"I must remind you that you signed the confidentiality papers. If you breathe so much as a word of what we tell you, then you'll be in breach of some of the most important laws in the EU, and you may receive up to thirty years in prison. This is about the security of the entire union. Do you understand?"

"Yes."

Breuer looked around the motorhome, seemingly searching for something with her gaze. Then she took a deep breath.

"Stay-Put was NATO's final line of defense against the Warsaw Pact. Bombs under roads, but also small atomic bombs that could be carried by individuals. The nuclear devices in West Germany have been recovered. The explosive that was detonated a few days ago was a smaller charge that was intended to block the road in the opening phase of any war. Perhaps those were left in place because we've never been able to trust Russia—not even after the end of the Soviet Union."

"The problem is that the USSR knew all about our defenses," Strauss added. "Thanks to their spies and moles."

"And the peace movement in the West," said Breuer. "Which mapped missile installations, mines, ammunition stores, roadblocks and nuclear warheads—all in the name of peace. Since they shared that information openly, it obviously fell into the hands of the Warsaw Pact, and they thought they had to respond in kind. The actions of the peace movement actually hastened the arms race."

"The American troops in the West made the Russians paranoid," said Strauss. "Those forces were supposedly there to defend Europe, but they could just as well have been used for attacks, according to Russian logic. A fundamental doctrine was that Hiroshima had proven that the Yanks wanted to make use of the weapons they had."

"Since there was a terror balance, the Warsaw Pact responded to NATO's initiatives," Breuer continued, "and naturally they wanted their response to be worse in order to serve as a deterrent. The arms race meant they buried their own explosives. But we've never found out where.

"East Germany wasn't provided with that information because the USSR wanted to retain full control. They didn't trust their vassal states, while simultaneously demanding blind loyalty from them.

"The two sides were in constant competition, and according to Soviet defectors, the USSR not only buried bombs to blow up roads, but they also buried explosives powerful enough to destroy an entire province."

"Atom bombs," said Strauss.

"And those are still in the ground?" said Sara.

She raised a hand in check, as if to pause the flow of information or to stop unwelcome insights. But the hulking policeman seemed to interpret it as a request for a refill, because he topped up Sara's cup. Breuer continued.

"The Russians say it's all gone, but that they don't have any documentation to prove it. Then Putin smiles scornfully and implies they have nuclear explosives in the middle of the EU. Both the EU and the USA have demanded to review the Soviet archives, but the requests have been refused. No diplomatic approaches have succeeded, and there's no desire to jeopardize the oil and gas supplies from Russia, so no one dares go too hard on them."

"And you think that the Soviet Union was willing to use those nuclear bombs?"

"The Warsaw Pact knew they needed a quick victory if they were going to invade," Breuer said. "They had to take West Germany before NATO had time to mobilize—preferably during the initial phase. But they also had a backup plan in case they failed. What would happen if NATO entered East Germany? The Warsaw Pact would be under threat, and by extension so would the USSR. They've always wanted buffer countries between themselves and the enemy—Hitler and Napoleon showed them that. It's a fear that's deeply entrenched in the Russian psyche—no more wars on their own soil. The strategy was for a proactive, advanced defense beyond Soviet territory. They were prepared to do whatever it took to avoid an invasion. The devastation of all of central Europe was a solution."

"Could it have happened?" said Sara.

"Yes," said Breuer. "Absolutely. It's actually rather strange that it didn't."

"But it's not too late," said Strauss. "If Abu Rasil finds out how to trigger the bombs."

"And that's why he's coming here?" Sara summarized, mostly for her own sake.

"He's probably already in the country," said Breuer. "Waiting for the all-clear from his handler. As soon as they're ready to detonate the charges, they'll notify him, and he in turn will give his signal to his contact here in Sweden that they're to meet for the handover of the necessary information."

"And that could happen at any time?"

"Any time at all."

33

Sara caught the Nockebybanan light railway and changed on to the metro at Alvik. She ended up in a carriage with a full graduating high school class, all resplendent in their white peaked caps. They were yelling, singing, laughing and crowing. Running back and forth, hugging each other. Behaving as if they owned the whole world.

And they did.

Right now, at least.

Sara chose to think about other matters.

For the first time since she became a police officer, she felt as if she'd encountered something she couldn't affect. She didn't know anything about spies or terrorists, or how to stop them. She knew a lot about Stellan, but apparently not the most important thing about him. His secret life.

He must have been eliminated because he'd known too much. If he'd been able to identify Abu Rasil, then perhaps he had constituted a threat. Was that why Ober had shot him?

Ober—who had once recruited him.

Maybe Stellan was no longer needed, and when the ring had been reactivated he had been a dangerous witness? Perhaps he'd told Ober that he no longer believed in the old doctrines?

Perhaps he'd simply refused to participate in the act of terror that was to follow?

Sara almost hoped that was it. It would make Stellan's betrayal of her and the whole Swedish population a little easier to bear.

Once she was back home in the apartment, she made herself a late lunch, having not realized until then how hungry she was. In the living room, the smashed guitar reminded Sara of the discoveries of the night before, as well as the explanations and Ebba's comments.

Her anxiety about atom bombs was replaced with one relating to a disaster in her personal life.

She felt that she couldn't be completely sure of Martin. But she wanted to be. She didn't want to just reach the most reasonable attitude through intellectual considerations—she wanted to feel convinced with her whole body.

She still had a few hours until she was due at work, so she decided to look into Nikki X some more. She took the metro to Tekniska högskolan, strolled past St. Giorgios Church and crossed the street to the 7-Eleven, where she bought a fresh pay-as-you-go SIM card that she slipped into her work mobile. Then she carried on walking north, before stopping a short distance from Birger Jarlsgatan 125. She wrote a text message:

Horny. How much for a home visit?

She got her reply after less than a minute.

Four thousand.

Sara answered:

Can you come now?
Where?
Blendavägen 27 in Täby.
There in half an hour.

Maybe it was stupid to pick Martin's friend Danne's address, but that was what she'd come up with when trying to think of addresses a long way out of town, and she wanted Nikki X out of her flat as quickly as possible.

While Sara waited, it occurred to her that Nikki might not still live in the flat where she was registered as resident. In that case, it was all for nothing. But after ten minutes, a taxi pulled up outside the door and an attractive, heavily made-up woman of around thirty came out. She was wearing a short skirt, a plunging neckline and towering stilettos. The driver rolled down his window, and Sara overheard him say, "Hansson?" as the woman climbed into the back seat.

As soon as the taxi was gone, Sara tapped in the police door code and opened the front door. She now knew it would say "Hansson" on the front door of the flat, and when she found one with that name she rang the bell, waited thirty seconds and then picked the lock before entering.

A heavy scent of perfume. White-painted walls in the hall, with shoes with needle-sharp heels lined up in rows as straight as arrows. Black-and-white photos of naked bodies. White drapes in front of a door that led into the living room and kitchen. There was a door off the hall, that Sara pushed ajar.

A window, curtains drawn, a bed with silk sheets, a stack of towels, rolls of toilet paper, bottles of oils and lubricants, a bowl of condoms. Had Martin been here?

Sara realized that it was effectively pointless, but she still wandered around searching for traces of Martin. Under the rug, under the bed, between the sheets, in the wardrobe. The fact that she didn't find anything didn't prove that he hadn't been here. Sara wondered what she was playing at, but still couldn't stop herself. There was something almost hypnotic about searching for clues she didn't want to find. If she'd had the equipment with her, she would have taken samples from the stains that were still on the sheets and walls, even though the room smelled like it was freshly cleaned. But that might have been taking it too far—cooking up a tale and sending DNA samples to the lab to check up on her own husband.

After twenty minutes, she received a text message on her new number.

I'm here.
Good. I went to get cash. Back in ten.

That bought her some time.

She'd gone over the room.

If she was interpreting the stains on the walls and sheets correctly, the fuck room was completely drenched in semen, while the rest of the flat seemed clean. No punters there.

Sara went into the bedroom.

Everything was white, with pale lilac and green detailing.

A bed from Hästens. Pillows, linens and candles from Versace and Hermès. Nothing but designer clothes in the wardrobe. Suits, dresses, tops, cardigans, skirts. A distinctly feminine style.

A dozen handbags from Prada, Marc Jacobs, Louis Vuitton and the like.

Expensive, shiny underwear. Even stay-ups and some sort of corset or teddy or whatever they called it. Maybe that was for escort clients who bought a full day or weekend. Not Sara's kind of underwear, anyway.

Perhaps that was why Nikki X was in her husband's mobile. Because Martin had always been turned on by stuff like that. But he hadn't been able to get her to wear it.

Would he not have slept around if she'd worn sexy lingerie a bit more often? No, it couldn't be that petty.

There had to be something else to it.

If he wasn't telling the truth, that was.

In the living room, she noticed something on a desk in the corner. There was an iMac with a keyboard, microphone and mixer. She pulled out a drawer and found a notepad with what appeared to be handwritten lyrics.

"Delusion," "Cold," "Promise to Live."

Bloody hell—she really was dreaming of becoming a pop star. It checked out.

Sara was thinking about whether to boot up the computer to listen to Nikki's songs when she heard a key turn in the front door lock. Sheer reflex made her step into the bathroom and shut the door behind her.

Then someone came into the flat.

Someone in high heels. It had to be Nikki.

Sara checked her mobile. Ten angry text messages and five missed calls. She had it on silent, and must have missed the vibration alerts.

What would she say if the girl found her? That she'd received notification of a break-in, and when she'd arrived the door had been standing wide open?

There were footsteps crossing the living-room floor, and then it sounded as if Nikki had gone into the bedroom. Sara crept to the front door as quietly as she could, opened it and stepped outside. She shut the door again without closing it fully, and heard steps behind her coming from the bedroom.

"Hello?" said a woman's voice from the flat's interior.

Instead of running outside, Sara crept up one story. Nikki emerged from the flat and stopped—perhaps surprised that the door wasn't shut—and then carried on downstairs to the main door. Sara assumed that she didn't have any immediate suspicions, since she soon returned and shut the door again.

Just in case the escort was peering through the peephole or the window overlooking the street, Sara waited half an hour.

That ought to be enough. She put her hand in front of her face as she stepped out of the main door, and walked as quickly as she could back toward the city center.

Wondering what on earth she was up to.

She was sitting in the car with David at Malmskillnadsgatan, trying to focus on the job at hand, but her thoughts wouldn't leave her be. Stellan, Agneta, Ober, the bomb in Germany, Abu Rasil. What exactly had happened, and what was going to happen next?

Sara stared into the summer night while she contemplated all this. She had plenty of thinking time during her shifts. There was lots of waiting. David didn't seem as upset with her any longer. He even bought her a coffee when he ran over to the nearest 7-Eleven.

But they still sat together in silence, because that was what they most often did. It was so easy to lose focus if they talked, and it could draw attention. Voices were audible on the street, but when you were silent passersby usually didn't notice that you were in the car. Sara was happy that things between them seemed to be better. She realized she'd gone too far, but with everything they saw, it was hard not to cross the line—at least sometimes.

Some cars circled for hours without stopping. Either the drivers didn't have the guts, or they got their kicks from looking and fantasizing. Feeling dirty. Or feeling like the women here were dirty. And they were the men's as soon as the men wanted them.

While they waited for an opportunity to intervene in a clear-cut offense, Sara began checking number plates against the vehicle database. She then took the names she'd pulled up and checked them out online, discovering that more than half of the men driving back and forth had wives at home, and sometimes even adult children. The system didn't show her children who were still minors, but some of the men probably had them, too.

What did they say when they got home? Did they think about the shag they'd paid for when they sat down to dinner? When their kids wanted to play with them? What excuse did they give for being late? Did they blame work, or a beer with the guys? Or a trip to the gym?

How did they justify paying for sex to themselves?

Because their sex lives had died after they'd had kids?

Because they just wanted some excitement?

That it was a mistake?

Just a stupid moment?

She'd heard every answer in the book. Everything that came after the degradation, and anger toward the police who'd caught them in the act. "You've ruined my life" was the most common reaction.

As if it was Sara and her colleagues who were forcing the men to break the law. As if it was the police force making them exploit Romanian women. Spit at them, strike them, rape them for money in the back seat of a car or against a gravestone in the Johannes cemetery.

A brand-new Volvo V90 that had done five or six circuits suddenly made a move. The driver pulled over in the small lay-by beside the entrance to the metro station, diagonally across the street from Sara and David's position in their car with its tinted windows.

The Volvo stopped level with Jennifer, a slender North African woman whose real name was probably something completely different. Sara was able to keep good track of all the women up here. Jennifer had always dismissed all offers of help or contact with women's groups, but without getting aggressive like some girls, who saw their income being threatened or who were worried what their pimp would do to them if they spent any time talking to social services. She usually took clients into her flat on Södermalm—a haunt that Sara assumed had been procured by a pimp. It was only when she needed cash desperately that Jennifer would head down to Malmskillnadsgatan.

The man in the car lowered the passenger-side window and Jennifer approached, bent down and spoke to him. While they were negotiating, Sara ran the plates.

Johan Holmberg, apartment in Vasastan. Wife and at least one child in their late teens. Maybe more younger ones, too. Sara googled him and pulled up his LinkedIn and Facebook profiles. He was a project manager for a construction firm. The coach of a junior boys' football team—so he probably had a younger son.

"We've got a sale."

Sara put down her mobile when she heard David's voice. The Volvo was pulling back onto Malmskillnadsgatan, heading toward Brunkebergstorg where it turned right onto Mäster Samuelsgatan. David slowly followed while notifying colleagues that they were on the move. Pål and Jenny remained in position, ready to carry out their own arrest.

Holmberg drove between the high-rises at Hötorget and turned right onto the narrow Slöjdgatan. He crept past Synsam, Lindex, the back door to the Sergel multiplex and then the Scandic hotel, before driving into the underground car park beneath Hötorget itself.

"Surely he isn't going to...?" said Sara.

"Maybe he's just parking and taking her into the hotel," said David, reporting to their colleagues by radio.

They followed into the car park but stopped one story above when the Volvo drove all the way to the bottom floor. Then they got out of the car and split up. Sara took the stairs, while David went down the ramp for cars.

She just had time to see the headlights turn off as she emerged from the stairwell. Holmberg had parked in the very far corner, which implied he was intending to make good on his purchase in the car park, rather than taking her into the hotel.

Sara crouched and peered under the cars. She soon saw David's feet approaching and she leaned forward between the cars to catch his attention, while still hunched down. She gestured toward the corner where the car had parked up, and pointed at her watch to suggest that they give Holmberg some time.

It was unfortunately necessary to let the punters initiate their sex acts before they were interrupted—otherwise they would simply deny everything, and it was almost impossible to prosecute them. Sara and her colleagues needed watertight evidence, even if they would have preferred to stop the buyers from the very beginning.

The car began to move, and Sara signaled to David that it was time. They crept toward the Volvo, peeked in and saw the man's back in the rear seats. His hips were moving back and forth in rapid bumps and grinds.

David took two steps away in order to cut off the escape route if the punter tried to run. A surprising number did leg it, leaving their cars in the hands of the police. Sketchy planning while panicking.

Sara had the hammer for the window ready when she put her hand on the handle and pulled. The car door was unlocked, so she didn't need to smash the window. Instead she yelled, "Police!"

Holmberg stopped his grinding and half-turned toward her. Then Sara caught sight of Jennifer underneath him, pushed down on her stomach, with Holmberg's hand tight around her throat and the side of her head pressed into a child's booster seat on the far side.

And she saw that it was the anus that he had been thrusting into so violently.

He was a thin-haired fifty-year-old with watery, staring eyes that didn't seem to grasp what was happening.

Sara struggled to master herself. You couldn't get emotionally affected—that might lead to a deterioration in the exercise of your duties. But she couldn't keep it together.

She pulled Holmberg out, dragged him onto the concrete floor and crashed her knee into his neck—guaranteed pain. Then David put him in handcuffs. Sara left Holmberg's trousers down while she leaned into the car to check if Jennifer was all right.

"Are you OK?"

"Yes. He was pretty violent, but I'm OK."

She pulled on her knickers and got out of the car and adjusted her clothes. She knew the drill. The police would take her witness statement and ask her to speak to a social worker, and when she declined their offer she was free to go.

"I haven't done anything," said Holmberg. "It's not illegal to have sex in a car."

"It's illegal to pay for sex."

"I haven't paid!"

Sara looked at Jennifer.

"Did he pay?"

Jennifer didn't answer. She merely pulled out three five-hundred-krona notes.

271

"I borrowed the car," said Holmberg. "From a mate. My name's Johansson."

"So it's not your car?" said Sara.

"No."

Sara bent down and checked his pockets. In the back pocket of his chinos, she found a black wallet.

"You can't touch that!" he shouted. "It's not mine! I found it!"

Sara pulled out a driver's license that belonged to one Bo Johan Holmberg, whose appearance was an identical match to the man under arrest. Sara showed the license to the man, who sighed and appeared to give up.

"Can I pull up my trousers now?" he said in irritation.

"Do you deny paying for sex?"

"No," said Holmberg. "I confess. And I want the letter sent to my PO box."

"Not your home address?" said Sara.

It bothered her quite how many people got away with it—the habituated customers knew exactly what to do so that they could carry on. The letter from the police would be sent to their place of work at their request, or, as in this case, to a PO box that had probably been procured precisely to receive this kind of letter. And then they paid their fines and they were soon back out on the streets again, ready to degrade yet another woman. Sara knew that it wasn't her job to punish—she only carried out the arrest. That was important enough.

But it bothered her.

Beyond reason.

After Holmberg's confession and acceptance of his caution and on-the-spot fine, he was released.

Yet another family man who went straight home from the red light district. Sara wondered whether he would think about Jennifer's face pressed down into the booster seat the next time he was buckling his kid into it. Probably not.

* * *

At the end of their shift, they headed back to the station to change and try to wind down. Although the passing of the years had hardened them, they were never entirely desensitized. It was impossible.

All these tragedies were far too dreadful to become routine.

A feeling of powerlessness was always threatening to take over, but they tried to follow up on the women they helped. Sara needed to remind herself that their work really did matter, and they began discussing old cases—girls who'd actually accepted help from social services or one of the women's groups that existed to assist victims of the sex trade. Sometimes they received letters from girls who'd got out of the world of prostitution—sometimes from minors, after their intervention had set them on the right track. Sara and David agreed they didn't need any gratitude, but the reminder that their work wasn't in vain was very valuable.

It could have an impact.

It could help the girls.

Sometimes, anyway. And it was enough to carry on.

"Cheers," said David, passing her a piping hot cup of coffee. Sara took it and touched it to David's cup.

"Cheers," she said, actually receiving a small smile in response.

It was weird drinking coffee in the middle of the night, but it had become their custom to round off the shift with a cup of hot coffee. It was almost a ritual—a caffeine kick to wake them up from a bad dream. At any rate, they did the same thing on this night.

Perhaps he felt they'd done something good, and that was why David had relaxed a bit. They were essentially both as committed to their jobs—they just had rather different temperaments.

"You were right," Sara began by saying, looking David in the eye. But she found it difficult to continue. She spent a long time looking for the words, and ended up being interrupted by a whirring sound.

Her mobile was vibrating in her handbag, and Sara pulled it out. Had something happened to Pål and Jenny?

No.

It was Hannah. Last name unknown.

The number was saved on her mobile, and belonged to one of the more down-and-out girls on Malmskillnadsgatan. Hannah often plied her trade in the doorways and side streets in order not to waste time having to move around. That allowed her to compensate for her poor rates through higher volume.

Sara had seen the men who bought Hannah. Fat, old, dirty, brutal and evil. The very lowest of lowlifes. She'd tried to help her, or even just sit down for a chat, but Hannah had always refused.

And now her name had appeared on the caller display. For the first time ever.

"You knew that bastard, too, didn't you?" was the first thing Hannah said. "Who was it that murdered him?"

"Who?" said Sara.

"The TV bastard. Uncle Stellan. I want to thank the person who shot him. And you should know who it was, being a pig and all."

"Why do you want to thank them?"

"Why do you think? Surely you know."

"Know what?"

"What he did," said Hannah curtly.

"Stellan?" said Sara. "How do you mean?"

"What he did to young girls. What the fuck else?"

Sara recollected that she'd once long ago talked about herself in order to try and get closer to Hannah. It had gone well until she mentioned that she'd spent her childhood at the Bromans' house. Hannah had spat on the ground and left.

"Can we meet?" said Sara.

"No. I'm working."

"I'll pay. Five hundred kronor for half an hour's chat with you."

"Five hundred? For half an hour?"

"Fifteen minutes."

"Ten. Where?"

"Golden arches on Vasagatan in fifteen minutes."

"I can do that."

"What did he do?"

Sara had started by passing over the banknote after they'd both sat down with a plastic tray of industrial fast food. The patrons around them took no notice of them whatsoever. They were all too drunk, too horny, too thirsty for blood. Fully occupied consoling themselves with trans fats, because yet another night appeared to be ending in solitude.

Hannah chewed on a few fries and looked at Sara.

"So you don't know?"

"No."

"Were you really friends with the family?"

"I was there all the time. I lived in the house next door."

"Yes, you said. But you also said you're from the hood. Which one's true?"

"We moved away from Bromma when I was thirteen. To Vällingby."

"So you're the pretty girl from the suburbs," said Hannah, giving her a wry smile. "And I'm the ugly girl from the pretty neighborhood."

"The pretty neighborhood?"

"I'm from Nockeby. Didn't I mention that? No, well, it's not something I bring up."

Sara digested Hannah's words. Nothing about her exterior divulged a background like that.

"That's how he came to fuck me over," Hannah said before falling silent.

"Explain," said Sara. "I've paid."

"Yes," said Hannah. "Fuck me, it's time someone knew. I was only thirteen years old. *Thirteen.* I met him by the square one day. I'd bought flowers, and he told me that he had lots of different flowers in his garden. And obviously I was impressed. It was bloody Uncle Stellan. He'd talked to *me*. We bumped into each other a few times and he invited me home. Said he had two daughters the same age as me. But when I got there, they weren't in. It was just him."

Hannah paused.

"Fuck, just think what would have happened if I hadn't gone there. One single, stupid decision…"

"Carry on," said Sara.

"I was a good girl. From a very proper, old-fashioned home. Didn't know shit about the world. I'd always been good at school. Bad at sport, good at Swedish and geography. You know. I wanted to be a teacher or a diplomat." She laughed. "Diplomat…Maybe I should send my application to the Ministry of Foreign Affairs…"

Sara contemplated Hannah's furrowed face, her arms covered in bruises, her mouth missing several teeth. The absent gaze of the heroin addict.

"What happened at Stellan's?"

Hannah stopped chewing and pushed the tray of food away.

"He raped me."

Raped?

Uncle Stellan?

Malin and Lotta's dad?

Sara didn't know what to think.

"He showed me his fucking garden and told me the name of every shitting flower. Hollyhock and amaryllis and fuck knows what else. Then we sat down in the sunshine and it was hot as hell, so he asked me if I wanted something to drink. But there must have been some shit in that, because I felt all groggy. He said we should go into the shade, and he led me into some shed. Then he pulled out a fucking cine camera and undressed me. I felt his disgusting hands all over my body and his fingers inside me, and then he took my clothes off and…raped me. I can still feel his skinny, white dick in my mouth, and how much it hurt when he pushed it into my cunt. I was bleeding and crying, but he didn't stop."

"And he filmed it?"

"The whole thing. With one of those fucking home camcorders. Super 8, or whatever they're called. And the thought of that film was almost the worst bit. In the early years, I was so scared the film would surface that I came close to killing myself. But when I starting smoking and drinking to numb the fear that my parents would find out, it mostly felt disgusting. For him to be there, jerking off to his own rape of a child."

"And you didn't tell anyone about it?"

"What the fuck do you think? I was ashamed. Felt disgusting. Worthless. My parents would never have believed me. Nor the cops, either."

Hannah spat a couple of chewed-up fries onto the floor.

"And afterward..." she added, "when he was done, he just got dressed and left. I was lying there, crying and throwing up. Completely bloodied. My whole fucking world ruined. *He* ruined everything. I just wanted to die. When I eventually got my clothes back on and crept out, he was on his knees in his bloody vegetable patch planting some onions. He even smiled and waved and said I should visit again. I should have taken that fucking hoe and put it through his head. Then I would at least have had a bit of self-respect left. Jesus—thirteen years old. I wasn't even old enough to be held criminally responsible. I wouldn't have gone to prison."

She paused.

"I left my new pink bike there. It hurt too much to sit on the saddle. And I didn't think I deserved it any longer after what I'd done."

"After what *he'd* done," said Sara, and Hannah gave her a quick glance. "Do you know whether he did that with anyone else?"

"No fucking way was it his first time. I can promise you that. I've been walking the streets for three decades and I've seen how horny old men behave. That was *not* his first time. What the fuck are you looking at?"

Hannah was staring at a drunk teenage brat who was grinning at her. She threw her drink at his face and he became furious, clenching his fists and getting up. When Sara flashed her police ID, he calmed down, although he sauntered away from them with the standard phrase: "Fucking cunt."

"The worst of it came afterward," said Hannah, the food making her burp. "One day the old bastard called my parents at home and asked for me. Asked whether I wanted to come to a party. I was terrified he would tell my parents about what had happened, so I did as he said. I went there, had a glass of wine even though I was only fourteen or something, and then he put me on the sofa next to some other old creep who was constantly grinning and topping up my glass. Once I was drunk, he led me upstairs to some room and raped me. I cried and said no, but that didn't make any difference. And when he left, he put three hundred kronor on the bed. I took the money and put it in a box at home. I felt so fucking sick every time I saw that box. Then one day I took the cash and went into town, clothes shopping. I got appreciation for my new clothes the next day at school, and then it felt a bit better. When I was beautiful on the outside, I could forget how dirty I felt on the inside. The next time the bastard called, I just thought about all the stuff I'd buy if I got more money. So I went there. To another disgusting bloke. And then again. And again. I was already worthless, so I didn't think it mattered. But do you know the worst thing?"

"No."

"I had friends who wondered where I'd got all the cash from. So I took them to him. Two or three girls who also got raped and broken. I ruined their lives. And all they wanted was to buy some nice clothes."

34

Sara hadn't been able to sleep. Martin had been snoring, but that didn't usually prevent her from dropping off. Unlike everyone else she knew, she thought snoring sounded quite homely, and she actually found it easier to sleep when she could hear her husband driving the pigs to market. Between the snores it was deathly quiet. The size of the apartment meant that the noise from the pubs down on Kornhamnstorg didn't find its way up to their bedroom.

Sara had been lying there, staring at the ceiling—a coffered ceiling in dark wood, one of the many stylish details that Martin was so uninterested in, despite having paid so much money for the flat. She'd taken the chance to enjoy having the whole family together, and realized that she had no idea how many more nights of this she would have. And she'd been sorry that she'd not had enough sense to appreciate these occasions sufficiently until now.

But above all, it had been what Hannah had told her that had been running through her head. It had been hard to take in, but Sara had felt it would be disrespectful toward Hannah to simply dismiss it. Was there any way of checking whether it was true?

Sara had been tossing and turning, wide awake, for a couple of hours, thinking it over before she got up. She realized she had to know—if only for her own sake.

So now she was back at the house. The fairytale palace of her childhood. Which was now a crime scene where she wasn't supposed to be.

She looked around, but no one was out and about this early. She still ducked slightly when she walked past C.M.'s house, which was closest to the road—the house they'd called "the factory" when they were little because of the strange name on his expensive Fabbri gun. It was funny that those kinds of oddities were still stuck in her head. It was obvious that it was impossible to choose what you remembered.

She went round to the back of the Bromans' house and retrieved the spare key from the usual spot before unlocking the door and going inside.

The house felt so different now. It had gone from lost paradise to crime scene, and now it was some sort of ghost house, with a secret hanging over it. A house of horror.

Stellan Broman had filmed his own rape of a young girl. If Hannah's story was true, Sara didn't think that Stellan would have got rid of that film.

And she'd worked in street prostitution for long enough to be convinced that the story was true.

She'd also been involved in enough raids of sex criminals and people in possession of child pornography to know that that kind of person never got rid of their collection. It became a fixation of sorts. They might have tens of thousands of videos and pictures— far more than they could ever look through—but they still always wanted more. It was almost manic.

As if they were the final liters of water on the planet.

But where had he hidden the film?

Sara had already searched the house and watched all the films she'd found. Generally speaking, a common method was to put a different label on the film—something dull like "lecture on Sarek national park" or "caravan holiday"—and hide it openly among other films.

But Stellan must have hidden it somewhere else.

She started from the top.

The attic was full of old furniture and boxes filled with Christmas decorations, Easter decorations, summer gear and the sisters' outgrown clothes. At the top of one box was the Wham! top that Malin had been wearing one of those times she'd said that Sara couldn't come to their house anymore because their real friends had returned. A Monday in late August, when the schools had just gone back.

As if she hadn't already known. The same scenario at the end of each summer.

Sara noticed that Agneta had also begun to save things belonging to her grandchildren. Box after box of old baby clothes, milk bottles, cuddly toys, bibs. Mini Rodini, Elodie Details and even Gucci. All neatly folded and labeled. There was even a printed photo of each grandchild as a baby affixed to their respective box.

But no films.

In the garage, there were oil cans, cleaning fluids and spray paint canisters lining the shelves. Winter tires for the car were neatly wrapped in plastic and stacked on top of one other. There were tools and a couple of old booster seats for the kids. No secret compartments, no films.

In the basement was the boiler room with its stench of oil, the laundry room, the stuffy rec room and a guest room that smelled of mold. And a small, dark larder.

She went through the rooms meter by meter. None of them seemed to contain any secret hiding place. Eventually, she flopped into the armchair in the rec room and checked the time on her mobile.

It had taken almost three hours.

And she had nothing to show for it.

She had to think this through. Everything was based on Hannah having told the truth. Sara had decided she was going to believe her. Otherwise there was nothing to search for.

The fact that she hadn't found anything wasn't all that strange in itself. If Stellan had filmed a rape, then it was highly likely that he'd hidden the recording well. A roll of film didn't take up much room. Not even one from an old Super 8 camera.

She had to go through the house again to search for secret compartments. She would have to open any kind of packaging that was big enough. Which room would Stellan have chosen to hide his treasure?

The garden shed? That was where the attack had happened.

No, he probably would have wanted it in the house, Sara thought to herself. She felt that that would have ensured greater control over it.

Not the kitchen. Not the living room. It could definitely have been the attic or the basement—but she'd already searched those.

She looked around.

Why not the rec room?

The projector was here, after all. He could be guaranteed privacy here.

Sara remembered how Stellan had needed to be left in peace for hours on end while he worked when she and the sisters were little.

And those hours had been spent in the rec room.

If he'd watched the film here, then it would probably have been easiest to keep it in the same place...

Sara looked around. She got up and tapped on the walls yet again, listening carefully for any echoing hollows. Then she moved the furniture, looked under the rugs and felt all over the stuffing of the armchairs and sofa with her hands.

It had to be here somewhere.

But where?

Inside the light?

Wouldn't fit.

Inside the stereo?

Wait.

The TV.

The old-style TV. The broken one.

A roll of film would definitely fit inside that. Several of them, in fact. And why else would it have been left here for all these years?

Sara had thought Stellan had kept it as some sort of memento of his golden era. But she no longer thought that.

With a slightly more adult perspective, why would Stellan have left an old TV rusting away there, year after year? Everything else in the house was carefully thought through and chosen. Why not just get rid of it?

Because it had value.

Contents.

Sara went into the garage and fetched all the screwdrivers she could find. Then she carefully removed the back panel from the set.

And there they were.

Not just one film.

There were several.

She took out the top case and read. "Madeleine—1." Then she got out the projector, raised the screen and rigged the roll of film into the equipment.

She realized she was nervous. Worried about what she would see. But she had to see it. She dimmed the lights and started the film.

The picture flickered and shook, and the colors were faded with age. Stellan was filming with the camera in his hand, and some of the shaking was possibly the result of his own excitement. The scene was the garden shed to the rear of the house, and he was documenting the body of a young woman.

Rather, it was a girl's body.

No more than fourteen or fifteen, Sara thought to herself.

A thin summer dress had been pulled up to her chin, so that the girl was left wearing only knickers and a bra. The camera slowly panned across her body. A man's hand appeared in shot and disappeared behind her back. Stellan's hand, with that wide gold wedding ring. Soon, the bra fell to the floor and Stellan zoomed in on a pair of young breasts. His hand stroked them, squeezed them and fingered them in an almost clinical way that turned Sara's stomach. For a brief moment, the camera drifted up toward the face of the girl and revealed a pair of distant but terrified eyes.

Then Stellan lowered the lens toward her hips, and Sara saw that he'd pulled her knickers down below her buttocks. He slowly pried the garment down to uncover her crotch. When his hand separated the girl's legs in order to get to her sex, Sara had to turn away. After everything she'd seen as part of the prostitution task force, all the disgusting men with disturbed sexualities who used women's bodies like slabs of meat, she'd thought she was immune.

But she wasn't able to cope with seeing this.

Such a young girl.

And the ice-cold, almost inhuman evaluation of the young body. She tried to look again, but she felt physically sick. She was on the verge of throwing up.

She was both surprised and relieved by the strong reaction. At least it meant she hadn't been desensitized.

Poor girl.

Girls.

Hannah had been convinced that others had been affected.

And there were a lot of rolls of film.

Now Sara understood why Stellan had placed sheets of plywood in front of the windows in the shed, and why he didn't want the sisters and Sara to be able to see inside. Why their spy games had met with such an abrupt end.

She glanced at the projector screen again, and saw the thrusting so typical of porn films and then the finish. This time onto a young, clearly unwilling body. Probably completely sexually inexperienced. The last thing visible in shot was Stellan's hand grasping a colorful towel and wiping the semen off her stomach.

Then the reaction. Sara vomited. Straight onto the rug in the rec room.

Repulsive bastard.

Bloody swine.

Her eye swept over the cases of rolls of film inside the hidden compartment.

How many people's lives had he ruined in this way?

Young girls who had probably never dared to report him. Not an adult, not someone so well known and respected.

Had they turned the hatred on themselves?

Had some of them thought that this was what it was like? Welcome to the adult world. Your body is no longer your own.

The silence had made all of this possible, Sara thought to herself.

When had this happened? During the hours when everyone thought Stellan was busy with his plants and flowers? Was that interest just a front? Was that why he'd hired a gardener? To conceal the fact that the only thing Stellan Broman did in his garden was rape young girls?

Sara went to fetch a mop and bucket and wiped up the sick. Not out of consideration to Stellan and his rec room, but because the stench was awful and she needed to stay there for a bit longer.

Then she went through a few more films, but she couldn't cope with more. She just watched the beginning of each one. Some girls seemed drunk, others terrified; the odd one seemed defiant. But even those ones had a completely different look in their eyes later. Empty, resigned, devastated.

He seemed to have been at it for years. Some girls reappeared, but this time they were markedly older.

In later films, Stellan had begun to make a habit out of documenting their faces in detail first. Perhaps it had given him a bigger kick when even that part of their bodies was his property—the object of his desires. He always did the same thing. Grabbed hold of the girls' chins and turned their heads back and forth for the camera. As if inspecting an animal at a livestock auction. Some of the girls looked up at him uncertainly, but most of them looked down. None of them looked into the camera.

A couple of the faces were ones Sara recognized—from school. She took photos of the projector screen with her mobile in order to look them up, if possible. But she wasn't up to watching everything in the hideaway. And perhaps she didn't need to, either.

Other films there had labels with men's names on them. And the containers were more worn—as if they had been subjected to damp. But the rolls of film appeared to be intact. So when Sara had had enough, she threaded one of the men's rolls into the projector.

Had Stellan done the same thing with young boys?

He hadn't, it transpired when the film finally flickered into life. This time, the scene wasn't the garden shed, but was instead the guest room in the house.

The room where Sara herself had slept on the odd occasion. Had Stellan filmed his attacks in there as well? She was on the verge of vomiting again.

But it wasn't Stellan who was visible in shot, but a range of men. They were largely middle-aged or older. And the camera wasn't shaky and handheld any longer but fixed—as if it were on a tripod. A full picture taken from a slightly greater distance.

But the girls seemed the same. Although now they weren't as passive. They seemed more indifferent and were more conspicuously inebriated. Sometimes almost senseless.

The men were in control in these films, too—they appeared to be giving the girls instructions to turn in different directions, to look turned on and eager, to do degrading things.

Film after film of Stellan's young girls together with grown men. Old men, sometimes. Sara took pictures of them with her mobile.

On the fifth roll of men there was a familiar face. Not from school, as had been the case with a couple of the girls, but from TV. He'd been a member of the government, or so she remembered. A fairly important minister. And now Sara was watching him have sex with a young girl. He was really het up as well, because after just a couple of minutes he was done. And when he'd dressed again, he took out his wallet and left a fifty-krona note on the pillow next to the immobile girl. Then he left.

A government minister.

Sara had to keep going, to see whether there were other high-ups who'd been recorded. She threaded roll upon roll of film, watched the beginning of each and took photos with her mobile of the men, noting the names on the labels.

Two more perpetrators were immediately recognizable to her.

First there was Thorvald Tegnér, the minister of justice. The old man she'd struck down in the brothel in Solna, but who hadn't reported her. And then a former prime minister. Who was clearly partial to very young girls. Judging by his reasonably young appearance, the film had been recorded before he took office—perhaps even before he had become leader of the party. But that was probably how Stellan had operated. He'd arranged to have a hold on as many people as possible moving in the right circles. You never knew where people would end up. Sara assumed that Stellan and his handler had made good use of that particular sequence.

She sat there for a long time, looking at the image of the former prime minister. He'd been married—Sara knew that. He'd had a somewhat father-of-the-nation style about him. How did someone like him manage to divide himself into two such different halves? Then it struck her that there was something off about the picture. A black edge was visible in the right-hand corner. She checked the other recorded encounters. The same thing. Sometimes the edge was a little wider, sometimes a little thinner. But it was there in almost every shot.

As usual, she couldn't stop when there was something she didn't understand. She left the rec room and went up to the guest room on the second floor. When she stepped into the room and encountered the very bed that she'd seen used for so many rapes, her head swam. She felt her knees tremble and she thought she was going to fall over. But instead she looked around the room and pulled out her mobile to compare.

The films had been recorded from an upward diagonal angle with a camera that must have been fitted into the wall.

Or behind it.

Sara pulled out a chair and scrutinized the wall with its medallion wallpaper. There—in the middle of the medallions—there was a hole. Just a few centimeters across. She stuck her finger in and felt around. Nothing. She tapped on the wall and then went to check outside. A few meters farther down the landing was the door to Stellan and Agneta's bedroom. Sara went in there and looked at the smooth wall adjoining the guest room. There was a built-in wardrobe at either end.

But the room didn't look as deep as it should. Sara paced out the distance between the doors out on the landing, carefully placing her feet heel-to-toe as she walked. Twenty-three steps. Then she measured the distance from the door to the wall of the guest room. Five steps. And then she compared it with the distance in the bedroom. Twelve steps.

There were six steps missing.

She went to the bedroom wall and tapped on it. It didn't sound like a very thick wall. Then she opened the right-hand wardrobe. Agneta's clothes.

The left-hand wardrobe was Stellan's.

Sara pulled all the clothes out and examined the wardrobe. Before long, she noticed that one wall could be pushed aside. When she peered behind the panel, she discovered a small space where a person would just have fitted at a pinch. Or a camera tripod. And just below the ceiling there was a hole in the wall through to the guest room.

The dark edge in the films was quite simply the part of the wall visible if the camera hadn't been placed sufficiently close to the hole. Stellan had stood here and rolled the camera while his guests had had sex with very young girls. So that he could extort them. On behalf of a foreign power.

He'd clearly exploited the girls himself first, and then got them to have sex with others and filmed that, too.

Perhaps he wanted to break them mentally to make them obedient tools. Perhaps he got off on breaking them down.

Was that how he conducted his espionage? By offering influential rich men sex with young girls, he acquired power over them?

Disgusting Stellan. Stellan the swine.

Other than the fact that what she'd seen had made her question her entire childhood—all the hours spent in the magical white palace—Sara realized that there might well have been another reason for Stellan's murder.

Revenge.

Every one of the girls who'd been filmed had cause for revenge. As well as their loved ones.

She needed help identifying the men, but some of the girls she would be able to find by herself. She retrieved the sisters' yearbooks from high school. She looked through the photos she'd taken of the attacks, and leafed back and forth between different classes.

She got three hits.

Camilla Skagerborg, Carin Larsbo and Maria Jonsson.

Three ordinary high school girls. In their class photos, they looked happy. Then Sara looked them up in the yearbooks from sixth form.

Only Carin was still there.

She didn't look happy. Anorexic, bags under her eyes and a gaze that almost seemed to be asking for forgiveness as it looked into the camera.

When Sara was done, she went down to the rec room and packed everything up again. It still smelled of vomit. That seemed fitting for the room, she thought to herself.

She checked that everything looked normal before she left.

Now she, too, had done the cleaning at the Bromans' house, just like her mother. But she had at least been cleaning up her own mess.

35

The postwar outer Stockholm suburb of Vällingby: an ABC town. At the time of its inception, it had been a proud symbol of modern, progressive Sweden. In Sara's eyes it was primarily a monument to lost happiness.

ABC stood for Arbete, Bostad, Centrum—jobs, homes and a town center. It had everything, so they claimed. The buildings were modern, unlike the cramped conditions and low standards found in the clamorous inner city. When Vällingby was completed in the 1950s, the pride of the politicians, architects and developers involved had been boundless. This was how the Swedes were going to live from now on. A young, newly married Olof Palme moved to the area with his wife Lisbeth. This was the future—the optimistic, successful, efficient Sweden the country was to become.

Later on, Vällingby largely came to be associated with crime and high turnover of tenants, before simply becoming a suburb like all the others in the midst of the current housing shortage—the only marker of note being its far-flung location, away from the city center.

Moving farther out of the city was, in Sara's eyes, failure. A capitulation that she'd transformed into victory when she'd made it out of Vällingby and into Stockholm's old town. Her mother, however, had said goodbye to Bromma and settled in Vällingby for good. And she'd categorically rejected all offers of help in making up the deposit for a flat that was closer to town. Why did Sara want to force her out of her own home? Jane would ask each time it came up.

So this was where she still lived after thirty years—in a tall tower block with white and beige facades. The same building where Sara had spent the darkest years of her life.

She recalled the feeling of having been dragged away from the party, having missed the train that was thundering away into the future with all her old friends on board. The impossible task of finding herself in a grim suburb during her sensitive teenage years, when everyone at school was brimming with hormones—a rootless maelstrom of emotions following a lonely summer.

Jane had dragged Sara away just before the summer holidays, which had made the separation even more traumatic. She'd spent the whole winter longing for the summer, when she would finally get the sisters back to herself again. She had been about to open the door to paradise when Jane had pulled her down into hellfire.

The doorbell sounded like it always had done—but inside the flat her mother had changed things around, as she often did. The fact that her home was in a state of constant change was the only consistent thing about it. Right now, the hallway was painted a pale shade of yellowish green, with framed typefaces and black-and-white newspaper headlines on the wall—framed prints Sara assumed had been on sale in some framer's. A gray pouf was positioned under the coat rack, and at least half of the shoes there had evidently been acquired since the last time Sara had visited. Granted, it had been a few years, she realized now.

Jane came and met her in the hall. She was just as well dressed as ever. Sara had never seen her in comfy trousers at home. Shirt, blouse, gold bracelet and a small watch on a chain around her neck. She had a new haircut again—this time it was cut short, and her hair was carefully sprayed with her fringe combed back.

Sara followed Jane into the kitchen. No matter how proud she was of her smart living room, her mother preferred to spend time at the kitchen table. She poured her daughter a cup of coffee and leaned back against the kitchen counter, just like usual. Sara didn't sit down this time, but remained standing. She looked at her mother for a while before speaking.

"I've seen films," she said. "Of Stellan." Jane blinked and Sara guessed that her mother knew where she was going with this. "In which he's raping young girls."

Jane didn't say anything.

"Girls that were at school with us—me and Malin and Lotta. Young. Some of them were minors."

"Yes."

"And he got away with it. He's never been reported?"

"No."

"Didn't anyone notice anything?"

"Some probably suspected."

"But did nothing?"

Jane shook her head.

"*You* didn't do anything," said Sara.

"Stellan and Agneta took me in when I fled. When I arrived with you in my belly, I was so young. And completely alone. I couldn't go to the police. Who would they have believed? Sweden's uncle, or a Polish refugee?"

"But someone else could have reported him. You could have asked someone else to go."

"I was afraid I'd be deported. He knew lots of powerful people."

"Did you know that he filmed it? You could have taken one of the films and handed it in. You cleaned up—you knew where everything was."

"Now you're talking like a police officer. I want to talk to a daughter."

"What do you mean by that? You mean that I should have some sort of understanding for what he did?"

"No. But for what it was like for the rest of us."

"You mean the ones who kept quiet and let it carry on?"

"I didn't know for sure. I could only hope it wasn't as bad as I thought it was."

"It was worse. Much worse. You should be grateful it didn't happen to you."

Sara looked at her mother, who averted her gaze. And at that moment, the insight hit her like a furious tsunami.

She stared at Jane.

"He took you, too," she said. "He used you."

Jane looked Sara in the eye, as if trying to calm and placate her daughter.

"Only in the beginning. Then I got too old."

"In the beginning? When I was an infant? Did he rape you when you'd had me?"

"The important thing was to protect you."

"Protect me? By letting me grow up with him?"

She was being tossed between feelings of boundless anger and helpless sympathy.

Which was worse—what had happened to Jane, or what could have happened to Sara? Or that Jane had let him do that to her?

But now Sara realized that was thinking like the enemy—blaming the victim. Just because Jane was allowed to live with him didn't give him any right to her body.

"As soon as he looked at you in that way, I left and took you with me," she said.

"What?"

It was as if the words weren't getting through. She could only stare at her mother. She was able to touch her hand, but that meant nothing compared with everything she wanted to say, all the questions she wanted to ask.

"Was that why we moved?"

"I could see it in his eyes. One day you were no longer a child. Not to him. You'd just turned thirteen and I saw the way he was looking at you. You had no idea. Couldn't have known. But when he invited you into that shed, I knew that you were no longer safe. I wouldn't be able to protect you if we stayed there. We had to leave."

"So that's why it happened so suddenly?"

"We moved right away. It was easier to find a flat back then. I called social services and said my boyfriend had thrown me out and that I was on my own with a teenage daughter. We got this flat the same day."

"Is that why you've never wanted to move?"

"Apart from you, this flat is the most beautiful thing I've ever had. It saved our lives. Just think—it used to be possible to get a flat that quickly then, even if you were a single parent and unemployed."

Sara was ashamed. For all the years of anger at her mother. For the way she'd punished her with silence and distance. She struggled to summon the words, but realized that she had to confess. Here and now.

"I've always thought you were jealous of Stellan and Agneta," she said, looking her mother in the eye. "And that was why you were so short with them."

Jane didn't seem surprised, which Sara found heartbreaking.

"A wolf can only bite you if it's allowed to come close to you," said Jane.

Sara pulled out a kitchen chair and sat down. She didn't know where to look.

Life could change so quickly. An unexpected death, overwhelming information, new insights. The big trauma in Sara's life—the move from Bromma—was now suddenly her salvation. The idol she'd missed was a beast who had come close to consuming her too.

"But what did it feel like for me to be round there so much?"

"What could I do? They had so much that I couldn't offer."

"But I'm your daughter. Didn't you want me to mostly be with you?"

"Is that how you feel with your own children?"

Sara didn't know how to answer. She had clearly never understood her mother, and never tried to understand her.

"Children do as they please," said Jane. "Trying to force love simply kills it."

"But surely you've always known that I love you?"

"That doesn't really matter. The important thing is that a mother loves her children."

36

An echoing stairwell and pale blue doors, most of them with burglar alarm stickers.

Sara approached the door with the sign "A & J Holmberg" on it, cracked the letterbox and got out the letter that bastard Holmberg had asked them to send to his PO box.

Sara had made sure not to seal it so that it would be easy for his wife to open it. Judging by their profiles on LinkedIn, she appeared to work from home sometimes. Hopefully today was just such a day.

Sara leaned forward and listened at the open letterbox. Yes, it sounded like someone was inside, typing at a keyboard. She pushed the letter through, let it go and left.

Now she felt a little better. When she emerged onto the street, the air was slightly easier to breathe.

It was too late to put Stellan away, but at least she could do something, she thought to herself as she headed for the car. By delivering the letter. She wanted to do this with every man they caught in future. All these men who thought they could just pay their fines and carry on like before.

Nothing was like before.

That feeling was very strong in Sara.

Just as she got into the car her mobile rang.

"Nowak."

"Hello—it's Mazzella. At City. I don't know whether you remember, but we were seated next to each other at the Christmas dinner a few years ago."

"Of course I remember."

Not.

"I've got a question for you, if you don't mind."

"Go ahead."

"Someone called Mia Hansson has reported a break-in."

"OK."

Mia Hansson, alias Nikki X. This was not good.

"Since nothing was stolen, I'm going to close the file, but I thought I recognized the woman in the photos."

"Photos?"

"Yes. You see, this Hansson has CCTV in her home."

Fuck. Shit. Hell.

"I'm looking at the pictures now and the burglar looks just like you, Nowak. Very strange. Do you have any explanation? Do you know if you have a doppelgänger?"

"No, I don't have a doppelgänger. It's me."

"Oh?"

Mazzella tried to sound surprised, but he was a bad actor.

"I was there. But I didn't break in. It wasn't locked. I rang the bell and then I saw the door was ajar, and since this Mia has been threatened, I was worried that something had happened to her. So I went inside. But there was no one there, so I left again. She sells sex, as you know. And she has some pretty unpleasant customers."

"I can well imagine. So she had been threatened?"

"Yes."

"By whom?"

"Some dodgy customer."

"And she reported it."

"No, I heard it from a girl on the street. They usually keep an eye on each other."

"So the door was open and you went in because this Mia had been the subject of threats?"

"Yes."

"And you'll have written a report on this?"

"No, not yet."

"If there's a threat against her, then we need to take it seriously. What if something happens to her?"

"You're right. I'll deal with it."

"Good. And Nowak…"

"Yes?"

"That means you think I can close this file?"

"Yes, definitely. And it might be best if Mia Hansson doesn't find out that it was me. She might not understand, and we need the girls' trust."

"Yes, I can imagine. Well, see you at the next Christmas dinner."

"Yes, definitely."

And then they ended the call.

CCTV.

Fuck.

Just as long as he hadn't told Lindblad. She would love this. The anxiety in Sara's gut didn't dissipate when she received an urgent text from Martin.

Where the hell are you? They're about to come out of the school building!

37

The thronging crowd, the pent-up expectations, the joy.

The feeling of community: we're here together.

The asphalt outside Norra Real school was packed like a Tokyo subway train. Everyone was staring up at the steps and the large pair of doors. They were carrying placards with pictures of the graduating students, and balloons, their own yellowing peaked graduation caps and bottles of sparkling wine. The school council had hired a DJ with a massive sound system playing the kids' selections as each class emerged.

There were so many people. Why were they so happy? Sara couldn't make head nor tail of it. Sixth-form graduation just meant that this part of life was over. Was that something worth celebrating?

People everywhere, heat and smells. Too much perfume on some, bad breath on others, the stench of sweat from many. Cigarette smoke. The pong of mouths filled with chewing tobacco. Someone had farted covertly. Humankind was certainly not pretty when it came together in a flock.

Sara was physically present, but her thoughts were completely occupied by Stellan, Holmberg and Nikki X. She realized that she had to pull herself together. She'd almost missed her daughter's big day, and suspected that Ebba was practically expecting her not to show up. After all these years of work and commitment to others, Sara was worried that Ebba didn't expect her to prioritize her own daughter. And following their thawing in relations at Caffè Nero the day before, she really didn't want to lose what she'd gained.

She'd managed to sort out a bloody placard, at any rate. Despite the stress. There were plenty of small businesses that made placards for graduation while you waited, and Sara had long ago picked a photo of Ebba as a baby and saved it on her mobile. All she'd had to do was email the place with the picture and caption. They sold balloons at extortionate rates, too. Sara had got the impression she wasn't the only one cutting it fine.

So here they were, waiting for their daughter, who was going to tumble out of school and childhood. Running toward her parents when she was actually leaving them. For her, life began now.

What kind of world awaited her?

Sara felt as if it was her responsibility to fix everything that was wrong. To make Ebba's journey easier than her own. She was proud of how much better a life she'd already been able to give her. At the same time, Sara couldn't help but be slightly envious of her daughter. There was so much she wouldn't have to do. And she couldn't help feeling that both her kids were rather ungrateful. They had no idea how good they had it.

On the other hand, young girls were much more vulnerable nowadays. They weren't just dealing with hormone-filled lads at school and horny old men out on the town. Now those men were online too—in a much more aggressive form.

The cloud of anxiety quickly cleared when it was finally time.

Ebba's class emerged onto the steps to the strains of Queen's "We Are the Champions." They were shouting and hooting, raising fists, thrusting their arms up into the air and taking a few dance steps. All the boys were in suits and the girls in white. There was applause and cries of hurrah from the waiting families. Then the class ran into the crowd and sought out their parents and siblings.

For the first time in several years, Ebba looked happy when she caught sight of her parents. Sara hoped that feeling would linger on somewhere in her daughter in future, too.

Ebba hugged and kissed her mother, father and little brother, then she let out a shriek of joy and ran into the street to the waiting student trucks parked up by Jarlaplan.

Sara stayed where she was and watched her daughter go, while keeping her arms around Olle, whom she would get to keep for a little longer.

Her mobile rang. Number withheld, but she picked up anyway.

"Sara."

"Hello, Åsa-Maria here. Lindblad."

Jesus Christ...And on Ebba's last day of school.

"Yes?"

"How are things?"

"Good."

"You sound upset?"

"No, no."

"OK, good."

"What did you want?"

"First, I just want to say that you're doing a fantastic job."

Sara didn't reply.

"Really," Lindblad continued. "You're an incredibly competent police officer doing a tremendous job. I don't know how many times I've showered you with praise when speaking to our chiefs and colleagues."

"But?"

"There's no 'but.' You're talented. You can keep that."

"Did you just call to say that?"

"Isn't that enough? Do you want more?"

"Just get to the point."

Martin signaled to Sara that he and Olle wanted to leave. Sara gestured at him dismissively. She needed to hear what this cow Lindblad wanted.

"Despite my praise, despite all the good things I've said about you, you do this."

"Do what?"

"What do you think? Break-ins that get you reported."

"That was no break-in. The door was open."

"I refused to believe it when I heard it. Not my Sara, I said. Never. But now that I've seen the CCTV footage...I feel so desperately sad. *You* are making me sad."

"Sad? Why?"

Sara flung her arm out and struck a couple of proud parents in mid-flow.

"Because you've put me in a tight corner. I've always defended you, no matter what you've done and how you've conducted yourself. And now that you've done this, I'm in a very tight spot."

"How the hell is that?"

"A police officer breaking the law is something that affects us all."

"I didn't *break* the law."

"Mazzella stared at me as if he couldn't understand how I didn't know what my team were up to. I couldn't defend what you did. And it felt awful."

Martin got bored and began to walk. Sara was a few paces behind him with her mobile glued to her ear.

"I've spoken to Mazzella," said Sara. "It's OK."

"You can't talk to Mazzella!"

"Why not? It was me in the pictures and he was the one who got them."

"It has to go through me."

"Why?"

"We're on the same team, Sara!"

"Same team?"

"Yes. You can be difficult sometimes, but I really like you. And then you do this. I'm so devastated. Deeply hurt. And since I've always taken your side, I'm also tarnished by your lack of judgment."

"So screw them. What does it matter?"

"A report like this is the last thing we need."

"She doesn't know that it was a police officer."

"But we know. People are incredibly worked up about you, Sara. The high-ups at the top. The public view of the police is incredibly important—you know that. Lots of people are angry right now. But I've found a solution."

"Good," said Sara, knowing that whatever Lindblad said, it would be the opposite of good.

"I can get them to calm down if you show some goodwill. Show that you know you've made an error."

"How so?"

"You'll have to resign. This is terrible. Such a shame that you've got yourself into this mess, but I'm glad I managed to find a solution."

"Solution?"

"Yes."

"There's not a problem."

"Listen to you. Not a problem? Breaking into someone's home and being caught on CCTV?"

"I told you, the door was unlocked. And there have been threats toward her. She's an escort. A prostitute. Those are the people we're meant to be helping."

"I can't look the other way," said Lindblad. "It would be gross negligence. I might get the sack."

"Of course you wouldn't. This will blow over. It's already been forgotten."

"Sorry, Sara. This is too serious."

"So I have to resign?"

"It's the only solution."

"And then you'll stay quiet?"

"I should be able to keep it quiet then, yes."

"And all the higher-ups will know, too?"

"If you do as we've discussed and show some goodwill, then yes."

"So you *can* look the other way? Both you and the angry chiefs? But only if I do what you want me to?"

"We just want to help you."

"Then you'll have to look the other way anyway. I'm not resigning."

38

The reception had gone well and Ebba had been happy. She'd been given some very expensive gifts by her paternal grandparents.

In addition to the new mobile phone and Cartier jewelry, Martin's father had also given her the keys to her own car—a VW Beetle Cabriolet in a metallic chocolate-brown shade. Ebba had shrieked and thrown herself around her grandfather's neck, then also given her grandmother a quick, dutiful hug.

A brand-new car was much too extravagant as a gift in Sara's eyes, and she couldn't help thinking about the paperback of Swedish poetry that she'd received from Jane on her own graduation day. That had been what her mother was able to afford, but the present had been chosen with care and love. Jane didn't read much, but she loved the poems of Tomas Tranströmer. Not that Sara doubted her parents-in-laws' good intentions, but she questioned the affordability. And wondered where Ebba would park the new car. She envisioned stacks of parking tickets that Martin would obligingly pay off.

After receiving the keys, Ebba crept off and changed the seating plan for the evening so that Grandpa Eric and Grandma Marie could join the top table, while Love and Mia from her class were consigned to a corner table farther back.

It was apparently very easy to buy love.

Sara looked for her mother in the hubbub in the big apartment. Relatives, friends, neighbors and Martin's colleagues all swept past her. Some old business acquaintances of Eric's had also made it—tanned and white-haired with self-assured smiles. Sara almost never saw her mother smile.

Jane was standing by herself with a wrapped gift in her hand.

"Is that for Ebba?" said Sara.

"She doesn't want it," said Jane.

"What?" Sara was angry immediately. "Did she say that?"

"No, but after being given her own car, this is a joke. Better to give nothing at all."

"Of course she wants it. You're her grandma."

Sara looked at her mother's parcel. Rectangular and hard.

"Do you know what?" she said. "She'll get much more use out of a book than a car. Give it to her."

Jane looked around the heaving apartment with an impenetrable expression. She didn't seem convinced of the value of her present.

Sara knew that Jane's mother had re-tailored her own bridal gown into a dress for her daughter when she'd graduated. To make sure she looked beautiful. Attractive. A book was much better. And longer lived. Sara could still quote lots of poems from her own collection.

"Wait here," she said, going over to the bookcase.

She searched for a while and then pulled out *Swedish Poetry*, a thick, dark blue paperback that was falling to pieces with age and wear. Then she returned to Jane and showed her the book.

"Look how it's almost been read to pieces. And I've still got it thirty years later."

Jane glanced at the poetry volume and met Sara's gaze, thinking for a second.

Then she went and placed her present on the gift table.

Sara looked at her daughter, who was the center of attention, surrounded by smiling people. She went to her and said, "Go and give your grandmother a hug."

And Ebba did, without really knowing what the hug meant.

Sara caught up with her daughter as she was heading back to her friends and whispered in her ear:

"Thank you."

Ebba stopped and looked at her mother.

"For what?"

"For thanking your grandmother. One fine day you'll realize that her present was the best one."

"One fine day? Why do you always talk about the future with me? I'm alive right now."

"Time passes quickly. If you only live in the now, then life might get away from you."

"Yes. Or you forget to live."

"I didn't meant to ruin your evening. I'm just... You'll understand when you have your own children."

"Perhaps. If I have children. But can't I forget about that tonight and just celebrate graduation?"

"Yes, of course."

Sara smiled at her daughter and patted her cheek, hoping that she wouldn't think her mother was ridiculous for doing so. Ebba made to turn away and leave, but then she stopped.

"Mum."

"Yes."

"Look at me."

And Sara looked at Ebba—in her glittering silver dress, her peaked student cap on her head and wearing two-inch heels. Her eyes were radiant.

"Am I beautiful?"

"Yes, very beautiful."

"Am I a good person?"

"What?" Sara was surprised by the question. "Of course you are. A really good person."

"In what way?"

"You're wise, kind, smart, ambitious, beautiful, stubborn. Bloody stubborn. And funny... You're good in all ways!"

"Thank you for that. That's to your and Dad's credit. You did that."

Ebba did a twirl in front of her mother to show the result of her parents' efforts. Then she smiled and ran over to Carro. She hugged her friend, and then they rang a bell to make themselves heard and they began to merrily herd the guests into their seats.

As she stood there looking at a happy Ebba, the center of everyone's attention, Sara was able to forgive her husband for spoiling their daughter.

The party that evening was a success, and Sara was grateful that she'd had the sense to book the day off work.

Martin and Carro's father were paying for the party, and had really beefed up the budget. They had hired the Swedenborg Hall at the van der Nootska Palace. Crystal chandeliers, tapestries and gilded wood paneling. Servers dressed smartly in black and white. All attendees in dinner jackets and cocktail dresses. All far too young to pull off the formal dress code, but endearingly proud of themselves. Speeches and songs in honor of Ebba and Carro.

There was a speech by Eric that was far too long, in which he completely and solely focused on Ebba's shining future in Swedish business life. And he concluded by raising a toast on behalf of both himself and his wife. Grandma Marie smiled and raised her glass.

The invitation had promised an open bar, and perhaps that was why the parents had to leave after dinner.

Martin insisted on paying for a taxi for Jane. They stepped out onto Hornsgatan and he hailed a cab, agreed a set price with the driver and paid in advance. But when Sara and Martin had said goodbye and turned to leave, Sara saw Jane jump out of the taxi and head for the metro.

"Why don't we get a glass of wine?" said Martin.

They stopped at the outdoor seating by the Hilton, where he selected the most expensive wine available by the glass—a habit of his. Sara didn't care.

"Did you know about the car?" she said, and it took a second for Martin to cotton on.

"No," he said, but he sounded more impressed than bothered. "What a present."

"Shouldn't he have asked us first?"

"It's his money. I suppose he can do what he likes with it."

Martin had never questioned or contradicted his father.

"I don't want her to think that life's like this," said Sara. "That everyone gets cars and luxury parties when they graduate. Very few people have this."

"Don't you think it's good that our kids have it? With the world in the state it's in, it's a bloody relief that we can give our children a secure upbringing and the best possible start in life."

"I think that leaves them very poorly equipped for life. If they're used to everything being served up to them."

"Not tonight, darling," Martin said, smiling. "Our daughter has graduated."

Then he leaned forward and kissed Sara.

"Our daughter," he said, looking Sara in the eye.

They finished their wine, then strolled past the eternal building site at Slussen and headed home.

Sara opened the windows and listened to the murmur of the summer night rising from Kornhamnstorg and the eateries there. People enjoying life and each other. Expectations, hopes, joy.

Martin opened a bottle of wine, but after just ten minutes they'd both fallen asleep in front of the TV.

39

The baritone voice of Loa Falkman shook the living room. Sara sat up in alarm, trying to see where the dreadful noise was coming from. The singing was coming from the morning news program on the TV, which was still switched on. She reached for the remote and switched it off. Were they really allowed to bellow out old classics at this time of the morning?

At the other end of the sofa, Martin was snoring away loudly. Sara placed a blanket over her husband, and then she carried the glasses with the remainder of their drinks from the night before into the kitchen and made herself a cup of coffee and scrambled eggs. Hangover food, even though her headache was tolerable after three glasses of wine.

Ebba's reception and party were over and done with. The relief was mixed with a gnawing sorrow that a chapter in her life had been closed—a milestone passed. She already knew that she would miss this time with the children many times in her life to come.

At least Sara could now focus on Uncle Stellan again. If nothing else, in order to distract herself. She pulled up the pictures she'd taken down in the rec room and emailed them to Hedin. To her surprise, Hedin called her straight back—at half past six in the morning.

"What are these photos?" she asked.

"From Stellan's home movies. Men having sex with young girls. Do you recognize them?"

"The first photo is Per Dieden. Justice minister in the eighties. Then there's Gösta Boström, the CEO of Svea Marin."

"What's that?"

"An industrial group that made defense equipment," said Hedin. "Including naval combat vessels. The third one is Mats Cajderius, editor-in-chief at *Svenska Dagbladet*. And you're telling me that all these men were filmed at the home of Stellan Broman while having sex with very young girls? Classic honeytrap."

"Stellan raped the girls himself first to break them in. Then he got them drunk or drugged them, and let these men exploit them."

"So that he had a hold over them."

"And look at the fifth picture," said Sara, who was also scrolling through her big game snapshots. The former prime minister.

When Hedin finally replied, she didn't sound surprised.

"That explains why the conservative governments didn't break away from the policy of neutrality when they came to power" was all she said.

Sara did her best to digest Hedin's words.

But it wasn't easy.

Had this roll of film dictated Sweden's security policy for several decades?

Well, why else would the conservative governments have stuck to a doctrine they didn't believe in? Why else would they have implemented a policy they hated?

One single man's warped sexuality had determined the fate of nine million Swedes.

"I can understand the prime minister," said Sara. "But why did Stellan want a hold over the others?"

"To bring more informants on board, to expand the ring, to show his handlers how good he was at his job. Or to obtain some specific information. Influence decisions."

"What kinds of information and decisions?"

"Neutrality, like I said. It was important in the struggle for the sympathies of Swedish subjects. Defense information. Political decisions. The recognition of the DDR as a sovereign state. These films may have helped to drive that through. In that case, it was a huge success for the spy ring. Getting a brutal dictatorship recognized when most other Western countries refused to. Think of the hundreds of people murdered when they tried to leave the country. While we got to see the Swedish prime minister shaking hands with the oppressor with a smile on his face."

Sara shook her head. But it was clear that Hedin was right. Given everything that had been kept from the Swedish people for so long—the truth about the Geijer prostitution scandal, the IB affair, the hospital spy, the collaboration with NATO—it went without saying that there was far more that had never been revealed. And this was possibly the greatest scandal of them all.

Should she take it to the newspapers? If she passed the material to the Security Service, it would probably just end up being classified before disappearing. Sara wanted it to emerge—wanted everyone to know. Not just that Stellan Broman had been a spy, but how he had worked—all the girls he'd exploited, whose lives he'd ruined.

Above all, she wanted everyone to know what these respected men had done. Not only had they raped drugged young girls—they had also allowed a foreign power to exercise its malicious influence. It would be a huge scandal.

"The Security Service knew about this," said Hedin.

"The girls?" said Sara.

"I went through the images of the files I got out of them and it matches the redactions in them."

"When did you do that?"

"Just now. In my head."

"Do you have a photographic memory?"

"I'm attentive."

"How does it agree?"

"Stellan's files from the MfS—the DDR Ministerium für Staatssicherheit—the Stasi—mentions decadent morals in connection with his working methods, and Säpo's files have redacted the sections about his working methods and the names of the people he exploited. However, it says in one place that they considered notifying social services, but opted not to, due to the risk that their knowledge of Geiger's identity as an IM would be revealed. And the social services only come up in espionage cases if they relate to—"

"Minors."

"Exactly."

"So they let him carry on with his atrocities out of fear that someone would find out that they knew he was a spy?"

"Something like that. And I suppose that's why they've gone to such pains to redact so much of his file. Not for his sake, or that of a foreign power that no longer exists. It's actually to conceal their own working methods. Have you found them? The girls, I mean. What have they said?"

"I've got some names," said Sara. "I'm going to try and find them. But there's something else... The cases for the rolls of film of the men were more worn. The ones that feature Stellan himself are in better condition. That has to mean that he kept them in different places. But they were all in the same place when I found them. Why?"

"Because the Cold War is over. At least he thought so."

"Might he have been murdered for the films? As revenge?"

"By one of the girls?"

"Or someone else close to them? Or maybe one of the men? What if he decided to start blackmailing them again and was using the films?"

"Regardless of the reason, it seems undeniable that he deserved to be shot," said Hedin before hanging up.

Sara sat, still thinking it all over, while the cup of coffee went cold in her hand and the leftover scrambled eggs congealed on the plate.

"Good morning."

Martin came into the kitchen, bleary-eyed and tousle-haired. He was still wearing his party clothes from the evening before. He kissed Sara on the top of her head and looked at the coffee maker hopefully.

"Is there any coffee?"

"Of course. Just not here."

An old joke from back when the kids were little had popped into her head and leaped out of her mouth. Martin smiled amiably, but not for long, at the familiar line. Of course, just not here.

"I had instant," said Sara.

"Then you need some proper coffee," he said, setting up the bright yellow Moccamaster. He had chosen the color on the basis that "Yellow makes you happy." Who knew, Sara had thought to herself.

"Yesterday went well," said Martin, sitting down opposite her.

"Really well," she replied. "You'd done such a good job."

"It was the girls who did everything. The dads just paid."

"You'd done such a good job paying," said Sara with a smile.

"Aren't you going to go back to bed?" said Martin. "I thought you didn't start until this evening?"

"I've got some things to do."

She got up, fetched her laptop and went into the living room with a fresh cup of coffee. And then she began searching for addresses and phone numbers for the people in the films.

Cajderius lived in Strängnäs, which was too far to go since Sara had to go to work that evening. Regardless of what Lindblad had to say about the matter.

Per Dieden had died in 2005, and his widow Margot said she didn't want to talk to the police.

Gösta Boström was in an old people's home in Lidingö, drooling, according to the indiscreet summer temp who answered the phone. The former CEO for the industrial conglomerate Svea Marin had major senile dementia, and was incommunicado.

The former prime minister was dead, which she couldn't do much about. The next rapist was one she'd recognized by herself. He'd been in the press a lot in his day, but she'd mostly met him through work. He was a user of prostitutes.

Henrik Carlsson Lindh.

Of course, he was much younger in the video. Dark-haired and good looking, unlike the hunchbacked figure he'd become. But there was the same jutting chin, the same raised eyebrows and half-lowered eyelids. The same sleepy smile.

Sara had googled him and found out that he was a former under-secretary of state for Foreign Affairs, had no family and had published his memoirs, *In the Service of Truth and Beauty*. She'd also found his home address, and now she made up her mind.

One shower and forty minutes later she was standing outside the perpetrator's home.

Stureparken 3.

Consistent with his station.

Lindh received Sara in tailored gray trousers, shiny patent leather shoes, a smoking jacket and a purple cravat tucked inside his white shirt. He sat down opposite her in the suite of Gustavian-style sofas and smiled kindly. He clearly recognized her, and didn't seem the least bit ashamed that he'd been arrested by his visitor on multiple occasions.

"Welcome. Nowak, isn't it? And what have I done this time, if I might be so bold as to ask?"

"Not now," said Sara. "Thirty years ago."

"Whoops," said Lindh. "Isn't that subject to the statute of limitations? Isn't the whole point of getting older that your sins are for-given and forgotten?"

"You were at the Ministry of Foreign Affairs," Sara continued.

"The Foreign Office, yes."

"As undersecretary of state. What can you tell me about Per Dieden, Gösta Boström and Mats Cajderius?"

"Dieden was justice minister. A good-for-nothing. It's a mystery why he was allowed to stay. Boström was the CEO of some indus-trial concern, I think? Not someone I had anything to do with. He may have been part of those delegations on occasion—you know, when Sweden wants to improve its trading relations and sends the prime minister, the king and the captains of industry with order books in their back pockets. It's rare that it leads anywhere, but the advocates for it are cheered on by the Wallenbergs and get to carry on with it. Who else did you say? Cajderius? Some newspaper hack. Not one of the writers who set the tone. Why are you asking about this odd assortment?"

"All of them—just like you—have been caught on film having sex with underage girls."

"Voluntarily or involuntarily? The capture on film, I mean."

"Involuntarily. And then the tapes were kept for the purposes of extortion."

"Does your team really take on cold cases like that?"

"This isn't to do with the prostitution team—it's about the murder of Stellan Broman."

"Was he a devotee of youth, too?"

"He organized the whole thing. Broke in young girls and used them as objects for perverted men."

"Did I sense a hint of value judgment there? Isn't all love beautiful?"

"How did it happen?"

"The sex?" said Lindh, raising his eyebrows.

"The honeytraps. What happened?"

"I've not been in any trap."

Sara pulled out her mobile and started the video of Lindh and his victim.

"Pretty couple" was the only thing he said.

Sara stared at him and then stopped the video.

"A teenager. Probably not even fifteen. What would have happened if this had come out? It would have been the end of your career, surely?"

"I never did anything I couldn't be held responsible for or that jeopardized the safety of the realm."

"How was this used? What did he get you to do? What did he make you do?"

314

"Nothing. Absolutely nothing. There were no traps. It was quite natural, innocent time spent with beautiful girls. Sexuality is a beautiful gift. Something you've probably forgotten, given all the sleaze you see in your line of work."

"Tell me how it worked. Practically."

"My dear, all of that is beyond the statute of limitations."

"Not to me."

"A gentleman never reveals his love secrets."

"A gentleman doesn't rape children."

"Oopsy daisy. You seem to have gone a couple of steps too far, inspector. Thank you for visiting, but it's time for you to be on your way."

"Tell me. I won't leave until you do."

"Is this really to do with the murder? Or is it actually that hearing about it gets you going?" Lindh had a lascivious look in his eyes. "You seem to have saved those videos on your phone. Maybe they have a stimulating effect?"

"I'm going to be completely honest with you. I'm not part of the investigation. This is personal. I'm going to solve this murder no matter what the cost, and if you don't tell me what you know, then I'll pass these films to the media. I don't think you want your legacy tarnished by a scandal like that. And you can tell me everything— as you said, it's all beyond the statute of limitations."

Lindh squinted at her. After a long pause, he leaned back, smiled slightly and said, "It was a wonderful time."

He took out two small stemmed crystal glasses and poured a nut-brown liquid into them from a carafe. Then he lifted the glass in a toast and raised it to his mouth and sipped it.

"A small circle of the initiated knew that Stellan Broman could rustle up young girls. I don't know how we knew about each other— there was no internet back then. But I suppose it was confidential late-night chats after a considerable amount of imbibing. Once the ice was broken, it was as if one had found a kindred spirit—so we would meet on a fairly regular basis. We knew we could talk openly. We shared tips with each other."

Sara grimaced, but when she noticed that it had distracted Lindh from his train of thought, she did her best to control herself.

"The origins of it all may actually have been Stellan's parties. They were huge. And there were plenty of beautiful women in addition to the nation's famous and powerful. I suppose you might say that the women at Stellan's parties were generally very…available. And sometimes you might help yourself. But for those of us who appreciated the unspoiled beauty of youth more than anything else, Stellan was a real gentleman and arranged small tête-à-têtes in his own home."

"So he could film?"

"That wasn't how he presented the idea—but with hindsight, one has to draw the sad conclusion that it was the actual purpose."

"Did he show the films to you?"

"No, but it wouldn't have made any difference. I'd notified my superiors of my weakness, and they had no objections. They merely asked me to be discreet. One was permitted the odd escapade in those days—just look at the Geijer affair. Those gentlemen were defended by the government tooth and nail."

"How long did this go on for?"

"I don't know," said Lindh after a few seconds' silence. "I socialized with Stellan for at least a couple of decades, I think. But for how long these dates were arranged, I can't recollect."

"You worked for the Ministry of Foreign Affairs when Sweden recognized East Germany as a sovereign state. Was that to do with the recordings?"

"Naturally, that had absolutely nothing to do with my little romances. My escapades were a private matter. The DDR was global politics. I don't think you can quite grasp the extent of it, little madam inspector."

"But you knew Stellan, who was in the pay of East Germany, and while you worked at the Foreign Office by day and slept with young girls at Stellan's by night, the ministry pushed for Sweden to accept the DDR as an independent state. Long before other democratic countries did the same."

"Stellan Broman was a great friend of the DDR, and he laid out his arguments in a forceful and persuasive manner. If I passed them on to my colleagues, it was because I saw reason in them—not because Stellan threatened me with the publication of private films made of me. That's not how Swedish politics worked back then."

"I'm just beginning to understand how things worked back then."

40

"It began when we were in Paris."

A feeling of unreality.

A vague sense of unease spreading through her body.

Paris.

Sara had found Camilla in Uppsala. She was the only one of the girls she'd recognized that she had been able to get hold of. Carin was dead, having committed suicide at twenty, and Maria had moved to the USA. She didn't know who the others were.

Camilla had suggested they meet right away, and had taken the train into Stockholm a couple of hours later. When Sara met her outside the station, it seemed as if she wanted to talk—as though there was something that had been torturing her for a long time that she needed to get out into the open.

"The trip to Paris the summer before year seven?" said Sara. "You and Stellan and Lotta?"

"Yes."

The trip to Paris that Sara had wanted to go on.

She'd nagged and fought and prayed and begged. Stellan had invited her, but the move to Vällingby had put a stop to it. Jane had saved her.

"He and Lotta had been fighting," said Camilla. "And Lotta locked herself in the single room, so he and I had to share. Just for a night, until Lotta had calmed down. We were out during the day, then we had dinner. I was allowed to have a couple of glasses of wine despite being too young. But he said that in France, all children drank wine with their meals. And when we got back to the hotel, he wanted to take a shower. He left the door open, and then he came into the room completely naked and said I should take a shower too. I didn't dare say no, and he continued talking to me while I got undressed. He even followed me in and watched me the whole time. While I was showering, I felt like I should draw the shower curtain, but when I finally had to get out, he passed me a towel and I saw that he had an erection. Then I felt his hands all over my body. And then he pushed me against the sink and penetrated me from behind."

Camilla paused. She seemed to be very distant and extremely present, all at once.

"I was a virgin—only thirteen years old," she said. "And it was incredibly painful. I cried out—I couldn't stop myself. But he just talked to me in a calm voice. He was quick, and then I could feel blood and semen running down my legs. He said I should probably have another shower—he even turned the water back on. When I came out half an hour later, after crying and throwing up in the shower and scrubbing my privates until I bled again, he was asleep. He had his back toward me and was snoring. I had nowhere to go, couldn't speak French, obviously had no mobile, so I got into the bed, too. As far away from him as possible. I hoped I'd wake up and realize it had all been a dream. It was at least a relief that he was asleep. I don't know how long I lay there crying, but eventually I drifted off. Only to be woken in the middle of the night by him raping me again. When I protested, he put his hand over my mouth and continued. I twisted and turned and tried to get free, but he was too strong. When he was done, he fell back asleep, and that's when I should have run down to reception and asked them to call the police. But I stayed there. And in the morning, when he raped me for a third time, I didn't make any attempt to resist."

"And then?" said Sara, although she didn't really want to hear any more.

"Nothing. We went out and had breakfast. He was in a fantastic mood, talking about Paris and his TV shows and all the celebrity guests he'd had on them. And there I was. Terrified that I might be pregnant. Horror-stricken. Later that day, Lotta turned up, but I couldn't say what had happened. It was her dad. And it was Uncle Stellan. No one would believe me. And when we got back home to Bromma, he invited me round about once a month and introduced me to various friends of his. They all got to use me. Some were OK, but others were...worse. The school nurse gave me birth control pills—I told her I had a boyfriend I loved. When I was due to start sixth form, I searched for a program of study that wasn't available in Stockholm and applied for that. Graphic design in Uppsala. Mum and Dad didn't understand why—they didn't want me to move to another town. But I dug my heels in, threw a few tantrums. My salvation was within reach. I think Mum could tell it was important, so eventually they let me move. And I was able to start over and become someone else. I'd almost managed to forget about Stellan when I read he'd died. I've got my family, and I actually work in graphics and like it. Maybe because it saved me from the monster in Bromma. It feels easier to come back here now that he's gone—now that there's no risk of me running into him."

The trip to Paris.

The trip she had been so jealous of Camilla for.

She didn't know what to say. She simply reached out with her hand and held Camilla's and squeezed.

And Camilla squeezed back.

41

Malin was still off work, in a state of shock due to the murder of her father and the disappearance of her mother. But she said she could come to her sister's office. So twenty minutes later, Sara was standing in reception at the Swedish International Development Cooperation Agency on Valhallavägen, announcing her arrival, and six minutes later Lotta came down to meet her. At the same moment, Malin entered through the revolving door.

Just beyond reception was the staff canteen. First there was a room with various buffet counters, and then four different queues to pay. Sara was hungry, but the others didn't seem to want to eat, so she said nothing.

She amused herself by noting how all the passersby threw hasty second glances at Lotta, sometimes involuntarily. She would have loved to know what they made of her childhood friend. What was she like as a boss? Lotta had been the one in charge even when they were little, but Malin and Sara had never engaged in the anonymous reviews that subordinates wrote in the adult world. Everyone had an opinion about their boss, and loved to share it with their peers. Views like that rarely went up the chain of command. It had been just like that when they were little.

Lotta's office was big, airy and equipped with light furniture. A Scandinavian feel. And she actually had a view right toward SVT's building. Stellan's old stamping ground. Malin's current one. This was the Bromans' corner of the world—at least professionally.

"What did you want to talk about?" said Lotta.

Sara had brought her iPad. She'd transferred the videos she'd taken of the assaults from her mobile and the picture quality wasn't the best. Old Super 8 footage filmed with a mobile and shown on a bigger screen...But it would have to do.

She said nothing when she started the film. But she scrutinized the two sisters' faces carefully.

Malin's eyes opened wide, and after a few seconds she looked away.

"Stop!" she said when Sara didn't switch it off.

But for once Sara didn't obey her.

"Why are you showing us this?" said Lotta, pushing aside the tablet. "Just a few days after Dad was murdered."

"Because this is to do with the murder."

"You're surely not involved in the investigation?"

"Your father filmed multiple rapes of underage girls."

"She's not underage."

"Under eighteen, in any case."

"And it doesn't look like he's holding her down or threatening her," said Lotta. "She's lying there completely of her own accord."

"What sixteen-year-old chooses to sleep with a fifty-year-old?"

"They exist. Believe me."

"We can watch more films. In some of them it's clear how terrified the girls are. And in others they're drunk."

"It can't be true!" said Malin. "Dad would never do this."

"It looks awfully much like he did."

"I suppose that's how they captured him," said Lotta. "Lured him into a trap. Now I understand why he would have helped the Stasi."

"You think he was tricked into doing this?"

"Yes, of course," said Lotta. "Dad was just as much of a victim as the girls."

"Do you want to see more?" said Sara, who was having a hard time stomaching Lotta's indifference.

"Watch away if it does it for you. But not with us."

"It's hard to comprehend," said Sara. "Isn't it?"

"Because it's not true," said Malin. "It's taken out of context."

"No. The context is a rape."

"Stop it!"

"And what are you going to do with this?" said Lotta. "Give it to the tabloids?"

"It's interesting from two perspectives. One, for the murder investigation, as a possible motive. And two, for the three of us here, who all grew up with Stellan."

"Possible motive?" said Lotta. "Do you think someone would murder an old lay thirty years later? Why? Who the hell hasn't kissed a few frogs in their time? Let's face it—in this girl's eyes, Dad was an old man. But that kind of thing happens. He was extremely famous, and it was probably exciting—but then she regretted it afterward, which I can understand. But she surely didn't shoot our father dead over it."

"Don't you see that it's an assault?"

"Honestly, I actually recognize her from school. She was special. Very sexually demanding. Sought out older men."

"What? So—"

"I don't mean that it was her fault, but you can sort of understand why Dad was tempted. She was probably pretty forward."

"Surely you can see she's scared?"

"Just unsure. He was probably the first person she propositioned—she didn't know how to behave."

"Propositioned? Are you out of your mind?"

"You've no idea how many women wanted to have sex with Stellan Broman," said Lotta. "You're forgetting that there weren't many celebrities back then, and the ones there were ended up being basically worshipped. There were only two TV channels, so everyone watched the same shows."

"I don't understand how you can't have any sympathy for the girls."

"We do," the older sister added. "But it's thirty years ago, and we're in the here and now, and I've just been offered a new job that will fall through if this comes out."

"It's your father you should be angry with."

"Have you changed your theory, then?" said Lotta. "What happened to the spying?"

"There's a connection to that. Other films."

Silence.

"What do you want?" said Lotta, fixing her gaze on Sara. Malin was simply shaking her head and looking away. "You know what this can do to me as a public figure. Do you want something to keep quiet? What's this actually about? Your sick obsession with our childhood? Isn't it time to grow up?"

"I...thought you'd want to know."

Sara began to wonder herself what exactly was driving her forward.

"No thanks. It changes nothing, and it really doesn't make anything better. Leo and Sixten are constantly asking for their grandmother and I don't know what to tell them. This is decades-old history. We're not children any longer—we're adults who have to try and process the fact that our father's dead and our mother's missing. And by 'we' I mean Malin and myself. Not you, Sara."

Lotta was right. Sara was ashamed. She'd gone too far. Had she simply never forgotten the feeling of subordination from her childhood, and thought she'd get her revenge now? She needed to take a step back, but she didn't want to admit her personal motives to Lotta.

"OK, but in that case I wonder whether you know anything about these films that may be of use in the investigation. Were there any threats? Did any of the girls threaten to report him?"

"It's not even your investigation!" Lotta went over to the window and her shoulders slumped.

"You work with whores," said Malin.

"I want to solve the murder," Sara replied.

"It's a bit much to come and show us a video like that just a few days after our father's been murdered," said Lotta, turning around. "Do your bosses know you're doing this? Or is this some kind of personal vendetta? If the film isn't part of the investigation, then you've obtained it by yourself, which means you've committed trespass. And tried to blackmail us."

"I thought you wanted to know who your father was."

"We know who our dad was," said Lotta. "To us."

"You've always been jealous of us," Malin interjected. "Mum was always saying we should be kind and play with you because she felt sorry for you. And then you tell us that Dad was a spy, and now that he was a pervert. What the hell is wrong with you?"

"I *was* jealous," Sara said honestly. "When we were little. But without any reason, I now realize."

"You ought to be a bit more grateful for what Mum and Dad did for you," said Lotta.

"For letting me come round? Because you played with me for two months a year when your friends were away? Or because my mother got the chance to clean your house and deal with your shit? Thanks a bunch."

"For not reporting you."

"For what?"

"For the garden shed."

The words hit her like a kick from a horse.

"What do you mean, the garden shed?"

"You tried to set fire to it."

"What?"

"When I went to Paris with Dad and Camilla."

Sara was silent.

"Did you think we didn't know?" said Malin. "Mum saw you."

"You'll have to excuse me," said Lotta. "I have to work."

Sara got up and left. Shaken.

The garden shed.

So they knew.

Had always known.

The memories that she'd tried to suppress and block out. How she'd taken the metro from Vällingby to Bromma, changed to the

Nockebybanan light railway and then walked the last stretch to the house. With a plan—or rather, a feeling—driving her forward.

A day when there had been bright sunshine and strong winds. The clouds slipping quickly across the sky. And she'd felt more alive than ever.

Jane had worked almost constantly that first summer when they'd just moved, to save money for furniture, food and rent. Sara knew no one in Vällingby, and her mother had forbidden her from calling the Bromans. The memory of being in that echoing, empty flat without any friends, without anything to do, with the thought of how fantastic it must be in Paris eating away at her.

The growing desire for revenge. For justice.

Forty-four-year-old Sara could picture her thirteen-year-old self opening the door to the Bromans' garden shed and getting out a bottle. Shaking it to make sure there was enough.

The lighter fluid that she'd sprayed over the outside of the shed.

Adult Sara couldn't stop young Sara, despite the fact that they were the same person.

Or were they?

One of them had lit the flame and run away, and the other one could yet again feel the soles of her cheap sandals slamming against the pavement as she ran away from the Bromans' house along the deserted summer streets.

High on her revenge for the non-trip to Paris, because the summers with the Bromans were at an end. She'd checked the papers for several days afterward.

Arson at the home of Stellan Broman—it should have been a big story. Made Sara important.

But the papers never said anything. The fire never took hold.

42

Spy or not, Stellan had been shot by someone he had caused harm to. A girl he had raped, or someone close to them. Sara was convinced of it.

This was the last time she was going to visit the house. She couldn't stand to see it anymore.

She could almost hear the desperate cries of the vulnerable girls. The panting of the men raping them.

Her image of her childhood was a lie that she'd swathed in rose-tinted summer memories. She realized that she hated the house.

Had she always hated it? But just in another way, for other reasons?

The police cordon was still there. Blue and white tape telling the world at large that something terrible had happened, but also that someone had dealt with it. "The terrible thing is on the other side of the tape. There's nothing to worry about on your side. We've limited the crime to this place."

Sara went round the back and looked down toward the water. Once again the picture of the three girls on the jetty sprang to mind. Three girls throwing sandwiches into the water and laughing hysterically.

But now she remembered. Now she could admit it to herself. It wasn't just that she'd been so hungry.

It was also the fact that her mother, Jane, had made those sandwiches for the girls. Instead of eating them, they'd thrown them into the water and laughed. And then they'd told Jane to make more, which had gone into the water, too.

Sara had met her mother's eye, but had quickly looked away.

It had been almost eleven in the evening, but it had still been light. Jane should have been allowed to go to bed. She had to get up early in the morning to prepare the breakfast.

But she hadn't been able to.

Because she'd had to make more sandwiches.

And covering it all, there had been that sticky, sweet scent of sun cream—intimately connected to the degradation of her mother. She felt Stellan's hands on her, slowly massaging the lotion onto her while talking about how important it was to be protected from the sun.

And then she'd sat there with the sisters and joined in with everything they did, even when that was humiliating her mother.

Sara returned to the present, rounded the house and unlocked the door.

The big, empty house. So strangely desolate.

Had it ever been inhabited? It was hard to believe, despite the fact that she'd been part of that life.

The house smelled stagnant. The summer warmth released odors from the walls, floors and furniture. All the distinct scents of the objects and materials—no longer being blended into a human presence. No smell of cooking, tobacco smoke, coffee, skin covered in beads of summer sweat or perfume.

What was going to happen to the house?

Would Agneta live here alone if she ever returned? What would the sisters do with it if the worst had happened?

Sell. Sara was convinced.

They weren't big on sentimentality.

The house had probably meant more to her than it had to Malin and Lotta.

Would she be able to live here?

Never.

Not now.

But once upon a time it would have been a dream for her.

Sara crept through the house carefully. The eternal guest, the one who didn't belong here. The silence was charged. The light didn't reach into every corner, and the twilight brought her imagination alive.

The parquet creaked and the walls groaned.

She felt a presence.

Someone close by.

As if there were a faint echo, she thought she heard the murmur of the past. Distant sounds lingering from all the big parties. All the happy guests. All the ruined lives.

A lonely saxophone made its way through the clatter and hubbub.

From the drawing room, she heard the hoarse voice of a long-forgotten femme fatale. Clinking glasses being carried away by the catering staff.

Someone throwing up in the guest toilet.

The final dance toward dawn. A handful of couples swaying to the soft jazz. The snoring of guests who'd fallen asleep on sofas and under tables.

Someone treading on broken glass and bleeding onto the white rug in the hallway.

Nothing that had happened in the house had been as it seemed.

She ought to burn the whole thing down. The way they pulled down the houses of serial killers and Nazis—an attempt to eradicate the evil. The evil energy, as Anna might have put it.

Sara wandered around, looking about. When she caught sight of the album labeled "Malin's graduation," she couldn't help herself.

She opened it and encountered photos from outside the school in Bromma, from the moment that could have been when Sara finished, too. Followed by the reception at home and the party in the evening. Her return to the Bromans' protection that had ended so badly.

She saw a younger version of herself beside Stellan. Martin was a few seats away.

She'd felt as if they had a thing when they saw each other again over drinks before dinner. It had been so easy to talk to him and laugh together. Suddenly the two-year age gap was nothing, and neither of them seemed to want to leave the other. But they were brusquely separated by an unsympathetic seating plan.

Her young love... What if they'd been able to keep talking that evening? If she hadn't crashed and Lotta hadn't been able to throw a spanner in the works...

Was that why Sara had later felt that she had to have Martin? To get one up on Lotta, who'd been turned down by him when they were in sixth form together? But then Lotta had hit on him again at her sister's graduation party, before dumping him as soon as he fell in love with her.

Perhaps Martin had been easy prey after that. Twenty-one years old, heartbroken and needing comfort and security. As far as Sara was concerned, it was still a victory.

Martin had become hers.

But now?

The firmer and clearer the past became, the looser the contours of the present became and the more unreal her life seemed. Was she really living in the present? Wasn't it all about what happened back then?

Didn't everyone cling on to their youth? The time when emotions were at their most powerful, when everything was important and possible, when people were eternal. Eternally beautiful or eternally ugly, eternally good or eternally bad. Less transient. Less ordinary.

She put the graduation album down and picked up "Janina 1972" instead. She opened it and examined the photos of a young Jane. Very young. In what must have been clothing from Poland. Then photos of her in new, probably Swedish clothes that she'd likely been given by the Bromans. They were really more Agneta's style. Janina. Jane. Sara's mother. With a happy smile that disappeared in the later photos.

330

Sara checked the spine of the album again.

1972.

That was wrong.

Her mother had come to Sweden in 1974. Stellan had got it wrong. Odd. Sara had always thought of him as a pedant, but perhaps the domestic help didn't matter that much.

She looked at the row of photo albums, and thought back to the childhood she'd witnessed but never really been a true part of. Now she knew she ought to be infinitely grateful for that.

"You've always been jealous of us."

Sara nodded to herself. A decision began to take shape.

Nothing could be undone, but it was possible to change your view of anything. Up in the attic, she rooted through the boxes until she found what she was looking for. She took the whole box downstairs and outside, where she set it in the middle of the lawn at a safe distance from any bushes and trees. Then she went into the kitchen and opened the cupboard that she'd known contained acetone, even as a child. She emptied the whole bottle into the box and then she lit it. She ignited the whole box of matches at once. The effect was like a miniature welding torch. A small fire lighting a bigger one.

The flames licked up the cardboard box intended for donations to the city mission.

Busnel, Chevignon, Moncler, Lyle & Scott.

Sara no longer kept up. But Malin's and Lotta's expensive jackets and clothes from their teens burned well. They let off an acrid, pungent odor.

In the 1980s, no one had bothered to try and avoid chemicals in clothes.

Sara turned around and contemplated the paving slab on the ground. The first of the twelve leading to the garden shed.

The slabs that Stellan had referred to as the "twelve-step model to a better life."

The words had taken on a completely different meaning now. The shed represented something else.

Sara chose to walk alongside the slabs as she aimed for the garden shed. She almost expected to see Stellan and one of the young girls inside when she opened the door.

Rake, lawnmower, jerrycan. Perfect.

She picked up the jerrycan in her hand and felt its weight. Almost full.

Then she unscrewed the cap and emptied the contents over the furniture in the shed. She flung the can about so that the walls were properly drenched. Top to bottom. Petrol splashed across her forearms. She'd never get the smell out of her clothes. It didn't matter.

When the can was almost empty, she put it to one side on the floor so that the few drips that were left could be reached by the fire. Then she put her hand in her pocket, but realized that she'd used up the box of matches.

Typical.

Well, she'd just have to get another one. She knew where the Bromans kept everything.

In the kitchen, she realized she was famished.

She couldn't remember when she'd last eaten. Oh yes, scrambled eggs at dawn.

She opened the fridge door and reviewed its contents. Something she would never have dared to do back in the day.

Now all she had to do was help herself. But there wasn't much she fancied.

Plastic bottles of mineral water, an open milk carton, margarine, cheese, liver pâté and salami. In the bottom drawer were rinsed salad in bags, organic carrots, onions and potatoes. Sara put two slices of salami in her mouth. That would have to satisfy the worst of her hunger.

The milk still hadn't gone out of date, so she grabbed the carton. Better for it to be drunk than left there to go off. Then she shut the door while she chewed on the salami and raised the milk carton to her mouth. She was amused to see the mixture of important and unimportant things stuck on the Miele fridge. Letters from the grid saying there was a scheduled power cut that had already passed, photos of the grandchildren, contact details for the GP, a magnet depicting the temptation of St. Anthony, and a calendar covering June.

"M & L back" was annotated against the day Stellan had been shot.

"Kids" was scrawled across the entire preceding week. "Theater" at the beginning of the month and "Bills" at the end. "Dentist" was noted against a date next week. It was unclear whom it applied to, but the visit most likely wouldn't be taking place.

And against every Sunday there was the word "Joa" noted. What did "Joa" mean?

Sara pulled out her mobile and called Malin.

Lotta knew more about her parents, but Sara wasn't up to talking to her right now. She got the impression that Lotta would somehow be able to work out down the phone what she was up to.

Would Malin pick up after the film screening at the office?

Yes—she answered. She probably hadn't got round to saving Sara's number, so she didn't know who was calling.

Malin changed her tone from neutral to suffering when she heard who it was, but she was still able to explain that "Joa" was Joachim—her parents' gardener. Did he come every Sunday, Sara asked. The younger sister was able to confirm that. Every Sunday for as long as Malin had been able to remember.

Then she called out to someone at the other end of the line and ended the call without saying goodbye.

Well, Sara had other things on her mind than her childhood friend's lack of manners.

Every Sunday for as long as Malin could remember.

But Joachim had turned up on the day Stellan had been shot.

It was a Monday.

The old phone contact book made from artificial leather was lying on the kitchen counter, a telephone gilded on the front cover. Inside, the pages were marked in the corners with letters in alphabetical order. It was the same book as when the girls were little— most of the numbers in it had been entered decades ago. Perhaps Stellan and Agneta, like most other people, had switched to saving new numbers and contacts in their mobiles, but they had still kept the old version. And since Joachim had worked for the family for so long he was in it. Under *J*.

Sara went to the landline phone on the wall, dialed the number and got an answering machine with a voice that she recognized as Joachim's, apologizing that he couldn't answer and providing a mobile number. She tried that. It rang out without being answered.

Why had he been there on the wrong day? On the day that Stellan happened to be murdered?

Sara checked Joachim's number in the phone book online, and found out what his last name was.

Joachim Böhme.

It sounded German.

Hadn't Joachim always had a bit of an accent...?

She had the same gut feeling that she got just before a fourth ace turned up in the river in a game of Texas hold 'em. She looked up Joachim Böhme online again and discovered that he lived out in Vaxholm.

That settled it.

You didn't come all the way from Vaxholm to Bromma every week for several decades just to mow the lawn, Sara thought to herself. Why even have a gardener when Stellan loved doing all those jobs? What kind of ordinary suburban garden needed the dedicated efforts of two men?

The problem with the recruitment and indoctrination of Geiger had been that Uncle Stellan was so well known. All those hours of education that had been reported by the leader of the spy ring, Ober—how would they have pulled that off without being spotted and without anyone around them becoming suspicious?

Hour after hour as they looked after beds, did the watering, planted seeds and pruned. Endless ideological discussions. Lessons.

Joachim Böhme was Ober.

As she jogged out of the house, she dialed Breuer's number.

Agneta Broman tracked Sara's rapid exit to her car from a distance of thirty meters.

In her hand she was holding Joa's mobile.

On the display it said: "Missed call: Bromans."

Agneta thought to herself: Run along, little Sara. Out of the house. Otherwise you may come to harm.

43

The task force were mobilized. A raid in Vaxholm.

They were pulling on their kit while simultaneously checking maps and satellite images, going through conditions on the ground and establishing their tactics. They were scheduled to depart in ninety seconds' time.

No one was worked up, no one was nervous.

They were all wired.

They knew the target was a potential suspect in two murders, and that if that were the case, then he would be armed and possibly dangerous. But as ever, the safety of those in the surrounding area was their top priority. Things usually worked out, but only as long as the team knew what they didn't have to worry about.

Sara, Breuer and Strauss were already in the Germans' BMW heading out of the city. Sara had wanted to leave in advance, since she thought the task force would drive much faster than them. But Strauss was doing 160 kilometers per hour on the E18 heading toward Norrtälje. He was weaving between lanes, almost brushing cars each time he switched. She was thrown forward and back in her seat as if she was a crash test dummy on a roller coaster.

Strauss had one hand on the horn all the way to make the cars ahead of him move. Sara wished he would keep both hands on the wheel instead.

She called David to let him know she might be late. She'd been forced to step in and help out German intelligence. She'd hoped that David would accept that explanation, but he didn't sound at all happy about it. He merely said that he couldn't very well go out on his own, and questioned whether she'd really thought he would.

Filled with equal parts expectation and guilty conscience, Sara ended the call, before looking at the satnav on her phone. She was pretty sure she knew the way to Vaxholm, but she didn't want to take any risks. It was easy to mix up the junctions on the motorway. When they left the motorway and joined route 247, Sara began to worry that Strauss would keep going at the same speed on this smaller road, but she was distracted by her mobile ringing.

It was Anna, who said that they'd done a search on the name Joachim Böhme ahead of the raid and got a hit from Uppsala University Hospital.

Apparently the Böhme they were looking for was there—dead after being run over in Roslagen. And inside the car that had hit him, they'd found a loaded AK-47.

"He's dead," said Sara.

"Shit," said Breuer.

"Run over by who?" said Sara to Anna.

"Don't know," she said. "Going to check."

"And the Kalashnikov? What does that mean?"

"That we should be very careful," said Anna, ending the call.

Sara couldn't avoid feeling somewhat gratified that Anna and her boss were finally taking her lead seriously. And they weren't even opposed to her accompanying the Germans.

"You should have found Böhme long ago," Breuer said to Sara. As if it were her responsibility.

"The question is what role he had," said Strauss. "Is he the third one to be murdered by the same perpetrator, or has he tried to get rid of the others but failed?"

"But who did it?" said Breuer.

"Could it just have been an accident?" said Sara.

Breuer simply looked at her.

Apparently not.

Before she had time to say anything else, Anna rang again.

"I spoke to Cederquist, who was the first officer on the scene. Böhme was apparently reversed over in the harbor at Räfsnäs outside Norrtälje. By an old woman who seemed to be confused and on the verge of a breakdown."

"An accident?"

"It looked that way. But when the police arrived she was gone."

"And the AK-47?"

"They've got no explanation for that."

An old woman who seemed to be confused, Sara thought to herself. Just like at Kellner's.

Was it a coincidence?

"And the car was registered to a man called Lennart Hagman in Sollentuna," said Anna. "But he lives in Thailand, and hasn't been to Sweden for twenty years."

"What does that mean?"

"Don't know. But here's the funny thing—witnesses on the scene told the police that Böhme called the woman who'd run him over 'Agneta.'"

Tied to a chair and two bullets to the head.

The pattern correlated with the murders of Kellner and Geiger, while Ober had been killed by other means.

Different perpetrators, or a murderer who mixed their methods?

Breuer had pulled up alarmingly detailed information about the four people in Räfsnäs with any form of ties to East Germany. An old theater director who had participated in cultural festivals there in the 1970s, and two middle-aged artists who had visited East Berlin in the 1980s and gone to underground clubs. But the most interesting person was one Elisabeth Böhme, raised in the DDR and sister of the deceased, Joachim Böhme. They had gone straight there.

When no one had opened the door, Strauss had simply kicked it down. The cabin was small and they found her quickly. Ober's sister. Shot in the head, and with a bucket of water and several damp towels next to her.

Strauss and Breuer searched the house before they let Sara call Anna to tell her about the body.

Then they handed over the police work to their colleagues and went to sit down in the harbor.

Strauss bought a Daim ice cream for himself and an ice cream sandwich for Sara. He didn't even ask Breuer. Perhaps he knew better from past experience. Sara accepted the ice cream and put it next to her on the bench, where she promptly forgot about it.

She surveyed the idyllic spot.

Archipelago, sun and seagulls. Families and their kids, weather-beaten pink-cheeked summer types and youths on the way out to the islands, perhaps for some summer job in one of the restaurants out there.

"Agneta?" Sara looked at Breuer.

Neither she nor Strauss said anything.

"Anna said that Ober said the person who'd run him over was called Agneta. Could he have meant Agneta Broman?"

Still no answer.

"Was it Agneta? Do you know something?"

"Anything is possible," Breuer said.

"Why would she do that? To avenge Stellan's death? Assuming it was Ober who murdered him?"

"It's possible," Breuer replied, pausing for a few seconds. "But Agneta Broman wasn't just the wife of a Stasi informant."

But?

What else could Agneta have been? Once the wife of Sweden's most famous man and a glamorous hostess at all his parties. Additionally, the mother of two evil girls and later a doting grandmother to her grandchildren.

Why run over Böhme?

Her gardener.

Her husband's colleague in espionage, codename Ober.

"Do you know what an 'illegal' is?" said Breuer.

Sara shook her head.

"A planted spy. Someone who lives under someone else's identity in another country while spying for their home country."

"You mean that Agneta…?"

Breuer picked up her white handbag, removed a file with elastic around the corners from it and passed it to Sara.

"This is for you."

When Sara opened the file, she found a copy of an article from a Swedish gossip magazine from the early 1970s, with a note containing a translation of the text to German. The headline read UNCLE STELLAN BAGS HIS YOUNG BRIDE FROM NORRLAND. The article was about Stellan and Agneta's wedding, and she was described as a beautiful, taciturn woman from the north who had tragically lost her parents in an accident when she was a child. The article was equally sympathetic toward Stellan Broman for taking in the orphaned beauty, who was in fact fifteen years his junior.

"And?" said Sara.

"The couple she gave as her paternal grandparents really did have a son who died in an accident with his wife, but the grandchild also died after spending many years in a coma. Someone acquired the entire house at auction after they died, and photos of both the grandparents and the young couple turned up in the home of Agneta Öman, and later with Stellan and Agneta Broman."

Breuer put down a wedding photo from the early twentieth century that Sara immediately recognized. It was framed in the Bromans' living room, and was one of the many pictures that she and the sisters had fooled around with as children. They'd made up their own stories about it. Now she understood that they hadn't been the only ones inventing stories.

After that, Breuer drew another sheet from the bundle, roughly A5 sized.

"Birth certificate" was printed at the top.

For Agneta Öman.

Her maiden name.

"Look at the signature," said Breuer.

The birth certificate had been issued by a pastor in Västerbotten.

It was Jürgen Stiller, the same man who was now a pastor in Torpa, just outside Tranås. One of the IMs that Hedin had written about. The one being guarded by the police in Östergötland.

"The KGB and GRU worked hard to get reliable people into the authorities and into organizations where they could be useful. Like this kind of assignment."

"So Agneta isn't from Norrland?" said Sara. "Is she East German, too?"

Breuer shook her head.

"This is where it gets complicated. And remember that you signed those confidentiality papers." Breuer stumbled slightly on the word. "Illegals were primarily used by the Soviet Union during the Cold War. They planted many spies under false identities in the USA and around Western Europe. In Sweden as well."

"So Agneta is from the USSR?"

Breuer's silence was reply enough.

It was too much to take in. Aunt Agneta was a Soviet spy with a false identity. She had completely duped those around her. She'd taken Sara in.

"Did Stellan know?" said Sara.

"We don't know," said Breuer.

"And the children?"

"Definitely not."

"You're sure?"

The German merely gave her a look in reply.

"So what was her mission? And what is she doing now?" Breuer's silence was suddenly harder to interpret. "Did Böhme know she was an illegal?"

"There are three theories," said Breuer. "Either she killed Böhme because he shot Stellan. Pure revenge. Or Böhme tried to annihilate the spy ring, and Agneta's mission was to stop him in order to help those under her protection to complete their missions and pass on the information to Abu Rasil. The KGB often planted so-called overcoats to monitor spies so that they could step in and help if necessary. Overcoats that the spies themselves had no idea existed."

"And the third option?"

"That she's the one getting rid of the spy ring. Just like Ober said."

Sara didn't know what to believe. Images of the Agneta Broman of her childhood flickered through her head. Agneta in the kitchen serving up sandwiches and hot chocolate to the girls. In a sun lounger in the garden, wearing sunglasses and clutching a Sjöwall–Wahlöö novel. At parties with a drink in one hand and a slender brown More cigarette in the other. The perennially smiling Agneta, who made almost everyone feel welcome. Who comforted Sara when she was sad more often than her own mother had done. But in a matter-of-fact, almost brusque manner.

"Why, then?" was all she managed to say.

"To stop it all. Alternatively, to get rid of everyone involved. Now that it's in motion, they don't want anyone left to testify."

"But why? The Soviet Union no longer exists!"

"There was a lot that changed in the world of intelligence when the USSR collapsed. We may have changed the names of our organizations, but the same people were still working for them. Take Robert Hanssen—he spent twenty-five years spying from 1979 to 2001, first for the USSR and then Russia. In his eyes, there was no difference—and the same went for the Russian bear. Remember that Putin was a KGB officer. He's never made an apology or opened any archives, and there's a tremendous thirst for revenge in the former KGB. They adapt. They used to control the far left in Europe, today they control the far right. Ideologies are of no interest. Realpolitik is everything. And in that regard, they consider Europe as a supporter of America. A supporter that must be removed in order to weaken the great enemy."

"What? They *want* the bombs to blow up?"

Given that they were surrounded by sun-seeking holidaymakers, the thought was hard to stomach.

"This is just a theory, remember. And we don't think the current holders of power in Russia would initiate an operation like this. But if someone else does it, then they wouldn't try to prevent it either— quite the opposite. Like if Islamists happened upon information about the bombs, and some old warrior from the Palestinian terror- ist groups is willing to get them the codes in return for payments. The Russians would hardly try to stop that. President Putin can actu- ally use rising levels of terror in Europe to justify harsher regulations at home. And he needs that, now that his popularity is plummeting and people are taking to the streets to protest. Seeing the detested West humiliated by rabid fanatics is just a bonus."

"So you think Agneta works for Russia?"

"It's important to remember that the FSB took over all of the KGB's resources."

"But why would she still be loyal to Russia after so many years? She has her children and grandchildren here."

"That was part of the mission."

"But it's a long time since it was given to her. A whole lifetime with her own family must have had an impact on her? Can you really pretend for so many years?"

Sara thought about her own children. There wasn't any single conviction in the world that would have made her regard them as merely a facade. She couldn't understand how anyone could ward off the emotions and instincts that their own children awakened within them.

"The illegals were brainwashed and drilled from infancy. The truth implanted in her then is the only thing she knows. That's her everything. It's the only thing she cares about. The KGB would often take orphans and raise them in their secret schools. So she probably has no trouble relating to her Swedish identity as an orphan. She probably regards her entire life in Sweden as preparation for what she's been trained to do."

"Which is?"

"Handling tricky situations."

Sara thought about it, but couldn't grasp it. She just couldn't imagine Agneta in any of the three scenarios.

"Then we have to find her," she said eventually. "Not just for her own sake, but for the sake of all the innocent people who'll die if we don't. We have to raise the alarm. Circulate her description."

Breuer thought about it for a while. Then she said:

"I think you need to do that."

44

At first she had been disappointed. She had been summoned to the secretariat in the middle of rehearsals for celebrations to mark the anniversary of the great victory over fascism. Every single member of the party leadership would be sitting up on the podium, and she was so eager to show how committed she was. How talented the entire troupe had become after a few bad apples had been forced out.

Nadia, who hadn't marched in time with everyone else; Jelena, who had sung too quietly; and Katryna, who had lacked any fire in her gaze.

Without them it was perfect.

The songs, the banners, the marching. The bright voices merged together into a strong, encouraging unit.

Sometimes, local groups of Young Pioneers were allowed to participate in the big celebrations in Moscow. That was what gave them the strength to keep rehearsing into the late hours each day. What made them forget about their fatigue, hunger and thirst.

The dream of demonstrating their commitment to the leaders in Moscow. The celebrations of that victory were everything.

She loved hearing what a role model she was. Not out of vanity— that was bourgeois and reactionary. No, it was because it showed how much could be achieved with willpower and discipline.

If she could do it, then so could everyone else. She held in contempt all those who failed to reach their full potential—who held themselves back.

Nothing was impossible.

Workers of the world, unite!

She had once sworn allegiance to that motto—to help change the world. To put an end to all evil. Together with the young in all countries, they would build a new world.

As she crossed the large courtyard, she glanced down at her clothes. It wasn't always easy to keep them clean when rehearsing in the large, dusty yard caked in dry mud. But they couldn't let the elements defeat humankind. Your outer appearance said everything about your inner appearance, and the new world wasn't going to be built with stains and wrinkles.

An alert gaze, straight-backed posture, clean and well-ironed clothes. That was how to honor the heroes who had saved the Motherland during the Great Patriotic War, as well as the sons of the Motherland who had once upon a time liberated the people of the Soviet Union from the shackles of imperialism and the tyranny of the tsars.

She stopped in front of the huge wooden door. Was she supposed to knock? Was she allowed to?

Yes. A Young Pioneer was fearless.

She clenched her small white fist and knocked three times, then she waited.

"Come in," said a deep voice.

She opened the heavy door and stepped into the semidarkness.

The chairman was sitting on a chair beside his desk. The light from the small window was reflected off his bare head, and in one hand he was holding a handkerchief that he was using to wipe his runny eye. No one knew what was wrong with it—all they knew was that it was always runny. Some said it was a war wound, others said it was punishment for a lack of commitment, while there were those who claimed that the eye was running because his soul was crying tears for the citizens of all those countries where socialism had not yet been able to liberate them.

Behind the chairman's gigantic desk there was a man she didn't recognize. He was wearing a uniform with a lot of gold on the lapels, and he was scrutinizing her with an intense gaze.

"Lidiya Alexandrova," said the chairman. "Do you love socialism?"

What a question!

"Yes, Comrade Chairman!"

"Do you want to see socialism victorious?"

"Yes, Comrade Chairman!"

"What ought we to do to ensure the victory of socialism?"

"Everything, Comrade Chairman!"

"Lidiya Alexandrova, will you contribute to the final victory? Will you dedicate your life to the most important of tasks? Will you participate in the salvation of the earth and its working masses?"

"Yes, Comrade Chairman!"

"I've had my eye on you, as you know."

The chairman had had more than his eye on her, but she chose not to mention anything about that. It was necessary to withstand anything to contribute to the final victory. Her suffering was nothing compared with the suffering on the battlefield—her body was a mere triviality by comparison.

"Yes, Comrade Chairman."

Perhaps she should have protested, shown herself to be humble. But she settled for answering concisely. Powerful men weren't to be interrupted with your own thoughts.

"You are a role model to all your comrades in the Pioneers. Your discipline, your stamina, your ideological maturity for one so young. You are an example and a very good servant to socialism and the global revolution."

"Thank you, Comrade Chairman. But this is only what the Soviet Union is entitled to demand from its sons and daughters."

"Comrade Bogrov here is very interested in young girls who set themselves apart. Assignments encompassing great responsibility are available to such girls."

"I've heard that you speak Swedish," said Bogrov, leaning forward as if he was awaiting the answer with anticipation.

"Just like everyone here," said Lidiya Alexandrova.

In the Swedish village, they were all the offspring of Swedish immigrants and had retained their language—something the Soviet authorities had not appreciated, but had benevolently allowed to pass.

"But not everyone has your conviction," said Bogrov. "And I gather you are alone in the world."

"My mother died in the service of the Motherland, and my father died as a result of his betrayal of the Soviet Union and her people."

"That is tragic," said Bogrov. "But all tragedies can be transformed into something good. What do you feel toward your father?"

"I regret his treachery toward my Motherland, but a child is not condemned by her parents' actions. Just as the freedom-loving Soviet Union rose from the ruins of the oppressed tsarist Russia, so I shall rise from the ruins of my father's demise and help to build a new society. I do, however, sometimes miss my mother."

Bogrov turned to Chairman Yuchenko.

"You were right to persuade me to visit."

The chairman mopped his eye, despite the fact that it was at that moment dry.

Bogrov leafed through a bundle of papers in front of him. The chairman produced a carton of cigarettes, but a look from the visitor made him put them away again.

"Lidiya Alexandrova, will you give your life to the realization of the idea and potential of socialism?" said Bogrov, looking the girl straight in the eye.

"Yes, Comrade Colonel!"

She knew her ranks, the visitor thought to himself.

"Are you prepared to leave everything in your old life behind and start a new life? One where you place the mission of socialism and the Soviet Union ahead of all else?"

"Yes, Comrade Colonel!"

"Are you prepared to leave behind your comrades here in Ukraine and start afresh in another country?"

"Yes, Comrade Colonel!"

"Do you promise to do your utmost to complete any assignment that your Motherland may ask of you?"

"Yes, Comrade!"

"How much time do you need to pack and bid farewell to your friends?"

"None. Sentimentality is a sign of weakness, and cannot be permitted to delay the advance of our struggle."

"Lidiya Alexandrova, your name is now Agneta Öman. You were born and raised in Sweden. You were orphaned at a young age. We will teach you your past so that you are able to recount it when we wake you up in the middle of the night, so that it is the one you cry out if the enemy tries to force the truth out of you with physical methods. Think only in Swedish. Your old self no longer exists. You are Agneta Öman. And your loyalty to global peace, the final victory of the working masses and the Soviet cause is complete. Is that understood?"

"Yes, Comrade Colonel!"

45

The view across the Västerbron and the island of Långholmen was breathtaking. Sara had never seen her city look so beautiful.

Fyrverkarbacken was adjacent to Marieberg, not far from the *Dagens Nyheter* tower, and it was just a stone's throw from the Russian embassy. From the outside, the building fulfilled all prejudices about Eastern bloc architecture. It was big, anonymous and completely lacking any joy. But when you stepped through the doors the impression was very different. Granted, the flats were dull. Like everything from the big bang social housing projects of the 1960s, the ceilings were low, the walls were thin, and there was no coving or plaster. But what the location offered was unparalleled natural beauty outside the window, which more than made up for the building's shortcomings.

Sara knew it would take time for Anna and Bielke to get to grips with what she and the Germans had concluded. But she wanted to move on—she wanted to know everything. Not least for her own personal reasons. Her online searches had only provided her with the historical background, and she'd thought long and hard about who might be able to help her—who might know more about the illegals and their role today.

Why not one of the leading figures of the Cold War in Sweden?

Sara knew that one of the former ambassadors from the Soviet Union, Boris Kozlov, still lived in Stockholm following his retirement at the time of the USSR's collapse in 1991.

She wasn't due at work for another couple of hours, and when she found Kozlov's number online and rang him, the former diplomat invited her to his flat in Marieberg without hesitation. Perhaps he was curious about what she had to say. Or maybe he was just a bored pensioner who missed the rough and tumble of big politics.

Just like many visitors, Sara was enraptured by the view. Magnificent.

"You were close to the embassy then," said Sara.

"Yes. It was good back then. Now the important thing is that I don't have to look at it."

He was right about that. All the windows faced the water, the park and the bridge. The Russian embassy was to the rear of the building.

"Is this the building they call the Erlander Building?" said Sara.

"Yes."

"Did he live here?"

"In this very flat."

It was impossible to tell whether it was an anecdote Kozlov enjoyed telling, or whether he just knew that Swedes liked to hear it.

"How long have you lived here?"

"Since he died. 1986. They were all rented flats back then."

The father of the nation, Per Albin, had lived in a terraced house, his successor Tage Erlander in this slightly sad concrete tower, and his heir Olof Palme had lived in an ordinary house out in Vällingby. Before the advent of the official residence at Sager House, none of Sweden's prime ministers had felt any need to live lavishly, so it seemed.

The purchase of Sager House had been precipitated by the murder of Olof Palme, so they said. But if it was just a matter of security, they could surely have found better solutions.

However, times had changed. Now Sweden was supposed to have leaders who lived it up. Even the rather ordinary Ingvar Carlsson had supported it, and neither Carl Bildt nor his successor Göran Persson had raised any objections. Naturally. It didn't matter whether you'd grown up in Vällingby or in well-heeled Östermalm—if you became prime minister, then you wanted to live well.

Kozlov set down a tray with coffee cups and two large schnapps glasses filled with transparent liquid.

"Is that vodka?" said Sara, astonished to encounter the legend in reality.

"It would be impolite to decline."

"I'm driving."

Kozlov merely looked at her. Sara decided to try and delay the issue of the drink.

"Thank you for agreeing to see me," said Sara.

"One does not say no to the police."

Sara couldn't discern whether Kozlov was speaking from a Soviet perspective, or whether he merely wanted to conduct himself appropriately in his new homeland.

"So how can I be of service?" said the former diplomat, sipping his coffee.

"Illegals," said Sara.

Kozlov put down his cup carefully and leaned back in the armchair.

"What am I supposed to know about them?"

"As ambassador, I should imagine you knew most things."

"The diplomatic core knew nothing. That was left to intelligence."

"You didn't get to be an ambassador without being part of the intelligence service."

Kozlov raised his eyebrows almost imperceptibly, as if to say "maybe."

"Many illegals stayed on in the countries they were deployed to," said Sara.

"Why do you say that?"

"It's common knowledge. Well documented in lots of articles and books. They also say that Russia took over the illegals from the former USSR. They are still on assignment. And still passing information to their handlers."

"Possibly. But I've left politics."

"I want to ask you about someone from your day. Agneta Broman—
Stellan Broman's wife. Was she an illegal? Is she still?"

Kozlov raised his schnapps glass.

"*Za zdorovie!*"

"No thanks," said Sara. "Not in the middle of the day."

"It helps me to think better."

"But not me."

"I won't drink alone. And if I don't have this, then I doubt I'll
remember anything, I'm afraid."

He seemed to mean it. A former ambassador, even briefly the
Soviet foreign minister, a personal friend of Gorbachev and Palme,
Kohl and Blair, who was now pressuring Sara Nowak into drinking.
Like a teenage boy.

Mad.

But she just had to go with the flow.

Sara raised the schnapps glass. It was big—probably at least a
quadruple shot. Kozlov downed his and Sara took a sip from hers.
A snifter.

"I'd rather tell you over a bite to eat," said Kozlov when he'd put
down his glass. "Let's go out to eat and I'll tell you everything you
want to know."

"I need to know now. If you tell me, then we can go out for a
meal another time."

"It's hard to concentrate when you look at me with those beautiful eyes."

"Are you flirting with me?"

Sara was completely dumbfounded.

"I was faithful for forty-five years," said Kozlov. "But now she's
gone, may she rest in peace."

"Agneta Broman first," said Sara.

Dear God—she couldn't get away from horny blokes even when
she was on a murder investigation. But the most annoying thing
was that almost every man seemed to be like that, except her own.

"Illegals," said Kozlov, draining his coffee cup. "Well, we had them." He sighed. "And yes, they're still around today. But back then it was for a purpose—they had a mission. To even up the odds. To help deliver progress. To make the world a better place, even if their methods were controversial. We believed in something. The current one—he doesn't believe in anything. Just power."

The current one.

The former ambassador was apparently unwilling to even say the current president's name.

"For those in charge, there's no difference," Kozlov continued. "It's the same empire. Slightly smaller now, but they intend to recoup their losses. Faith in the Motherland is at the heart of it. Communism was a passing phase, but Mother Russia endures."

"The illegals," said Sara. "What did they do? What can they do today?"

"Gather information. But back in the day it was for preventative purposes—to avoid being taken by surprise by the enemy. Now, it's industrial espionage that is the order of the day—defense secrets. Everything is about money. Ideology is dead."

"To avoid being taken by surprise by the enemy?"

"You must have heard the people who spent years bleating on that the USA and its allies should have attacked the USSR after the defeat of Nazi Germany. Even that they should have used atom bombs, like they did on Japan. To crush the evil empire. You would never have succeeded—of that I'm certain. It would merely have caused millions of deaths."

"Was Agneta Broman an illegal?"

Sara felt it was time to apply some pressure to get to the truth.

"I didn't know Agneta. I would greet her at the Bromans' parties— she was a very beautiful woman. But I never really conversed with her."

"That wasn't my question. Was she an illegal?"

Sara swapped Kozlov's empty glass for her own almost-full one.

Kozlov waved his hand in front of him like a conductor summoning the attention of the orchestra. Then he took Sara's glass, drained it in one and set it back down.

"I can tell you about Desirée."

The dead wife, Sara supposed. She regretted tricking him into the second giant vodka.

"The illegal Desirée," Kozlov continued. "Born in Ukraine, orphaned at a young age, recruited by the intelligence services for her fiery patriotism. Raised in the Swedish village in Ukraine—so she spoke Swedish from infancy. Albeit somewhat dated Swedish. Deployed into Sweden with a stolen identity, as a Laestadian child from the far north without any family. Trained in social skills, instructed to work on her appearance, and then assisted onto the social scene in the capital. After a couple of brief engagements to prominent industrialists, she finds the winning ticket. She attends a party at the home of the country's most famous television personality, where the entire social elite are to be found. And not only that—they're on such a rampage that they're targets for all sorts of influence. This becomes Desirée's mission—send home information about all the guests. Get them to talk while drunk, while in bed, photograph their papers. Find out everything about their lives."

"Agneta?"

"I'm merely recounting the story I've heard within KGB circles. I have no name for Desirée."

"Did she work together with Stellan?"

"Sara," said Kozlov, putting a hand on her knee. She pushed it away, at the risk that he would be angry. But he didn't seem to care. "In the world I'm talking about, secrets and double-dealing were at the very heart of it. Espionage and counterespionage went to great lengths to avoid two agents being aware of each other's existence. There are countless examples of spies and informants and illegals who worked side by side for years without knowing about each other. Especially when it came to an East German informant and a Russian—we would never have told them about our personnel. Better to let them act as supervisors and secondary informants. It made it easier to find out if someone became a double agent and started reporting to the West, or was trying to plant disinformation. You can't imagine how paranoid we were."

"You spied on your own spies?"

"We spied on everything."

Kozlov paused and seemed to be daydreaming.

"Desirée was special," he said. "I hope she's well."

"Special?" said Sara. "In what way?"

Kozlov looked at Sara as if considering how much he could tell her. How much he wanted to tell.

"She went against her handlers to help me. As a straightforward favor to a friend. I don't think that's ever happened in the history of the Soviet Union."

"What did she do?"

"You're aware that I was the foreign minister?"

"Yes," said Sara.

She knew that. Even if Kozlov had only held the role briefly.

"When Gorbachev was deposed in the coup, Desirée advised me to speak up for him, even though it was her senior chiefs at the KGB who had ensured he lost power. I did as she told me—then Gorbachev returned, and as thanks for my support he appointed me foreign minister. Not a bad career for a little orphan farm boy from Kyrgyzstan! How she could have known, I have no idea. Later on, I'm afraid, Yeltsin went against Gorbachev—and when Gorbachev fell, I fell, too. But thanks to Desirée I've still been one of the most important leaders in one of the world's biggest, most feared countries."

"Impressive," said Sara.

"But today it's all gone," said Kozlov.

It was not altogether easy to digest that Aunt Agneta had played such a major role in history. The question was whether this might have any connection to Stellan's death.

"And if Desirée were to be activated today," said Sara. "What reason might there be for that?"

Kozlov leaned his head back and appeared to be thinking.

"It's absolutely certain that they have younger resources they can use. And Stellan Broman's contacts are not current. It would have to be something that only she was able to do. A skill of some kind. Or personal connections, of course. Current events in some other sector tied to her active years would likely give you a clue."

"Stay-Put," said Sara.

She'd signed the confidentiality paperwork and knew what was at stake. But she had to try it out. Stay-Put was no secret. It had been known about in the 1980s. And the magic words worked.

Boris Kozlov's face cracked into a wolfish grin.

"Why are you here if you already know everything?"

"Is this to do with Stay-Put?"

"Yours or ours?"

"So you had your own?"

"NATO had Stay-Put, so of course the Warsaw Pact had Stay-Put. We responded in kind."

"How did it work? Is it still active?"

Kozlov looked at Sara for a long time, then he straightened himself up, looked at the ceiling and began to deliver a small lecture. She hoped that he would get to the point sooner or later.

"Monitoring of the western side of the Fulda valley was primarily handled during the seventies by the American Fifth Corps under the command of General Starry," said Kozlov. "His reasoning was that it had to be possible to attack the Warsaw Pact's forces in East Germany, Poland and Czechoslovakia before they had made it to the battlefield, to ensure that in the event of any attack there was no need to use nuclear weapons that would impact their own forces and the West German people. A strategy adopted by NATO which made us in the East assemble the same radical defenses—we planted explosive charges in the ground at roadsides and key locations. But the chiefs weren't content with just ordinary explosives."

Kozlov paused for effect before continuing.

"They went for nuclear explosives," he said, letting the words resonate around the room. "To make the ground impassable and secure Soviet borders through a wide, radioactive buffer."

"The devastation of Europe?"

"A corridor straight through Europe, running along the border between East and West. The military probably felt they were simply responding in kind—after all, we had all of NATO's war plans. I can tell you that much, because they were found by Western powers in the Stasi headquarters in Berlin when the Wall fell—so it's public knowledge. The Warsaw Pact knew exactly what NATO was thinking. And they responded to it all."

"So you buried atom bombs in the ground."

"You could say that."

"And the atom bombs...?"

"Have never been found. Most Soviet archives remained sealed, unlike in the DDR. The KGB and GRU managed to keep their secrets."

"Could the information about them have leaked out by any other means? Could it have been sold? Would the current Russian powers be interested in the bombs being detonated?"

"Let me answer each part separately. The information could have been sold. Most things were sold when the Soviet Union collapsed. It could also have been sold in East Germany, which was—after all—the intended scene for this devastation. But in that case, there would have been only a very few people who knew about it. To your final question—would Russia have anything to gain from the atom bombs being triggered today?"

Kozlov paused.

"Yes. Well, the country's leaders would certainly have an interest in information about the bombs being leaked. It would cause panic and undermine society in a string of European countries. And you know that Ivan likes destabilization. And if responsibility was shouldered by some terrorist group—say, an Islamist cell that obtained the information from their Palestinian brothers... Well, I think our friends in the Kremlin would be unlikely to cry tears of blood over that."

"So a Russian illegal could very plausibly be tasked with cleaning up all trace of any such operation, and helping to realize it? But what type of information might be here? Something someone has to come here to collect?"

"After having seen the complete disappearance of East Germany, there were many who hid important information in neutral locations because they were worried the USSR would go the same way as the DDR. Some wanted to protect themselves, others wanted to use it as a weapon in the struggle against developments or quite simply to sell it and earn a bundle. Everything was sold when the Soviet Union went down. Tanks, submarines, transport planes, warheads. It's a miracle more of them haven't turned up. Either the quality was too poor, or we've been extraordinarily lucky. But it's not too late. Munitions keep for thirty years. Easily."

"So Desirée was guarding the information?"

"Perhaps."

"Why is she getting rid of the entire East German spy ring, then?"

"Is she?"

Damn. Now she'd said too much.

"That has to remain between us," said Sara. "At least until it's official."

"It'll never be official. No matter how many die."

"But why is she killing them all?"

"To cover up tracks, if you ask me. Perhaps the East German spies were originally assigned the mission, but now that it's actually happening she's tasked with cleaning up and ensuring that no one can talk. After this many years, they won't dare rely on people's loyalties. Or perhaps they're just afraid that some old spy with dementia will start babbling in their golden years. In the good old days, no one ever expected a spy to see old age—but there are actually rather a lot of them who made it."

Sara took a sip from her coffee and tried to formulate her next question, but thoughts were spinning in her mind.

A Soviet stay-put. With hidden atom bombs that no one knew the locations of.

Or rather, a few people knew.

The wrong people.

46

With her walking poles almost dragging along behind her rather than working rhythmically, she drew no attention. Just another old lady who thought a pair of sticks would compensate for a lifetime of being sedentary. As yet, no one had guessed that the anonymous old woman who had been wandering around the neighborhood in recent days was the wife of the murdered Uncle Stellan, currently being searched for by every police force in the country. Their neighbor. Unrecognizable. A complete stranger in her own neighborhood.

And then it occurred to her that she had always been that. Stellan's fame had, in a way, given the street its profile. It had set the tone. If you lived there, you lived in Stellan and Agneta's neighborhood.

And yet she'd felt like a visitor—never at home. As if she'd been hopping spiritually from foot to foot on the front step, waiting for an invitation that never came.

Had she pretended for all those years? No, she had been Agneta Broman.

But now she was someone else.

Faithful to her mission, Agneta had ensured she carefully documented everything to do with Geiger. Given that she'd been active long before the East Germans had managed to recruit their inform-ant, it had been easy to identify Geiger's instructions. Her own agency had been worried, and classified Geiger as a risky recruit. But the East Germans had been overjoyed. A prestige signing with access straight to the heart of Sweden's corridors of power. But they were more interested in being recognized as a state in their own right than they were in defeating the great enemy.

Agneta was certain that her family had never guessed the truth, which meant she'd been able to monitor everything that the East

Germans' secret informant had done. In the beginning, all the information had been in writing—contrary to all instructions. But that was what it was like working with amateurs. The advantage for Agneta was that she'd easily been able to photograph the notes. She noticed that once Geiger had memorized the information, the notes had been destroyed. But by then she'd already documented everything and sent it on.

That was why she knew, among other things, where Geiger's "letterbox" was: the public place where a handler or other spies could leave messages. It could be chalk marks on a building wall, stones arranged in a certain way in the flower bed or drawing pins stuck into a tree trunk, where the different colors of the pins meant different things: "Contact your handler," "Everything is going according to plan," "You've been exposed" and so on.

Geiger's drop was on the promenade by the water's edge a few blocks away. She turned onto Tällbergsgränd and used the poles to maneuver herself toward the path that ran through the small wooded area. On the fifth tree trunk, part of the bark had been peeled off. Just a couple of centimeters, but that was enough.

After three days, the message had finally arrived.

She'd begun to have her doubts.

Despite the fact that she knew that much of the assignment was about waiting, uncertainty—and last-minute changes to the plans. Despite the fact that she knew it was important for an agent in the field to retain their focus. Not to forget, not to hesitate, not to stop. Wait, be ready and then act with lightning speed when the time came.

But after so many years of inactivity, she had to ask herself whether anything could really happen now. She'd begun to lean toward the idea that it wouldn't.

But now there was a message.

"We need to meet."

Abu Rasil.

He'd finally received the all-clear from his handlers that they were ready. So he wanted to meet Geiger to obtain the codes.

But he wasn't expecting Agneta.

Desirée.

How long had it been? Forty years?

At one of the training camps, when they had been on the same side.

Today, Agneta was on her own side.

It was time.

And she was ready.

She plodded back toward the house, careful not to give away her eagerness. She unlocked it with the borrowed keys. She put down the poles and immediately felt twenty years younger. Then she checked what was in the fridge and freezer. She didn't want to cut corners with her food—especially not when it might be her last meal.

Then she went down to the basement and into the boiler room.

"How does minced veal with cream sauce and rowanberry jam sound?"

He didn't reply—merely stared at her. He was, perhaps, still having trouble grasping how the woman who'd recently given herself to him with such passion suddenly had his life in her hands.

There wasn't much he *could* say either, from where he was sitting. But he could at least have nodded. The ropes and the gag didn't prevent him from nodding.

"Well, that's what it's going to be," said Agneta. "You can have a glass of wine with it if you like. I've got to work, so I'll have to abstain."

Agneta didn't know whether her words were being registered.

She looked at her captive. Bound and locked into his own home. The question was, what would she do with him when it was time?

A bullet would be easiest, but he hadn't actually done anything to her or otherwise impeded her mission. On the contrary, he'd given her some pleasure and enabled her to monitor the meeting spot.

Perhaps she should just leave him there, and let luck and chance determine his fate?

47

With Kozlov's words resounding in her head, Sara wandered through the large police complex at Kungsholmen.

Agneta, an illegal.

A Soviet citizen who'd been living in Sweden under a false identity.

She couldn't help comparing it with her own life when the children had been younger. She'd lied about what she did at work so as not to frighten them.

To protect them from the sordid world that she encountered every day.

Could she, too, have been a spy? An illegal? Would she have been able to turn off her true self completely and live as someone else?

Lying to the children hadn't been difficult. Would she have been just as happy to live her life alongside people who had no idea who she really was?

Never being able to say your real name to your children, never talking about your childhood, only repeating memories learned by rote. Or details from the childhood of some stranger.

Oddly enough, it was the children that she thought of. Deceiving your husband didn't seem as strange. That was something you already did to a great extent—especially at the beginning of a relationship. The problems usually cropped up when you stopped pretending, when you wanted to be seen for the person you were.

Like so many other women, Agneta had completely adapted to her husband's interests and lifestyle. But she'd done so for a clear purpose: to achieve something. Something that malevolent men had demanded from her.

Sara stepped into the locker room, changed into her more durable work clothes and gathered her equipment. Pistol, handcuffs, truncheon, pepper spray, gloves, the compact comms radio and the small but powerful torch. Sometimes it was handy to be able to blind the punters when they were caught red-handed—it increased the confusion and further paralyzed their ability to act rashly. Fewer of them tried to escape or fight.

"All the animals come out at night."

Sara looked up at David, who had just entered.

"Whores, skunk pussies, buggers, queens, fairies, dopers, junkies," he added.

Sara wasn't sure *Taxi Driver* was a suitable source of inspiration in their line of work, but she was glad that he seemed willing to put their row behind them.

When they got down to the car park, she got into the driver's seat. It would be good to drive—to think about something else.

Then they headed out to the most notorious street in the country. It was undeniably the road in Sweden with the most similarities to *Taxi Driver*.

"Not much action yet," said David, and Sara looked around.

It wasn't that late, and the bright summer evening gave the red light district a completely different feeling to a black November night. But in a way, it was sadder like this. So much grime and brutality was to be found even in beautiful summer Sweden. The Sweden that they'd all thought was paradise while growing up.

The light, enchanting nights. The warm breeze. The suddenly outgoing and happy Swedes. All the parties and festivals, all the encounters with new people, all the outdoor seating. Suddenly everyone was open, pleasant and beautiful.

Even on this infamous street, there were young, innocent partakers of nightlife stumbling past on their way to or from the bars. Or perhaps they'd their sights set on city hall for a night-time dip in the midst of a quiet and peaceful city. Simply walking through Stockholm on a summer's night was an almost supernatural experience, Sara thought to herself. Provided you didn't happen to be right here.

"He wasn't just a spy," said Sara without any warning. "He was a sex offender, too. He filmed himself raping young girls. And he filmed loads of other men as they did it. So that he could blackmail them."

"Jesus Christ!" said David. "Uncle Stellan?"

"Basically serves him right," said Sara. "That he got shot, that is."

David looked at Sara, unsure what to say.

"He was just like all the other men we see out here every single day. But worse. Sick. How do you end up like that?"

"Don't ask me."

"And he had two daughters the same age as the girls he was raping."

"I've never understood how they function," David said. "Rape, assault, degrade. Then back home to the family."

"Imagine being his child."

"Do the daughters know about it?"

"Yes."

"Pity he's dead," he said. "It would have been bloody good to put away someone like that."

"A celebrity?"

"A dirty old man who thought he could get away with anything."

They fell silent. They watched the three girls they could see were waiting for clients. Jessica, Nana, Sahara. Made-up names, obviously.

When they headed out at the start of the evening, did they ever consider that they might not come home again? Prostitutes being murdered was fortunately not that common in Sweden, but it wasn't unheard of.

And no one knew how many disappeared and were never reported missing.

What was it like to be someone that no one cared about?

"We've got a bite in progress," said David.

Sara followed his gaze and saw a tall, broad-shouldered man in a baseball cap speaking to the black girl, Jessica. A bit of small talk before making up his mind? Strange behavior. But Sara was pretty certain. The punters assumed a different posture when they began the actual negotiation. Well, asked for the price. There were those who tried to haggle or get more for their money, but not many.

The man in the baseball cap was nodding to himself while Jessica answered a question he'd asked.

"Does it help?" said Sara, while following the conversation outside the entrance to the metro station.

"That he small talks?" said David.

"What we do. Does it help? It never ends. There are always new faces. There are just more and more victims of trafficking."

"Think about what it would be like if we *didn't* do something."

A marginal difference, she thought to herself.

"Show time," said David, and Sara saw Jessica and the man begin to head toward Sankt Johannes Church.

David got out of the car, stretched and then began to follow the pair at a distance.

Sara opened the door, but before she could get out, her mobile rang.

She really ought to have hurried along behind her colleague, but she chose to stay where she was as she answered. As if she could tell that it was important.

It was Hall.

Their superintendent.

In the middle of the night.

Sara whistled to David and signaled that he should wait.

"Nowak."

"Tom Hall here. I'm, er... It's come to my attention that you have got involved in a murder investigation in Västerort. Because you knew the murder victim."

Bloody Lindblad. She always got lazy old Hall to do exactly as she wanted, even though he was her boss.

"Got involved...?" repeated Sara. "In my spare time, I've gained access to information that may be relevant, and I've passed it to the investigation. Anna Torhall, who's working on it, is an old friend and course-mate from the Police Academy."

"But when you were in possession of important information about a missing person, you contacted German intelligence rather than our own security service or your friend on the investigation."

"I…" Sara began.

"That's bad enough, but I've also been informed that you broke into the home of a private citizen, and additionally harassed Stellan Broman's children by showing them shocking films of a sexual nature that depicted their murdered father. Is this true?"

Lotta had apparently decided to hit back.

"I didn't break in and the case has been closed. And I didn't harass Lotta and Malin. It was pertinent to the investigation—"

"An investigation that you aren't a part of. And films that came into your possession by means that remain unclear and potentially criminal. There are no excuses for this kind of conduct."

"I'm sorry if they took it badly. It was with the best of intentions."

"Surely you realize that I have no choice?"

Sara didn't reply. *Could this really happen?*

"You're suspended with immediate effect."

"We're out on patrol. I'm needed here. We're about to arrest a man paying for sex."

"Leave that to your colleagues and go home. Immediately. You're suspended. And you may be terminated if the investigation proves that the accusations against you are founded. Return your weapon and badge."

"Now?"

"No." Hall sighed. "The office is closed. As soon as you can in the morning."

"Well then, I can finish my shift."

"No. You're to go home. And if you refuse to adhere to the suspension, then you'll be dismissed without any further investigation. Is that understood?"

Sara processed the information.

"Is that understood?" Hall repeated.

"Yes."

48

Streets and squares flickered past, people moving in public places at top speed. Cars, bicycles, but above all, pedestrians. Dressed for the summer, dressed for work, stressed, wandering aimlessly. The cast of a major city.

There was really no reason to watch the films that the program was analyzing, but Breuer still preferred to follow them on a screen so that she knew the computers were actually doing their job. It might be an old-fashioned approach, but she didn't care.

Working together, the computers in the portable command center in the motorhome could search six hours of CCTV footage each minute. Back at base in Pullach, they would have been able to work at ten times the speed. The limitation meant that they had to concentrate on the cameras positioned at the most frequently visited locations, metro stations and in the city's taxi cabs.

So far they had nothing.

Breuer couldn't understand these people. Everyone had an individual personal identification number that was registered all over the place—records that went back centuries and listed everything that had ever happened to each and every citizen, and a legal principle of transparency that meant that anybody could find out anything about anyone of their choosing. But they didn't have facial recognition cameras.

The Brits, who used nothing but their postcodes as identification, had cameras all over the place. And thanks to facial recognition, they'd been able to prevent a string of terrorist acts.

China based its entire apparatus of control on this technology.

But in this Orwellian post-socialist state, around halfway between Britain and China in Breuer's eyes, they refused.

That was why the computers weren't able to find any faces that matched with any of the possible Abu Rasils that Breuer had pulled up over the years. Four different men who *might* be Rasil. Even that was a long shot, since there wasn't a single photograph that they knew for certain depicted the terrorist. And everyone who claimed to have met him was dead. It was like hunting a whisper, as Strauss put it.

If they got hold of Agneta Broman, that might be a way to Abu Rasil. But they couldn't find her either.

"No hits at the airports, railway stations or ferry terminals. None of our informants have a clue where Abu Rasil is, or where the meeting place might be."

Breuer heard the doubt in Strauss's voice.

"But they say Rasil is here?"

"Yes," Strauss replied. "But isn't it just wishful thinking? They've built up a myth about the elusive Abu Rasil that's grown over the years he's been gone—so now there must be something huge happening to justify the long wait. A bit like Christians awaiting the resurrection of Christ."

"You're forgetting Hattenbach," said Breuer.

"But perhaps that was all they had? Maybe there was only one bomb left?"

"In the West, certainly. But we know nothing about the East. Except that the bombs that were once there were enormous. And that there's nothing to indicate their removal. This is just about who could trigger them, and who is actually willing to do so. The blast in Hattenbach was presumably just a taste of what's to come—to show they have the ability. That was why they picked a small bomb. They want payment for the big ones."

Strauss looked heavy-hearted. Although he'd been involved in preventing terrorist attacks on several occasions, and had dealt with presumed terrorists, this was on an altogether different scale. Hundreds of thousands of deaths—perhaps millions.

"All you have to realize," said Breuer, "is that given all the terrorist attacks in Europe in recent decades, there are plenty of people who would be willing to set off those bombs. You of all people should know that."

"But how do you stop a shadow?" Strauss asked.

"Don't forget how close I've come several times," said Breuer. "I know how he thinks. How he works. He's in the country. The handover is tonight—or tomorrow night at the latest. Believe me."

But Strauss didn't know what to believe.

49

Suspended.

The punishment itself didn't bother Sara. She'd never been career-focused, and she was uninterested in what her bosses thought of her. But she thought it was idiotic to pull an experienced officer off the street just because Lotta wanted to screw with her. And above all, it bothered her that she was excluded from the investigation. It was just like when they were kids. Suddenly she was no longer allowed to participate.

The murder inquiry had turned out to have plenty of points of contact with her own life and childhood, but it was really all about every Swede's life. The entire population had grown up with Uncle Stellan as a unifying figurehead, as the only indisputable positive force in the country. Politicians were crooked and athletes could let you down when it came to the crunch, but you could always rely on Uncle Stellan.

Sara sent a text message to Anna.

Suspended. Let me know if anything happens.

She received a thumbs-up emoji in reply.

She was certain that Anna hadn't said a word to Hall or Lindblad about Sara being involved in the investigation. Not even to Bielke. While Sara was angry with Hall, Lindblad and Lotta Broman, she was in equal measure glad to have her friend.

But now she was completely at a loose end on an involuntary basis. Sara had messaged the kids to say she was at home and wanted to see them. So far, neither had replied.

While she waited, she summarized the situation. Geiger was dead. Kellner was dead. Ober was dead. What was going to happen next?

What was Abu Rasil up to?

Did he even exist?

What was Agneta up to?

No, Sara thought to herself. She couldn't spend her whole evening ruminating on the Bromans. They'd taken up far too much of her life already.

Where were the kids?

Eventually, Sara messaged both Ebba and Olle:

Come home! Now!

And she received in return, respectively, an ironic message and an angry smiley.

There was really no need. Just doing nothing felt good. If the summer evenings hadn't been light, she could have sat in the twilight. Let the darkness slowly envelop the apartment without switching on any lights. Bow down to nature. Sitting in the twilight was one of the most peaceful activities in existence, as far as she was concerned. But she could just as well sit in the light.

Her thoughts moved on.

What would have happened if Jane hadn't saved her from Stellan? If Sara had also become a victim? She would hardly have been likely to become a police officer. She might instead have become one of the girls that she and her colleagues tried to help.

Or would she have managed to bury that within her? The #MeToo movement had shown just how many women had their own stories of assault that they had never shared. Sexism and unpleasant comments during her own teenage years were something that Sara could testify to, as well as manipulative playmates in her childhood. But she had been spared downright assault. She'd never understood how close she'd come—what her mother had done for her.

Where did it emanate from, that anger toward all the men who paid for sex that she encountered through her job?

Perhaps it was just a completely normal and healthy reaction to the payment of money for someone else's body—to use others however one pleased, often exerting violence over them. A response to the contempt for human life that was so palpable to Sara and her colleagues. She supposed the rage had built up over the years.

Long ago, she'd tried to have some understanding. She'd believed the myths about the lonely and unwanted people who paid for sex because they would never obtain it by any other means. Before she became a police officer, she'd largely looked at it according to the principle that buying sex was a voluntary arrangement between two adults. But no explanation held water. She'd learned that after just a few days on the job.

She needed to think about something else. She picked up the novel she was reading from the coffee table and realized it had lain untouched for a couple of months. But if she was going to resume reading, she would need to switch on a light, and she didn't like doing that. She also thought it would be challenging to engross herself in a fictional world when the real one was so turbulent. She knew that Anna loved to lose herself in novels precisely so that she forgot about daily life and its troubles, but it didn't work the same way for Sara. She needed peace and quiet in her mind in order to get to grips with fiction. Sara had to make do with holding the book. The hardback binding, the shiny dust jacket, the many thin pages inside. She ran her fingertip along the print and thought she could feel the small bumps of the printed letters, although perhaps she was just imagining that. She put the book to her nose and smelled it. They said that the other senses were heightened if you stopped using one, and right now Sara thought that both her fingers and her nose were decidedly more sensitive than usual. Perhaps it was just a matter of being attentive.

Sara thought that some classical music might be a fitting addition to the darkness. She took out her old violin and put the bow to the strings, but she couldn't bring herself to move her hand.

The way she felt now, she would never be able to play it again.

Why? Because it had been given to her by Stellan? Or because the last few days had snuffed out the small tendril of joy and creativity that she'd retained?

She wanted to smash it to pieces.

That probably wouldn't make anything better, she thought to herself. But then she realized that it wouldn't make things worse, either.

If nothing else, it was a good deed. A memory of Stellan Broman being erased from the surface of the earth.

She grasped the violin by the neck, raised her hand and then smashed it against the coffee table, splintering it into pieces.

Now it was 1–1 between Martin's instrument and hers. She struck the violin another half a dozen times against the table, so that it would be impossible to repair.

And then she sank to the floor and leaned her neck against the table.

She'd sat down on a splinter of violin that was cutting into her backside, but she didn't feel able to move.

Let it hurt, she thought to herself. That way I know I'm alive.

After half an hour, both the kids returned home. They complained because it was so dark. Olle settled down on the sofa and turned on the TV. Sara turned it off. Ebba came in with a plastic carrier bag from a convenience store and pulled out a large bag of crisps and a big bottle of cola. Hung over, Sara thought to herself, and let her be.

"So, what is it?" said Olle. "Why did we need to come home?"

"So that we can spend some time together. Ebba might be moving out soon, and then we won't be able to hang out together very often."

"Great. Can I have her room, then? You can sit there in your one-bed flat in Tumba," said Olle, smirking at his sister.

"There's nothing wrong with Tumba," said Sara, feeling overly politically correct.

Dear God, she had inner city kids. Maybe she should have taken her kids to see Jane in the suburbs more often. They were now both at an age where her admonitions effectively had the reverse effect.

"I'm getting a flat on Södermalm. Dad said so."

"Did he?"

"We've already been to view it. It's at Mosebacke."

Jesus Christ, Martin. A flat . . .

"What do I get, then?" said Olle.

"You can have a new mobile," said Ebba, smirking back at Olle.

She saw the words had an effect. Siblings knew which buttons to push in each other, Sara thought to herself. She'd never had a sibling—just Lotta and Malin, whom she would never have dared be mean to, out of fear that she'd be excluded. There was a security to being able to be mean to each other while still knowing you'd always have the other person there.

"If she gets one, then I should get one too!" said Olle, looking at his mother.

"You don't just get a flat," said Sara.

"Why not?" said Ebba. "Dad promised. I need somewhere to live, after all."

"But that costs millions of kronor. You don't get that."

"Why not? We've got money. It's like a poor family giving their daughter a tent for a hundred kronor."

"Listen to yourself!"

"But relatively. Three million isn't much for Dad."

"Six million, because I need one, too," said Olle.

"What's wrong with you? What sort of upbringing have we given you?"

"None whatsoever," said Ebba, stuffing a fistful of crisps in her mouth.

The words stung.

"I've got a very guilty conscience over the fact that I've worked so many late evenings and nights, but can't we try and make up for lost ground now? I can work less. You'll soon be a grown-up, and then it'll be too late."

"So what are we going to do then? Go to the kids' museum at Junibacken?"

"Go out for a meal?" Sara suggested.

They weren't children any longer, even if they were *her* children, and going to a restaurant sounded appropriately grown-up.

"There's no point," said Olle. "It'll never happen."

She sighed. But she didn't have much to offer by way of counter-arguments.

"Why don't we just talk?" said Sara. "I know I've been gone a lot, but do you remember how proud you were when you were little about the fact that your mum was a police officer? Aren't you proud anymore?"

"Well, how much fun do you think it is to hear that your own mum works on Malmskillnadsgatan?" said Olle.

"What? Who says that? People at school?"

"Yes."

"They're just trying to be funny," Ebba said in a tired voice. "They know you're a police officer, but that you work on Malmskillnads-gatan. Like the whores."

"Don't say whores! It's a bloody horrible word. And tell those idiots at school that this is a real damn job. I'm trying to help girls that no one else cares about. They're subjected to dreadful things."

"Yes, yes…"

"Surely there are other people who can help," said Olle. "Who don't have kids."

"Yes. But right now I'm trying to find the person who murdered Uncle Stellan, too."

"Why? He was rotten."

"Who said that?"

"Grandma. He thought she was worthless because she was a cleaner."

"Did she say that?"

"Yes."

"But they took care of her."

"What do you mean, 'took care of'?"

"Mum escaped from Poland. Surely I've told you that—don't you remember?"

"You've started to tell us lots of times, but then you've always had something else important to do. Why did she escape?"

"It was a dictatorship. And she didn't want to live there. She'd got pregnant with me and my father didn't want to know about it. Her own family rejected her and the communists thought she was immoral. They wanted to take me away from her and put her in an institution, so she fled. And when she got here, she had no money and didn't know anyone. Stellan and Agneta needed a housekeeper and placed an advertisement. Someone in social services spotted it and wanted to help Mum out."

"Is that right?" said Olle, putting his hand in the pocket of his hoodie.

"No mobiles," said Sara.

Olle pushed the phone back into his pocket again. It couldn't be any clearer that the story didn't exactly engage a fourteen-year-old.

"I'm sorry we haven't talked about this sooner, but remember it sometimes. You have it so good—a secure family, an amazing home, no money worries. But your grandmother fled a dictatorship without a penny to her name. And she cleaned 24/7 to provide for herself and her daughter. Because she wanted me to have a better life than her."

"Don't you want us to have a better life, too?"

"Yes."

"So let Dad give me that flat then."

Open goal.

"That's not the same."

"Surely it is."

"Were you ashamed?" said Olle.

"Of what?"

"That Grandma was a cleaner."

"Of course not."

Cleaning woman.

Suddenly an old quote from a movie cropped up in Sara's head. Why?

Cleaning woman! Cleaning woman!

A memory emerged. Sara and Malin and Lotta were sitting there screeching *Cleaning woman!* And then they threw rubbish on the floor where Jane had just cleaned. And when she picked it up, they threw rubbish somewhere else that she'd also cleaned. And called for Jane.

Cleaning woman! Cleaning woman!

And her mother had come and cleaned again.

And all the girls had laughed.

Sara hadn't thought about it since then. Not once. Effective self-censorship. And so far as she could remember, Jane had never spoken about it. She'd never reproached her daughter. She could have yelled at her, forbidden her from playing with the sisters. In fact, she *should* have told her off and stopped her from seeing them.

Why didn't she say anything?

Did she think that Sara would tell Stellan and Agneta? Had she started to count her own daughter among the masters of the house? She'd definitely acted that way, if Sara was honest.

There was something about Jane, it occurred to her. What was it? Something that didn't make sense.

Jane and childhood…

Exactly.

Sara looked at her two children. Ebba was yawning and Olle was absorbed by a game on his mobile.

"Look, you two, there's no need for you to sit here with me. I'll have to work less, and we'll have to try and use the summer to hang out together some more."

Relieved, the children went to their rooms.

Sara watched them go, and then surveyed the living room. The hut in the Bromans' garden that she and Jane had lived in would have fit into this room several times over. She noted that her own children had ended up with a better life than she had. Just like Sara's mother had given her daughter a better life.

She pulled out her mobile, checked her recent calls and hit redial.

"Yes?" said Jane in a slightly irritable tone—as if Sara was disturbing her. Her mother had some rather particular telephone habits.

"What was he like?" said Sara.

"Who?"

"Stellan. What was he like?"

"How do you mean?"

"To you. Olle said that you'd said he was mean to you."

"Well, there's mean and then there's mean…"

"Was he?"

"He had so much on his plate. I suppose he didn't have the energy to be pleasant to a cleaner."

"But what about all his talk about solidarity with the workers?"

"I never heard anything like that. I suppose he didn't want to disturb me while I was cleaning and doing the laundry and cooking."

"And what about Agneta?"

"Well, what can I say? I don't think she had it easy being married to someone like that."

"Was she unpleasant to you?"

"She wasn't very…warm. A bit harsh. It sometimes felt like she would force me to clean in the evenings so that I couldn't spend time with you. I don't know why. She had two daughters of her own, so she had no cause to be jealous."

"Why did you stay?"

"You were so attached to the girls."

"It was for my sake?"

"Yes. And you must remember how angry you were when we moved."

"But I didn't know then how they'd treated you, or what Stellan did to girls. But you knew that."

"I didn't know. I suspected. And I didn't want to soil your young world with ideas like that—I wanted to protect you from even having to know about those kinds of things."

Just like she had tried to protect her own children from what she saw in the line of duty, Sara thought to herself. She had more in common with her mother than she had been willing to recognize.

"I was so angry at you for so many years...I behaved like a spoiled brat. You've done so much for me and I'll always be grateful for that, but it's awful that the swine managed to die before the truth came out. You should have said something when I was an adult."

"Yes, yes. I made a mistake. It's not easy."

"I didn't mean to give you a guilty conscience. And I understand this is hard to talk about. But I've got a question—something I'm ashamed to ask."

"There's no need to be."

"Yes, there is. Do you remember how Lotta and Malin used to drop rubbish just after you'd cleaned. And how I latched on to them?"

"It was always rowdy with two kids in the house. Three, including you."

"But we did this intentionally. As soon as you were done in one room, we would go in and mess it up. And then we'd call for you. 'Cleaning woman.' Do you remember that?"

"No."

"I want to apologize for it anyway. It was an awful thing to do."

"I was just glad you were playing so nicely with the girls."

"So you do remember?"

"I don't know. It doesn't matter now."

"Mum..."

"How are things with you, then?"

Talking about emotions wasn't Jane's thing.

"Good. Listen, I found something. I've just watched loads of home movies at the Bromans'. Not only the disgusting ones of the rapes, but the ones from their trips and parties and of general family life. And photo albums, too. And I saw one from when you'd just started at the Bromans', but the year was wrong. You were pregnant when you fled Poland, right?"

"Yes, by an unpleasant man—I didn't want you to grow up with him."

"But the album is from 1972. And I was born in '75."

"It must be wrong."

"No, I don't think so. The old king was visible in a newspaper. And he died in '73—I've checked. Did you come here in 1972?"

There was silence on the line.

"Mum?"

No answer.

When Sara pushed the phone to her ear, she could hear her mother crying.

"Mum," she said quietly. "What's the matter?"

Jane sobbed, then she whispered, "Sorry..."

"For what?"

No answer.

"What does it matter which year you arrived? Except that you weren't pregnant when you fled..." Sara stopped herself. "That happened in Sweden..."

The realization hit her like a goods trains ramming a caravan. Total destruction. Everything beyond repair.

Jane had fallen pregnant in Sweden. If she arrived in 1972, then she had only been sixteen years old.

To Stellan's tastes.

"Mum..." said Sara.

"What was I supposed to do? I was afraid they'd send me home."

"You were just sixteen."

"He stopped when I got pregnant. You say that I saved you, but you saved me first, Sara. When you came into the world, he stopped."

"But then Stellan was my..."

Sara could hear Jane crying on the phone as if through a thick, stifling mist.

"Sorry..." she said in a faint voice. "Sorry."

But Sara couldn't understand.

Sorry.

For giving her a father.

No. For giving her *that* father.

50

Life—her real life—had begun the day Lidiya's mother had told her about her father.

What had happened to him, and who had done it.

The party and its functionaries.

In the name of the global revolution.

They had knocked on the door at half past four in the morning, told him that he was under arrest and dragged him away.

Much later on, her mother had found out that he had spent three weeks in an ice-cold cell. Constantly hungry, with no blanket to warm him or mattress to sleep on. And then a trial. Lasting all of twenty minutes, and consisting largely of a list of accusations.

He was convicted of opposition to the Soviet state, in accordance with article 58 of the Criminal Code of the Russian Socialist Federative Soviet Republic. Then he was taken away and executed. His body was cast into a mass grave with others from the purge.

One of many purges.

Her father had always been loyal to the revolution. Dedicated. He had preached its necessity and positive impact on the country. But he had wanted to discuss methods of production and collective ownership. He wasn't opposed to them—he merely posed questions. For reasons of pure agricultural romanticism. But Ilya Petrovsky, who bore a grudge against Viktor Andreyev, didn't hesitate to report him.

All of this was told to Lidiya.

Ilya Petrovsky had recounted the course of events to Lidiya's mother with ill-concealed delight, and she had told it to Lidiya.

And her mother had withheld no details.

She wanted her daughter to know exactly what had happened. Who was guilty. She even told her that Ilya Petrovsky had offered her his bed. That had cost him an eye.

Lidiya remembered asking her mother what she could do to punish the men who had killed her father.

"Become one of them," her mother said.

Lidiya thought she had misheard, but her mother repeated it. She looked her straight in the eye and nodded.

"Become one of them.

"Get them to trust you. Learn everything you can. Let the years pass. Become trusted. Advance. And then, at a critical moment, exact revenge. Strike as hard as you can against the entire system.

"But a little girl can do nothing. You must train. You must become resilient. Start by becoming the best. Get their attention. Never rest.

"Praise the party above all else. Proclaim its might with each waking second.

"Ensure your eyes are radiant when you talk of Comrade Khrushchev, about the Soviet system, about the Pioneers' tributes to the working masses and the dictatorship of the proletariat. Praise the heroes from the great war for the Motherland. Learn the names of all the fallen generals. Do not learn the names of those who ended up in disgrace and were brought to justice under the great Stalin.

"Ensure you change your views at the very moment the party does. Report comrades who do not do their best, or who doubt the overarching Soviet system. Identify friends who may be receptive to counterrevolutionary propaganda, and watch them closely. You need enemies, not friends, so that you personally appear reliable.

"They must never find the slightest crack in your facade.

"You must believe it yourself.

"Conceal the truth in a small compartment deep down that you can bury under all the layers. Not in your heart—a heart can always be pried open.

"Hide it at the very back of your mind, behind the secrets that you are most ashamed of. The ones you would never tell anyone. Behind all the shame and guilt that you carry, all the things you would rather die than tell to anyone. A small, hard kernel of truth."

And Lidiya—or Agneta—had committed her life to crushing the system by first becoming a trusted part of it. She had become Desirée. She had played her role so well that she had been entrusted with the Union's most secret and important missions. She had accomplished them to the best of her ability while waiting for the right moment.

The person who was to become Agneta Öman had been trained to spread devastation, to dissimulate, to deceive. To intrigue, to analyze and attack the weakest points. Knowledge she had assimilated in the hope of one day avenging her father's death.

And she had been an exemplary pupil.

51

The apartment was dark now. Deafeningly silent.

Sara had been sitting there, completely immobile, for hours.

The truth had shaken her to her very foundations. Changed everything. She was another person now.

Why had she dug into this?

Why did she always need to find the truth?

What was she supposed to do now?

Who was she?

Stellan Broman was her father.

Stellan Broman the rapist.

The schadenfreude that Lotta and Malin's beloved and admired father had turned out to be a monster and traitor had come back to get her. All three of them shared the same origins.

She knew there was nothing she could do about that, but she couldn't help feeling guilt. Why?

Was that why so many sexual predators got away? All those businessmen, politicians, movie moguls, TV celebrities, directors and artists—the ones who'd attacked so many over the years and got away with it. Was it because all those girls had blamed themselves?

Because they had known that no one would listen to the weaker party?

Jane had been scared of being deported to communist Poland. Being returned there would almost certainly have meant prison for her, and her daughter would have been taken away from her. By staying with the man who'd raped her, she could keep her child. She just had to conjure up a story about another father.

But how had Janina Nowak managed to carry this with her for all these years? She'd simply stayed quiet and taken it whenever Sara had erupted with rage about the move. Without saying a word.

Sara felt grateful for the darkness in the room. It helped her to hide. Right now, she didn't want to be visible; she almost didn't want to be found. She didn't know where to go—she didn't have the strength to carry the burden of her new knowledge. Now she completely understood how self-absorbed she'd been for all those years. How ungrateful she'd been. And she'd had the effrontery to be upset with her mother for being a little edgy over the years. Of course, Sara hadn't known, but she hadn't asked herself whether there was a reason behind her mother's gruffness, either. Dear God, it was a miracle she hadn't had a breakdown and disappeared beneath the surface. Sara guessed that the only reason Jane hadn't let herself crumble, the only reason she'd stayed on her feet and kept working for all those years, was to protect her daughter.

If Sara thought that she'd made an effort for her children, then it was nothing compared with what her own mother had done for her.

And she'd never said anything. Not when Sara had joined Lotta and Malin in their mockery, nor when Sara had directed her ire at her because their lives weren't like those of the Bromans, nor when Sara had hated her for moving them away from Bromma.

Not a word about how ungrateful her daughter had been, what she herself had gone through or what she'd saved Sara from.

She never told her that Stellan had almost succeeded in forcing himself upon her.

His own daughter.

He must have known that she was. Sara supposed he just hadn't cared.

Not then, when he had been about to lure her into the garden shed.

Until then, he had perhaps looked upon her with a certain tenderness. But one day she was no longer a child in his eyes. Perhaps he'd never regarded her as his child. Perhaps she had just been an annoying reminder of his encroachment.

It occurred to Sara that she was actually evidence. It was possible to determine paternity, and given her mother's young age and vulnerable position at the time of conception, it had been a crime. Jane had said he had stopped when she fell pregnant. So she must have been abused by him for some time.

All these primitive beasts who merely regarded young women as items for consumption…Self-appointed alpha males, completely driven by their sexual desires. Hidden behind a thin veneer of civilization and success. For a few minutes' pleasure, they destroyed a young person's life. Considered it their right. A complete lack of empathy.

Had Sara inherited any of that?

Her uncompromising approach, her strong desire to win, her conviction that she was in the right. Did that come from Stellan?

She realized that she was doing it again. Searching for fault in herself.

There was only one person to blame here, and that was Stellan.

How could a person care so little about others—about his nearest and dearest? Who was Sara now? Everything she'd believed about her own life had been wrong.

She cried, for the first time in several years.

She sat in the darkness and let the tears flow.

It was a sorrow she hadn't known about, that had lain buried deep within her, a long, long way down, and it was now slowly emerging.

Her mobile vibrated.

In her distraught state, she thought something must have happened to the kids. Then she remembered they were at home and were probably asleep. Then she worried about Martin. He was out entertaining, and there were so many testosterone-fueled arseholes out there who wanted a fight.

Sara picked up.

"Yes?"

"He's going to beat me to death!"

The voice was no more than a whisper, but it was shrill, almost desperate. It sounded as if the person was struggling to produce any sound at all. Sara checked the display.

Jennifer.

OK.

Suddenly Stellan didn't matter. He was gone from her head.

"Who?" said Sara. "Who's hitting you? Is he still there?"

Sara assumed it was her pimp, but she didn't know who that was. She would need a name, and for the woman to testify against him. It didn't usually happen.

But it wasn't the pimp.

"The guy you arrested," said Jennifer.

"Who?"

"The guy in the car park," she sobbed, before whimpering with pain.

Sara tried not to think about what he had done to her.

"Where are you? Is he there?"

"I'm at home. He's left. I think."

"I'm coming. Where do you live?"

"No! He's still here!"

The anxiety in Jennifer's voice was unlike anything Sara had heard before. Pure mortal terror.

She ran to her weapons cabinet and pulled out her pistol. The one she'd not yet had the opportunity to return. The one she wasn't really allowed to use. But she didn't care about that now.

"Where do you live?" Sara yelled into the mobile.

"No, *no*...!" Jennifer cried out.

Then the call was cut off.

Sara tried to call her back, but no one answered.

Where the hell did Jennifer live?

Hadn't they been there and caught buyers on several occasions?

Tanto.

She attached the holster to her waistband and ran outside.

52

Sara screeched to a halt in front of the gigantic semicircular high-rise building. A concrete ghetto in the middle of the city. She leaped out of the car and ran to the door, tapped in the police entry code and hurried inside.

She stopped at the list of residents on the wall.

What the hell did it say on Jennifer's door?

Von Otter.

There—thirteenth floor.

Sara wondered whether the von Otters knew what was going on in the flat they had rented out.

Once she was in the lift, it struck her how stupid she'd been to simply set off without calling in reinforcements. She pulled out her mobile, but just as she'd brought up her speed dial list, the lift reached the thirteenth floor. When she stepped out, she saw that the door to Jennifer's flat was open. And there was one hell of a mess inside.

She stowed the mobile again as she ran into the flat.

"Jennifer?"

No answer.

Then she realized Holmberg might still be there, and drew her gun.

"Jennifer?"

So far as Sara could remember, Jennifer had two bedrooms. One where she hosted clients, with more vulgar decor—black silk sheets and a door straight into the hallway. And one where she actually slept—almost hidden on the far side of the living room.

The first bedroom—the one for punters—was empty.

Sara glanced into the kitchen as well as she passed.

No one there.

In the living room, there was furniture tipped onto its side, smashed vases, framed pictures torn off the walls and fresh blood on the floor.

The trail led into the private bedroom—as if a heavily bleeding person had dragged themselves that way. Or had been dragged.

"Jennifer!" Sara called out again, approaching the bedroom door with a bad gut feeling.

When she passed the bathroom door, a baseball bat suddenly crashed down on her hand. The pain shot up from her wrist through her arm and into her shoulder. The pistol flew out of her hand.

Sara twisted and met Holmberg's gaze.

Staring, watery eyes. Creamy brown tan acquired in a tanning salon.

He was furious. Inhuman. Bestial.

Like a rabid dog. Impossible to reach.

At that moment, he struck again, missed her head but got her shoulder.

It was pure luck that he didn't have room in the cramped hallway to take proper aim.

But the blow still had an impact. She cried out, lost her balance and collapsed. She panicked. She definitely didn't want to be lying on the floor.

"Fucking cunt!" Holmberg screamed. "Do you know what you've done?"

He raised his arm to strike her again, but apparently he had something to say first.

"They've gone! My wife's left me! And the kids won't talk to me! I said I wanted the letter to my PO box!"

Sara could see that it said "Simon Holmberg" on the baseball bat. It was written in childish handwriting. She tried to get to her feet, but he kicked her over again. All she could think to herself was that Holmberg had brought his own son's baseball bat. And now he was going to beat her to death with it.

When she curled up into the fetal position, he struck her on the ribs. He must have broken one of them, because the pain slicing through her body was unendurable.

She fumbled for her holster, found that it was empty and remembered that he'd knocked the pistol out of her hand.

Why the hell hadn't she called for backup?

"I'm a police officer," said Sara, trying to shield her head with her hands.

"No, you're a whore!" Holmberg shouted, taking aim with the bat again.

Pure reflex made Sara withdraw her hands to protect them. And then Holmberg hit her on the head.

But she didn't have time to register that before everything went black.

53

"Are you awake?"

Sara returned to consciousness slowly. Very slowly.

It was like gliding up to the surface from the bottom of the sea.

She opened her eyes. Or had someone opened them for her? She could see, at any rate, but she was still numbed by the pressure down in the depths. She was struggling to adjust.

A man in a white coat was looking at her. He had a shock of thick, dark hair, steel-rimmed spectacles and a friendly smile.

"Mmm," Sara replied, shifting her gaze from the doctor to the hospital room.

Everything was fuzzy. Each time she'd been to hospital—in her own time, when she'd given birth, and for work, when she'd accompanied girls who'd encountered prostitute-beating monsters—she'd struggled to get a grip on the atmosphere. The simultaneous feelings of suffering and alleviation were both painful and comforting.

But if there was a doctor standing in front of her—Doctor Mehra, according to the name badge—that meant she'd survived and received expert help, which was something to be grateful for.

Had someone found her?

Had Holmberg reined himself in?

"Jennifer?" said Sara in a hoarse voice.

"Who?" said Mehra.

"Is she dead?"

"The girl you saved?"

Saved. Did that mean she'd made it?

"She's not called Jennifer—her name's Leila Karim," Mehra added. "She's in surgery right now. No trauma to her head, like in your case—she's mostly got injuries to her lower abdomen. But they're pretty serious."

"Jesus Christ…"

"Yes. You might say that." Mehra paused. "He's also on the operating table."

Sara's brain felt like she was wading through treacle.

"Who?"

"Holmberg," said Mehra. "She shot him with your gun. Probably saved both your lives."

Sara nodded slowly.

"How bad?"

"Holmberg? She got him right in the head. I can't imagine he's going to end up anything other than a vegetable. Going to cost society a fortune for years to come."

"Bastard."

Mehra smiled.

"Now that you're awake, perhaps you're ready to receive visitors?" he said.

Visitors? For a second in her groggy state, Sara thought it was Stellan Broman who'd come. But then she quickly brushed away that unpleasant thought.

"Of course," she said.

Mehra nodded and left the room.

Half a minute later, the door opened again and Martin rushed in.

"Sweetheart! Tell me how you feel! You could have died."

He pulled a chair up to the side of the bed, sat down and took her hand. He fumbled a little, and she noticed that his gaze was almost overly emotional. He'd been out entertaining, and was probably much drunker than he wanted to give away. Emotions were made stronger by booze, but Sara was still touched when he patted her on the cheek and stroked her hair and even shed a tear. He had really been scared. Perhaps there was still some of that original first love between them.

Sara lay still. Her head was splitting, even though she knew she must be brimming with painkillers. *Jesus.* Head injuries weren't child's play.

"You can't do things like this," said Martin.

But it wasn't the danger she'd put herself in that was occupying Sara's thoughts. Perhaps it was the blows to the head; maybe it was the morphine or whatever they'd stuffed into her. But there was only one thing on her mind.

"I burned their clothes," she said.

"What?"

"All of Lotta's and Malin's old designer clothes from high school. I carried them down from the attic and burned them in the garden."

Suddenly it felt like a horrible onslaught. Those clothes would have made her happy back then, and now they were just gone. She felt like a murderer.

"I wonder if Lotta will report me," said Sara.

Martin stared at her.

"Lotta? I hardly think she cares about designer clothes."

"That was all she cared about."

"When she started high school, sure. But not during sixth form. Then all that mattered was Palestinian scarves."

"Lotta?"

"Yes. Communist-Lotta."

"'Communist'? Lotta?"

"Christ, yes. Did you miss that? She completely changed during sixth form. Demonstrations and boycotts and flyers and all that jazz. She was bloody lonely in sixth form, I can tell you that."

"But hang on...You're telling me that the fashion snob Lotta Broman became a communist?"

"Yes. She completely changed, overnight. Then she changed again a couple of years later—but for a while she was a fanatic. Didn't you know?"

Sara felt even groggier, if that was possible. It was insane. But it was true that she'd not really kept up with life at the Bromans' after the move.

"But I don't think she ever let go of it," said Martin. "I remember when the Wall came down. She kept droning on about it being the fault of imperialism. Peace haters. And when Germany was unified, she was crazy about the fact that the people who worked for the Stasi were going to be prosecuted, but not the people who worked for the West German Stasi—whatever they were called."

"The BND."

"She said something about how she couldn't understand that everything good about East Germany was just going to disappear. What a waste it was."

"Lotta?"

"Yes, it was really weird. She was completely transformed. Suddenly, it was all about how the USA had ordered a hit on Palme. She didn't give a shit about that when it happened, but when the Wall fell, everything was the fault of the USA and capitalism, right away."

Lotta. A fanatic.

A DDR supporter.

It all fell into place.

Lotta who had worked in the garden, side by side with Stellan and Böhme.

Böhme, who had taught Geiger. Schooled him. Indoctrinated him.

All of Stellan's films with the young girls in the garden shed.

He hadn't been educated by the spy, Ober. He'd been kept out of the way with the help of those young girls.

The same girls that he had raped first and broken down, and then used as bait to tempt Swedish politicians and other holders of power into a fall.

Girls from Lotta's school and the neighborhood.

Who controlled the social scene at school?

Lotta.

All those hours that Ober had spent schooling Geiger—it hadn't been Stellan that Böhme had been teaching. It had been Lotta. Suddenly it was clear to her: why had Sara wanted to start playing the violin? Because her idol Lotta did.

Lotta the violinist.

Geiger.

54

Only Malin had eyes for anything else. Her Barbie dolls. It was a bit late to be playing with them at fourteen, but her parents left her to it.

The rest of the family were sitting in front of the TV watching events unfold in silence.

The Berlin Wall fell. It was hacked to pieces by exultant East Germans who were assisted by jubilant West Berliners.

People helped pull each other up and began dancing on the wall that had until then represented mortal danger if they even approached it.

Grim-faced East German border guards merely stood by and watched. The reporter acted as interpreter for the entire world's astonishment that this was allowed to happen.

That the guards weren't dispersing the crowds. Shooting at them.

In Hungary, the border obstacles had been removed during the summer, although in China the popular uprising in Tiananmen Square had been brutally crushed—with tanks and dead freedom fighters as the outcome.

The anti-imperial protective ramparts were falling without anyone attempting to defend them.

Lotta was shaken by the betrayal. The Wall was to protect the DDR and its people. Her friends, the ones she'd met so many times on trips with her family. She'd made friends with them, played music with them, played sport with them, talked politics with them.

All they wanted was to live in peace and work toward a better world together. But the USA and the capitalists couldn't let them do that. They couldn't allow an alternative to the buying frenzy and materialism in the West. The people weren't allowed to see that another path was possible, because then they might not accept the status quo of market-driven slavery.

"Dad," Lotta said, almost pleading.

"Yes," said Stellan. That was all.

His commitment went no further than that—his willingness to fight for a better world. For peace.

Being celebrated and awarded medals was fine. But actually making an effort was something that didn't interest him. It wasn't by chance that Ober had picked her instead, and let her take over the work to secure material to blackmail those in power and strategically placed civil servants. He'd seen her dedication and resilience. He had honed her, drilled her and trained her.

Her father hadn't had the focus and conviction required for battle. But the decadent Western pleasures he'd engaged in had at any rate made it possible for Lotta to exploit his friends and acquaintances for her own ends. For something much greater.

Lotta had noticed that if Stellan got to meet a few girls from school, then it came in useful for her later on. And that had allowed her to perform better than even Ober had. She'd managed to gather compromising materials on a vast swathe of Sweden's officialdom, had managed to secure political and business decisions that benefitted the DDR and socialism in all manner of matters. Just like Stellan boasted that he'd got the Swedish parliament to acknowledge East Germany as a sovereign state. But that was the only thing he had achieved.

And now? What were they supposed to do with all this material now?

She needed to contact Abu Rasil and see whether she could be of assistance. The Palestinians' struggle was continuing, even if they'd lost an important ally in the DDR. The concept of socialism wasn't dead. She hadn't given up.

One beautiful day, the bell would toll for imperialism.

55

It had been Lotta all along.

Since when?

Her teens? Eleven or twelve? No, it was impossible.

Her father had laid the foundations through his work for the DDR. Flattered, deceived, vain man. Then Lotta had stepped in with her tough personality, drilled by Ober, while the monstrous Stellan was allowed to carry on with his attacks because it provided them with holds over the right people. Because he was providing his home and his contacts.

Because he was Lotta's father? Did Lotta care about that kind of thing?

Once again. Just a young girl. A girl who'd sold her country down the river, who'd sacrificed girls her own age. She had rejected others' choices. She had betrayed everything for an abstract concept.

A child.

How had the East Germans agreed to that?

Had Ober simply lied to them about whom he'd recruited? Had he bragged and just pretended it was Stellan? Or didn't it matter, so long as Geiger was alive?

Sara remembered Hanne Dlugosch, whose mother had tried to leave the DDR but had instead been imprisoned and had died. Was it Lotta who had reported mother and daughter to the East German authorities? After Stellan had mentioned their situation at home? Perhaps Stellan really had meant to help them, but Lotta had got there first?

How many other people's lives had she ruined?

Everything was cast in a new light.

Hadn't Malin said that it was Agneta who'd picked up the phone? If Lotta was Geiger, then naturally the people calling were expecting a woman to answer. Hence the operation continued.

It was no surprise that the rolls of film had different levels of wear and tear. They'd been kept in different places. Quite simply because the rolls of film from the garden shed were Stellan's, while the ones from the guest room were Geiger's. Lotta's.

She'd filmed everything in the guest room, filmed the powerful men exploiting young girls. Stellan had only filmed himself with the girls.

Lotta was the secret spy. Stellan was the useful idiot.

Instead of reporting her father for the rapes, she had helped him. She would invite girls that she could use once Stellan had broken them.

A toxic duo.

Lotta must have left her films together with Stellan's to strengthen suspicions against her father and establish that he was Geiger. To protect herself.

If Agneta had killed Ober, was she the one who'd killed Kellner and Stellan, too? And why Stellan, if he wasn't Geiger?

Sara had waited until Martin left. She'd told him she was tired and wanted to sleep. Then she waited another ten minutes, dressed and made her escape.

She caught a cab outside the main entrance to the hospital and gave Lotta's address. She was still fuzzy from the painkillers and the attack, but firmly resolved to confront her childhood friend and hold her accountable.

When they reached Eastmansvägen, the taxi pulled over and Sara passed the driver her credit card. While the charge went through, she saw Lotta come out of the main door of her building and head in the opposite direction, toward her car.

Where was she going?

She asked the driver to put the meter back on and follow Lotta's car at a distance. She really ought to have called Anna, and she ought to have called Martin to tell him she'd left the hospital. But they would only have tried to stop her.

A left turn onto Dalagatan and then along Sankt Eriksgatan to Fridhemsplan, then Drottningholmsvägen toward Bromma. When they reached the Tranebergsbron, Sara began to guess where they were going. She had the feeling something was happening. That it was all drawing to a close.

Was Lotta going to meet Abu Rasil?

Sara called Breuer—despite the ban on her being involved in the investigation. Despite the fact that she was suspended.

"Stellan wasn't Geiger," said Sara as soon as Breuer picked up. "It was Lotta. His daughter. She's on her way to Bromma. I think she's going to meet Abu Rasil."

"We're coming," said the German, hanging up.

Sara was relieved that Breuer had believed her straightaway. It was a matter of urgency if they were going to catch Abu Rasil. And Breuer probably realized that.

And Agneta?

What was her role in all of this?

Who on earth was she?

56

Eventually, grown-up Agneta had been given her opportunity to take revenge on behalf of little Lidiya for her father's death.

After having waited and watched for decades, she had discovered cracks in the evil structure. Cracks that she could exploit, strengthen and enlarge. And by that stage she had been a trusted source for a long time, following thirty-five years of dutiful service on behalf of global socialism. A generation.

In East Germany the Wall had fallen, and in the Soviet Union the new general secretary Mikhail Gorbachev had begun to open up the Soviet system to give it a chance of survival.

Agneta knew that change and adjustment were always equivalent to vulnerability, and she began to seek out points of attack.

Via her handler, Yuri, Agneta knew that opposition to Gorbachev was widespread within the KGB—right to the top. There were strong differences within the mighty apparatus of power. And differences could be exploited.

It took little time to identify the key players. There were two factions, one on either side of the secretary-general. On the one side was KGB chairman Vladimir Kryuchkov, and the reactionary forces surrounding him. On the other side was Boris Yeltsin, member of the Supreme Soviet and former first secretary of the Moscow *gorkom*—appointed by Gorbachev and forced into resignation from the Politburo because he thought that perestroika was advancing too slowly. Yuri was able to tell her that Yeltsin was bitter and filled with a thirst for revenge. He was aiming for the post of president of the constituent Soviet republic of Russia, and once he was there he would become very useful.

When news reached them that Mikhail Gorbachev was to visit Sweden in June 1991, Agneta realized her chance had arrived. She requested direct contact with someone as close to Yeltsin as pos-sible, and Yuri put her in touch with Gennady Burbulis, one of Yeltsin's closest advisers. Once that connection was established, she could focus on her plan.

Convincing her vain husband to invite the Soviet leader to their home via his old drinking buddy, the cabinet minister, hadn't been difficult. What a triumphant return to the limelight! Once the seed was sown, Stellan handled it all by himself.

Offering the prominent guest some relaxing company in a pri-vate setting was deemed desirable. But since Sager House still hadn't become the prime minister's residence, and Ingvar Carlsson lived in a very plain terraced house in Tyresö, the suggestion of dinner at the home of Stellan Broman was gratefully accepted. Stellan lived in a fine house, and his commitment to the peace movement had always been appreciated by Moscow, so the Soviet advisers accepted the Swedish government's proposal.

Agneta had taken Lotta and Malin on a mini cruise to Lenin-grad and the Hermitage Museum, and once there she didn't take long to complain of sore feet and settle down in front of da Vinci's *Madonna and Child*. While her daughters continued their tour of the enormous museum, Agneta was able to meet with Yuri in peace and quiet and receive the equipment she'd requested—equipment that she had no problems whatsoever bringing into the country, since back then she was still recognized as Uncle Stellan's wife more or less everywhere. No Swedish customs officer was going to look inside Agneta Broman's bags.

Ahead of the distinguished visit, she had plenty of time to plant hidden microphones—in the dining room, on the terrace and in the living room. Even in the sauna, just to be sure. And dur-ing the evening she gently asked leading questions of the Soviet president until she felt she had everything she needed. It was all well disguised by Stellan's enthusiastic talk of disarmament and nuclear-free zones.

The day after, she'd listened through all of it, picked out the parts that were useful and wrote new questions. Then she'd called Gunnar Granberg, an impressionist who'd made his breakthrough on Stellan's show with his parodies of politicians and celebrities. Agneta confided in him that she was secretly preparing a surprise for Stellan's birthday, and she asked Granberg whether he would do an impersonation for her. She asked whether she could record him imitating Prime Minister Ingvar Carlsson speaking English. Of course he had agreed. Anything for Uncle Stellan. When Carlsson later lost the election, Agneta was able to tell Granberg that this was why the recording had never been used.

In practice, she'd used the equipment provided to her by Yuri to cut together the Granberg imitation of Ingvar Carlsson's questions with the real Gorbachev's answers to her own. She even included a recorded phrase from the real Carlsson first, in case the intended recipients carried out any kind of voice identification checks. But then she built her own story.

Agneta's question to Gorbachev, "Have you given up on Lenin and Stalin?" was replaced by Granberg's Carlsson saying, "You have strong opponents in the form of Kryuchkov and the KGB." And she joined this together with Gorbachev's answer about the former leaders: "They have played their part and belong to another era. We must move on. We must build the new Soviet without them."

After a couple of days, Agneta was in possession of a completely sensational dialogue between Sweden's prime minister and the president of the Soviet Union. Under the pretext of visiting invented relatives in the far north, Agneta flew to Helsinki. There she met with Yuri and passed on the tape with the faked exchanges to send further up the organization's chain of command—top priority. Yuri was a traditionalist, and just like his bosses, he'd long wanted to see the reformer Gorbachev toppled. He gratefully accepted the opportunity.

Just as planned, the recording had seriously shaken opponents in both the government and the KGB. Now they could hear for themselves that they were to be swept away, and the powers at large in the USSR were well acquainted with the meaning of the word "purge."

When Agneta was told of the reactions, she went behind Yuri's back and made contact with Yeltsin's adviser Burbulis, explaining that Gorbachev was under threat from opponents within the KGB and the party. This was the ideal opportunity to support the president and push through more of the reforms that Yeltsin advocated.

In July, Gorbachev and Yeltsin had signed an agreement for increased reforms.

In the eyes of the opponents, this was the final evidence that Gorbachev was selling out the Soviet Union, and that their own days were numbered.

They had to act, and in August they saw their chance.

Satisfied that he had an ally in the shape of Yeltsin, Gorbachev departed Moscow to rest at his dacha in Crimea. This was exploited by the conspirators to place him under house arrest and notify the people that he had been deposed. A junta comprising nine people took power, led by Prime Minister Valentin Pavlov, Defense Minister Dmitry Yazov and KGB chairman Vladimir Kryuchkov.

The group acted in panic based on information from the illegal Desirée and the unholy alliance of the former sworn enemies, Yeltsin and Gorbachev.

The coup demonstrated with absolute clarity who was on the side of the opposition and wished to preserve the old Soviet Union. Something which suited Desirée perfectly.

While Yuri focused on the perpetrators behind the putsch, she rekindled contact with Burbulis. She revealed to him that the recording with Gorbachev was fake, and with this trump card Burbulis was able to persuade Yeltsin to act.

The vengeful Yeltsin immediately saw the opportunities at hand. He also saw the risks, but they didn't bother him.

By heading out into the streets during the coup, climbing up onto a tank and urging soldiers to lay down their weapons, Yeltsin transformed himself into a man of the people. Once he had the military on his side and was able to prove that the recording of Gorbachev was false, he made the coup plotters back down. Half the battle was won.

With Gorbachev under arrest, President Bush of the USA had no choice other than to support Yeltsin to avoid a return to the Cold War. Not to mention the risk of what he described as "Yugoslavian chaos" occurring within a nuclear superpower.

Yuri quickly became a turncoat and gave Yeltsin his full support, but he realized that he'd been deceived by Desirée, and it soon became apparent to all that the coup had failed.

Gorbachev, now released, had had his wings clipped and was unable to stand up to the new strongman, Boris Yeltsin.

Given that Desirée's intelligence had been fortuitous thus far, Burbulis advised Yeltsin to continue listening to her. And since Agneta knew through Yuri that Ukraine and Belarus wanted to strike out alone, she proposed a secret meeting between Yeltsin and the presidents of the two countries, Leonid Kravchuk and Stanislav Shushkevich, so that they could then quite simply present Gorbachev and the Soviet Union with a fait accompli.

The three met under cover of great secrecy in a hunting cabin in the forest in the Belarusian Belavezhskaya National Park, where they signed the agreement declaring the dissolution of the Soviet Union and its replacement by the Commonwealth of Independent States. Gorbachev declared it an illegal coup d'état, but he was unable to halt events and a few weeks later he was gone.

Yuri was furious at the fall of the Soviet Union, and he deeply resented Agneta's role in it. But as a new follower of Yeltsin, there was nothing he could do. He didn't even protest when Yeltsin established the "Hero of the Russian Federation" medal as the highest decoration in the land, and awarded it to Desirée in recognition of her assistance.

The party that had killed her father had been crushed, the country that had ruined her life no longer existed. Evil had been conquered.

It was like a story. One single little girl had defeated the monster.

After the victory, Agneta had given herself a new mission. One that was to last for the rest of her life, and that she approached with tremendous dedication. But when the phone had rung that Monday, everything had been threatened with collapse.

Her final battle was to secure the future for those she loved the most.

And now it was time.

She was ready.

Pills of every color of the rainbow lay before her. Perhaps her final ones. The blue blood-thinning warfarin, the yellow lercanidipine for her blood pressure, the atenotol and atorvastatin for her heart. If she didn't make it, then at least it wouldn't be her own body giving up on her.

She swallowed them all with a glass of water and then headed for the door. She stopped and wondered what would happen to C.M. if she didn't come back.

She quickly found a pen and paper and wrote "help me" on it. Then she affixed it to the front door and left it unlocked. By the time a newspaper delivery boy, bin collector or Jehovah's Witness saw it, tonight's encounter would be done and dusted.

Agneta was surprised by her own softness. Was it old age?

She went over to her own house. Not that it had ever been truly hers.

There she was.

Lotta.

Just as Agneta had feared. Her daughter's conscientiousness surpassed even her own.

Lotta looked up but didn't seem surprised.

"Mum" was all she said.

"You have to leave," said Agneta.

"Where've you been?" Lotta asked.

She nodded to the neighboring house.

"With C.M.?" said Lotta. "The whole time?"

"A couple of days."

She looked around. Time was not on her side.

"You need to leave," said Agneta. "Think of the children."

"I need to know something."

"What?"

"Who shot Dad?"

"I did."

"Why?"

"To protect you and your sister. And your children."

"From what?"

"From this. From Geiger."

"What do you mean?"

"Let your dad be Geiger."

"What do you know about Geiger? How can you know?"

"I've always known. My assignment was to keep my eye on you. The Stasi never realized that Ober was lying about his novice, but we knew. We let it go on for as long as you delivered."

"'We'? Are you KGB?"

Lotta grappled with what this might mean for her outlook on the world, but deep down she knew it was true.

"Not any longer. Now I'm just a grandma. And I want you to be a mum and nothing else. Leave this place. Now. Before it's too late."

"Do you know why I'm here?"

"Yes. I know who you're meeting. And I know why. But if you do this, then there's no way back."

"That's the point. Help me. If you're committed. You must surely believe in the same things as I do."

"I've always had my own convictions."

"We've got a chance now to set it all right. To correct history."

When Agneta didn't reply, Lotta continued.

"Look at the state of the world. The schisms, the injustice. Money governs everything. Evil men have become dictators in Hungary, Turkey, Poland and the USA. We can stop it. We can create a new world. We can tear down the old ruins and vanquish the predators, and make room for something amazing in its place."

Sara got out of the taxi a few houses away from the Bromans', crept into the nearest property and cut across the neighbors' gardens. It wasn't long before the white villa was looming before her. It was a light summer's evening, so she didn't have much in the way of cover from darkness—she hoped that no one would happen to be looking out just as she passed.

Sara entered the Bromans' property to the rear of the house and swept her gaze across the façade and garden.

Empty.

Slowly, she crept up to the house. When she got close to the front, she saw Lotta together with an old woman with buzz-cut gray hair.

She continued to observe them, and after a minute or so she realized it was Agneta she was looking at. Short hair, no makeup and completely different body language.

But that was her.

It took a while to sink in.

Agneta in the flesh.

Together with Lotta.

Two of the idols of her childhood, uncovered as spies for foreign powers.

Sara waited, unsure what she should do, but she realized she couldn't let them disappear. She had to keep them here, somehow. She stepped out of the darkness and approached the two women.

"Agneta" was the first thing she said.

She didn't know what reaction she'd been expecting, but when the two women turned toward her they didn't look at all surprised. Agneta's face was completely blank and Lotta seemed to be mostly annoyed.

"Little Sara," said Agneta. "You can't be here."

Sara was glad she was alive. She realized that now. Agneta had been a mother figure of sorts to her. Yet at the same time she believed what Breuer and Kozlov had said about her. So it was hard to know how to act.

Instead she turned to Lotta.

"I know. I know everything."

For the first time in her life, she truly had the upper hand over her old childhood friend.

Lotta looked at Sara without saying anything.

"You're Geiger," she continued. "All the rapes of those young girls in the guest room, all the films for blackmail purposes. You exploited the girls that Stellan got hold of so that you had a hold on people. You organized it all. And Joachim trained you."

"Yes," said Lotta, without looking in the slightest bit surprised. "He began and I took over."

"Sara, leave," said Agneta. "You don't know anything about this."

"Stay-Put," said Sara, looking her in the eye. "The Soviet equivalent. It's still active. But I don't know whether you're trying to stop it or deliver it. You're an illegal."

"No, not any longer. Not since the fall of the Wall. Now I'm just a grandma."

"What do you mean?"

"Sara, I'm here to put an end to this. To bury my daughter's secret. Her children shouldn't have their lives destroyed by the choices of others, like Lotta and I have."

Sara tried to make out whether Agneta meant what she was saying. Had she surrendered her old convictions? But if so, why had she executed four people?

"My grandchildren won't have to grow up and read that they're the children of a spy," said Agneta.

"Was that why you shot Stellan? So that everyone would think he was Geiger?"

"Yes. And for all the awful things he's done. I was forbidden to intervene. And while I couldn't undo all the awfulness, I could at least avenge the girls with my shot."

Sara barely recognized her. The amenable, docile Agneta of her childhood was gone. This was someone else entirely.

Desirée.

"If the ring hadn't been activated, then I would never have had to clean everything up. But my hand was forced," Agneta added. "When the worst happened and the call came, I didn't hesitate for one second. The only things I care about now are my grandchildren. Everything else is unimportant. And regrettably you're in my way, little Sara."

Without Sara noticing, Agneta had pulled out a pistol that was now aimed at her.

Instinctively, she shifted her hand to her own holster, but then remembered she wasn't carrying one. And no gun either, since that was currently evidence in a case of attempted murder against herself.

Sara looked at Agneta and Lotta.

"Do you really know what you're doing?"

"You shouldn't have come here," said Agneta.

"Do you understand what will happen? How many will die?"

"You've never seen the big picture," said Lotta.

"It's thirty years since the Wall fell. You have a completely different life. You have children."

"It's them I'm thinking of. They shouldn't have to grow up under the tyranny of commercialism. It's impossible to save a rotten building. Sometimes you have to knock it down to build something better."

"I'm your sister."

It felt so strange to say the words.

Sara looked at Agneta.

"You must have known. You must have seen Mum with her growing belly and realized who the father was. Did you say anything? Did you do anything?"

No answer.

"Mum was sixteen!"

"There were many who had it much worse, back in those days," said Agneta.

"You can't do this. You're my second mother. You can't shoot me," said Sara, pleading.

"I was able to shoot my husband," Agneta said flatly. "Some values are more important."

Sara looked at Lotta.

"Lotta, we have the same father!"

"Why do you think I've always hated you?" Lotta said with contempt in her voice.

The words were like a kick to the stomach, and Sara knew instinctively that it was true. She turned to Agneta.

"You can't let her detonate the bombs!"

"We'll see. But I'm afraid that, either way, you have to go."

Agneta took a step closer and raised her hand so that the muzzle of the pistol was pointing right at Sara's forehead. It took only a split second for Sara to realize that she was deadly serious. But it felt like a lifetime.

Images flashed through her head.

Ebba. Olle. Martin. Her colleagues. Anna. Jane.

Now she was never going to see them again.

Would they ever find out what had happened?

What would happen to her body? Would Agneta leave Sara lying there in front of the house until someone found her, or would the body simply disappear?

How would Martin react when he realized that Sara had sought out her own executioner, thus depriving his children of their mother? Or what if he never found out what had happened to her?

As if in slow motion, Sara thought she saw Agneta's finger begin to squeeze the trigger. Not a shadow of doubt was visible in her gaze. Sara was merely an obstacle in her way. A technicality.

Was this how it was going to end?

A couple of quick footsteps was all that she heard. Then Agneta fell to the ground with a cry.

Strauss leaped to his feet with astonishing speed and grabbed her weapon. He had tackled her to the ground with a rapidity that was surprising, given his body weight. Now he took aim, while Breuer stepped out of the shadows. She was wearing a bulletproof vest, and had a Glock in her hand, and a Heckler & Koch MP5 slung over her shoulder.

Sara thanked her nonexistent God for giving her the foresight to call the Germans. Breuer looked from Agneta to Sara to Lotta.

"The codes" was all she said.

Lotta looked at Breuer blankly, then she turned around and went to the beginning of the garden path. Using a bar propped against an apple tree, she flipped over the first paving stone on the path to the shed.

Something was carved into the bottom of the stone: "F473B12."

"There's a code under each slab," said Lotta.

Breuer nodded, raised her pistol and shot Strauss in the back of the head. He hit the ground with a thud, like a felled bison.

The world froze for a second and Sara tried to understand what was happening.

Breuer had shot Strauss.

Lotta didn't look at all surprised.

There was only one explanation.

An impossible explanation, but also the only one.

"Abu Rasil" was all Sara managed to say.

Breuer smiled.

"In a world dominated by men, the best disguise is to be a woman. I've always said I knew exactly how Abu Rasil thinks."

"Well, that means my mission is almost over," said Agneta, getting up.

Breuer looked at her. It took a little while for her to recognize Agneta with her new appearance.

"Agneta Broman," she said, searching her memory. "Desirée?"

Agneta nodded.

"We've met before," said Breuer.

"A couple of times," said Agneta. "And while they may be thirty years old, my instructions are to help you."

"That's great, Mum," said Lotta. "We're so close now."

Breuer turned to Sara.

"And then there's stubborn Sara. If you hadn't called, I could have come here without Strauss. His life is on your conscience."

Breuer raised her weapon to fire.

"Wait," said Agneta, nodding to the neighboring house, where a light had come on in a window. "Don't shoot now."

Breuer lowered her weapon. Sara couldn't work out whether Agneta was trying to help her, or was genuinely being cautious.

"We need to transmit the codes," said Lotta.

"*Genau.*"

Breuer glanced at the glowing lamp in the window of the neighboring house. She kept the automatic aimed at Sara, and used her other hand to fish out her mobile, photograph the first code and send the image.

She could hardly believe it after all these years.

The codes were at her feet.

Her pension.

Her house in the Caribbean.

But above all, her revenge on those who'd once crushed her dreams of a better world—the victorious powers who'd spat on her commitment, and degraded her and all her comrades in the struggle.

Now she was glad that she'd never given up, but had continued on a freelance basis, or whatever you wanted to call it.

All these years of waiting had paid off.

She was grateful that there were others like her. Not only Geiger, but also Desirée, even if she hadn't been counting on any help from that direction.

She had never been given access to the codes—her handler didn't want to risk her writing them down or learning them by heart.

That was why they'd been stored in Sweden, in a well-heeled suburb. An analogue backup in the safest possible setting. With two guard dogs—Geiger and Desirée. And Breuer had had to wait like a lamb for the signal from her handler that they were ready for the handover before she made contact with Geiger. She had to pretend to be tracking Abu Rasil in Stockholm in order to be ready, which once again provided her with the perfect alibi. Abu Rasil's most dogged opponent, always on his heels but once again conquered by the legendary terrorist.

Lotta turned the next slab over. "HX329K1."

Carved in stone. Breuer would never have guessed.

She took a photograph and sent it.

Twelve stones, twelve codes, twelve steps to hell.

"Joachim and I were the only ones who knew," said Lotta.

Proud.

Breuer's true identity had shaken Sara, but now she was steady once again.

She realized she couldn't just stand here and watch. Watch the beginning of the apocalypse.

When Breuer bent down to photograph the third slab, she saw her moment. She was thinking about the German's two weapons as she sprinted off, but all she needed was a chance to get away.

To call for help—to find something to defend herself with.

She ran faster than she'd ever done before.

Away from Breuer and the Bromans.

Toward the road.

Despite her body aching after the serious assault. She shut the pain out.

But Sara hadn't taken many steps before she heard the sound of a shot hitting a tree a few centimeters from her.

Breuer had probably fired as quickly as she could, and hadn't had time to aim properly. The next time she would be guaranteed not to miss.

And it would be quick.

Her only chance was the garden shed.

Sara tore open the door and threw herself inside, turning the key in the lock. At exactly the same moment, a second shot was fired. A bullet penetrated the door and went into the rear wall.

Breuer approached and tried the door.

Locked.

And the shed was solid. She didn't have time to break the door down. She needed to send the codes. When she'd notified them that she was going to meet Geiger, the entire operation had been initiated and now there wasn't much time. Far too much was at stake for her to take any risks.

Using her neatly compact but deadly efficient MP5, she fired a cross shape at the shed to leave as little room as possible for Sara to hide in. It didn't matter whether anyone heard. She had her police badge to flash if anyone turned up.

She emptied the first magazine, quickly changed to the second and carried on.

A white angel of death.

Inside the shed, Sara threw herself to the floor, tipped the old wheelbarrow on its side and curled up behind it.

The automatic gunfire continued. A few bullets hit the barrow and left huge dents—despite the fact that they had already passed through the thick wooden wall.

The metal wouldn't hold for much longer, and Sara scanned the space for protection.

She was interrupted by a velvet-soft thud. One of the bullets had hit the jerrycan she'd left there previously. It was downright luck that it wasn't full—if it had been, then it would have exploded.

The can started to burn, and an infernal odor of petrol and smoke spread throughout the shed's interior. The outside wall burst into flames with a sound that was almost like a dog barking. And then the side walls. And the back.

Walls that Sara had drenched in petrol.

Now she was stuck inside a fire trap that she herself had set.

The heat was already savage, like opening an oven door and putting your face right to the opening. A searing pain that made you instinctively back away.

But there was nowhere to back away to.

The shooting had stopped, and Sara ran to the wall where the tools hung. It was on fire, too, but with the help of a rake, she managed to knock an ax from its position on the wall.

She couldn't get out through the door. Breuer was waiting for her there.

Using the ax, she began to hack at the wall where there was the least fire.

But the planks of wood were solid, and the wall was thick. Stellan had wanted it to be warm even in winter.

She tried the floor, but faced the same issue. Thick, solid boards that she could only make small indentations in.

She could no longer breathe. She prayed to God and the Devil and the Buddha and Allah and all of Anna's spirits for salvation. She crouched, putting her arms over her head to shield herself from the heat. She threw herself around the space in a panic, but it was just as hot wherever she went. The same infernal heat.

The panic and pain made her scream.

Death was everywhere around her, and soon it would conquer her. Destroy her. There was nowhere to escape to.

Her lungs were on fire; the heat was stinging her skin as if she were being flogged. The acrid stench of burned hair was mixed with petrol fumes and smoke.

There was nothing left to hope for.

She wouldn't see Olle finish school. She would never give a speech at Ebba's wedding. She would never see any grandchildren.

Sara sank to her knees and looked around one final time.

Door, roof, floor, walls.

Window.

The boarded-up window.

Sara got up, grabbed the ax and threw herself at the rear wall. She roared with pain as she stepped into the flames and hacked at the sheets of chipboard that had been placed across the back window.

The boards gave way on the first attempt.

She tore away the cracked pieces of wood, smashed the glass with the ax and threw herself through the opening, screaming. A desperate, primal cry.

The beauty bush at the back didn't do much to cushion her fall. Sara landed heavily on the ground, hitting her shoulder so hard that her arm throbbed. She rolled around in panic, trying to extinguish the fire that had taken hold of her clothing.

And she sucked the cool air into her lungs.

The cool, life-giving summer air.

At the front, Breuer heard Sara's screaming fall silent as the shed was engulfed in flames. She turned toward Lotta.

"The codes. What's the next one?"

"Think about Leo and Sixten," Agneta said in a low voice that Breuer wouldn't hear. "You're their mother."

Lotta stopped. She looked as if she was performing a mathematical calculation in her head, rather than thinking about her sons.

The flames from the garden shed lit up the scene with a hot, flickering yellow glare that was spreading across the lawn and the shrubbery.

Agneta looked at her daughter. Leo and Sixten's mother.

She had chosen a struggle that had died long ago ahead of her own children and her sister's. A brutal and belated revenge for the fall of an evil empire, instead of an untarnished future for her sons. For Agneta's grandchildren.

"The codes!" Breuer cried out, and Lotta grabbed the bar again.

Agneta's pleading had been in vain.

Somewhere, someone was entering the codes into a firing system that would soon kill tens of thousands of Europeans, and kill hundreds of thousands in the long run.

It would sink the entire EU.

It would change the balance of power in the world forever.

It would ensure the victory of the repressive powers.

The same kind of system that had taken Lidiya's father from her was now going to take Agneta's grandchildren away from her.

Was everything she had done in vain? All those years of readiness. All the preparations and all the work when the call had arrived. All the killing afterward. Was it all for nothing?

Was she truly prepared to allow Breuer to win Lotta over to her side? If the cost was Agneta's family and the grandchildren's childhood?

No.

She'd managed to persuade Breuer that she was still committed to her mission. She had to exploit that. And there wasn't much time.

As quietly as she could, she pulled out her Cold Steel knife and kept it concealed behind her thigh as she approached Breuer.

At the moment the white-haired woman turned around, Agneta aimed the tip of the knife at her midriff and stabbed. The intention was to go deep and then damage as much as possible, but Breuer's reactions were quick despite her age, and she twisted out of the way.

"No!" Lotta cried out when she realized what was happening.

The knife penetrated into the German's side, but didn't incapacitate her.

Breuer's hand automatically went to the wound, making her drop her automatic weapon. She looked around and ran toward the house with the white facade. Agneta grabbed the MP5 and chased after her. Lotta stood irresolutely where she was by the paving slabs for a moment, then she hurried after the other two.

"Mum!" she shouted, both pleading and reproachful.

Breuer turned the corner of the house and Agneta raised her weapon, thinking the German would be easy prey in the narrow space to the side of the building.

But Breuer came to a sudden halt, pressed herself against the wall and pulled out her pistol. When Agneta rounded the corner, Breuer put two rapid shots in her chest and one in her head.

She fell to the ground just as Lotta caught up with the others. Dumbstruck, the daughter witnessed her mother's death throes.

Agneta fumbled in her pocket for the object she'd been carrying—the secret weapon that would win the battle for her.

When Breuer saw that she was moving, she once again raised her weapon.

With her final ounce of strength, Agneta managed to pull out what she had been carrying ever since the call for Geiger had arrived, and she'd been forced to resume life as Desirée.

Breuer was about to squeeze the trigger, but stopped herself when she saw what Agneta was holding.

A yellow rag doll in the shape of a banana with a red mouth.

Agneta's eyes closed and the doll fell out of her hand.

Once Breuer had confirmed that her opponent was out of action, she turned to Lotta.

"The codes."

Lotta was immobile, her eyes shifting from Agneta to Breuer, as if she was trying to process the course of events. But then she began to head back toward the garden path. After just a few steps, Breuer stopped her with a movement of her hand and silenced her with a finger to her lips.

They listened.

And they heard a sound from the garden.

Rapid footsteps heading down toward the water.

Breuer immediately hurried toward the sound.

For Lotta, it took a second to make the same decision.

Sara was making her way along the jetty when she heard steps behind her. Running as quickly as she could, she reached the edge and dropped the heavy paving slab.

The splash when the slab hit the water was like a gunshot. She'd hoped to sink it without Breuer and Lotta noticing anything, praying that it would disappear without a trace.

She had at least managed to shift a second slab to one side, so that Breuer wouldn't know which order the final slabs had been in, even if Sara had only had time to sink one of them.

Breuer raised her hand as she ran. It was as if she was pointing at her, and Sara collapsed before she registered the sound of the subdued gunshot. She didn't feel the pain from the bullet that had entered her body.

She spun round and landed on her back. She saw Breuer come onto the jetty, her pistol still raised.

The shot had hit her shoulder.

It was a good hit, given that the shot had been taken with a pistol at such a long distance and while running. It hadn't started to hurt yet, but the injury had been a shock to her entire system.

Sara was lying on the jetty, frustrated that she couldn't think clearly. She shut her eyes, and when she opened them again Breuer was standing in front of her. Above her.

"She threw one in the water," she said to Lotta, who appeared behind her.

"I'll retrieve it," said Lotta, jumping into the water.

The sound of the splash when Lotta jumped in reminded Sara of throwing sandwiches in their youth. She'd been so fortunate to have the opportunity to apologize to Jane, she thought to herself. It was just a shame that they wouldn't get to talk more about the life they'd shared. Soon it would all be over. Unless she thought of something very quickly.

Lotta spent a long time searching in the water, diving at different points and feeling her way around. Then she had to struggle to grasp the heavy slab and heave it up onto the jetty.

"What order were they in?"

"No idea," Lotta replied, and Breuer looked at Sara.

"What order?"

When Sara didn't reply, Breuer fired a shot right beside her. The sound made her eardrums ring.

She knew she was going to die if she stayed lying on the jetty. There was only one direction in which she could escape.

She pointed at the slab, as if she was going to tell them. And that made Breuer look at it on reflex.

Sara quickly rolled over the edge and into the water.

The dark, warm water.

It was the first time she'd swum off the jetty, she thought to herself as she sank to the bottom. Up on the jetty, Breuer emptied the magazine into the water, taking aim at the air bubbles.

When she was out of bullets and there were no more bubbles rising to the surface, she turned to Lotta.

"Are you sure you don't know the order?"

Lotta nodded, and Breuer thought the situation over.

Time was in short supply, and the obstacle was unexpected. But if she sent nothing at all, then defeat was a certainty.

She pulled out her mobile and took a photograph of the recovered slab. Then she went back to the garden path with Lotta in her wake. She photographed the other slabs in order and sent the photos.

The apocalypse was ever closer.

Revenge.

Punishment.

Finally, there remained just the two slabs that Sara had moved.

A 50–50 chance.

She chose one at random and began to enter the code into the message.

Behind her, the fire—spreading toward the house via trees and bushes—formed a dramatic backdrop.

The garden shed was completely in flames and almost gone. The fire had new targets. It always had to move on.

The flames were licking at the facade of the white house, and from a distance sirens were audible. It would soon be over.

"They're coming," said Breuer.

Lotta looked toward the sound, and when she turned around Breuer was aiming her pistol at her.

"I can help you," Lotta said, panic in her voice. "I'll be a member of the government."

"I don't need any help," the German said. "I'm retired."

"But surely this is just the beginning?" said Lotta. "We're going to rebuild the world!"

"No," said Breuer. "This isn't the beginning, it's the end. Nothing personal."

Then she smiled and squeezed the trigger.

At the same moment, Breuer's arm flew up in the air so that the shot went into the sky.

And at the same time, her head exploded.

Dark red liquid splashed everywhere for meters around her. Onto the lawn, the paving and Lotta.

When Breuer's body fell to the ground, Sara was standing behind her.

Out of breath and drenched from her swim. With an extremely expensive shotgun from Fabbri in her hands.

One that had been held by King Carl Gustav himself.

"I stopped by C.M.'s," she said.

And the flashing blue lights of half a dozen patrol cars illuminated the garden and the old childhood friends.

Acknowledgments

I want to thank my publisher Jonas Axelsson, my editor Annie Murphy and my agent Sofie Voller. Without their wisdom and superpowers, this book would not have been possible.

About the Author

Gustaf Skördeman was born in 1965 in Sweden and is a screenwriter, director and producer. *Geiger* is his literary debut.